# PRAISE FOR TAWNA FENSKE

## NOW THAT IT'S YOU

"A funny, poignant reminder that the baggage our exes leave can't stop love from moving us forward."

—*Kirkus Reviews*

"This is a heartwarming story with well-developed, artistic characters."

—*Publishers Weekly*

## LET IT BREATHE

"This charming romp from Fenske evokes the best of romantic comedy, with its witty characters and wacky but realistic situations."

—*Publishers Weekly*, Starred Review

## ABOUT THAT FLING

"Fenske's take on what happens when a one-night stand goes horribly, painfully awry is hilariously heartwarming and overflowing with genuine emotion . . . There's something wonderfully relaxing about being immersed in a story filled with over-the-top characters in undeniably relatable situations. Heartache and humor go hand in hand in this laugh-out-loud story with an ending that requires a few tissues."

—*Publishers Weekly*, Starred Review

## THE FIX UP

"Extremely charming and undeniably sexy . . . I loved every minute."

—#1 *New York Times* and *USA Today* bestselling author Rachel Van Dyken

"Sexy banter in the boardroom, romantic movies with a sexy alpha geek, and humor that will leave a smile on your face until the very last page."

—*New York Times* and *USA Today* bestselling author Kelly Elliott

## MAKING WAVES

Nominated for Contemporary Romance of the Year, 2011 Reviewers' Choice Awards, *RT Book Reviews*

"Fenske's wildly inventive plot and wonderfully quirky characters provide the perfect literary antidote to any romance reader's summer reading doldrums."

—*Chicago Tribune*

"A zany caper . . . Fenske's off-the-wall plotting is reminiscent of a tame Carl Hiaasen on Cupid juice."

—*Booklist*

"This delightfully witty debut will have readers laughing out loud."

—*RT Book Reviews*, 4 1/2 Stars

"[An] uproarious romantic caper. Great fun from an inventive new writer; highly recommended."

—*Library Journal*, Starred Review

"This book was the equivalent of eating whipped cream—sure, it was light and airy, but it is also surprisingly rich."

—Smart Bitches Trashy Books

## BELIEVE IT OR NOT

"Fenske hits all the right humor notes without teetering into the pit of slapstick in her lighthearted book of strippers, psychics, free spirits and an accountant."

—*RT Book Reviews*

"Snappy, endearing dialogue and often hilarious situations unite the couple, and Fenske proves to be a romance author worthy of a loyal following."

—*Booklist*, Starred Review

"Fenske's sophomore effort is another riotous trip down funny bone lane, with a detour to slightly askew goings-on and a quick u-ey to out-of-this-world romance. Readers will be enchanted by this bewitching fable from a wickedly wise author."

—*Library Journal*

"Sexually charged dialogue and steamy make-out scenes will keep readers turning the pages."

—*Publishers Weekly*

## FRISKY BUSINESS

"Up-and-coming romance author Fenske sets up impeccable internal and external conflict and sizzling sexual tension for a poignant love story between two engaging characters, then infuses it with witty dialogue and lively humor. An appealing blend of lighthearted fun and emotional tenderness."

—*Kirkus Reviews*

"Fenske's fluffy, frothy novel is a confection made of colorful characters, compromising situations and cute dogs. This one's for readers who prefer a tickled funny bone rather than a tale of woe."

—*RT Book Reviews*

"Loaded with outrageous euphemisms for the sex act between any type of couple and repeated near-intimate misses, Fenske's latest is a clever tour de force on finding love despite being your own worst emotional enemy. Sweet and slightly oddball, this title belongs in most romance collections."

—*Library Journal*

"*Frisky Business* has all the ingredients of a sparkling romantic comedy— wickedly clever humor, a quirky cast of characters and, most of all, the crazy sexy chemistry between the leads."

—*New York Times* and *USA Today* bestselling author Lauren Blakely

# THIS TIME AROUND

# ALSO BY
# TAWNA FENSKE

## Standalone Romantic Comedies

*Now That It's You*

*Let It Breathe*

*About That Fling*

*Eat, Play, Lust* (Novella)

*Frisky Business*

*Believe It or Not*

*Making Waves*

## The Front and Center Series

*Marine for Hire*

*Fiancée for Hire*

*Best Man for Hire*

*Protector for Hire*

## The First Impressions Series

*The Fix Up*

*The Hang Up*

*The Hook Up*

## Schultz Sisters Mysteries

*Getting Dumped*

*The Great Panty Caper* (Novella)

# THIS TIME AROUND

## TAWNA FENSKE

Montlake
Romance

Published by Montlake Romance, Seattle

www.apub.com

Amazon, the Amazon logo, and Montlake Romance are trademarks of Amazon.com, Inc., or its affiliates.

ISBN-13: 9781503943209
ISBN-10: 1503943208

Cover design by Rachel Adam

Printed in the United States of America

*Dedicated to all my loyal readers, especially those who've taken the time to leave online reviews, chat with me on Facebook or Twitter, subscribe to my e-newsletter, send fan mail about one of my books, or telepathically communicate your fondness for a character I've written. You're the reason I keep going on days I think I should throw in the towel on this author gig and become a pirate.*

# CHAPTER ONE

"You go ahead. I'm saving room for those currant scones with Devonshire cream." Allison Ross took a sip of her Earl Grey and used the tip of one French-manicured finger to nudge a plate of dainty tea sandwiches toward her mother.

That's how it went in her mind, anyway.

In reality, the tea was a can of tepid Diet Coke, the plate was a pile of legal documents, and the cozy tearoom of her childhood memories was now the noisy visiting room of a federal prison.

At least the French manicure was real.

"It's all right there, Allison," her mother said, shoving the documents back across the table. "My attorney brought them yesterday when we were working on my appeal."

Allie looked down to see the papers hadn't morphed into tea sandwiches or scones or anything else she'd fantasized about since she was a little girl. This was not the life she'd imagined with herself in a starring role as a grownup lady who sipped tea with her mother and red wine with her handsome husband and apple juice with their two adorable children.

It had never occurred to her how many of her youthful fantasies revolved around beverages. It was also possible she was losing it.

"Allison, are you paying attention?"

She snapped her focus back to her mother, who was clad head to toe in prison khaki. "I don't understand." Allie blinked back tears as she met her mother's cool green gaze. "I just had lunch with Grandma last week. She was totally fine! And she's never said a word about—about—about *this*." She gestured to the paperwork, unable to process it any more than she could process the thought that she'd never again see her grandma's handwriting on a birthday card. Would never hear the story of her own father's birth, which her grandma had promised to share *"someday when you have your own baby, dear."*

"I didn't even get to say goodbye," Allie said.

Across the table, Priscilla sighed. "Your grandmother always did know how to make a dramatic exit."

"But why wouldn't she have mentioned the B&B? She talked about how she wanted me to have her china and Aunt Gretchen's wedding rings, but her *house*?"

"Look, your grandmother was always a little flighty, Allison. And clearly she didn't realize she was going to drop dead playing mah-jongg at the senior center."

Allie flinched at her mother's words, but pressed her lips together to keep from saying anything she'd regret. Her visitation time at SeaTac Federal Detention Center was limited. There was no reason to spend any of it getting hung up on her mom's insensitive remarks. Priscilla Ross was doing time for orchestrating a Ponzi scheme that had robbed dozens of families of their life savings. Ambivalence to people's feelings was kind of a given.

But her mother seemed to realize she'd overstepped, because she put her hand over Allie's and softened her tone. "Look, your grandmother clearly appreciated all the time you spent having lunch with her every week and fixing her hair and running her around to appointments all the time. This was her way of rewarding you for that."

"But that's not why I did it!" Allie shook her head and looked down again, feeling her throat tighten at the sight of her mom's prison-weathered hand covering her own. Of course, Priscilla's knuckles were still smooth and dainty, and she somehow managed to maintain the perfect French manicure behind bars, so *weathered* was a relative term.

"I didn't spend time with Grandma so she'd leave me money or property or anything like that," Allie continued, swallowing the thick lump in her throat. "I did it because I loved her."

"Then think of it as the icing on the cake, dear. You know, real estate in the West Hills is very valuable. If you like, I could have my attorney contact some investors about—"

"No." Allie's voice came out harsher than she intended, but there was no way she'd let her mom go down that path. She may not have loved the ostentatious bed-and-breakfast her grandma had owned in Portland's elite, historic neighborhood, but she did love her grandma. It was clear from the paperwork that she'd wanted Allie to have the Rosewood B&B.

"It's fine, I'll deal with it," Allie said. "I haven't been there since she left those caretakers to run it. I'll email them to see if I can stop by after work sometime to check things out."

"Work," her mother repeated, drawing her hands back and folding them on the table. "Yes, how is that going?"

To an untrained ear, it might have seemed like a pleasant career inquiry. But Allie's ears had been trained by years of her mom's disappointment, so the subtext was clear. *If you'd finished law school like your father and me, you'd have a distinguished-sounding job title and a fat bank account instead of an eighteen-year-old car and a job you're stuck explaining to everyone.*

Or maybe that was all in Allie's head, too. It was hard to tell sometimes.

"Three minutes."

They looked up at a guard wearing a dark-blue uniform and a bored expression. At a table next to them, a woman sniffled and wrapped her arms around an inmate with dandelion-fluff hair who had the same crinkle-edged green eyes as Allie's grandmother.

Allie took a shaky breath and swung her gaze back to her mother. "Daddy says to tell you hello."

Priscilla's expression softened almost imperceptibly, and she twisted her fingers together on the table. "Tell your father Frank's hoping to get a court date next month and that he should make sure his appeal doesn't overlap with mine and that he should wear the gray Armani, not the blue one." She bit her lip. "And also that I love him. And I'm sorry about his mother. Victoria was a lovely woman."

The sound of her grandmother's name brought tears to Allie's eyes, but she nodded and stood up with the paperwork clutched in one arm. "I will." She wrapped her free arm around her mom's slender shoulders. "Dad said his lawyer thinks he has a good shot at a reduced sentence for all the time he's spent helping other prisoners write appeal letters."

"Hmph." Priscilla hugged back with surprising warmth, and Allie could have sworn she caught a whiff of Chanel N°5. It was probably Allie's memory playing tricks again, though it wasn't outside the realm of possibility that Priscilla had found a way to smuggle perfume into a federal prison.

"Writing appeal letters is not how I imagined your father and I using our law degrees," her mom continued, "but we do the best with what we have."

"I love you, Mom," Allie murmured into her mother's hair. Her mom squeezed tighter, and Allie closed her eyes to breathe her in. "Stay strong."

Her mom sagged a little against her. "You, too, Allison."

Before Allie could say more, the guard was herding her out of the room. A familiar numbness inched through her veins as she shuffled through the well-worn ritual of frisking and pat-downs, then the dizzying ride to the airport where she got patted down some more.

It was the most action Allie had seen in a long time.

She stayed dazed for the forty-five-minute flight back to Portland, grateful for the last-minute-fare sale that allowed her to fly this time instead of fighting traffic for four hours between Portland and Seattle. When she'd gotten word on Sunday that her grandma had passed, she'd jumped in the car in her pajamas to make the hour-and-a-half drive to visit her dad. Halfway there, she remembered visiting hours had ended at the penitentiary in Sheridan and she'd have to come back the next day. Preferably not wearing pink flannel pants.

But seeing her mom was more complicated, since the lack of a women's federal prison in Oregon meant Priscilla was doing her time in Washington. In six years, Allie had put more than a hundred thousand miles on her car.

Taking a deep breath, she slung her small carry-on bag over one shoulder and pushed through the revolving doors that led into the cloud-washed afternoon outside Portland International Airport. She inhaled the comforting scent of mud puddles and cherry blossoms as she scanned the idling cars. Spotting a metallic-gold convertible, she did a mental eye roll, then fixed her expression into one of proper gratitude as she trotted over and opened the passenger door.

"Thanks so much," she said, as she lowered herself into the passenger seat and hugged her carry-on to her lap. "You don't know how glad I am not to have to fight traffic today."

Her best friend, Wade, grinned at her from the driver's seat, his mirrored sunglasses flashing dual images of Allie looking tired and drawn. She'd have to remedy that before dinner.

"No problem," Wade said. "The weather's been nice, so this was a good excuse to get the Jag out and put the top down. And before you say anything about it being a compensation car, I should tell you last night's date texted this morning to say I was the best she's ever had."

"I'm going to assume you mean best *attorney*," Allie said as Wade pulled away from the curb. She slipped on her own sunglasses, though the thick, wooly cloud cover rendered them mostly unnecessary. "I don't need to know about your sex life. Besides, I wasn't going to say anything about the car. Or your junk."

"Because you have fond memories of the glory that is my massive meat pipe?"

Allie snorted. "Ugh. No, but thanks for that visual." She shook her head, but couldn't help smiling. His silly dick jokes normally jostled her out of her post-prison blues, but not today.

Today, she had other things on her mind.

"No offense, but I barely remember your meat pipe," she told Wade as she gazed out the window at the blur of cars moving past. "I've erased it from my memory since we broke up."

"That must be hard for you. Speaking of hard—"

"Enough!" Allie barked, but she was laughing now. "Really, thanks, Wade. I'm grateful. For the *ride*. And for what you're doing tonight. I wouldn't trust anyone else to be my fake boyfriend."

Not for the first time, Allie wished she'd had some real romantic chemistry with Wade. Even when they'd dated, it felt like dipping her toes in a lukewarm Mr. Turtle Pool. Pleasant enough, but not the sort of bone-deep, bubbling heat she felt in a Jacuzzi or when she'd been with Jack—

*Jack.* Allie's stupid, traitorous heart clenched. Dammit to hell.

"So remind me again how we're playing this," Wade said as he steered the car onto I-5. "Are we an affectionate, can't-keep-our-hands-off-each-other kind of couple, or cool and aloof lovers?"

"Can we play it by ear? Let's see what Jack and his wife are like together and we'll cue off them."

"Roger that." Wade changed lanes to pass a slow-moving Prius following another slow-moving Prius. "Tell me the wife's name again so I don't forget."

"Paige," Allie said. A fizzy ball knotted in her gut, the same one she'd felt every time she'd said or thought the name since she'd gotten Jack's email a week ago.

*I'll be in Portland next week for my college reunion. If you're free Wednesday or Thursday, maybe we could have dinner and catch up. Would love for you to meet Paige and to hear what's new in your life.*

Just like that, out of the blue. She'd heard he got married a few years after they split, but she never knew his wife's name, or even that he'd gone back and finished college after dropping out their sophomore year. The last time she'd seen Jack Carpenter, he'd been sitting on a sagging futon with a video game controller in one hand and a can of beer in the other. He'd worn a paint-stained shirt and a dumbstruck expression that was as likely a reaction to something in the game as it was to Allie's request that they pull the plug on their engagement.

*"We want different things out of life,"* she'd told him back then.

*"Not really,"* he'd replied, shaking his head in disbelief. *"We just have different ideas about how to get there."*

"So what are we having for dinner?" Wade asked, jarring Allie back to the present.

"Seafood *en brodo* with tarragon pesto," she said. "And bourbon-roasted peach cheesecake for dessert."

"Pulling out all the stops."

Allie shrugged, not wanting to admit how much thought she'd given the menu. How she'd remembered their sophomore year in college when she and Jack dug change out of the overstuffed sofa to find enough gas money to drive to the coast. They'd rolled up their pant legs and walked barefoot in the sand, digging clams until they had enough to fill their small red bucket. Later, they'd nestled together in an ocean of pillows on their living room floor, licking butter from their fingers in the flicker of candlelight.

"The meal is no big deal," Allie said as she pulled out her phone to review the evening's menu for the millionth time. "I just needed something I could make in advance. The *brodo*, the pesto, the dessert—I did it all last night. All I have to do is heat it up, add the shellfish, and drizzle in the pesto."

"I grabbed a loaf of that bread you asked for. The crusty stuff." Wade reached over to tousle her hair. "You'll do fine, Albatross. Stop worrying."

*Albatross.* Wade had given her the nickname several years ago after Allie threw in the towel on yet another relationship that wasn't going anywhere. Allie Ross the Albatross, the bird who'd rather fly alone.

It wasn't entirely true, but Allie had liked the way it made her sound strong and independent instead of like a loser whose romantic aspirations never turned out the way she thought they would.

"Go get ready," Wade said, and Allie looked up, startled to realize they'd arrived at her small, shoebox-shaped duplex already. "I'm sure you need to preen before your long-lost ex arrives, and I need to text Francesca."

"Who?"

"My date from last night."

"I thought her name was Vanessa."

Wade waved a hand. "Something like that."

Allie hustled inside and threw her bag down on the bed, grateful to have a few minutes to herself before Jack and Paige showed up. She glanced at the antique clock on her wall, calculating the primp time required to craft an image that said, "My life's fantastic! How about yours?"

She only had an hour, so she'd settle for, "I'm fine, thanks. Pass the wine?"

She wriggled into her Spanx, then zipped herself into a sheath dress in plum silk. The color brought out the green in her eyes, and the cut showed her Pilates-toned arms while assisting the Spanx in hiding her not-so-toned tummy. There was no hiding the laugh lines around her mouth and eyes, so she didn't bother trying. Her hair still looked good, long and loose around her shoulders with caramel highlights she'd got-ten at the nearby beauty college because it was cheaper than the fancy downtown salon she'd frequented in her other life. The life her wealthy parents had wanted her to have.

Allie turned and surveyed herself in the mirror. Sucked in her stom-ach. Turned to the side. Not bad. Not fantastic, but not terrible. She'd aged pretty well in the sixteen years since she'd last seen Jack Carpenter, all things considered.

*Things*, meaning her parents' arrest and imprisonment, a career path that hadn't gone according to plan, and a love life that never seemed to match the one she'd always imagined.

Allie turned again in front of the mirror, swaying a little on heels she'd almost forgotten how to walk in. Back in college, she expected to strut into courtrooms on her Louboutin stilettos, then kick them off at home so her handsome husband could rub her feet by the fireplace.

Her little house didn't have a fireplace. And though she loved lob-bying and planning and developing public health policy in her role as a Certified Association Executive for a state medical association, she knew the job title itself sounded made-up, and that heels were too impractical at her stand-up desk.

Allie swept some bronzer over her cheeks, then stabbed herself in the eye with an eyeliner pencil. Started over. Her hands were shaking, and she cursed herself for giving a damn what Jack Carpenter and his wife thought of her. In sixteen years, she'd never once Facebook stalked him. She hadn't cared, or at least that's what she thought before she got his stupid email about coming to town for his reunion.

"Hey, Albatross," Wade called from the other room. "A car just pulled in. I think it's them."

Allie took a deep breath and stepped back from the mirror. *Showtime.*

She turned and pushed open her bedroom door and strode down the hall, projecting a confidence she didn't really feel. If nothing else, she knew how to fake it. That had always been her superpower, the skill that proved more useful than any law degree would have.

Wade gave a low whistle as she marched into the living room. "Lookin' good," he said from his perch on her sofa. He shoved his phone in the pocket of his jacket and stood. "Want me to hover possessively beside you, or go fiddle around in the kitchen like a devoted fiancé?"

"Just hang back," Allie said as footfalls echoed up her front steps and she wished, not for the first time, that she had a peephole on her front door. She hated the clamminess in her palms as the footsteps got louder. "If I signal you by tugging my left ear, it means lay it on thick with the affection. If I signal you by tugging my right ear, play it cool."

"Should I write this down somewhere?"

"Hush."

Allie took a shaky breath and glanced at the crystal vase of lilies she'd set out the night before. The doorbell chimed and she reached for the knob, then hesitated, not wanting to look too eager. She took a few more breaths as her heart thudded in her ears and she ordered herself to smile warmly, to greet Jack with a firm handshake and his wife with a friendly hug. Or maybe a double cheek kiss, European style?

Her fingers were sweaty as she gripped the doorknob and twisted right, then pulled open the door. Her gaze landed on the two people standing on her porch.

She stumbled back, too stunned to form a polite greeting.

"Oh," she said, and clapped a hand over her mouth.

# CHAPTER TWO

Jack took one look at Allie's face gone pale as a soda cracker and wondered what he'd done this time to make her throw up.

"Here, use this." He set down the bottle of wine he'd brought and yanked the plastic off the bouquet he was holding, offering it to her as a makeshift barf bag. He'd made similar offerings in college when nerves or emotion got the best of his stoic fiancée and she turned this exact shade of white.

But Allie just stared at him like he'd lost his mind.

"I'm not going to throw up," she said, waving the bag away. "I'm fine. I just—" She took a sharp breath, and her gaze darted to Paige.

*Paige.*

He felt a surge of pride seeing his ten-year-old daughter standing beside him looking cheerful and well-mannered in the blue dress she'd picked for the occasion. She'd French-braided her own hair in some complicated twist Jack could never figure out. Sensing his gaze on her, his kid gave him a grin so wide he saw the gap from the newly lost molar he'd hidden in a silk pouch in his sock drawer.

Emotion welled in his chest, so Jack looked back at Allie. She'd recovered some of her color, which probably had something to do with the possessive male hand resting on her shoulder.

"Jack," Allie began, licking her lips. "I'd like you to meet my fiancé, Wade."

The guy slid his palm from Allie's shoulder and reached out to shake Jack's hand. Jack returned the handshake, impressed with himself for not feeling any twinges of jealousy at the word *fiancé*. He was over her, obviously. Had been over her for years, long before he'd gotten married and had a kid.

The reminder prompted Jack to offer his own introduction. "Pleasure to meet you, Wade," he said. "This is my daughter, Paige."

Paige stuck out her hand, beaming like she always did when given the opportunity to socialize with grownups. Still looking dumbstruck, Allie grasped the small hand in hers and gave it an awkward shake.

"I'm Paige Carpenter," his daughter announced, her dimples on full display as she looked from Allie to Wade and back again. "It's very nice to meet you."

"Paige." Allie gave her a nervous smile. "It's a pleasure to meet you. Such nice manners. How old are you?"

"Ten. How old are you?"

Allie laughed, breaking the spell that seemed to have held her for the last thirty seconds. Her face creased into familiar crinkles around her eyes and mouth, into laugh lines Jack couldn't help noticing had grown deeper in the sixteen years since he saw her last.

Laughter he hadn't been part of. God, had it really been that long?

"I'm thirty-six," Allie said, answering Paige's question at last. "Same as your dad. Please, come on in."

She stepped back, and Jack tried not to notice the way the wine-colored dress swept around her thighs and moved over her hips. Hips that were still full and beautifully rounded. Hips he used to grip with both hands as she moved over him, her breasts bare and—

*Jesus Christ*, was he really doing this? With his kid standing beside him, and Allie's fiancé next to *her*?

Jack looked at the fiancé, reminding himself that Allie belonged to someone else now. The guy's suit screamed *lawyer*, which made perfect sense. Allie had obviously gotten what she'd wanted out of life.

*So did you*, his subconscious reminded him. *That's why you're here, to rub her face in the fact that you turned out great without her.*

It was a shitty thing to think, but there it was. Jack squeezed his daughter's shoulder as she stepped through the front door. He followed behind her, bringing him closer to Allie than he'd been since he was twenty years old. He stepped back quickly and turned to pick up the wine. Then he moved past the lawyer fiancé and into a living room that was well-decorated, but small. Smaller than he would have expected. Silky-looking throw pillows lined a leather sofa that looked vintage. There was a crystal vase of lilies on the coffee table, and an earthy-looking clay vessel on a nearby bookshelf. Jack remembered it from their college apartment. Her grandma had made it, and Allie used to keep it on her desk to hold dried flowers from the first bouquet he'd ever given her.

It held something metallic now. Daisies? Stems of copper twisted up to meet petals made of iron and steel, an effect that was both artistic and tasteful. And expensive. Probably very expensive.

He looked back at Allie and handed her the bouquet of sunflowers he'd brought. "Thank you for inviting us to your home."

Too late, he remembered he'd taken the bag off the flowers and they dripped water on her shoes. The Allie he used to know would have freaked out about ruining the leather, but this one didn't seem to notice. Or maybe she had plenty of other pairs of fancy shoes in her closet. That seemed likely.

Jack cleared his throat and held out the bottle of wine, feeling a little like an asshole for deliberately leaving the wine shop's price tag on the edge of the label. "I brought this, too."

The fiancé took the wine and gave him a pleasant smile that looked genuine. "Very nice," Wade said. "I had this one at a tasting event for New Zealand wines. This will be perfect with Allie's seafood *en brodo*."

Jack glanced at Allie, who was watching Paige like she was some kind of exotic butterfly that had fluttered into her living room. Seeming to sense his eyes on her, Allie turned toward him and offered a sheepish look. "Sorry, I didn't realize—I, um." She licked her lips. "Does Paige eat seafood? If not, I'm sure I can throw together chicken fingers or peanut butter and jelly or—"

"I love seafood!" Paige looked up from the collection of photos she'd been studying on a bookshelf and grinned at Allie. "Especially salmon and shrimp."

Allie blinked. "That's great. You have a very refined palate."

"Thank you," Paige said automatically, even though Jack was pretty sure she didn't know what *palate* meant. In that moment, he felt so damn proud of his kid he wanted to pick her up and squeeze her.

"You'll love the wine," Paige continued solemnly. "It's very itchy with notes of tulip stem and green Crayola."

The fiancé barked out a laugh that made Allie jump. Paige beamed, pleased with the reaction from her audience. Jack hustled to explain.

"It's our inside joke," he said. "Paige and I try to see who can come up with the craziest descriptors for wine. Things like 'old shoe leather from a 1978 Birkenstock' or 'mango Trident gum found under the third-row bleachers at Autzen Stadium.' Stuff like that."

He didn't add that they'd started the ritual after watching some hoity TV show about food and wine pairings recommended by snobby rich people. He'd wanted Paige to know she didn't need to aspire to be the sort of woman who sipped tea with her pinky up and spoke in condescending tones about the amuse-bouche.

From what he could guess, Allie had grown up to be one of those people.

"It's great you're such a fan of wine." The fiancé was talking to Paige, not him, which made him like the guy and also made him resolve to use his name instead of branding him *the fiancé* like a character in a play. "I always love talking with a fellow connoisseur," Wade continued, smiling at Paige. "Maybe you could give me some good pointers on wine."

"I don't actually drink wine," Paige said, pronouncing *actually* with an extra syllable the way her mother used to do, which was crazy. Paige barely remembered her mom, so there was no way for phonetics to have fixed themselves in his daughter's memory.

*Focus on the present,* Jack ordered himself as he felt a familiar tightening in his chest.

"I like grape juice, though," Paige was saying. "And seltzer. And root beer."

"I'm pretty sure we have at least one of those things in the fridge," Wade said. "Would you like something to drink?"

His daughter looked back over at him, a question in her eyes. Jack nodded once before glancing at Allie to see her exchange a questioning look of her own with Wade. Allie gave the guy a quick nod, and the next thing Jack knew, he was standing alone with her in her living room.

Alone. For the first time in sixteen years. It felt awkward. And familiar. But mostly awkward.

"So," Allie said, resting her perfectly manicured hands on the back of the sofa. "It's wonderful to finally meet your daughter. She's adorable. Just like I pictured her."

Jack snort-laughed. He couldn't help it. "Liar."

Allie frowned. "What?"

He shook his head and took a step closer, lowering his voice so Paige wouldn't hear. "Until five minutes ago, you had no idea I even *had* a daughter."

"That's not true!" Allie tossed her hair. "She looks just like her mother. Very beautiful."

Jack rolled his eyes. She sounded so convincing, so sure of herself. If he hadn't seen her face when he'd stood there on the doorstep, he might have even believed her.

"Paige's mother died when she was eighteen months old," he said, making Allie's face go pale again. "And you might still be the world's best liar, but you can't fool me. Admit it—you haven't cyberstalked me once in the last sixteen years."

Allie folded her arms over her chest and met him with a level gaze he remembered with something less than fondness. "So what? Are you accusing me of that like it's a *bad* thing?" She frowned. "I meant the stalking, not the lying. And I'm sorry about your w— about Paige's mother."

"Thank you."

Her expression softened again, something he hadn't seen often when they were together. The Allie he remembered never backed down, never apologized. "I mean it," she said. "I'm really sorry."

It was on the tip of his tongue to say, "Me, too," but he realized she wasn't apologizing for anything sixteen years ago. She felt bad for bringing up the dead mother of his child. He appreciated that Allie didn't ask for details, didn't even press to find out if he'd actually been married or if Paige was the result of some drunken fling. It would be just like her to think the worst of him, even now.

Jack volunteered nothing. He didn't want to tell his sad story and see any trace of pity in Allie's face. What he wanted to see was awe. Respect. Maybe embarrassed shock that he'd turned out successful, despite her predictions to the contrary. Jack Carpenter had made something of himself, dammit.

Why the hell did he need her to know that?

Jack cleared his throat. "I'm actually running my own company now," he said. "Started out working on video games and sold one a few years ago for a pretty nice profit."

"Wow. That's great."

He knew his words sounded like boastful assholery, and he ordered himself to shut the hell up.

But his tongue didn't obey. "After that, I founded Clearwater App Development," he continued, somehow unable to stop the flow of stupid words. "I'm actually killing two birds with one stone coming out here for my reunion. Paige and I are making the move to Portland and I'm finalizing a deal to move our headquarters from Silicon Valley, too. The tech sector is really booming here."

He wanted to pick up those stupid metal flowers and stab himself right through the eyeball to skewer his brain. Why the hell was he giving her his fucking résumé?

Allie stood silent for a moment, looking pleasant and polite. Then, ever the gracious hostess, she gave him a warm smile. "That's wonderful. Congratulations. It sounds like you've done very well for yourself."

He nodded, not trusting himself to open his mouth again for fear of what might come spewing out. Maybe he'd start talking about bank balances or how much he'd spent on his last car.

He should probably ask her about her own career, since she'd posted surprisingly few details on her Facebook page over the years, leaving him pretty much empty-handed when he *had* tried to cyberstalk her. Or maybe he could talk about something benign like food, since that's a subject she'd always loved. He was preparing himself to ask about good restaurants in the area when Paige burst into the room.

"Daddy! Don't forget to call your girlfriend at seven."

◆ ◆ ◆

Allie kept her face frozen in a mask of practiced nonchalance. In a ten-minute span, she'd gone from thinking Jack Carpenter had a beautiful wife named Paige, to realizing he was a widowed father, to knowing he had a girlfriend serious enough to require a phone call in the middle of a dinner party.

She held the most neutral expression she could, unwilling to let any of that rattle her. She was secure with herself and her place in the world. She didn't need a man or a million-dollar bank account or an adorable daughter with dimples that matched Jack Carpenter's.

There was no trace of the dimples as Jack turned to her with the tiniest hint of sheepishness in his expression. Or maybe Allie was imagining it. He held Allie's gaze for an uncomfortable instant, then looked back at his daughter. "I don't have a girlfriend, sweetheart."

He was talking to Paige, but Allie sensed the comment was meant as much for her. She said nothing, though she was holding her breath, not wanting to miss a word of this conversation.

"*Dad*," Paige said with the exaggerated patience of a preteen girl. "Lacey. Lacey is your girlfriend and you said you'd call her at seven."

Jack shot another glance at Allie, and she concentrated on looking bored, like she didn't care one way or another if Jack Carpenter had a girlfriend. Or if he had *a million* girlfriends. It made no difference to her.

Not now, anyway.

"She's been on this kick lately," he said to Allie. "Her best friend's mom let them binge-watch a bunch of old *Full House* episodes and now she's obsessed with boyfriends and girlfriends and wanting me to date someone and—"

"Hey, it's none of my business." Allie shrugged and glanced toward her kitchen. Wade stood there looking like he might explode with laughter, which meant he'd heard the whole conversation.

For a lawyer, Wade had a surprisingly lousy poker face. She shot him a warning look and turned back to her guests.

"No worries if you need to make a phone call," she said. "I need to put the finishing touches on dinner, so you can make the call outside or step into the guest room. It's the second door on the right down that hall."

Jack looked at her a moment, then nodded. "Thank you."

Paige gave a smile that made Allie's ovaries ache just a little. "Do you need any help with dinner?"

"I think I have it covered, but let me check." Allie bit her lip, stupidly unsure of herself. Was it okay to let a ten-year-old slice bread or snip the stems of the sunflowers Jack had given her? She had no idea, but it was probably best not to hand her any sharp objects until she knew for sure. She hated how undone she felt at the sight of a kid. Allie had always assumed she'd have children of her own by now, that she'd instinctively know what sort of snacks they ate or what activities were age-appropriate.

But instead, she was thirty-six years old and completely clueless about kids. And Jack Carpenter wasn't. How the hell did that happen?

"You can help yourself to the tapenade," Allie offered. "The um—the stuff right there on the table? It's really good on those crackers."

Did kids eat tapenade? Paige looked dubious.

"Thank you," the girl said politely. She glanced at the fig and olive mixture Allie had stayed up late making the night before, then picked up a cracker.

Allie let her gaze drift to the glass clutched in Paige's other hand, and she grimaced at the words printed on the side. *You can't drink all day if you don't start in the morning.*

She glared at Wade, who pretended not to notice. Feeling like the world's worst hostess, she marched into the kitchen and began bustling around, trying to ignore the way her hands were shaking. She snipped the ends off the sunflowers and stuck them in another crystal vase her parents had somehow managed to save when the Feds liquidated their estate.

She set the flowers on the dining room table, then turned to start pulling things out of the fridge—clams, broth, the tarragon pesto sealed up tight in a glass container. She flipped on her gas stove, wondering if she should just stick her head in the oven and get it over with.

When a hand touched her elbow, she jumped.

"Easy there, Albatross," Wade said. He shoved a glass of white wine in her hand and Allie wrapped her fingers around the stem.

"Thanks." She took a fortifying sip.

"You okay?"

Allie nodded, then darted a glance toward the living room.

"Don't worry," Wade murmured. "She's in the bathroom throwing up the tapenade, and he's rifling through your underwear drawer."

"Wade—"

"I'm kidding. He's still on his phone in the guest room, and the kid is drinking apple juice and flipping through your *Glamour* magazine in the living room."

Allie frowned. "Where did you get apple juice?"

"That big brown bottle in the fridge. Smelled like apple juice, anyway."

"Wade! That's kombucha. Doesn't kombucha have alcohol in it?"

He took a step back and held up his hands in defense. "Like a tiny little fraction of a percent. Less than orange juice that's been left out on the counter too long."

"I wouldn't give her that to drink, either!"

"I'm sure it's fine. I see kids drinking kombucha all the time."

She shook her head as guilt pooled in her belly. "And that issue of *Glamour* has a bunch of celebrities posing topless. Jack's been here less than ten minutes and I've already gotten his kid drunk and showed her porn."

"Allie, relax." Wade caught her elbows in his hands and gave her a squeeze. "You're doing fine."

Allie closed her eyes, and her brain filled with that first glimpse of Paige. God, she'd had no idea. A kid? And a dead wife? Why hadn't she done some homework the instant Jack reached out instead of assuming she knew how his life turned out?

Jack used to chide her for doing exactly that back in college. *"To assume is to make an* ass *out of* u *and* me.*"* Had she learned nothing these last sixteen years?

She opened her eyes to see Wade watching her. "Tell me honestly, did I look like a total idiot when I opened the door?"

"You hardly batted an eyelash."

"You're a good friend, Wade."

He grimaced. "Please remember that when I tell you I'm going to have to sneak out early to meet Vanessa."

"Wade!"

"Sh! It's just that she's leaving town tomorrow for two weeks and this thing she does with her tongue—"

"You promised!"

"I know! And I'll stick around through dinner, honest. Maybe even dessert. But now that there's a kid, maybe you won't want to stay up late anyway."

Allie sighed. "Fine. Manwhore."

Wade grinned and squeezed her arms. He started to let go, but tightened his grip as Jack rounded the corner into the kitchen.

"Oh, sorry—didn't mean to interrupt anything." Jack's gaze darted to Allie's and she inched closer to Wade, doing her best to look like a woman being pawed by her fiancé instead of a woman whose best friend was trying to keep her from losing her shit.

Maybe it was the same look.

It had been often enough when she and Jack dated. They'd always loved the clichés about marrying your best friend, certain the fact that they'd been friends in high school before they started dating would be their ticket to happily ever after. Every sappy pop song, every *Love Is* comic strip convinced them they could ride that lustful camaraderie to a land of blissful togetherness.

She'd wanted so badly to believe the fairy tale. God, she'd been dumb.

"Dinner's almost ready," Allie told Jack as Wade planted an awkward kiss on her forehead. She hoped their total lack of chemistry didn't show. Back when she and Wade had dated, it was one of a dozen reasons they realized they weren't meant to be anything but friends. Her toes had never curled when Wade kissed her, but they'd damn near rolled into a spiral when Jack used to touch his lips to hers.

She said a silent prayer Jack couldn't read her mind.

"Need me to help with anything?" he asked.

"Thanks, but we've got it." She handed Wade the loaf of bread he'd picked up earlier. "Can you slice this up, sweetie pie?"

"Sure thing . . . uh, babycakes."

Jack laughed and leaned against the kitchen counter. "I see a few things have changed since college."

Allie blew a lock of hair off her forehead as she tumbled the clams into the simmering broth. "How so?"

"It drove you nuts when couples called each other pet names," Jack said. "You rolled your eyes anytime I tried it."

Allie smiled at the memory as she settled the clams to the bottom of the pot and used a wooden spoon to nudge them around. "That's because your pet names were ridiculous."

Jack grinned and began piling Wade's bread slices into the basket she'd set on the counter, the evil dimples making Allie's gut clench. "My pet names were not ridiculous," he insisted.

"Lovey yummers?" she reminded him.

"Well—"

"Puddin' knickers?"

"You have to admit—"

"Canned peach half in heavy syrup?"

Allie didn't realize she'd started laughing until she caught sight of her own reflection in the copper-rimmed mirror next to her kitchen sink. She wiped a smear of pesto off her cheek and glanced at Wade, who was regarding her with an odd expression. Allie tried to shoot him a loving glance, but probably just looked like she had something in her eye.

"So how did you two meet, anyway?" Jack asked.

Allie started to answer, but Wade spoke first, leaving her to telepathically communicate the importance of being vague while sticking close to the truth.

"We met at my office," Wade said. "My law firm handled her parents'—"

"Wills!" Allie finished, cutting him off before he could air too much dirty laundry.

Wade said nothing, but Jack gave her the familiar eyebrow lift. "I know about your parents, Allie."

"Oh?" she stirred the broth, silently insisting her heated face was the result of standing over a gas burner and had nothing to do with the conversation. Maybe Jack didn't know the whole story.

"It was in the news," Jack said. "I kept seeing headlines about the trial whenever I'd check *The Oregonian* online."

"Right." She stopped stirring and put the lid on the pot, desperate for something to do with her hands.

"How are your folks doing?" Jack asked.

"Okay. Under the circumstances, I mean."

"I'm glad. It can't be easy."

"It is what it is."

God, what an inane statement. What did that even mean? Jack stepped closer, and suddenly everything else fell away. Wade, the clams, the fact that Jack had a ten-year-old daughter and a whole history she knew nothing about.

"It's fine, Allie," he said. "We all have skeletons in the closet. Secrets, mistakes, things we don't like to talk about."

She nodded, not sure she could find her words, but certain she shouldn't speak the ones tumbling around in her brain.

*You don't know the half of it, Jack Carpenter.*

# CHAPTER THREE

"Everything was delicious, Allie." Jack reached over from his spot on the sofa to grab his coffee mug off the side table, wincing as Paige rolled over in her sleep and kicked him in the nuts.

Allie gave him her serene smile and sat down on the adjacent love-seat, a good three feet of distance between them. Maybe more. Paige had dozed off a few minutes after dessert, with Allie's fiancé making an exit a few minutes later. Something about an urgent oral presentation at work, though Jack had seen Allie roll her eyes when she thought he wasn't looking.

So it was just the two of them now, plus one unconscious child. As Jack shifted his daughter's feet on his lap, Allie balanced a pale-blue teacup on a saucer, stirring it with one of those dainty little teaspoons she always used to leave around their apartment. Jack breathed in the faint scent of Earl Grey, not sure what to say to the woman he'd once been ready to marry.

"Is your coffee okay?" she asked.

"It's great, thanks." He hadn't taken a sip yet. "Actually, I should probably get going." He set the mug on a coaster and tried to figure out how to move Paige without waking her.

"You said you wanted coffee."

Allie's tone was normal enough, but something accusatory rang in it. Or maybe that was Jack's imagination. Too many years of veiled and not-so-veiled accusations about how he could never decide what he wanted. Never commit to a college major or a career or even what he wanted for dinner. Anything but Allie. Right up to the day she left, he'd always been sure about her.

It hadn't been enough. Not for her, anyway.

Jack hesitated, then settled back against the sofa. What the hell, it had been sixteen years. A few more minutes of making small talk wouldn't hurt. He cleared his throat. "Nice place you have here."

"Thank you."

"Been here long?"

"Oh, I guess about four years. Something like that."

She wasn't offering much, but then again, he was asking pretty dumb questions. Conversation used to flow better between them. Had they changed that much, or were they just out of practice?

He took a sip of coffee, then tried again. "Does Wade have to work late a lot?"

Something flashed in those dark-green eyes, and he tried to decide if he'd sounded judgmental on purpose. No, of course not. He was just making small talk.

"Wade's in a position to make partner at his law firm," she said. "It's important to show everyone he's committed."

"Of course," Jack said. "Gotta climb the ladder."

Was he baiting her? He wasn't sure, but certainly his words smacked of insults he'd hurled years ago. *It's all about the money, isn't it, Al? That's all that matters to you.*

He'd both hated and loved the way her eyes glittered with anger. *Well, someone has to figure out how to keep a roof over our heads, and you're too busy playing video games to contribute anything.*

He'd showed her. Not then, admittedly. Not when it mattered, not until years after they'd split, but still. He started to apologize—for his snark just now or for not pulling his weight sixteen years ago, he wasn't sure. But before he could say anything, Allie spoke.

"You remember that time we went camping?"

The question startled him at first—an olive branch? He found himself smiling. "Yeah. It was your first time. Camping, I mean. I couldn't believe you'd never slept outside."

"Please," she said, lifting her cup for a sip of tea. "You met my family. Our idea of being outdoorsy was using the crosswalk instead of the Skybridge to get around Pioneer Place."

Jack smiled. "You were a pretty good sport about it."

"Yeah, right up until the moment we were attacked by that giant swarm of mosquitoes and you realized you'd packed air freshener instead of bug spray."

"It did smell nice." He picked up his coffee and took a small sip. "And all the bugs made for good fishing."

"I suppose so."

"Which would have been better if I'd remembered to bring anything to cook with. Or matches."

"I wasn't going to bring it up." She smiled over the rim of her teacup, and Jack had a flash of memory. Allie looking calm and unsurprised in the midst of his latest screw-up—forgetting to register for classes? Not budgeting enough to pay the water bill?

After years of her nagging, it was her eventual calmness that bothered him most. The moment she'd stopped looking disappointed by his failures and started looking like she expected them.

"Well, it's water under the bridge," he murmured, not sure whether he was talking about the camping trip or the bigger picture.

"Right. And hey, we got to figure out how to make fire without matches."

"I still can't believe we pulled that off."

"It took half the night, and a little bloodshed."

"Man make fire," he said in a caveman voice that always used to get her laughing. "A good life skill for our résumés."

She smiled and took a dainty sip of tea. She was quiet a moment, and Jack wondered what she was thinking. He didn't have to wait long to find out. "I was cleaning out my parents' old storage unit the other day and found one of your boxes."

He didn't have to ask what she meant by that. Back then, his idea of housekeeping involved shoving everything off counters and tables and piling it into a box. Junk mail, bills, half-empty packs of gum—all of it got stuffed in a box and lugged to the garage to be dealt with later.

How the hell was he supposed to know there'd be no *later* for the two of them?

"What was in the box?" he asked, almost afraid to hear.

"Lots of things," she said. "A pile of clues you made for me. Remember how you used to do those treasure hunts?"

He nodded as something squeezed tight in his chest. "I remember."

"You'd leave them all over the house. Things like, 'If you want some good lovin', go look in the oven.' And when I'd check there, I'd find another clue that said something like—"

"'Our love isn't creepy, so go look by the TP.'" He grinned. "That was my personal favorite."

"I remember they all led to where you'd hidden that bucket list thingy you made."

"The bucket board," he said. "Patent pending."

She gave a small smile and Jack remembered how much bigger her smile had been when she'd found it. He'd fashioned the bucket board from a buddy's cast-off corkboard and some leftover Christmas gift tags.

*"Every year on our anniversary, we'll write down our bucket list goals as a couple,"* he'd explained, *"things like 'have sex under a waterfall' or 'think up names for our kids.'"*

*"Or, 'start a savings account,'"* she'd offered. *"Maybe 'pass the bar exam.'"*

*"Sure, that's fine."*

As Jack snapped his attention back to the present, he noticed Allie wasn't smiling anymore.

"There were other things in the box," she said, glancing down at her lap. "Tons of paperwork. I'm not sure how it ended up with my parents' stuff, but there it was—unpaid power bills, an old credit card bill, a third late-payment notice for your student loans—"

"Right," Jack grunted. "Keeping track of that stuff was never my forte."

She frowned. "There were a ton of collections notices. I never realized how many late fees you racked up and how many credit cards there were."

"Allie, come on." He set his mug down hard on the end table, deliberately missing the coaster. "Maybe I could have done a better job paying my bills if you hadn't insisted on that insanely expensive apartment with the heat blasting all the time and those ridiculously expensive HOA dues to cover the on-site fitness center and the trendy zip code and—"

Paige kicked him in the nuts again, and Jack shut up. His voice had risen along with his frustration, but his daughter slept on. He took a deep breath, then reached down and stroked her hair. His little girl smiled in her sleep, and Jack felt himself go calm again.

When he looked up, Allie was staring at him. "My apologies." Her voice was tight. "Sorry if I happened to like having nice things."

Jack felt his blood pressure rising, but he kept his voice low this time. "And I'm sorry if I didn't mind the romance of learning how to be broke together. Ramen noodles, cheap beer, a crappy sofa scrounged out of the landfill instead of some fancy Pottery Barn number."

Allie glared. "I'm so sorry to have deprived you of that experience. Bedbugs and Bud Light sound like tremendous fun."

Jack gritted his teeth, annoyed with himself for falling back into this pattern with her. Annoyed with her for being who she was and with himself for being who he was, even though he felt pretty sure he wasn't the same guy she remembered.

But mostly he felt annoyed that he still gave a damn what she thought of him.

He watched Allie tuck a strand of hair behind her ear and remembered the feel of those silky threads between his fingers. Her dark-green eyes flickered with annoyance, and he watched her gaze drop to his hand. She stared for a long time, eyes fixed on his knuckles.

Or was she looking at Paige? At the small polka-dotted stockings cupped in his palm?

Jack cleared his throat. "I should get going."

He shifted his daughter's legs off his lap, and stood up. Paige grumbled in sleepy protest, but didn't wake up. He leaned down and scooped her into his arms, deliberately avoiding Allie's eyes. His little girl flopped like a rag doll, but didn't wake up. How much longer would he be able to hold her like this? The thought that she wouldn't always be this small made his chest ache.

When he turned to face Allie again, she was standing, too. Something in her eyes made him stop. It looked a lot like longing, or maybe he was imagining things.

"Thank you for having us over," he said. "Dinner was excellent."

"My pleasure." She opened her mouth like she wanted to say something, then stopped. When she closed it again, Jack knew that was the end of the conversation.

"It was good seeing you again," she said at last.

"Likewise." He shifted Paige in his arms and started to turn toward the door. He looked at Allie again, saw her hands twisting in the side seam of her dress, saw uncertainty flicker in her eyes.

"You're still beautiful, Allie," he murmured. "For what it's worth. More beautiful than you were sixteen years ago. That's saying a lot."

He wasn't sure which of them felt more surprised by his words. Did her eyes look misty, or was it just a trick of light?

She didn't say anything for a long time, and Jack stood there with his sleeping daughter in his arms wondering if he should have waited to pick her up. He'd missed his chance to hug Allie goodbye, but it was probably for the best.

"Thank you," Allie said at last. "You look good, too. Congratulations."

"On?"

"Your career. Your daughter. Your amazing, perfect life. Everything."

They were the words he'd wanted her to say, the reason he'd come here in the first place. But they didn't make him feel smug.

They made him feel hollow.

She gave him a small smile, and the hollowness filled with something warm. "I'm glad you're doing well," she added.

"You, too," he said, though it occurred to him they'd hardly talked about her life at all. About what she was doing now. God, he was such a self-centered prick.

"Hey, if nothing else, it was a good chance to remember why we're lucky we didn't end up together," he offered.

She gave a bark of laughter and tossed her hair. "That's for damn sure."

Her answer stung a helluva lot more than he expected.

◆　◆　◆

The first thing Allie noticed when she stood on the front porch of the Rosewood B&B was the heavy brocade drapes. Faded and dusty, they were the same ones her grandmother had ordered from Paris at least a dozen years ago.

The second thing she noticed was the swath of tiny holes marring the cedar trim over the window. It looked like someone had jammed a kebab skewer into the wood over and over again. Allie squinted at the holes, wondering what the hell could do that sort of damage.

She didn't realize someone was staring back at her until she heard the squeak.

"Aaah!" She jumped back, nearly knocking herself off the porch. She grabbed hold of the railing and peered through the window at a cat who peered right back with clear disdain.

"Jesus," Allie muttered. "I didn't see you there. Who are you?"

The cat didn't answer, probably because it was a cat, and also because it had better things to do than converse with a thirty-six-year-old single woman standing on the porch of a B&B that looked a lot rattier than Allie remembered. The cat looked ratty, too. It was the color of an old gym sock, and had fur that stuck out in all directions. Her grandmother had always had a cat or two around, but Allie didn't remember this one.

Bored by the human attention, the cat lifted one paw and began to clean behind a ragged ear.

"What's wrong with your paw?" Allie stared at it, trying to remember if cats were supposed to have thumbs. This one had at least three extra digits on the left front paw, and on the back—

The door flew open and Allie tore her gaze off the cat to size up the woman standing in the doorway. "Hi." Allie smoothed down the front of her navy sheath dress and tried to look presentable.

"Hello," the woman replied as she studied Allie with a curious expression.

The long, dark hair she wore loose around her shoulders had a few cobalt-blue streaks running through it. Her feet were bare, and her flowy, tie-dyed dress looked like she'd been attacked with a paint sprayer. Her face bore no trace of makeup, and she had a porcelain complexion with a smattering of freckles. Allie couldn't begin to guess if she was eighteen or forty-eight.

The woman scrunched her brows a bit and regarded Allie with a curious expression. "Can I help you?"

"I'm Allie." She stuck out her hand, and the woman took it with a firm shake. "Allison Ross. My grandmother is Victoria Ross." She closed her eyes, and swallowed back the wave of grief that threatened to grab her by the throat. "*Was* Victoria Ross."

A pair of warm arms enveloped her, and Allie opened her eyes to find herself wrapped in a patchouli-scented hug.

"Oh my God, I'm so sorry," the woman said. "Your grandmother was such an amazing woman. I just adored her. I can't believe she's gone. You must be so heartbroken."

"I—yes, thank you." Allie tried to spit out the woman's hair, not sure how to disentangle herself from the hug. She'd never loved physical affection from strangers, but there was something about this hug that felt familiar and warm, so Allie relaxed and let the woman hang on for a few extra beats. "I didn't catch your name," Allie said.

"Oh, sorry." The woman drew back and tucked the wild curls behind her ears. "It's Skye. Skye Collins. I guess that didn't show up in the email we exchanged?"

"No, just the info@rosewood address and the signature lines at the bottom—all the stuff my grandma's web guy must have plugged in years ago."

"Right," Skye said. "Sorry, it's been a little crazy around here."

"Were you not expecting me?" Allie glanced at her watch to see it was half past five, right on the dot. "We did say Thursday at five-thirty, right?"

"Yes, of course, it's my fault. I was studying for exams. I'm a student at the Aesthetics Institute. Hair, nails, facials, that sort of thing. I guess I lost track of time. You know how it is."

Allie wasn't sure she did. Punctuality had always been her forte, and she kept track of her appointments in duplicate using both her iPhone and her Erin Condren LifePlanner.

But Skye seemed warm and sweet, so Allie gave her a smile. "So you're one of the caretakers?"

Skye's smile seemed to falter just a little. "Oh. Well, yes. But it's just me. I'm the only one who lives here."

Allie frowned. "I thought my grandma said she hired a couple to look after the place."

"Yes. Um, she did. But Brody—that was my boyfriend—he moved out a few months ago. Things weren't working out between us and—well, anyway. It's just me."

"Oh. I'm sorry to hear that."

"No, it's fine, really. I mean, I've been doing my best with upkeep and everything, and Brody wasn't much help anyway. I'm managing just fine on my own."

Allie nodded and wished there were a way to rewind and start this conversation over. She hadn't meant to pry into the other woman's love life so soon after meeting her. Eager for a subject change, Allie tilted her head toward the window. "What's wrong with that cat's feet?"

Skye followed the direction of Allie's gaze and laughed. "Felix? You mean the extra toes? He's a polydactyl. They all are. Come on inside so you can meet them."

"Them?"

But Skye was already walking through the foyer of the historic West Hills home, her bare feet slapping on travertine floors that looked clean, but more weathered than Allie remembered. She hesitated, then followed Skye into the parlor. She stopped on the threshold of the arched doorway and looked down at the rose-printed carpet. She remembered how she used to hop from flower to flower while her mother shushed her and her grandma laughed and said, *"Oh, let her be a little girl, Priscilla."*

Allie looked up to see Skye standing in the middle of the room. She held an orange tabby cat cradled in her arms, and two more cats—one black and one gray—stood on the back of the sofa, one of them batting at Skye's elbow with a paw that looked like an oversized catcher's mitt.

"Oh my God," Allie said.

Skye laughed and set down the cat, who gave a growl of displeasure before wandering off. Tossing her hair, Skye scooped the gym-sock-colored cat off the windowsill and looked around the parlor. "Isn't it great? Vicky had the cat playground built about three years ago so they'd all have somewhere to play. It's a little extravagant, but it's what she wanted."

Vicky? Cat playground?

Allie looked up to see an intricate network of ramps and sisal-covered walkways lining the top edges of the walls. There was a cat door that appeared to lead out to the sunroom, and a bay window with a birdfeeder tacked to the other side. Another cat sat perched in a corner, its left ear looking like someone had bitten off the tip.

Allie looked back at Skye, trying to piece everything together. None of this was making any sense, nor was the fact that she had no fewer than three mutant-pawed felines twining themselves around her ankles. She stared at the cats, trying to figure out if these were some of the ones she'd already seen. Good Lord, how may were there? A black-and-white one looked up at her and gave a plaintive meow.

Allie looked back at Skye. "Cats," she said, wetting her lips as she realized how moronic she sounded. "How many cats are there?"

"Let's see, there's Matt, Luna, Sassy, Ferrell, Kenny, Barabbas, Maestro, Maggie, Boo, Marilyn, Felix—"

"And they're all—what did you call them?"

"Polydactyl. Extra toes. Yes, every single one of them."

"And they belong to you?"

Skye cocked her head to the side, her expression somewhere between amused and perplexed. "No, of course not. They're your grandmother's. She just hired me to be the caretaker."

"Of the B&B," Allie said slowly, still not understanding. "Taking reservations and cleaning rooms and—"

"Oh dear." Skye frowned and set the cat down. The feline scampered across the carpet and out into the foyer, its baseball-mitt paws skidding across the travertine. "So Vicky didn't tell you?"

"Tell me what?" Allie struggled to remember someone—anyone—daring to call her grandmother *Vicky*. She'd always been Victoria or Grandma, but Vicky?

"She hasn't run this place as a B&B for years," Skye said. "Said she didn't have the time or the energy anymore. She turned it into a cat sanctuary about a year ago."

"A cat sanctuary? Like—for cats?" Allie grimaced, knowing she sounded like an exceptionally dense child, but this wasn't adding up. "I mean she was always into animal advocacy, but I didn't realize—I mean, she never said—"

"I did sort of wonder why no one from the family came by to see it." Skye gave a sympathetic head tilt, and Allie knew what was coming next. "She told me about your parents—about the whole prison thing? I guess I figured you all had your hands full."

Allie swallowed hard, trying to understand. "She never wanted me to visit her here after I got older. And then when she moved into assisted living, I used to take her out to lunch all the time. I always offered to bring her here to see the old place, but—"

She trailed off, hating where that thought was taking her.

*She didn't want me to know. She knew I'd tell Mom and Dad, and she knew they wouldn't approve, but she went and did it anyway and made sure we wouldn't know until she was gone.*

There was something utterly heartbreaking about that. About her grandmother feeling a need to hide her own act of charity or impulsiveness or whatever this whole cat thing was.

Skye had gone quiet, seeming to sense Allie's need to process. When she finally spoke, her voice was soft. "It started with only a few cats, but she took in a few more," she said. "Then it turned out a couple of the originals weren't spayed or neutered. It's mostly under control now, and I have a vet come in every few months to make sure they're all healthy."

Allie nodded, still numb. "I mean, I guess I can kind of see why she'd do it. My grandmother loved cats, and she always had one or two, but—"

"Not fourteen?"

Allie blinked. "Is that how many there are?"

Skye nodded. "Vicky left enough in her will to keep them fed and cared for at least for a little while, but of course I'll be leaving as soon as I graduate."

"What?" Allie shook her head. "You're leaving?"

Skye smiled. "Well, I wasn't planning to live here forever. This is your place now."

"My place," Allie repeated, too dumbfounded to form words of her own.

"I know it meant a lot to your grandma for you to have it," Skye said. "She wanted you here."

Allie surveyed the room and wondered how long it had been since the sofa was cleaned, since the walls were repainted, since the floors were scrubbed or resealed.

And wondering how she'd gone from being Allison Ross, budding lawyer, potential wife and mother, to Allie Ross, instant crazy cat lady.

◆　◆　◆

Jack took a step toward the door, then hesitated and turned back to his mother. "You're sure you're okay with this?"

His mom smiled at him from the mostly empty living room of the three-bedroom house Jack had rented for the next couple months. "Sweetheart, of course I am! I'm just happy to see you two again. It feels like it's been ages!"

"It's been three days," Jack pointed out. "But I really appreciate you watching her on your first day here."

"Nonsense," she said. "You're going through all the trouble and expense of moving me out here and setting me up in that nice new place. The least I can do is watch my granddaughter every now and then."

The granddaughter in question had run down the hall to put Louise's suitcase in the guest room, which is where she'd be staying until all her furniture arrived and her new place was ready. Jack had wanted her to wait until he had her all set up in the posh apartment he'd rented for her at a nearby retirement village, but his mom had insisted on coming early. She'd missed them too much since they'd left California, and the loneliness had gotten the best of her after only a few days.

The thought of his mother alone sent a small surge of rage through him. It was like that anytime he thought of his father walking out thirty years ago, but he tamped it down. Now wasn't the time for old grievances.

"Grandma!" Paige came bounding down the hall like an excited puppy, her long, dark braid bouncing behind her like a tail. "Want to see the dance routine I've been working on?"

"Absolutely! Where would you like to do it?"

"Upstairs. Come on, you can sit on my bed and work the iPod."

The idea of his mother serving as a DJ to a ten-year-old made Jack smile, or maybe that was the sight of his mom and his little girl looking so happy to see each other. Paige didn't have a close relationship with Caroline's parents, who lived in Florida and visited once a year at best. The girl saw her aunt Missy—Caroline's sister—a couple times a year, but the visits had become less frequent as more time passed since Caroline's death. That left Jack's mom serving dual roles as primary grandma and the lone, consistent female presence in Paige's life.

Considering she'd raised Jack alone, he knew she was up to the task.

Paige and her grandma were halfway up the stairs now, Jack completely forgotten. It was just as well, since he needed to head back to the temp office he'd rented so he could nail down the final details of Clearwater's move to Portland. He had contracts to review, moving trucks to coordinate, job postings to consider, transfers to—

"Hey, Daddy?"

Jack looked up at the top of the stairs where his little girl was biting her lip. "I think I left my sweater at Allison's house last night."

—*and sweaters to retrieve*, he added to the growing to-do list.

"What have we talked about, Paige Anne?" he scolded. "About being more responsible for our belongings?"

God, he sounded like a parent, or like Allie used to sound when he'd lost his damn keys for the hundredth time.

The thought of Allie made him realize that Paige's forgotten sweater gave him an excuse to see her again. He couldn't decide whether to feel pissed off or giddy, or pissed off at himself for even *thinking* the word *giddy*. Was he sixteen?

"I'll go get your sweater," he said. "But you're going to have to do an extra chore from the chore list to earn it back."

"All right," she said. "I'll do it before you get back. Then me and Grandma will make that chocolate mousse you like."

"Grandma and I," he corrected without thinking.

"Nope, just us. Ladies only!" She giggled and ran up the stairs before he could say anything else. It was just as well. He was glad they'd be spending time together. Paige needed more girl time in her life, more female influence than he'd managed to give her in his years as a single dad.

He headed for the door and out to the silver Toyota he'd rented until the moving company brought his Audi out with the rest of their things. He didn't go for ostentatious sports cars, but he did like nice automobiles. Not that there was anything wrong with the Toyota. He'd owned one in college, though that had been covered in rust spots and sporting an odometer that had keeled over somewhere around three hundred and fifty thousand.

He spent several hours at the office going over contracts, then hit Fred Meyer for a few groceries and toiletries they needed at home. The route back from there took him right by Allie's place which was a good excuse to grab the sweater. Halfway there, it occurred to him he should probably call first, but he was on the interstate and didn't have the hands-free option set up in the rental car. Hopefully she was home, and she wasn't writhing beneath Wade in the throes of ecstasy. The thought made him a little queasy, so he pushed it out of his mind as he turned off the ramp and onto the little side road that led to her place.

As he pulled into the driveway, he noticed a blue BMW that looked like the one she drove in college. That seemed odd. It had been a nice car then, brand new when her parents gave it to her as a high school graduation gift with a personalized plate that read *anus tart*.

At least that's how Jack had read it until Allie's mom sniffed and pointed out that *a nu start* was a celebration of their baby's departure for college. Jack hadn't said so at the time, but he guessed it also under-scored their hope Allie would set off for her new life and leave her deadbeat boyfriend behind. Jack got the last laugh there. For a little while, anyway.

As he parked beside it now, he knew it was definitely the same car. The license plates had changed, of course, and it showed a bit of age. Eighteen years was a long time to keep a car, especially for someone with the sort of taste Allie had.

He got out and surveyed the fading paint, the body style that har-kened back nearly two decades, and wondered why he hadn't noticed the car the night before. Peering through the back window, he felt an unexpected rush of nostalgia. He knew that backseat well. He recalled fumbling and groping and having sweaty, passionate sex too many times to count that summer before they started college. Back when they were young and dumb and full of hope and hormones.

Jack clicked the alarm on the rental car and turned to Allie's place, taking the steps more quickly than he had the night before. He was starting to think showing up unannounced was a dumb idea, and if he hurried, maybe he wouldn't change his mind. It was a habit he'd started after Allie dumped him and he dropped out of college. In a rare moment of nostalgia, he'd tracked down his father's number and called him for the first time in years. He'd been hoping for a meaningful father-son talk, maybe even a few words of wisdom.

*"Get your shit together, son!"* his dad had barked over the phone. *"The road is paved with flattened squirrels who couldn't make up their minds."*

It was one of the last times he'd spoken to his father.

Jack shook off the memory and steeled himself to knock on Allie's door. He waited, hearing footsteps on the other side.

She answered faster than she had the night before, almost as though she'd been standing right next to it with her hand on the knob.

But as Jack took in her appearance, he decided that was unlikely.

She wore baggy sweatpants with a pink stain on the thigh. Her hair was in a sloppy topknot, and her entire face was covered with something that looked like split pea soup. The television over her shoulder blared something that sounded like *Real Housewives of New York City*.

Allie gaped at him. "Holy shit."

And with that, she slammed the door in his face.

# CHAPTER FOUR

Allie leaned back against her front door with her eyes closed, listening to the blood pounding in her head.

Or maybe that was Jack knocking.

"Why are you here, Jack?" she yelled through the door.

"Paige forgot her sweater."

*Great.* Of course she did. Allie gritted her teeth.

She'd assumed she'd never see Jack again after last night, and she sure as hell wasn't in any shape for entertaining. The mud mask she'd smeared on her face smelled nearly as bad as the blue silk tank top she'd pulled on before realizing it had hollandaise on the hem. But she hadn't had the heart to remove it—the shirt or the sauce—because she'd gotten both on a brunch outing with her grandmother just a few months ago.

"Allie?"

"I'm thinking."

Crap, where was the sweater? She glanced around the living room before remembering she'd stashed it in the coat closet at the far end of the hall like a stupid fucking perfect hostess.

She sighed. "How about I mail it to you?"

On the other side of the door, Jack stayed quiet. She thought for a second he'd gone away, and it annoyed her that she felt the tiniest hint of disappointment. She should probably just grab the damn sweater and toss it to him. It would take all of thirty seconds, and then he'd be on his way and out of her life for good.

"Allie, come on. Don't be vain. I've seen you looking worse."

"Thanks, Jack. That makes me feel much better." Her cheeks burned hot with embarrassment, but she'd infused her voice with enough steel to cover it.

"Just toss it out the door," he coaxed. "I won't look at you, I swear. Or just have your fiancé bring it out."

Something bubbled hot and shameful in her chest. She felt tired and embarrassed and really, really exhausted. Maybe it was the stress of planning her grandma's funeral. Maybe it was the evening spent surveying the dilapidated B&B. Maybe it was something else entirely. Something that had been brewing long before last night's silly game of make-believe with Jack.

Before she realized what she was doing, she turned and flung open the door.

Jack jumped back, startled either by the door opening or by her appearance again. Probably both. "Allie—"

"Look, I've had the week from hell," she snapped. "My grandma died on Sunday and I had to visit both my parents in prison to tell them, which was about as much fun as ripping off my own eyebrows with duct tape. I just spent my whole evening crawling around in basements and crawlspaces to realize I've just inherited a massive tax liability filled with dry rot and woodpecker holes and cat fur. Pardon me if I'm not thrilled by unexpected company."

Jack blinked, his expression ashen. "Your grandma died?"

The sympathy in his voice was enough to make her eyes sting with tears. Allie nodded, afraid to trust her own voice.

"God, Allie. I'm so sorry." He started to reach for her, then seemed to stop himself. "Your dad's mom? The one with the B&B?"

Again she nodded, and felt something thawing in the center of her chest.

"Shit, I'm so sorry. I know how much you loved her. Why didn't you say something last night? We could have cancelled dinner or—"

"No, we couldn't, Jack." Allie shook her head, feeling deflated. "I wanted everything to be perfect. I wanted you to see how fabulously awesome my life has turned out without you. I wanted to impress you and your gorgeous wife, so I cleaned my house and faked a fiancé and squeezed into Spanx so tight I still can't feel my thighs, all so I could spend an enchanting evening listening to you talk about your amazing, perfect life."

Jack just stared, and it occurred to her she hadn't meant to say any of that out loud. She sounded like a crazy person. Looked like one, too, considering the mud mask and hair that looked like she'd been electrocuted. God, she was pathetic.

"My amazing, perfect life," he repeated, looking a little dumbstruck. He nodded once, then turned. "Wait here."

He jogged off down the driveway, and Allie stared after him. She should probably shut the door. This was her chance to lock it behind him and pretend none of this had happened. Last night, right now— hell, maybe even sixteen years ago.

But instead she turned and walked down the hall, leaving her front door wide open. It was probably a dumb move, though not much dumber than opening it in the first place when she looked like this. She opened the coat closet. The little cream-colored sweater was right in front, and Allie pulled it off the hanger.

It had daisies stitched around the collar and on the front pocket, and a silly pang of longing rattled through her chest. She'd always imagined herself buying clothes like this for her own daughter, laughing and smiling as they sipped Italian sodas at the coffee shop next to Nordstrom. She folded it over her arm and walked back to the front door.

Jack had already returned from wherever he'd gone, and had set up camp in her living room. He'd closed the front door and parked himself right in the middle of her sofa with a shopping bag on the coffee table in front of him. He looked up as she walked in, and gave her a smile that made her traitorous heart surge in her chest.

"Hi," he murmured, and her heart thrummed faster.

"Make yourself at home," she muttered, trying to muster up some indignation. In truth, she wasn't that annoyed. It felt good to have another living, breathing human in her home, someone who wasn't looking at her like she was crazy or pathetic despite all evidence to the contrary.

"Please join me," he said.

"Just let me change into—"

"No."

The forcefulness in his voice surprised her, and she was about to tell him to stop bossing her around in her own home. That's when he reached into his shopping bag and pulled out a box of Crest whitening strips.

Wordlessly, he opened the package and peeled the back off one of the strips. He pressed it against his front teeth, using his oversized fingers to smooth out the edges. He repeated the process on his bottom teeth, then worked his way around the sides.

Allie stood watching, fascinated, not sure if she'd entered some sort of *Twilight Zone* episode or if she'd finally gone crazy.

"You're whitening your teeth," she said unnecessarily.

"Yep," he said, applying another strip to his teeth. "Would you mind shutting off the TV? This is the episode where Ramona looks at real estate, and I've already seen it."

"You've watched *Real Housewives of New York City*?"

"Yep. It's my guilty pleasure after Paige goes to sleep. Can I have some of that green face goop?"

Allie stared at him a moment, then picked up the remote and switched off the TV. "Why are you doing this?"

"So you stop feeling embarrassed and exposed and sit down on the damn sofa with me and have a snack." He put down the box of whitening strips and turned to grin at her.

Allie felt something soften in the center of her chest. "You look like a dork."

"Yep. That's the idea."

The corners of her mouth twitched up, threatening to morph into a smile. "And you can't eat snacks with those things on your teeth."

"Ah, that's where you're wrong." He reached into the shopping bag again and pulled out a can of non-dairy whipped topping. He popped the top off and opened his mouth, aiming straight down his throat.

The hollow, foamy sound was both familiar and foreign, and Allie tried not to remember the times in college when she'd walked in to find him doing this in the kitchen. Or the other times when he'd brought the can of whipped cream into the bedroom and—

"All right," she said, stepping around the sofa. "You win." She sat down beside him, her butt landing a little closer to him than she'd aimed for. Her thigh touched his, but it would be awkward to move away, so she grabbed the can of whipped cream out of his hand. She hesitated a second, then squirted it straight onto her tongue.

"Nice," Jack said.

"This is disgusting." She lifted the can again and took another hit, enjoying the creamy sweetness more than she expected.

Jack grabbed the can back and squirted another mouthful, smacking his lips. Then he set the can down on the table and rested one massive palm on her knee, just like it belonged there.

"Look, there's nothing I can say about your grandma that will make this hurt any less," he said. "Anything I have to offer will just sound trite and clichéd and won't cancel out the fact that you won't bake cookies together again, or hear her tell you how much she paid for the antique carving set at Thanksgiving dinner. You'll never get to hug her or smell those fancy roses she put all over the house. You'll go to buy Mother's Day cards and you'll realize you need to buy one less than you did the year before, and you'll end up standing there in the aisle at Target bawling like an idiot while people bump into you with their shopping carts, and it's going to suck like you wouldn't fucking believe."

He held her gaze with his, and Allie felt a tear slip through the green goo on her cheek. "Hypothetically speaking," he added softly.

"Hypothetically speaking," Allie whispered as the tear dropped onto the leg of her sweats, making another discolored spot. "Thank you."

"You're welcome."

"You get it."

"I do."

She bit her lip, then thought better of it when she tasted minty clay. "Want to talk about it?"

"Not really," he said. "I've spent enough time telling random strangers how one shitty car accident left my kid motherless and made me a widower. I don't need to relive it."

"I'm sorry." Her throat felt thick again, but it was clear from the look on Jack's face that he didn't want her to ask more questions. "And I take back what I said about your amazing, perfect life. You've obviously been through some tough stuff."

He nodded and picked up the whipped cream can again. He tilted his head back and took another hit, and Allie felt her shoulders relax for the first time since she'd gotten the call about her grandma.

When they looked at each other again, there was something different between them. Allie couldn't put her finger on it, but it felt like things had shifted.

"So . . . Wade—" Jack prompted. "Not your fiancé after all?"

Allie shook her head, grateful to the green goo for hiding her flaming cheeks. "Not my fiancé. Sorry. I spent yesterday evening worrying you'd notice the engagement ring I was wearing was an old pinkie ring my grandmother used to wear."

He laughed. "Yeah, I kept close track of your grandmother's pinkie rings." He picked up her left hand, an absent gesture, but one that sent goose bumps up Allie's arm. He studied her bare hand, turning it from side to side before setting it back on the sofa. His palm rested lightly on the back of her hand, and Allie wondered if it was force of habit or something else that left his fingers touching hers.

"So Wade's just a friend, then?"

Allie hesitated, then nodded. "Yep. Just a friend."

"So you're not sleeping with him?"

"Of course not," she said. "Not that it's any of your business."

"Hey, we're putting it all out there, right?"

Allie shrugged and took the whipped cream from him. She fiddled with the nozzle. "Wade's just a great friend. The two of us have zero chemistry."

"I kinda noticed."

Allie snorted. "Thanks."

He shrugged and took another hit of whipped cream. "Figured we're being open and honest and everything."

Allie glared at him, though she wasn't actually annoyed. Mostly just ready to move on with the conversation. "So who is Lacey, anyway?"

He quirked an eyebrow at her. "You told me last night that you didn't care."

"I don't," she said, pretty sure that was true.

"She's not my girlfriend, like I said."

"That's fine." Allie shrugged with as much nonchalance as she could muster. "It's really none of my—"

"But that's because she doesn't want anything serious, so we've had a friends-with-benefits thing going for about a year now, which is obviously something I'm not willing to explain to my daughter."

Allie cleared her throat and nodded, not willing to admit how much it annoyed her to think of Jack having sex with some leggy blonde whose casual attitudes about sex probably meant she was amazing at it. Really, it meant nothing to Allie. Nothing at all.

"So you've moved to Portland." She wasn't sure if she meant it as a subject change or a question about whether the friends-with-benefits thing would endure a six-hundred-mile move.

"Yep. The rest of my team will be making the move over the next several weeks, but I've already started getting the company up and running in its new location. And we visited Paige's new school yesterday morning, so she'll start next week."

"It's so strange seeing you as a dad," she admitted, looking down at her lap again. "I guess I didn't expect that."

He laughed and took another hit of whipped cream. "Neither did I. Wasn't exactly planned, if you know what I mean."

"Oh." Allie kept her expression guarded, not sure if that tidbit of information made her feel better or worse.

"But I love being a father. She's the best damn thing that ever happened to me. Gave me a reason to be a better guy than I had been." He cleared his throat and set the whipped cream down. "Enough about me. You said your grandma left you the bed-and-breakfast?"

Allie nodded and took a shaky breath. "Yes. My grandparents started it back in 1949. It used to get written up in all kinds of travel books."

"I remember it. Yellow, right? With those fancy arch-top plantation shutters you always loved. And there was that huge table they always bragged about importing from France or Italy or someplace like that."

Allie nodded, surprised he'd remembered any of that. "Right. Only it's not actually functioning as a B&B now. Just a home for about six hundred mutant-toed cats."

Jack frowned. "Come again?"

"Mutant cats. The place is overrun with them."

"What do you mean *mutant*? Like radioactive or something?"

Allie laughed and shook her head. "They have all these extra toes. It makes their paws look like catcher's mitts."

"Oh, you mean Hemingway cats?"

"What?"

"That's what they're called, I think. Ernest Hemingway used to own a bunch of extra-toed cats, so that's where the name comes from."

"I guess so. I didn't know that." She shook her head, pretty sure the fact that they'd spent this long discussing cats officially qualified her for crazy cat lady status.

As if owning fourteen felines hadn't already accomplished that for her.

"So it sounds like your job's been going great," she said, eager to steer the subject away from felines. "Congratulations."

"Thanks. I had a few years of being a lazy dumbass before I met Caroline. She urged me to get my shit together, so I went back to school and had just about finished the degree when we found out she was pregnant with Paige."

"Wow." Allie kicked herself for not formulating a better response, but that was all she could come up with. The back of her throat was stinging, and she wasn't sure if it was the knowledge that he'd been willing to shape up for another woman, or if it was something else entirely.

*Something else entirely*, her subconscious said, but Allie ordered herself not to go there. She grabbed the can of whipped cream and took a hit.

"So are you a lawyer now or what?" he asked. "I tried to Facebook stalk you over the years, but you never really posted much. I couldn't make it to our ten-year high school reunion, so I'll admit I'm kind of clueless what you do for a living."

Allie laughed and swallowed the whipped cream. "You and most people."

"What do you mean?"

"I'm a Certified Association Executive," she said. "I know it sounds like a made-up job, or like a glorified secretary or something."

"I wasn't going to say that."

"It's okay, I get it a lot."

"So what does a Certified Association Executive do?"

"I oversee a state medical association, organizing membership campaigns and public advocacy and planning education events. That might sound boring, but I really love it. No two days are the same, and I get to use a lot of negotiation and people management skills. It's so much better than the political campaign stuff I was doing before."

"So did you finish your poli-sci degree?"

"Undergrad, yes. But I only got through one year of law school before I quit."

She wasn't sure if she'd ever said those words—*I quit*—out loud before, and she braced herself for Jack to say something snarky. To rib her for not being able to hack it or to give her crap for not heading down the path she'd been so certain was meant for her.

Instead, he reached for her. Well, not for her. For the whipped cream can in her hand. He pulled it from her grip, tilted his head back, and took a hit. "Delicious," he said.

Allie smiled. "Thank you."

"Why? Did you can it yourself?"

"No. I mean—thank you for not being a dick about me dropping out of school. Or faking a fiancé or having jailbird parents or—"

She stopped there, not sure how much he knew about that. Not sure how much she wanted him to know.

"So it sounds like life didn't turn out quite like either of us expected sixteen years ago," he said at last.

"Nope." Allie pressed her lips together, then nodded. "I guess not."

"And we're also not exactly who we pretended to be last night."

"Guilty as charged." Allie shifted on the sofa, bumping his knee with hers. "So where does that leave us?"

"Friends?" There was a hopeful note in his voice, a tone Allie recognized from a long time ago. Years before they'd even dated, back when Jack was the sweet boy in math class with sad eyes. The boy whose father had walked out and left him alone with his mom and a whole heap of trust issues.

She wondered if he'd ever gotten over that.

"Friends," she repeated, nodding a little. "That sounds good."

"Excellent." He leaned back against the cushions, splaying his arms out across the back of the sofa. "So is there anything else you want to confess?"

"What?" Her voice cracked just a little, but she forced herself not to flinch. "What do you mean?"

"Well, we've kinda opened all the floodgates here. The fake fiancé, the career paths that didn't go like we expected. Your law-breaking parents, my shotgun marriage—it's been very therapeutic getting it all out in the open."

"Oh. Right. Yes, it has."

"So I just wondered if there's anything else either of us wanted to share."

Allie felt her cheeks heat up, but she was determined not to let him notice. "You've seen plenty of embarrassing stuff from me tonight. Speaking of which, I need to go rinse off this mud mask."

"And I should probably get this crap off my teeth. Is there more than one bathroom in this place?"

"Yeah, go ahead and use the guest bath you used last night. I'll wash up in the master."

She stood up and headed down the hall, wondering if she should have seized the chance to tell him goodnight and bid him farewell. She rinsed her face quickly, then toyed with the idea of smearing on a little lipstick. She decided against it, ruling out the hairbrush, too. It seemed pointless now. He'd seen her at her worst already.

She turned and walked back down the hall to find Jack standing by the door with his shopping bag in hand. He flashed her an exaggerated grin, showing teeth that no longer bore the film of whitening strips. "Better?"

"Definitely," Allie said. "Here, don't forget your whipped cream." She hustled around the couch to grab it off the table, then met him back at the door and thrust it into his hand.

"You sure?" he asked. "I wouldn't want to deprive you."

"Deprive me, please. I don't need the extra calories."

"You look perfect to me."

She laughed. "It's the sweatpants. I know they're a turn-on, but please try to control yourself."

He grinned at her and reached up to tuck a stray lock of hair behind her ear. It was an intimate gesture, and one so unexpected that Allie realized she wasn't breathing.

Jack seemed startled, too, and he stepped back a bit. He didn't say anything for a second, and Allie wondered if he was waiting for something. He scuffed his toe on the carpet, then cleared his throat. "Look, if you need any help with the B&B, give me a call."

"What do you mean?"

He shrugged. "We're friends now, right?"

"I guess so."

"You know what I was doing for some of those years before I got my shit together and went back to college?"

Allie shook her head. "No." She grimaced. "We've already established that I'm a self-absorbed bitch who couldn't be bothered to look you up for the last sixteen years."

"I never said that."

"No, but I did. For the record, it wasn't that I didn't care. I just needed closure, I guess."

"Yeah," he said. "I hear you." They stared at each other for a moment, and Allie started to lose herself in those silvery-blue eyes.

"So anyway," Jack said, breaking the spell. "I did a lot of handyman work in my time away from college. Drywall, roofing, painting. That sort of thing. I'm also a pretty decent carpenter. And while I hammer out all the final details of moving my company out here, I have a little bit of free time on my hands. I might as well give you a hand with the B&B."

Allie swallowed, not sure what he was offering. What sort of price tag came with a favor like that?

"Jack, you can't—"

"Allie, you want to know the best thing about not marrying you?"

She blinked, then shook her head. "What?"

"That you don't get to tell me what I can and can't do anymore." He smiled. "Now what time can I come look at the place?"

◆ ◆ ◆

Jack wasn't sure what the hell had gotten into him offering to help Allie with her grandma's B&B. He hadn't slung a hammer to do anything but hang pictures since Paige was still in diapers. He already had plenty to do moving his damn business and setting up in a new city, not to mention everything involved in getting his daughter ready to start at her new school. Besides that, his reunion was tomorrow night.

Did he really need another thing on his plate?

*Hell yes,* he thought as Allie opened the door looking flushed and lovely and holding a big gray cat in her arms.

"*Mrrrw-ow,*" said the cat.

"Hi there," said Allie, looking a little embarrassed.

"Good morning." He nodded at the cedar trim above the window. "Please tell me those aren't bullet holes."

"Those aren't bullet holes."

"Termites?"

She shook her head. "Woodpecker. At least that's my suspicion, based on internet research."

"No kidding?" He whistled low and surveyed the damage again. "Impressive that a bird could do all that."

"*Impressive* might not be the word I'd choose. I've been online all morning trying to figure out how to put a stop to it. I don't suppose you have any sticky resin like Tanglefoot or Roost No More in that tool belt?"

"'Fraid not. How about a roll of duct tape?"

"I'll pass, but thanks."

She stepped aside to usher him in, and Jack caught a hint of her perfume. It was new, not anything she'd worn in college. A little like Chardonnay, with hints of oak and vanilla and honey and melon. Jack's stomach flipped over, though it probably didn't have much to do with a craving for wine.

"Thanks so much for coming," Allie said. "Careful. The cats are everywhere. This one keeps trying to get out the front door."

"Maybe they'll go after the woodpeckers."

"Not a bad idea, but I don't think they're very street smart. The cats, I mean. Jury's still out on the woodpeckers."

Jack closed the door behind him and Allie set down the gray cat she'd been holding. It scampered a couple feet to the right and took a swat at another cat that had a mottled-looking coat. That one had splotches of tan and orange and white and looked a little like a disco ball.

"Hey, disco kitty," he said, bending to scratch behind its ear. "Mind if I take a look at your house?"

"Disco kitty?" Allie laughed. "How did you know that's BeeGee?"

"Lucky guess." He turned in a slow circle, breathing deeply. "You know, I've gotta admit, I expected it to reek of cat pee."

"I'm glad it doesn't. I think Skye's done a good job keeping the litter boxes tidy, plus there's a catio with a huge garden where a lot of them go."

"I'm not sure whether to ask about Skye or the catio, but both sound intriguing."

Allie bent down and scratched the mottled-looking cat under the chin as another cat—this one a black-and-white tuxedo—came up behind her and head-butted her calf. Jack did his best not to stare at Allie's ass while she was bent over, but he wasn't having much luck. He felt a mix of relief and disappointment as she stood up and turned to face him and the tuxedo cat trotted off with its oversized paws making a soft thumping sound on the travertine floors.

"Skye is the caretaker," she said. "The one my grandma hired to look after the place. And a catio is—"

"A patio for cats?"

"Bingo, smart guy."

Jack grinned. "We college dropouts have some smarts."

"I thought you went back and got your degree."

"I did. But I don't recall learning about catios or home repairs."

Allie smiled at him, and Jack felt something stirring in the center of his chest. He hadn't expected to remember much about the house, but standing here in the entry was filling him with an odd nostalgia. He'd only been here a couple times, but he recognized the familiar patina of the alder wainscoting and the tinted slabs of sunlight streaming through the parlor windows onto a piano Allie's grandmother used to play. He remembered her belting out bawdy show tunes after a few glasses of sherry one Thanksgiving. Allie's father had hustled in to try and quiet her down, but there had been no stopping Victoria Ross.

"Do you remember coming here with me for Thanksgiving that one year?"

Jack looked at her, wondering if she'd read his thoughts. "Yeah, I remember," he said. "Our freshman year in college. We were supposed to alternate between your family one year and mine the next. My mom's still pissed she never got her turn."

"Really?"

"Not really. But she did tell me to invite you over for dinner when she heard I was coming here."

That wasn't all his mom had said, but Jack figured it was best not to share. When he'd told her about helping Allie out with this place, a familiar crease had appeared between his mother's brows.

*"Are you sure that's a good idea?"* she'd asked, glancing down the hall to where Paige was busy organizing supplies for her first day at her new school on Monday. *"After everything she put you through—"*

*"That was a long time ago, Mom."*

*"I know, but it still had an effect on you. First your father abandoned us, and then Allie left. Between that and Caroline passing away, I just worry about you setting yourself up for more heartache."*

*"Relax,"* he'd told her, planting a kiss on her cheek before turning to grab his tool belt. *"I'm nailing up some loose decking, not nailing her up against a wall."*

He'd only said it to make his mom laugh and swat him with a dish towel. But seeing Allie now in a pink V-neck sweater and jeans that made her ass look like a dream, he couldn't pretend it didn't cross his mind.

"I always liked your mom," Allie said, which kinda killed the sexy thoughts Jack had been having.

"My mom liked you, too. She thought you were a good influence on me."

"And mine thought you were determined to corrupt her innocent angel."

"She was right." He grinned. "Which is why my daughter isn't dating until she's thirty."

Allie laughed. "Good luck with that."

Jack looked around the parlor, a little amazed by all the ramps and cat perches built along the walls and all the way up to the ceiling. Cat beds jutted out from each window, even the ones twelve feet off the ground. It was an impressive feat of engineering; he'd give it that.

"So," he said. "Where do you want to start?"

"I guess I can give you a quick tour of the place," she said. "I don't imagine you remember much from sixteen years ago."

"I remember plenty." He didn't realize until after the words left his mouth that it sounded more meaningful than he'd intended. Like a commentary on how they used to be together, which wasn't what he meant at all. Or was it? "But I'm sure tons of things have changed over the years," he added. "About the house, I mean."

"True," she agreed, holding his gaze for a moment before turning to walk down the hall.

She spent the next hour leading him around the grand old home while a parade of cats trailed behind, mewling and occasionally snarling at one another. Jack followed along, taking notes while Allie pointed out warped spots in the myrtlewood moldings in the guest rooms and patches of sagging drywall in one of the guest baths. Most of it was cosmetic and fairly easy to repair. All things considered, the place wasn't in the poor condition Jack had expected.

Several times he stopped to take measurements or poke at a loose piece of trim. Each time, Allie bent low over him. It gave him a nice glimpse down the front of the pink sweater, which was even more pleasant than the rear view she offered as she led him down hallways and up stairwells.

*You agreed to be friends*, he reminded himself. *Friends don't ogle friends.*

A convincing argument, but not one that registered with Jack's libido. By the time they'd reached the third floor, there wasn't much blood left in his brain.

"Do you think you can get it up?"

Jack shook himself out of his testosterone-fueled trance and tried to figure out what the hell Allie was saying to him. "I beg your pardon?"

"The ladder." She pointed at the ancient-looking wooden A-frame leaned up against the wall, and it occurred to him she'd probably been telling him about it while he was busy staring at her ass. "I spent an hour this morning trying to set it up so I could see what's in the attic, but the damn thing's stuck."

Jack bent down and picked up the ladder. It was rickety as hell, and common sense told him he probably shouldn't attempt to climb on it even if he could get it open. But he'd already said goodbye to common sense the second he offered to help his ex-fiancée with her home repairs, so Jack yanked a small can of WD-40 out of his tool belt.

"There," he said as he squirted each of the hinges. "Just needed a little lube to get the legs open, that's all."

Hell. He didn't mean that to sound suggestive, but maybe the pheromones were short-circuiting his brain. He saw Allie flush a bit, but she said nothing as he eased the ladder open and set it up beneath the trap door to the attic. He tested the first couple rungs by putting a little weight on them, which convinced him the ladder was stronger than it looked. It wasn't that far to fall anyway, so he clambered the rest of the way up and reached for the handle on the attic door.

"You coming?" he called behind him.

"Yes," Allie said. "Just taking my turn staring at your ass. I figure it's only fair, since that's what you've been doing to me for the last hour."

He grinned over his shoulder at her. "Yours has aged rather nicely."

"Same to you."

Jack laughed and pushed open the door to the attic. Okay, so they were flirting like old friends sometimes did. Casual, easy, fun. He could do this.

He got the attic door all the way open and crawled inside, grateful he'd had the foresight to stuff a Mini Maglite in his tool belt. Not bad for the guy who'd once forgotten half the supplies on a camping trip.

"I didn't forget condoms, though," he said.

"What?"

"On that first camping trip," he said. "The one we were talking about the other night? I might have forgotten bug spray and cooking stuff and matches to make fire, but I didn't forget condoms."

He turned around in time to see Allie rolling her eyes. "Typical eighteen-year-old guy."

"No argument there."

She clambered up behind him, taking the rungs one at a time. "So what the hell were we thinking planning a life together? We couldn't even plan a camping trip."

"We were young and dumb." Like that explained everything. It didn't, not even close, but Allie was nearing the top of the ladder now and Jack was too busy keeping an eye on her to elaborate.

"Careful," he said. "A couple of the rungs near the top are a little wobbly. Here, take my hand."

He reached out to her, expecting Allie to insist she had it under control and that she didn't need him at all. Instead, she put her palm in his.

"I forgot how small your hands were," he remarked as he hoisted her up.

He waited to see if she'd respond with a comment about the size of his hands. He'd seen her looking last night, so maybe things like that still registered on her radar. But Allie just righted herself on the floor of the attic and dusted her hands on her jeans.

"Thanks for the help."

"Probably want to shut the door," he said. "You don't want a dozen cats climbing the ladder."

"Good idea."

While Allie pushed the hinged flap closed, Jack surveyed the space. Someone had laid long pieces of plywood across the rafter beams, but they looked old and a little warped. The space wasn't as dim as he expected, mostly due to slatted vents and a couple small attic windows on either side. Still, he was glad he'd remembered a flashlight.

"Careful," he said as Allie took a tentative step onto one of the flat spans of plywood. "We don't know how stable those are."

She tested one out, pressing the toe of her shoe against the board. "Do you think it's safe to walk on?"

"Maybe. Keep your weight on the rafter beams just to be safe."

Jack pivoted, surveying the rest of the space. He guided his flashlight beam in a slow arc, illuminating dark corners with the narrow yellow ray of light. The room smelled like cardboard and old mothballs, and he could see dust sparkling in a sunbeam that filtered through a small window at the peak of the ceiling. There was a seventies-era tinsel Christmas tree along one wall next to a creepy-looking dressmaker's mannequin wearing a scuba suit. Near that was an old steamer trunk like the one his own grandparents used to have, and he wondered how the hell someone had lugged it up a ladder. Maybe some sort of pulley system.

"Do you know if she's had this place checked for black mold or asbestos or any other environmental hazards?" he asked.

"Not sure. Is that expensive?"

"The inspection won't be, but dealing with any hazards could be. What is all this stuff, anyway?"

"I think Grandma mostly used it as storage space. I have no idea when she was last up here. Years, probably."

Allie took a few cautious steps toward the wall where the mannequin and steamer trunk sat, which was smart. The floor looked reinforced over there, so it should be safer. Jack watched as she balanced on one of the plywood-covered beams, making her way across the dim space. The dormer window illuminated her path, but Jack pointed his flashlight there anyway, hoping to give her a little extra help.

"Take it slow," he called.

"I know, I know."

He watched her take two more steps, her hand reaching out to brace her against the bare wood beam. Her hair fell over her face as she looked down at a pile of boxes stacked three high, each the size of a large microwave.

"I guess I should look inside some of these," she said.

"Need a box cutter?"

"No, they're not sealed." She was already unfolding the flaps of the top box, sending little puffs of dust into the sunbeam from the window above her. Jack took a few steps closer, aiming his flashlight beam at her hands.

The instant her shoulders tensed, Jack froze.

"Holy shit."

# CHAPTER FIVE

Allie stared into the cardboard box, hardly believing her eyes. She started to reach inside, then yanked her hand back. Did she really want to touch it?

"Allie? What is it?"

She turned and looked at Jack, then shook her head. "Nothing. Just some old clothes my grandma wore when I was a little girl. I hadn't seen them for years, so it caught me by surprise."

Good, that was a good lie. Close enough to the truth that he wouldn't feel the need to investigate.

Either her lying skills had slipped over the years or Jack had gotten better at recognizing them, because the next thing she knew, he was striding across the attic toward her. Allie hurried to push the box flaps closed. Maybe she'd get lucky and he'd slip off the rafter he was balancing on and go crashing through the ceiling below.

She didn't want him hurt. Just distracted enough not to ask more questions.

Allie pivoted and pointed to the old steamer trunk near the window. "Let's see if we can get into that trunk. It looks pretty old." She kept her back to the pile of boxes, feeling the contents burning through her spine. "You know, I think that's the same trunk I hit my head on when I was six or seven. Bled all over the place. It used to be in one of the bedrooms downstairs, so maybe the keys are still—"

"Allie."

"What?"

"What's in that box?"

"What box?"

"The one behind you."

She tossed her hair, doing her best to look casual. "Like I said, just some old clothes I remember Grandma wearing when—"

"You're full of it."

He was close enough now to touch her, close enough that she saw flecks of silver in those pale-blue eyes. Obviously she wasn't fooling him, so she dropped her hands to her sides with a sigh. She turned around and peered at the box.

The flaps had sprung open again like the world's most terrifying jack-in-the-box. They both stared into it for a good long time before either of them spoke.

It was Jack who broke the silence. "Old clothes your grandma used to wear, huh?"

"Right."

He reached into the box and pulled out the first item. "Funny, I don't remember your grandmother wearing a crotchless mesh bodysuit at Thanksgiving dinner."

Allie felt the heat creep into her cheeks. "I'm sure there's a perfectly reasonable explanation."

"Sure there is." He set the bodysuit down and reached into the box again, this time pulling out a froth of black-and-white satin and lace. "It gave her something to wear when the French maid costume was being cleaned."

"I really don't think—"

"Hey, check this out." He'd pried the box all the way open and was poking around, not picking anything up this time, thank God. "Looks like Grandma liked ball gags. And anal beads. And leather paddles with embedded spikes. And—"

"Please stop touching things." Allie swatted his hand off the edge of the box, but Jack reached in with the other and picked up something that looked like a riding crop. He turned it over in his hands with a look of fascination mixed with amusement.

Allie cringed. "I'm sure it couldn't belong to my grandmother."

"Was her middle name Elizabeth?"

"No, it was Elena. Why?"

Jack flipped the riding crop over and held it out so she could read the *VER* monogram on the end. "Either this belonged to her, or she was in the habit of storing sex toys for guests who shared her initials."

"It was a very busy bed-and-breakfast at one time. I'm sure—"

"Allie."

"Yeah?"

"Cut the crap."

She sighed and grabbed the riding crop out of his hand. "Good Lord." She tried shoving it back in the box, but she must've had the angle wrong, because the flaps wouldn't close. She gave up, letting the top spring open again. "I can't believe this."

"Believe it, babe. Grandma was kinky."

She grimaced and closed her eyes. "Pardon me while I jot that down so I can include it in her obituary."

Jack laughed. "I never would have guessed the woman who lectured us on living together before marriage had a treasure trove of BDSM gear in her attic."

"Well, she always was very . . . vivacious."

"That's one word for it."

"She had this prim and proper side to her, but inside—" Allie shook her head, not sure whether to laugh or cry. "Did you know she married my grandfather on a bet?"

"I don't think I heard that."

Allie nodded, keeping her eyes averted from the box of sex toys. "She walked past a shop where he was working as an auto mechanic. He had a car torn up in a million pieces and she bet him he couldn't have it put back together and running by the end of the week."

"And he did it?"

"Yep. So she married him. They were together fifty-two years."

Jack gave a low whistle. "So that's the secret to a long, happy marriage, huh?"

"You mean a total lack of foresight and planning?"

He laughed. "Something like that."

Allie glanced back at the box of sex toys. God, what was she going to do with all this?

Jack pointed at the mannequin behind her. "I thought that was for scuba diving," he said. "Who knew they made crotchless latex bodysuits with a full hood?"

Allie was almost afraid to look, but she turned and stared at it anyway. *Yep.* The nipple tassels were a nice touch. She turned back to Jack. "You can't tell anyone about this."

He quirked an eyebrow at her. "There go my plans to invite CNN for a tour of your grandma's attic."

"I'm serious, Jack. She'd die if—" She stopped there, closing her eyes. "I can't believe I just said that." She opened her eyes again and took in the mannequin, the box, the dozens of other boxes she was afraid to open now. "This is so—so—"

"Enlightening?"

"Not the word I was looking for. I just never imagined this side of my grandmother."

"It's not a big deal, Al. Everyone has sex. Some just have different tastes." He took a step closer and lowered his voice. "As I recall, you used to like me tying you to the headboard with silk scarves."

Allie felt the heat creeping into her cheeks. "That's different. My grandma—"

"Was a sexual person, too. When did your grandpa die?"

"Eight years ago. A few years after that, Grandma introduced us to her special friend, a man named Harvey. We thought they were just playing mah-jongg together."

"I don't know what mah-jongg is, but if it requires anal beads, you were right."

"Ugh." She covered her face with her hands. "I can't un-see this."

Jack laughed and pried her fingers away from her eyes. He didn't let go of her left hand right away, and Allie felt his touch like a brand. "I know it's not the image you had in your mind for your grandma," he said, "but I think it's kinda cool. Isn't it at least a little exciting to know she had a happy, healthy sex life?"

Allie frowned at him, but said nothing. He probably had a point, but she'd prefer not to think about it.

"Maybe it needs to sink in a little more." Jack glanced at the mannequin, then looked away quickly. "On second thought, maybe you're better off not giving this too much thought."

Allie waved a defeated hand around the attic. "I was planning to go through all these boxes to see what I might be able to sell to pay the back taxes on this place. Now I'm afraid to open anything else."

"Just a hunch, but I don't think the going rate on used bondage equipment is all that high."

She rolled her eyes. "Seriously, what am I going to do?"

"Look, odds are pretty slim she had two hundred boxes of sex toys. Just pick another one. You're bound to find something useful. Just keep poking around."

"Poking around," she muttered, trying not to think about the sort of poking around her grandmother might have been doing. "Okay."

Jack let go of her hand, and Allie tried not to feel disappointed. She stepped away from the stack of boxes, relieved to put a little distance between herself and the creepy bondage mannequin.

And Jack, come to think of it. Having him this close, this big and strong and solid beside her was reminding her that it had been an awfully long time since anyone besides prison guards had run their hands over her body.

He still smelled good, dammit. He'd never worn cologne, and she didn't think he was wearing any now. But he'd always had a certain aura about him. God, that sounded so cheesy when she thought of it like that, but it was true. He smelled like the Oregon desert after a thunderstorm, earthy ozone and damp sage, and if she kept standing next to him, she'd probably say or do something stupid.

He was already pawing through another stack of boxes on the other side of the mannequin, so Allie used the chance to slip over toward the steamer trunk.

"This one's not so bad," he called. "Looks like a bunch of old magazines. Home and garden stuff, not porn, in case you're wondering."

"Thanks for the report."

She knelt in front of the trunk. It was definitely the same one her grandma used to keep in the blue bedroom on the south side of the house. She remembered trailing her hand over the top of it as a little girl, the bumps and ridges like a topographical map under her fingers. She'd never paid attention to the lock on it before, and had just assumed it required a key. Studying it now, she realized it was a combination lock. She thought about asking Jack if he had a lock-picking kit in his tool belt, but right now she needed a little space between her hormones and Jack's tool belt.

The little dial looked rusty, but the numbers spun without much effort. She moved the digits to form her grandma's birthday, then pushed the lever. Nothing. Of course. Victoria Elena Ross had been savvier than that. Then again, she hadn't been savvy enough to burn her bondage equipment before moving into an assisted living facility. It was all relative.

Allie's hands were sweating, which probably had more to do with Jack's proximity and the heat of the attic than a fear of finding more sex toys. She wiped them on her jeans and tried again. This time she dialed in her grandfather's birthdate, conscious of Jack still pawing through boxes behind her.

Nothing. She tried her grandparents' anniversary, followed by her own father's birthdate. Nope. Same for her parents' anniversary and every common series of numbers she could think of like 1234 or 6666, though would Victoria Ross have thought to plug in the sign of the beast?

Unlikely.

Then again, Victoria Ross had owned a ball gag.

Allie tried 6969, just to be sure. She was relieved when it didn't work.

Behind her, Jack was whistling something. She thought it might be a Barenaked Ladies song, and her brain flashed to the memory of them listening to one of their albums in college. They'd danced together in their apartment living room, not caring that the blinds were wide open and anyone in the world could see them. She'd tossed her hair and shrieked with laughter as he spun her around while the downstairs neighbor pounded on the ceiling.

Allie turned the numbers on the combo lock again, forming her own birthdate. This time, something clicked. A shiver chattered down her spine as she pressed the lever and found it moved easily. She hesitated, not sure she wanted to open it.

Behind her, Jack had stopped whistling. She heard footsteps and knew he'd noticed the change in her demeanor.

"Please don't be more sex toys," she murmured as she slowly lifted the lid. "Please no more sex toys. Please no more sex toys. Please no more—"

"Holy shit."

It was Jack who said it this time, and Allie couldn't help but point out the obvious. "I already said that," she breathed as she stared into the trunk. "Try something more original."

"Are those twenties or hundreds?"

Allie leaned closer to peer at the large stacks of bills, each one bound with a tidy yellow ribbon. "Hundreds." She swallowed hard, pretty sure she'd never seen this much cash in her whole life. "There must be at least—"

"A million dollars."

She turned and looked at him, wondering if she looked as stunned as he did. "How do you know?"

"I saw a video once." He swallowed and Allie watched his throat move. "Paige asked me what a million dollars in cash looks like, so we Googled it. We found this YouTube video showing all the different configurations and how it would stack up." He nodded at the steamer trunk, and Allie realized he was a lot more shaken by this than he'd been by the sex toys.

Allie stared at the money. She didn't feel excited. She didn't feel giddy. She didn't feel rich.

She felt utterly terrified.

♦ ♦ ♦

"Holy shit," Jack said again as he stared at the stack of bills.

It had to be connected to Allie's parents, right? He glanced at her, wondering if she was thinking the same thing. Her face was paste white, and he knew from experience what was coming next.

"Um, here." He fumbled for a plastic Easter basket on a shelf overhead, pausing to dump out the painted metallic eggs. They bounced and wobbled across the floor, one of them bumping Allie's knee as he thrust the basket into her hands.

She took the basket with a bewildered stare. "What's this for?"

"You looked like you might puke."

She looked down at the basket, then back up at him. "I told you the other night I'm not a nervous puker anymore."

But she was definitely nervous. Jack could feel the tension radiating off her like shockwaves. It felt odd to have her on her knees in front of him, but she hadn't made any move to stand up.

"Anyway," she said, in a breezy tone that sounded a little forced, "I really don't think a woven basket is the best receptacle for vomit."

"Pardon me for forgetting my waterproof bucket. I'll pick one up on my way home."

"That would be helpful."

He waited for her to say something else, but she'd gone quiet again. Her gaze was back on the cash, and she started to reach for one of the tight bundles.

"Wait!" he said. "Do we need to call the police or something?"

She turned and stared at him, hand poised over the stack of bills. "What for?"

"If this is connected to a crime, won't they need to dust for fingerprints?"

Allie frowned. "A crime."

"Right."

He wasn't going to be the one to say it. He didn't know all the details of her parents' trial, except that they'd been convicted of bilking investors out of hundreds of thousands of dollars. This had to be tied to it, right?

Allie didn't respond right away, but she did drop her hand to her side. When she looked up at him again, she had more color in her cheeks.

"This has nothing to do with my parents." Her voice was firm, and the fact that she'd read his thoughts in the first place should have been damn convincing. The old Jack would have taken her word for it. Would have just assumed his smarter-than-average fiancée with two lawyer parents would know more about law and finance than he would.

But the Jack who'd been through a failed engagement, the death of his wife, and a decade of single parenthood had a little more confidence in his own instincts. A giant trunk full of cash was a big deal.

Besides, he'd seen the look on Allie's face when she'd opened that trunk. She was as freaked out as he was. "Look, I'm just saying, you probably want to look into the legal side of things," he said. "You know, make sure this won't get you into any sort of trouble."

"I'm confident it won't," she said, not sounding very confident. "I'm sure there's a perfectly logical explanation."

"Or a perfectly criminal one. You won't know until you dig a little deeper, maybe talk to a lawyer."

Something that looked like anger flashed in her eyes, and Jack wondered if he'd overstepped. But hell, he'd read the articles during her parents' trial. From what he understood, her mother had been the ringleader, though her dad had at least been complicit in the scam. That made sense, based on what Jack remembered of the woman he used to call the Ice Queen and the friendly, good-natured guy she'd always seemed to bulldoze. How many families had they bilked out of their life savings? Didn't Allie owe it to the families to make sure this wasn't connected?

Allie studied him a moment longer, her expression more guarded than anything. Maybe he'd imagined the anger. She gave a tight nod, then closed the lid on the trunk. Wiping her hands down the legs of her jeans, she stood up and looked him in the eye.

"You're right," she said.

"What?"

"About looking into the legal aspects of it. I'll do that, thank you."

Something was off here. He wasn't used to hearing *you're right* coming out of her mouth. Had she ever said that before? Not once, he was pretty sure. Then again, how often had he actually *been* right? He'd be the first to admit he hadn't been the most astute eighteen-year-old on the planet. He'd made mistakes, plenty of them, but then again, so had she.

His addled brain was so focused on the novelty of her words that he didn't realize she'd moved closer. That Allie was standing near enough for the side of her breast to graze his arm as she reached past him to put the Easter basket back on the shelf. Her sweater rode up, exposing a swath of pale skin on her low back. He saw something that might've been the top edge of a tattoo, but that seemed unlikely, and he was more interested in the hint of a lacy lavender thong above her jeans. God, did she still wear sexy underwear? It had always driven him wild, the thought of her all buttoned-up in conservative slacks and cashmere turtlenecks, while underneath, she was gift-wrapped in satin and lace.

She set the basket on the shelf and stood facing him, eyes locking with his. She was so close, close enough for him to feel the heat of her abdomen against his bare forearms. He watched her rub her lips together slowly, the way she used to just before he kissed her, and Jack wondered if her pink sweater was as soft as it looked.

"I'll deal with the chest later," she murmured. "Right now, we should stay focused." She made no move to step away, and he could feel her breath against his throat.

"Yes," he replied, aware of a buzzing sound in the back of his own brain. Of the static swirling in her hair and the smell of vanilla and honey enveloping him in a cloud of lust.

Allie didn't move back toward the boxes. She moved closer, and for an instant, Jack thought she was reaching for him. Instead, she stretched up again, breast pressing into his arm once more as she stood on tiptoe to inspect the shelf over his shoulder.

"Hmmm, this box looks familiar," she said.

God, the sweater *was* as soft as it looked. Or maybe that wasn't the sweater. There wasn't much blood left in Jack's brain, and he took a deep breath, flooding his senses with her.

"My grandma used to keep old letters in a box like this," Allie was saying, though Jack could hardly make out the words through the buzzing in his head and the feel of all that softness pressed against him.

Her hair was tickling the side of his neck, and Jack breathed her in again, knowing full well that was just compounding the problem. She lowered herself to her heels and stood looking up at him. Those dark-green eyes fixed on his, and he looked deep into them, thinking of shaded forests and dark, warm places.

He reached for her without thinking, palming the curve of her waist and pulling her tight against his body. He watched her pupils dilate, her lips part.

"Allie."

"Hm?"

Her lashes fluttered, and Jack tightened his hold on her waist. "That was a very nice try."

She blinked. "What?"

"The boob graze. The hair tickle."

"I don't know what you're talking about."

"It was a good trick when we were eighteen." He reached up with his free hand to brush her hair off her forehead, rewarded by her sharp intake of breath. "Back then, the boob graze would have distracted me from an appendectomy."

He watched her eyes darken, and she licked her lips again. "You're saying I'm not hot enough to be a distraction at thirty-six?"

He almost laughed. "I'm not saying that at all." He was still gripping her waist, and he leaned in to brush his lips over the top of her ear, triumphant when he felt her shiver beneath his palm. "You're still hot as fuck."

He drew back, half expecting her to slap him. He probably deserved it. He was being cocky as hell, and rude, too. She had every right to haul off and smack him.

But he watched her throat move as she swallowed, and knew from the flush in her cheeks that she wasn't unaffected by her own attempt at seduction. She'd gotten to herself, too.

"But I'm smarter now," he said. "Smarter than I was at eighteen, anyway."

"I noticed," she whispered.

Something flashed in her eyes that he'd never seen before. Awe, maybe. Respect. All the things he'd wanted to see when he'd shown up to gloat the other night.

But he hadn't expected to see those things up close. Not like this, with his hand on her waist and her pelvis arching toward him. He wasn't sure if she was responding to a desire to distract him from the contents of the steamer trunk or plain old desire. Did it matter?

He pulled her closer. She came willingly, head tilted back, breasts curved toward him. He was kissing her before he'd made up his mind to do it.

The momentary shock of it melted into something else as Allie arched against him, arms lifting to twine around his neck. What had started out as a game had morphed into something else, and it took every ounce of Jack's self-control not to get swept away.

He was still kissing her and the sensation was both foreign and familiar, like revisiting the scene of a party where he'd had too much champagne. She was soft everywhere—lips, breasts, thighs—every place where her body pressed against his was warm and yielding.

"Jack," she gasped, grinding against him.

He broke the kiss and reached for the clasp above his hip. "For the record, that's my hammer." He let the tool belt drop to the floor and reached for her again, pulling her tight to his body.

Her eyes widened a little and she glanced down before smiling up at him. "But that's not."

"Nope."

He kissed her again, remembering all over again what this felt like. He'd almost forgotten, or tried to, anyway. Not kissing—he'd done plenty of that—but kissing Allie, all her sharp edges giving way to something softer as she curled her whole body into his.

She made a soft moan in the back of her throat, a sound so subtle he would have missed it if he hadn't been listening for it. But he was listening. He was listening to the thrum of his own heartbeat in his ears, the whisper of her hair sliding between his fingers, the soft patter of rain on the oak leaves outside.

She broke the kiss just long enough to murmur, "Don't stop," before moving her lips back to his. He agreed without words, sliding his hand around to cup her ass. He would have remembered the curve of it anywhere. He could have picked it out of a lineup of a hundred asses, a visual that jackknifed through his brain and made him dizzy all over again.

He let his other hand drop from her waist to the hem of her sweater. He lingered there for a moment, giving her a chance to pull back. To say this was a bad idea. It probably was, though he'd forgotten why.

Her eyes flashed with assent so Jack slid his hand up under her sweater. He let his thumb graze the edge of her breast, lightly at first. She pressed into his palm, and he moved his whole hand over the softness to lay claim to it.

This time she did pull back, but only for an instant. Just long enough to level him with those molten green eyes as she reached for the hem of her sweater. Her wrists crossed in a delicate X as her fingers gripped the pink fabric. Her gaze was locked on his, and her cheeks were flushed deep pink.

"I want you," she said.

"Okay," he replied dumbly as she began to lift the sweater. It happened in slow motion, and Jack stared mutely as her navel came into focus, the soft hollow he'd kissed hundreds of times. Then he saw the smooth ridges of her ribs, one, then the next, and another until they rounded up to perfect cups of lavender lace and—

*Clack-clack-clack!*

The sweater dropped back, and Allie let go of the edge. She stared at him, eyes wide, face flushed. Jack stared back, trying to figure out what the hell was making that racket.

*Clack-clack-clack!*

"The ladder!" He turned and leapt across the beams, moving as fast as he could toward the attic door. The clacking was moving away, which meant someone must have been dragging the old wooden ladder down the hall. Jack dropped to his knees beside the opening in the floor. He heard Allie clomping behind him, and she landed in a heap next to him with her thigh pressed against his. Each of them grabbed an edge of the attic door, fumbling to get it open.

The door swung up and bonked him in the head. Allie went sprawling backward as light flooded the space around them. She righted herself and leaned down through the opening to call out.

"Skye!" she yelled as Jack grabbed the back of her jeans to keep her from falling through the attic door. "Wait!"

He set Allie back on her heels and leaned through the opening himself. A freckle-shouldered brunette in a long rainbow-striped skirt looked up at him from halfway down the hall. She'd folded the ladder neatly and was dragging it down the hall. She had the wooden rails gripped in both hands and an alarmed look on her face.

It probably wasn't every day she saw a strange man peering down at her from the ceiling.

Allie stuck her head out further and the woman's face lit up. "Allie. Oh my God, I'm so sorry. I didn't know you were up there. The door was closed."

"We were looking through some of my grandma's things and wanted to keep the cats out." Allie shot him a look that told him it would be unwise to say more about what else they'd been doing up there. Was she worried about the money or the kissing?

Jack wasn't sure which of the two had shocked him more.

Allie gestured awkwardly between him and the befuddled-looking woman. "Skye, meet Jack. He's an old friend from college." She looked back at him. "Skye is the caretaker I was telling you about."

"Caretaker, of course." He tried not to think too hard about the *old friend* label, or the fact that she'd described Wade with exactly those words. But he could still taste Allie on his lips, and he wondered if she kissed all her old friends like that. Did she press her body against them and reach for the hem of her sweater with a look of—

*None of your fucking business,* he told himself. *You're being a dick.*

"Nice to meet you," he managed, offering Skye a smile he hoped wasn't too stiff.

"It's great to meet you, too. Sorry, I was just putting this away." She gestured to the ladder, then smiled and pushed her hair off her face, showing Jack a few flashes of blue woven through her dark curls. "Are you from Portland?"

"Not originally, no," Jack said. "But Allie and I went to middle school and high school and college together here, and I'm in town for a college reunion."

"That's awesome! I didn't realize you had a reunion this weekend." It took Jack a second to realize she was talking to Allie, not him. "You have to let me do your hair and nails for the event! Please? I just passed the final for both, but I need the practical experience. I'd do it for free, and I promise I'll make you look like a million bucks."

"Oh," Allie said, glancing at Jack. "Actually, I'm not—"

"You should do it." The words were out of Jack's mouth before he'd thought them through. The look on Allie's face told him they surprised her as much as they did him.

But the idea wasn't half bad, so he kept talking. "I know I ended up graduating five years after you did, but I think you'll still know a few people. Remember Kent Rogers? He was a freshman our sophomore year, but had to quit for a few years when his dad got sick. And Trista Madden? The girl in the next apartment who drove the—"

"—pink Volkswagen, of course." Allie cocked her head. "She's going to be there?"

"Yeah, she married someone from my graduating class. I think there are a few others, plus a few professors you might remember. Come on, it'll be fun."

Allie gave him a dubious look, and he didn't blame her. He was feeling rather dubious himself.

But a small part of him wanted her there. Wanted the comfort of an old friend, even if he'd just compromised the friendship by groping her in the attic.

More than anything though, he wanted a buffer. Wanted an attractive woman by his side so people would think twice before approaching to put a hand on his arm and gaze at him with a look of deep concern. "I was so sorry to hear about Caroline," they'd say, wrapping him in a tight hug before he had a chance to flee. "How are you doing?"

The thought of going through that once, twice, a dozen times over the course of an evening was enough to make him break out in a cold sweat. He was sweating now, or maybe that was still the result of kissing Allie. It was tough to tell.

Allie was still looking at him oddly, so Jack shrugged like it was no big deal. "It's up to you, but I think it'd be fun. Dinner's at Bumble."

"I always loved Bumble."

"I remember."

She seemed to think about it a moment, then nodded. "It's tomorrow?"

"Yeah. Six o'clock."

"Okay. Yes, I'll go."

"Great!"

He probably sounded way too eager, but Allie didn't seem to notice. Several feet below, Skye was still looking up at them.

"So can I do your hair and nails? I mean, you probably have a regular person you go to, but—"

"Actually, that's perfect." Allie smiled. "I usually go to the beauty college closer to my apartment, so I've never been to the one where you're training."

"I thought you always went to that fancy place downtown," Jack said.

Allie raised an eyebrow. "I'm not allowed to change beauty routines in sixteen years?"

"No. I just thought—"

He stopped himself from saying whatever the hell he'd been about to say. Probably something like, "You'd still be a snob," or "I thought no one but Francois was allowed to touch your hair."

She was right. A lot could change in sixteen years, and beauty habits were probably the least of it.

Sensing this was a dead-end conversation, he looked down at Skye. "Any chance you could put the ladder back?"

"Oh. Yes, of course." Skye pushed her hair out of her eyes again and hurried over, ladder in hand. "I'm so sorry. I didn't mean to trap you up there."

"Not a problem," he said.

"Not your fault," Allie added. "We should have left a note or something, but I didn't think you'd be back until late."

"My client didn't show, so I came home early." Skye unfolded the ladder and righted it under the attic door before glancing at Jack. "I'm pretty close to graduating from the Aesthetics Institute."

"But she's going to keep looking after the B&B until then," Allie added.

"And the cats." Skye grinned. "Have you met them yet? They're just the sweetest."

"They're pretty impressive," Jack agreed. "All those toes." His heart rate was almost back to normal now, so at least all this benign banter was good for something.

"Vicky used to say they're all descended from some famous cat in Florida," Skye said. "Or maybe it was the Bahamas."

"Like a show cat?" Allie asked.

"I'm not sure. Anyway, she just loved the polydactyls. The way it looks like they're all wearing mittens. They pet each other sometimes, did you know that?"

"I didn't," Jack said, trying not to think about how much he wanted to retreat back into the depths of the attic for some heavy petting of his own.

But a quick glance at Allie told him there was little chance of that happening. She tugged down the hem of her sweater and folded her arms over her chest.

"Right, well, I'm going to go feed everyone now," Skye said from below as two tortoiseshell cats twisted themselves around her ankles and meowed. "A couple of them get pills, too, so it's a bit of a chore. It was a pleasure meeting you, Jack."

"Likewise. Thanks for putting the ladder back. We might have been trapped up here forever."

Which wasn't the worst thought in the world, though the look on Allie's face told him she felt otherwise.

Skye hustled off down the hall, a stream of cats yowling behind her. When she was out of earshot, Jack sat back on his heels and turned to Allie. "So," he said. "I take it you're keeping your shirt on?"

Allie's cheeks went pink, and she tugged at the hem of her sweater again. "Right. Um, I think we kinda got caught up in the moment."

"Not the first time."

One corner of her mouth tilted up, and he could tell she was trying not to smile. Trying not to remember that summer after their senior year in high school in the backseat of the car, windows fogged up, hair wild, Allie's skirt pushed up around her hips as Jack—

"That would be dumb." Allie's words jolted him back from the memory. "Fooling around, I mean."

"Right," he agreed, nodding for emphasis.

"We already know we're an awful match," she said. "No sense going down that path again."

"Agreed. Nothing but potholes and landmines and slugs on that path."

"Definitely."

The certainty in her expression told him she believed it. So did he, dammit. There was no reason to even toy with the idea of starting anything with Allie Ross again.

But his brain flashed to the memory of her mouth on his, fingers twisted in his hair, a small moan in the back of her throat.

Right now, he couldn't say for sure if the memory was sixteen years or sixteen minutes old.

# CHAPTER SIX

Allie looked across the table at her father, wondering how it was possible he'd aged twenty years in the six he'd been here at the Sheridan Federal Correctional Institution.

"It's so good to see you, Alliecakes." Her dad squeezed her hand across the dark-gray table between them, and Allie bit the inside of her cheek to keep the tears at bay.

"You, too, Daddy. I've been thinking about you a lot since I was here Monday. You're sure you're doing okay?"

Less than a week had passed since Allie had come to tell him his mother had died, and that she wouldn't be bringing Grandma Victoria to visit on his next birthday like they'd planned. He looked tired, more tired than he'd looked on her last few visits. His eyes seemed red, but maybe it was seasonal allergies. He probably wasn't getting allergy-reducing acupuncture treatments in prison.

"I'm okay," he said. "It's been a rough week. But it's been nice seeing you twice in the same week."

"That's true." Allie cleared her throat. "I saw Mom."

She watched his eyes light up, and a pang of sadness rattled her ribs. Yes, her parents had bilked people out of thousands of dollars. Allie knew that. They'd done it together the way some couples took up tennis or wine tasting in middle age. That still didn't make it any easier for her to see them separated by two hundred miles and masses of steel bars.

"How's your mom doing?"

"Good. She was sad to hear about Grandma. Wanted me to send you her condolences."

"I sure do miss her."

Allie wasn't sure who he meant, but didn't want to ask. Didn't want to make this any harder than it was.

But her father had always been able to read her mind. "I miss your mom, and I miss your grandma." He squeezed her hand again. "I miss you most of all. Miss seeing my little girl whenever I want."

The tears fought their way forward, and Allie fought back. Her dad didn't need to feel worse than he already did. She stared at the tall ficus in the corner, grateful for the greenery scattered throughout the visiting area. It gave her something to look at when the sight of her father in prison garb threatened to unravel her. She'd always been a daddy's girl, and had never gotten used to seeing him behind bars.

Taking a deep breath, Allie glanced at the guard hovering three feet away. He wore a dark-gray uniform and stared straight ahead, though she knew he was listening to every word of their conversation.

That made it tougher for her to fish for information. To find out if her dad knew anything about the contents of the trunk in the attic. But her time here was limited, so she needed to get to it.

Allie shuffled her feet on the floor and ordered herself to keep her tone casual. "Did you know Grandma left the Rosewood B&B to me?"

He shook his head. "No, but it doesn't surprise me. She always loved you so much."

"Right. I mean, I guess there wasn't anyone else to leave it to." She stopped, wishing she could take back the words that probably sounded unkind. If her dad weren't behind bars, she had no doubt he would have inherited the property.

But her father didn't seem fazed. He sat with his hand covering hers, wearing the same sad little smile he'd worn every time she'd visited him here. "You deserve to inherit it, Allie. I'm glad the old place will stay in the family."

"Me, too." Allie cleared her throat, ready to try again. "So, Daddy. Did your lawyer ever talk to you about Grandma's will? About her assets or anything?"

He shook his head. "Not really. From what I understand, there wasn't much left. I know that assisted living place ate up a lot of her savings, and all the legal stuff a few years ago—"

He glanced at the guard, then back at Allie. "I do feel bad about all that."

Allie nodded, not sure what else to say. Not sure what she *could* say. She knew he'd been working on an appeal, just like her mom was. That made them both pretty tight-lipped about the details of the crime that had put them both behind bars.

Allie tried again. "So Grandma never talked to you about her other assets?"

"You mean like stocks, bonds?"

"Sure, anything like that."

Her hand felt chilly beneath her father's warmer one, and she willed him to read her mind, to know what she was driving at. He'd always been so good at that.

But he just shook his head and frowned. "Nothing I know about. Why?"

"No reason. Just being thorough."

He squeezed her hand again. "That's my girl. Always dotting every i and crossing every t."

"Right. That's me."

"So have you been back to the place? The B&B, I mean."

"I have." Allie glanced at the guard again, trying not to notice the lethal-looking club on his belt. "Did you know Grandma turned it into a cat sanctuary?"

"Sanctuary? Like a church?"

"No, not a church. Like a residence for homeless cats."

He gave a small, fond smile. "She always did like cats. Remember that orange one with the weird ears? And that gray one she had, Stumpy?"

Allie nodded, dimly remembering Stumpy. "That's right. The one with the white feet and the meow that sounded like a smoker's cough."

Her dad laughed, already on his way down memory lane. "I remember she got him as a gift from someone. She never said who, but that always seemed like a pretty weird present."

"Maybe it was a gag gift," Allie suggested. Then she grimaced as her brain flashed back on the image of the ball gag she'd found in the attic. "Do you remember if Stumpy had extra toes?"

"Not that I can recall, why?"

"Most of the cats there now have extra toes. I was wondering if maybe they're all relatives or something."

He looked thoughtful. "Could be. I don't know much about the toe thing, but I suppose if it's some sort of congenital abnormality, it could be recessive. Like you might have a cat with normal paws who carries the gene and produces kittens with the extra toes."

"It's no big deal." Allie shrugged, still trying to figure out how to steer the conversation to the topic of the steamer trunk. "I didn't mean to go all crazy cat lady."

"No, it's very interesting." He grinned. "Besides, it doesn't sound like there's much chance you'll be making me a grandpa anytime soon. This might be the closest I get."

"Right." Allie brushed her hair off her forehead and tried not to let the words sting. "Just call me your spinster daughter with fourteen cats."

"Fourteen? Are there really that many?"

"Apparently."

He whistled low under his breath. "That's a lot of cats. I bet the place stinks to high heaven."

"Actually, there's a caretaker who's been looking after them. She keeps the place pretty clean, and the cats have these fancy robotic litter box contraptions. You really don't notice the smell."

Good Lord, is this what her life had come to? Discussing litter box smells with her incarcerated father?

She almost didn't notice her dad's face had changed. He was frowning now, and it took Allie a moment to realize it had nothing to do with feline odor control.

"Wait, you said there's a caretaker?" His frown deepened. "You mean someone's been living in the house?"

A faint prickle fluttered down her spine. Her dad looked worried. Allie licked her lips, wanting to tread carefully. Did her dad know something about the money?

"Yeah, I guess when Grandma went into the assisted living place, she hired a student to look after things. She didn't have the bandwidth to handle the B&B, so she just looked after the cats. Seems like a nice girl. Skye something."

Her dad was still frowning, and Allie watched his face for any hints that he knew about the money. He seemed to be considering something.

Then he cleared his throat. "I don't suppose you've been up in the attic?"

Allie held her breath for a second, not sure how to answer. She'd thought about it all the way here, framing questions and subtle hints in her mind, but she hadn't anticipated being asked about this outright. She glanced at the guard, then at the couple seated on the other side of them. No one was looking their way, but that didn't mean they weren't listening.

She chose her words carefully, struggling to keep her tone casual. "Is there something in the attic that you wanted me to look for?"

"No. I just—" Her father sighed, then rubbed the bridge of his nose. When he looked at her again, he seemed resigned to something. "I suppose you may as well know."

Allie could hear her heart pounding hard in her ears, and she forced herself to keep her expression neutral. She lowered her voice to reply. "Know what?"

Her dad glanced at the guard, then leaned closer to her across the table. "There's something stored up there that's rather—*private.*"

"What is it?" Her voice was barely a whisper.

Her father's hand still enveloped hers, and Allie couldn't tell if he was shaking or if she was.

"It was something I didn't want your mother to know about," he said slowly.

Allie held her breath. "Are you able to tell me?"

He seemed to hesitate. Another glance at the guard. "You've already been up there?"

She knew she hadn't actually said, and wondered if this was one of his old lawyer tricks. He'd always been good at getting her to confess, at making her admit something she didn't want to without her even realizing it. Like the time she toilet-papered the neighbor's house with two girls from French class her freshman year and he knew right away she'd done it. Or the summer before college when he noticed a streaky handprint on the glass in the backseat of her car and asked, cool as could be, if she'd been having difficulty rolling down the window.

Allie decided to answer truthfully. "Yes. I was up there yesterday."

"I see. And did you find anything . . . noteworthy?"

Another glance at the guard. Allie's hands felt clammy, and she wished she'd worked out some sort of secret code with her dad before they'd hauled him away. How the hell was she supposed to know she'd find a huge chest of money and need to covertly discuss it?

Allie took a deep breath. "Are you talking about that old steamer trunk Grandma used to have in the blue bedroom downstairs?"

Her dad frowned. "Steamer trunk? Oh, you mean that thing she used as a coffee table in the blue room?"

"Right."

"You found that upstairs?" He shook his head. "Wonder how she got that up there. It had a lock on it, right?"

Allie nodded, not sure if he was testing her or genuinely unsure. "Yes. It had a combo lock."

She waited for him to ask if she'd gotten into it. Her brain raced with how best to answer, how not to arouse suspicion with the guard.

But that's not where her dad took the conversation. "Nah, the thing I'm talking about is a cardboard box. With some stuff inside that might be a little—" He cleared his throat. "Embarrassing."

A little ripple of queasiness moved through her. "Oh."

She waited for him to fill in the blank. To confirm what she'd just realized and give her an indication how willing he was to discuss it.

But he said nothing.

"So you're talking about what was in the *other* box," she tried.

She fixed her face into an expression of nonchalance and neutrality. *No judgment here*, she tried to telegraph. *None at all.*

"Right." Her dad looked uncertain. "The *other* box."

"Look, it's no big deal," she said. "Plenty of people have stuff like that lying around. Heck, I used to have these silk scarves—"

She stopped herself, not sure why the hell she'd brought that up. She'd forgotten entirely until Jack mentioned it the day before. Now here she was discussing her history of bondage with her father.

*That's what you get for letting Jack Carpenter back into your head.*

Allie took a shaky breath and looked her father in the eye. "Don't worry about it, Daddy. I only glanced at it quickly, but it doesn't make me think any less of Grandma."

Her dad frowned. "Why would it?"

"Um—I guess I assumed it all belonged to her. I mean, I saw her initial on something. Just a quick glance, though. Maybe I was wrong."

He frowned. "Could it have been an N instead of a V? Nathan Ellington Ross?"

"Uh—I guess so." Christ, what was her dad suggesting? And did she really want to know this? "Look, Daddy, I don't need to know details. If that stuff belongs to you—"

"Of course it belongs to me." He lowered his voice, adopting an almost reverent tone. "Well, your mother and me."

"Oh." Allie bit her lip. "Right. Well, plenty of people are into that stuff." She tried a casual laugh, not wanting her dad to feel embarrassed. "Paddles, whips, toys—all those things are pretty mainstream right now."

Her dad blinked. "What?"

He looked genuinely baffled. What the hell? Allie leaned forward, lowering her voice again. "The sex toys. That's what you meant, right?"

His eyebrows rose like white caterpillars arching to climb a tree branch. "What are you talking about?"

"Um—nothing." Allie laughed, hoping it sounded less stilted to him than it did to her own ears. "I was kidding. Just—you've heard about *Fifty Shades of Grey?*"

He raised an eyebrow at her. "A few of the inmates got their hands on a copy last year. Let's say it was well-read."

"Right. I was just making a joke. A *Fifty Shades* joke. A highly inappropriate—"

"Sweetie, don't take this the wrong way, but you've gotten a little weird lately."

Allie sighed. "Thank you, Daddy." She cleared her throat. "So what box were you talking about?"

"It's not a huge deal or anything. Just—some old letters, okay?"

"What kind of letters?"

"Love letters."

Allie felt her pulse kick up again. "You mean you had a mistress?"

"What? No, of course not! I'd never cheat on your mother."

His voice was loud enough that several inmates and their guests looked over. A man with tattoos up both arms stared for a long moment, then shook his head and went back to his own conversation.

"Who are the love letters from, Daddy?"

"Your mother and me." A faint flush had crept into his cheeks, and Allie watched with curiosity as he dropped his gaze to the table. "They're from when we first dated, back in college."

"I don't understand. Why is that a secret?"

"You know how your mom is." He shrugged and gave a small smile, meeting her eyes again. "Not very sentimental. She was always throwing things out, doing spring cleaning and fall cleaning and purging. You remember when she threw out your old teddy bear?"

"Right. Well, I was sixteen, so—"

"Doesn't matter. Sometimes you want to hold on to things like that." He shrugged again and glanced down at their hands. "Anyway, I didn't want her to chuck those in one of her cleaning binges, so I hid 'em up there in Grandma's attic maybe seven or eight years ago."

"So that's it?"

He frowned. "What were you expecting?"

She shook her head. "Not that, I guess."

He gave her hand a squeeze. "Thought maybe you'd found them and read them. You had kind of a funny look on your face earlier. Like you were hiding something."

"Right." Allie shook her head. "I wouldn't read your private letters, Daddy."

He laughed and bumped her knee with his beneath the table. "Nah, you're welcome to read 'em. Heck, you might even learn something. Good stuff about life and love and courtship—all the stuff your mom and I were still figuring out back when we were eighteen."

"Did you figure it out?" The question came out breathless, and Allie realized she genuinely wanted the answer.

He laughed. "At eighteen? Nah, we were all dumb hormones and lofty ideals back then. We didn't really figure it out until we were well into our mid-twenties. After you came along and we started to get our careers underway."

"Oh."

"But those letters—those early bumbling attempts at love? They're worth remembering. Even if it's not where we ended up, they're part of how we got where we were going. That means something."

Allie nodded, not sure what else to say. She'd been witness only to parts of her parents' love story. The parts that included her, and the ones she saw through the trial and their prison separation. Her chest felt tight as she considered how much more there was to the story. Those long ago memories that belonged only to the two of them. Wasn't that the core of intimacy?

Her dad squeezed her hand again, and Allie felt something twist in the center of her chest. "You sure there's nothing else, Alliecakes? You seem like you have something on your mind."

She hesitated. A movement in the corner of her eye made Allie turn to see the guard had changed positions. He'd moved four or five feet down the wall, a better position to keep a close watch over the heavily tattooed couple holding hands across a gray table identical to theirs.

Allie looked back at her dad. If she kept her voice low, she could probably confess what she'd found. What she was really hiding.

But the words that came out of her mouth had nothing to do with the money. "Jack Carpenter is back in town."

A look of understanding flashed across her father's face. "Ah. That makes sense."

"What makes sense?"

"Why you seemed so—undone, I guess."

She started to argue, but took a deep breath instead. "He got married," she blurted, not sure why she was confessing all this to her father. She knew she'd never tell her mom any of this, and it felt good to confide in one parent. "But his wife died a couple years later."

"I'm sorry to hear that," he murmured.

"They had a kid. A daughter. She's ten years old and Jack's been raising her alone. I think he's grown up a lot."

Her dad nodded, and gave a soft little laugh. "That'll change a man. Having a daughter."

She smiled back, relieved to see him looking happy again. "Yes. I imagine it would."

"Always felt sorry for the guy, truth be told," her father said. "That'll do a number on a kid, having his dad walk out like that. What was he, six, seven?"

"Six," Allie said, surprised her father remembered, since she and Jack hadn't known each other then. But she'd told her dad the stories, wanting her father to care about Jack the way she did. Wanting her parents to love and accept him like she had.

"It definitely shaped his personality," Allie said. "Always expecting people to walk or disappoint him."

Her dad squeezed her hands. "You can't blame yourself for any of that, sweetie. You were right to break things off when you did. The two of you were just kids."

"I know," Allie murmured, but her voice was small. She wanted to change the subject, and felt a wave of relief when her dad did it for her.

"Listen, sweetie—maybe you should stay out of the attic for now. Are those rickety old boards still up there?"

"Yes, but I've been trying not to step on them. I'm being careful."

"Still. I'm not sure it's safe. I'd hate to have you go crashing through the ceiling or something."

"I'll be careful," she promised. "Besides, I'm not sure I have much of a reason to go up there again anyway."

"Good." He squeezed her hands. "Always such a good girl, Allie."

She smiled and tried to ignore the knot in her gut.

◆  ◆  ◆

Of the items on Jack's list of quintessential Portland experiences to have now that he was back in Oregon, getting a straight-razor shave from a heavily tattooed guy wearing lumberjack plaid and sporting a Fu Manchu mustache ranked right up there.

"Dad! Hold still. I want to take a picture for Instagram."

Okay, having his ten-year-old photographing the experience added an extra element of weirdness. Maybe that made it more Portlandesque.

"Make sure you get a good shot of all my gray hair," he said as Paige angled up on her knees in the adjacent barber chair. "Since you're responsible for most of it."

She giggled. "You mean there's a color besides gray in there?" Plunking back down in the seat, she began to scroll through the images.

The guy with the mustache—whose name, according to both the sign above his workstation and his knuckle tattoos, was Bam—paused with his narrow scissors poised over Jack's overgrown sideburn.

"You can tag Union Barber if you want," Bam told Paige.

"Okay, if my dad lets me. He's super strict about that stuff."

"Poor abused child," Jack said. "One accidental tagging of a strip club instead of a playground, and suddenly your evil father monitors your every online move."

Paige grinned as she typed with impressive speed. "The struggle is real."

Man, when did his kid get to be so witty? She'd always been clever, a born comedienne, just like her mother. But lately there was a sophisticated quality to her humor that left him floored.

In the waiting area behind her, a man and a woman—or was it two women?—were having a boisterous conversation about a date one of them had the night before. The taller one sported fuchsia hair and more piercings than Jack could count. The other had a buzz cut in mottled hues of blue and green. They chattered loudly over the blare of an Avett Brothers song on the overhead speakers, and Jack inhaled the familiar scent of pot and patchouli wafting from their direction. He'd almost forgotten marijuana was legal in Oregon. Not that he smoked it these days, but he'd blazed a joint or two in college. If it had been legal back then, would he and Allie have spent less time bickering about his recreational use?

Probably. They'd certainly never had a shortage of things to squabble over.

He glanced back at Paige, who was still engrossed in her phone. As an app developer, he couldn't be too annoyed by her reliance on the gadget. As a dad, he could be as annoyed as he wanted to be.

"Paige," he warned as Bam combed down his right sideburn. "Remember this counts toward your thirty minutes of screen time."

"Even if I'm doing this for Grandma?"

"I can assure you Grandma won't be that excited about my haircut." Which probably wasn't true. His mom lived for the tiny minutia of Paige's life, routinely posting emoticon-heavy comments with the screen name "PaigesGramma." Allowing grandmother and granddaughter easy contact with one another was the main reason he'd gotten her the phone in the first place.

"You can show it to her tonight when I'm at the reunion," he added. "You ladies can play with that new app that lets you turn people's faces into butts."

"That does sound fun."

Paige shoved the phone into her backpack, which was pink plaid with kittens on it. She'd pleaded for it at the start of the school year, but within three months had declared it *"babyish."* He'd insisted she keep it for a few months after that, but now that she'd be starting at a new school, he was willing to concede that something more mature would be fine. He'd let her pick it out herself if they had time to hit the mall before he had to pick up Allie for the reunion.

"We're going to do a little hot towel treatment now," Bam told him.

"Sounds good."

The couple in the waiting area laughed about something as Bam marched in heavy Doc Martens to a contraption in the back corner of the room. He returned with a hot, damp towel that smelled like limes and some spice he couldn't identify. Coriander, maybe? Allie would know.

The thought of Allie drifted through his mind like a wispy ghost, and Jack closed his eyes as Bam tilted Jack's chair back and began to wrap the towel around his face.

"Too hot?" he asked.

"Nope. It's fine."

"Daddy, you look like a mummy."

He grinned beneath the towel and tried to think of a daddy/mummy joke that wouldn't fall flat or remind her that she'd spent most of her life as a motherless child.

"That'll save me the trouble of finding a Halloween costume in a few months," was all he could come up with.

Bam finished wrapping the towel and rested his hands on the sides of Jack's face. "I'm going to leave that on there for just a few minutes. Let the steam do its thing."

Jack nodded, feeling a little silly with nothing but his nose sticking out of the warm, scented towel. It was quiet under here, with sounds muffled by the damp terrycloth. It bothered him just a little not being able to see Paige. What if someone snatched her or she wandered out the door or—

"Daddy?"

"Yes?"

"What does *shaving your boobs* mean?"

He replayed the question in his mind, trying to make sense of it. "Um—"

"Or poops. Maybe it's *shaving your poops*."

"I have no idea."

Behind him, Bam chuckled. "Pubes. The word is *pubes.*" He cleared his throat and raised his voice. "Keep it down over there, ladies. We have children in the house."

"Sorry!" The two voices came from the waiting area, which answered at least two questions pinging around in Jack's mind.

Jack sighed. "*Pubes* is a short way of saying *pubic region,*" he said, feeling ridiculous delivering this information with his face wrapped in a towel. For all he knew, he had a full audience listening to this little father-daughter moment.

But he knew Paige was waiting for a response, and he'd promised her a long time ago that he'd always answer her questions promptly and honestly. Might as well get this over with. "Remember that book we read together a couple months ago?"

"The one with the monkeys?"

"No, the other one. The one about what's happening to your body."

"Oh. Yeah. That one."

He pictured her sitting there with her cheeks turning faintly pink. He opened his mouth to suggest they continue this conversation later, but she surprised him by pressing on.

"I liked that book," she said, a little quieter now. "I learned some stuff I didn't know."

"It's a great book," Bam offered. "One of my favorites."

Paige was quiet a moment, probably thinking. "So why would someone want to shave pubes?"

Jack was still trying to formulate a response when Bam beat him to the punch.

"Shaving's a personal choice," the barber said. "One for when people get old like your dad."

"Thank you." Jack stopped there, hoping the response settled his daughter's curiosity instead of inviting questions about anyone else's pubic grooming.

But Paige just said, "Oh," and fell quiet again.

He hoped he hadn't dissuaded her from asking questions of a sexual nature. The older she got, the more obvious it would be that she didn't have a mom to answer increasingly tough questions. He loved that she still felt comfortable coming to him with inquiries about everything from breast development to if he thought he could eat fifteen oranges in one sitting. He always did his best to answer truthfully.

Bam began unwinding the towel from his face, and Jack breathed deeply. He glanced over at Paige, who flashed him a grin. "Your face is all red."

"Probably because you're making me discuss pubes in public."

She laughed as Bam began to lather his face with a thick foam that made his cheeks tingle. Had he ever had another person shave his face like this? Seemed like one of those things that always happened in romantic movies with the woman propped bare-legged on the counter wearing nothing but the man's shirt.

The mental picture jogged his memory, reminding him of the time Allie had asked to try it in college. She'd been wearing gray sweatpants and a little red tank top with no bra underneath. Her hair had been loose around her shoulders, cool as silk between his fingers as she patted shaving foam on his face, then wrapped her legs around his waist and—

"Daddy?"

"Yes?"

"Did you have a girlfriend when you were my age?"

Jack held off on answering while Bam finished smoothing the foam around his jaw.

"Nope. Didn't have a girlfriend until I was a lot older."

"How old?"

"Mm, fifteen? No, sixteen."

"What was her name?"

"Sarah Williams."

Paige was quiet a moment, and they both watched as Bam put a fresh blade into his straight razor. The handle was some sort of carved wood, very beautiful. He glanced at his daughter to see if she looked nervous. About the razor, about the girlfriend, about anything. She didn't look worried, but she did look like she had something on her mind.

Seeming to sense his gaze on her, she turned and looked at him. "Was Sarah the first girl you were in love with?"

"No."

"Who was?"

An achy little knot appeared unwelcome in the center of his chest, but Jack was determined not to let it get to him. "My second girlfriend. The one I started dating when I was seventeen."

"What was her name?"

"Allie."

He waited for Paige to connect the dots. Bam slid the razor blade into the contraption and tested the edge with his thumb. Beside him, Jack could hear his little girl breathing heavy, the way she did when she was deep in thought.

"Was it Allie whose house we visited the other night?"

"Yep."

"You loved her?"

"At one time. A long, *long* time ago."

"Before Mommy?"

"Yes. This was before Mommy. A few years before."

Bam cleared his throat. "Okay if I start the shave now?"

"Go right ahead," Jack said.

Beside him, Paige was silent. He wondered what had triggered all the questions. She'd always been inquisitive, but this wasn't her usual line of questioning. She'd been watching a lot of lovey-dovey stuff with her grandma and one of her little friends in California, but maybe that's what little girls did at this age. He'd have to look it up in one of his child-development books. It made sense she'd be starting to think about things like boyfriends and girlfriends, but it had never occurred to him she'd take any real interest in *his* life.

"Daddy?"

"Mm?" He was careful not to move his face as Bam glided the blade across his right cheek.

"That book we read? The one about bodies and how babies are made and stuff?"

"Mmhm." No movement, very good.

"I was just wondering." Her voice was small, but determined. "Did you do that stuff with other people besides Mommy?"

"Whoa!" Bam jumped back, yanking the razor away from Jack's face an instant before he flinched. "You're lucky I saw that one coming, man."

"Thanks." Jack moved his jaw from side to side, relieved not to feel any nicks or cuts. He turned to his daughter. "Why do you want to know that, sweetheart?"

She shrugged. "I just do."

Jack cleared his throat. "Well, that's one of those questions that's very personal. A lot of people don't like to share that kind of information with other people."

"Right," she agreed. "But we're not other people. We're family."

"Can't argue with that," Bam said.

Jack shot him a look. "Not helping."

"Sorry, man."

He turned back to his daughter. Her expression was earnest and he reminded himself he'd promised honesty. He might not have that much to offer as a parent, but he had that.

"Yes," he said at last. "There were other people besides Mommy. But this is a conversation we can have when you're a little bit older, okay?"

"Okay." She bit her lip. "How come?"

"Because love and sex and making babies—those are all really big and powerful things, but it's important to be mature enough to think through all parts of it. The physical stuff, but also the emotional stuff. Does that make sense?"

Paige nodded. "Uh-huh."

"Totally." Bam cleared his throat. "Good talk, guys."

"Thank you for being part of it." Jack sighed, pretty sure he'd never gazed upon his infant daughter and imagined serious conversations with her might include a guy sporting a neck tattoo of an octopus.

Bam looked at him in the mirror. "Mind if I start shaving again?"

"Yeah." Jack glanced at Paige. "No more sex questions for right now, okay? After we're done, we'll go do some school clothes shopping for you and we can talk about anything you want."

"Okay."

"And you'll be able to do it without me slicing Daddy's jugular," Bam added.

Paige sat quiet for the next twenty minutes, and he knew it probably drove her nuts not to have her phone for entertainment or the opportunity to badger him with questions. By the time he'd paid and ushered her out the door, she was beaming up at him again.

"You look good, Daddy."

"Thank you. So do you."

She giggled as he ruffled her hair, and Jack wondered how much longer he'd be able to do that. Grabbing his hand, she started to skip down the sidewalk, even though he hadn't told her which direction they were headed. He steered them into downtown Portland toward 10th Avenue as a smattering of rain started to fall. He flicked open the umbrella he'd brought along, grateful he'd had the foresight to grab it before leaving the house. At some point he'd gone from being a guy who forgot his own house keys to a guy who remembered to pack snacks and umbrellas when he was taking his daughter out for the day.

Paige scooted under the umbrella with him, still skipping as she swung his hand back and forth.

"Are you excited about starting at your new school?" he asked.

"Yeah. Kinda. Maybe a little nervous."

"What are you nervous about?"

She shrugged. "Bullies, maybe. Bigger kids."

A flicker of rage burned in his chest, but he ordered himself to stay calm. "Have you been bullied before?"

"No. But it's still scary."

"That it is," he agreed. "You know you can always come talk to me about stuff like that, right?"

"Uh-huh. But not about pubes."

"You can talk to me about pubes, too. Just not in a public place next time, okay?"

She grinned and swung his hand back and forth a few times. "Got it."

He stopped in front of the high-end thrift shop and gestured toward the mannequins decked out in clothes Jack guessed had originally cost more than his first car. "This is the shop I was telling you about."

He pushed open the door, taking in the sight of bright dresses and fancy handbags. This shop hadn't been here back when he was in college, but he'd read about it online. Caroline would have loved the place. Scoring designer clothes for a tiny fraction of the original cost had been something of a hobby for her, and Jack had learned everything he knew about bargain hunting from her. Back when Paige was just a baby and money was tight.

Thinking of his late wife didn't make him ache the way it used to. It was more of a soft pang, somewhere between nostalgia and fondness. She would have appreciated a shop like this for the same reasons he did. There was something thrilling about knowing rich suckers were spending hundreds of dollars for the same shirt he could find in a boutique thrift store for twenty bucks.

He surveyed the shop, his gaze swinging between racks of handbags from Coach and Prada, past a rack of barely used Armani suits, skimming over the woman in a red dress with lush curves and caramel hair and—

"Miss Allie!"

The woman jumped, and Jack looked down to see his daughter waving with excitement. "It's me, Paige! We ate clams at your house. We were just talking about you."

# CHAPTER SEVEN

Allie stared at the little girl who held the hand of a tall, handsome man, dimly aware she knew them both, though not quite in this context.

"Jack," she croaked out, finding her voice at last. "Paige. It's so good to see you two again. What brings you here?"

"School shopping!" Paige chirped. "Daddy says this is a smart place to buy stuff if you want to dress like a rich snob but not spend stupid amounts of money."

"Those may not have been my exact words." Jack stepped closer, looking as surprised to see her as Allie felt seeing him. Which was saying something. He nodded at the cluster of hangers gripped in her hand. "Doing some dress shopping?"

Allie looked down at the froth of dresses looped over her arm, the silky fabrics a little too bright now that she looked at them with Jack standing this close to her. There was no point pretending she was shopping for someone else, so she shrugged like it was no big deal.

"Someone sprung a college reunion on me at the last minute, so I had to find something appropriate to wear."

"Never figured you'd shop in a place like this."

"Like what? A high-end boutique thrift shop?"

He shrugged, and Allie wondered if he was baiting her. Trying to make her defensive or to imply how far the mighty had fallen.

Or maybe she was reading too much into it.

"Oh, this one's pretty!" Paige gripped the hem of one of the dresses Allie held, a fluttery, silk chiffon Vera Wang number with a V-neck and a draped skirt. "It looks like the green part of a peacock feather."

"It kinda does," Allie agreed. "That's the one I like best. I'm crossing my fingers it fits."

Paige beamed at her. "My favorite color is green, too."

Allie glanced at the dresses, every one of them a slightly different hue of green. Heat crept into her cheeks, and she could feel Jack's eyes on her. "Yes, uh—they do all seem to be green, don't they?"

"A green dress?" The teasing note in Jack's voice made her look up at him, and she wasn't surprised to see traces of a smirk on that obnoxiously handsome face.

Allie straightened her spine. "Yes. A green dress."

He grinned wider. "Is that in honor of our song? The one by the Barenaked Ladies?"

"No, I just—I like this color, that's all."

But that wasn't all. Jack was right. She knew the song well, the one that used to make her laugh each time it got to the part about the green dress. The Barenaked Ladies had sung about the things they'd buy if they had a million dollars, and she and Jack used to sing along with them, twirling through the living room of their too-small apartment. They'd substituted words like *textbooks* and *phone bill* in place of items the singer claimed he'd buy for his sweetheart in the event of a financial windfall.

Allie felt the smile starting slow in her belly and spreading across her face. She saw the corners of Jack's mouth tug, too.

Then he stopped, a frown wiping out the smile before it even appeared.

Her memory zipped from the living room of their old apartment to the attic at her grandmother's house. To the million dollars tucked in a trunk up there, and uncertainty of what to do about it. As Jack stared at her, she wished for the hundredth time he hadn't been there when she opened that trunk.

"So," she said, brushing hair off her forehead. "I didn't even realize they had kids' stuff here."

"I can wear women's extra-small stuff now," Paige boasted. "And size-six shoes."

"Impressive!" Allie smiled at the little girl, who wasn't actually that little. She came up to Allie's shoulder, probably four foot seven or eight. Was that above average for a ten-year-old? "You must have inherited your dad's height."

The second the words left her mouth, Allie wanted to kick herself. Good Lord, the girl's mom was dead, and might have been a pro basketball player for all Allie knew.

But Paige just shrugged and looked up at her dad. "Can I go check out the jeans over there?"

"Sure. Looks like the smaller sizes are on this side. Remember what we talked about, okay?"

"I know, I know . . . nothing skintight."

"Right."

Paige wandered toward the opposite side of the store, leaving Jack and Allie alone. Allie held the dresses aloft. "I guess I should try these on."

"You should. For the record, the skintight rule doesn't apply to you. In fact, I encourage it. The tighter the better."

Allie rolled her eyes. "You haven't changed a bit."

"Yes, I have. I brought an umbrella. That makes me a responsible, upstanding citizen." He held it up to show her, and Allie laughed in spite of herself.

"I stand corrected."

She turned and headed into the dressing room, conscious of Jack's gaze following her. Pulling the door closed behind her, she took a shaky breath and ordered herself to get it together.

*The man saw you eating whipped cream from the can. Is it really a big deal if he sees you shopping in a thrift store?*

Or maybe that wasn't what bothered her. Maybe it was the fact that he'd called her out on choosing a dress in a hue that held a special memory for both of them. She'd figured he wouldn't remember. That it would just be her little inside joke, or a hat-tip to nostalgia. Obviously, she'd been wrong. She'd been wrong about a lot of things.

She stripped off her red jersey-knit dress and kicked her sandals under the bench, grateful at least that she hadn't gone shopping in old sweatpants. Her underwear wasn't great—gray cotton, not remotely sexy—but it's not like he was going to be seeing it.

"Hey, Allie?"

She froze at the sound of his voice so close to her ear, then covered her boobs with her forearm. "Yes?"

"You planning to show me those?"

"My boobs?"

"What?"

The dresses, of course he meant the dresses.

"Um, I wasn't planning on it." She yanked the first one off the hanger and pulled it on, struggling in the taffeta for a few moments before realizing she had it on backwards. She righted the dress, then reached behind her to do up the zipper.

Crap! She couldn't reach. Since when had her arms gotten too short to do up a damn zipper? She wriggled and stretched, wishing like hell she'd made a better effort to do Pilates more regularly. She just didn't have time and—

"Need help with any zippers?"

"Dammit, are you spying on me?"

His laugh bounced through the small dressing room space, and Allie felt her cheeks grow hot. "It's a solid door, Allie. Floor to ceiling, and no keyhole. No, I'm not spying on you. Paranoid much?"

She tossed her hair, not sure whether to be more flustered with herself or with him. She tried the zipper again. Dammit to hell.

"Fine," she said, yanking open the door. "I could use help with the zipper."

"Funny, I didn't hear a *please* in there."

"Please." Allie sighed and turned to present her back to him. He was silent a moment, and she glanced in the mirror to see his eyes cast downward toward her ass. Embarrassment bubbled in her gut, but she tried to cover. "Yes, I'm wearing granny panties, okay? Sue me. I haven't had time to do laundry all week and—"

"I wasn't judging your underwear, Allie. Just admiring the tattoo."

"Oh."

"When did you get it?"

She bit her lip. "A year after college."

His fingers grazed the small of her back, and for an instant, she thought he was touching the tip of one of the small, orange flames. Then she realized he was reaching for the zipper. He dragged it slowly up her spine, and Allie focused hard on keeping her stomach pulled in, wondering if her muffin top was showing over the top of her awful gray panties.

"It's very nice. The tattoo, I mean."

"Thank you." His hand was still on the zipper, even though she was pretty sure he had it all the way up. The heat of his hand made her shiver.

"What does it mean?"

"The tattoo?" She shrugged, trying to look casual as she smoothed down the front of the dress in the mirror in front of her. She didn't look up, not wanting to see Jack's eyes. "It doesn't mean anything. Just a pretty, fiery design, that's all."

"I know you, Allie." His voice was low in her ear, so close she could feel his breath ruffling her hair. She let her gaze stray up, and she locked eyes with him in the mirror. "You wouldn't permanently ink something on your body if it didn't have meaning."

She stood frozen with her gaze locked on his, not daring to speak. Desperate to break the spell, she turned to face him with an expression she made as blank as possible. "Maybe I *would* get a meaningless tattoo. You knew the nineteen-year-old version of Allie, not the twenty-three-year-old one I was when I got the ink."

He raised an eyebrow at her. "Or the thirty-six-year-old one, apparently." He studied her for a long while, gaze locked with hers, and Allie found she couldn't look away.

She nodded. "A lot's changed."

"That it has." He was standing close, too close. He was practically touching her. She *wanted* him to touch her. Just a tiny step forward and—

"Oh, wow! That's super pretty!"

Allie blinked and took a step back as Paige peered out from under her father's arm. She smiled up at Allie and reached out to touch the hem of the dress. "You look nice."

"Thank you." It occurred to Allie that she'd barely looked in the mirror yet, so she turned to study herself in the full-length one behind her. Not bad. Not bad at all. A little snug around the chest, but it was probably supposed to be. There was a little armpit fat poking out at the top, but the hemline made her legs look good, and fluttered nicely when she turned back to face Jack and Paige.

"Looks like you got lucky on the first try."

Allie shifted from one foot to the other, not trusting herself to meet his eyes again. "Looks like it."

"Who was your first boyfriend that you loved?"

Allie blinked and looked at Paige. "Wow. That's kind of random."

Jack laughed and ruffled his daughter's hair. "Not totally. We were just talking about it at the barbershop. We were also talking about how some things are personal and not appropriate questions to ask, weren't we?"

Paige gave a solemn nod and looked up at Allie. "That's true."

Jack gave Allie his slow, lazy smile, holding her gaze for a few beats too many before turning back to his daughter. "Did you need something, kiddo?"

Allie said a silent prayer of thanks that Jack had a talent for distracting his daughter. The girl nodded and held up an armful of clothing. "I wanted to try these on."

"Looks like someone's in the room next door," Jack said. "You'll have to wait your turn."

Allie reached behind her neck, fumbling for the zipper. "Hang on, you can have this one. I don't need to try on the rest of these. I know what I want." Her fingers gripped the zipper and her shoulder creaked as she tried to pull down. "Just let me get out of—"

"Allow me." Jack grabbed her by the waist to hold her still, then tugged the zipper down with a bit less finesse than he'd used to slide it up. He stopped just above the small of her back, and Allie wondered if he was preserving her modesty or trying to keep his daughter from seeing the tattoo.

But the kid clearly had eagle eyes. "Is that fire on your back?"

Allie turned around, holding the back of the dress together with one hand as she stole a look at Jack. Discomfort was etched on his face, but he wasn't meeting her eye. Allie looked at Paige.

"Yes, but I didn't get it until I was a grown-up," she said. "The decision to get a tattoo is a big one, so it's not something you even want to start thinking about until—"

"It looks just like one my dad has."

"What?"

Paige nodded and pointed to her father's ribcage. "Right there. Beside his tummy. He has fire, too, only his has—"

"Why don't we let Allie finish getting dressed?"

Paige looked up at her dad and shrugged. "Okay."

Something in Jack's expression must have let the kid know he meant business, because the next thing Allie knew, he was pushing the door shut and murmuring quietly to Paige on the other side of the door. Allie couldn't make out what he was saying, though she thought she heard the word *private* at one point.

Allie wriggled out of the dress and cast a quick look at the other ones she'd brought into the dressing room. She frowned. Was she deciding too hastily, settling on the very first one she'd tried?

Her mother's words were a faint buzz in the back of her head. *"You shouldn't settle down with the first boyfriend you've had, Allie."*

*"But that's what you and Daddy did, and it worked for you."*

*"Trust me, sweetie—you're going to regret it if you don't spend some time spreading your wings."*

Allie shook her head and put the chosen dress back on the hanger. Hesitated. Then grabbed the next one, a green-and-black velvet number with cap sleeves and a swirly skirt. She pulled it on, adjusting the shoulders but not bothering to zip it up all the way.

She frowned at herself in the mirror. "You look like a kid getting ready for the school Christmas pageant." With a sigh, she stripped the dress off again. She glanced at the rest of the dresses she'd brought with her into the stall, but none of them did anything for her. Not like the first one had.

"Dammit," she muttered under her breath, not sure why that frustrated her so much.

She got dressed again and pushed open the door. Jack and Paige were standing a few feet away looking at a rack of shirts. Jack's head was bent low, and he was talking to his daughter in a quiet voice.

"But Lauren wears a bra already," Paige said. "So does Piper. She showed it to me on our last playdate before we moved. It had yellow and black stripes and looked super pretty."

"And why exactly do you need your underwear to look pretty? Who are you planning to show it to?"

Jack's voice sounded strained, and Allie took a step back, not wanting to intrude. But Paige looked up and shot her a pleading look.

"Allie knows! Tell him, Allie—tell him it's important to start wearing a bra when you get to be ten."

Allie opened her mouth to reply, then shut it. No way was she getting in the middle of this one.

But Jack had other plans. "Actually, that's a good idea." He straightened up and folded his arms over his chest, and Allie did her best not to notice how impressively his pecs had aged. "What are your thoughts, Allie?"

She stared at him, then glanced at Paige. The little girl gave her an imploring look, so Allie directed her attention back at Jack. "You want my input on when a girl should get her first training bra?"

Jack frowned. "That's another thing. What are you training them to *do*, exactly?"

"Dad!" Paige rolled her eyes and shot Allie another pleading look. "When did you get your first bra, Allie?"

Allie grimaced. "You sure like the personal questions, don't you, kiddo?"

"We're working on that," Jack muttered.

Allie looked at him again, trying to gauge whether he was looking for an ally or the truth. His expression was steely, but he didn't look like he was trying to communicate anything to her. Just like a guy who didn't want to be having this conversation in the middle of a thrift store.

Allie chose her words carefully. "Well, I think I was in fifth grade," she said, trying to remember exact details. "Let's see, I was in Mrs. Schaffer's class, so yes—fifth grade."

"I'm in fifth grade now!" Paige announced, looking pleased with herself.

"Right, but there are other factors," Allie said cautiously. She glanced at Jack, hoping like hell he wouldn't make a jackass comment about his daughter not having enough to actually fill a bra. Allie would probably punch him in the nuts if he said it, even if it was the truth.

But Jack said nothing, and Allie silently commended his sensitivity as a single dad.

She took a few steps closer, not wanting to embarrass anyone. "Look, there's a certain age where things get a little tender and it can hurt to have your shirt rubbing up against you," she murmured. "Sometimes it's about that, and sometimes it's about wanting to cover up a little bit. Like if other kids are starting to notice and tease. And sometimes it's just about not wanting to be the only girl at a slumber party who doesn't have one."

Jack stared at her. "Wow." He looked down at his daughter for a moment, and Allie saw him lift his hand as though to ruffle her hair. But he stopped himself and looked back at Allie again. "I didn't—huh." He lifted his hands in a gesture that looked almost like surrender. When he met her eyes, his gaze was almost sheepish. "I guess I didn't know that."

"Most of that wasn't in the book," Paige said.

Allie looked at Jack. It was the first time she'd seen him so undone this week, and the fact that it was over underwear was almost comical. But Allie didn't dare smile, not wanting Paige to think anyone was laughing at her. She glanced at the girl, who seemed to be studying her.

"Maybe you could help me buy a bra?" Paige's voice was small, almost hopeful.

Allie bit her lip. "I think that's something that you and your dad could—"

"No!"

The father-daughter chorus was strong enough to make Allie take a step back. The fact that they'd answered in unison seemed like a pretty good indication they meant it. "Okay." She looked at Jack. "Are you sure this isn't a job for her grandma?"

Jack smiled a little at that. "My mother is convinced Paige still needs someone to cut up her meat and read her a bedtime story every night."

"It's nice and stuff," Paige said. "But she still reads me *The Very Hungry Caterpillar*."

Allie laughed, which seemed to dissolve the tension somehow. Before she knew it, all three of them were cracking up beside a rack of Alexander McQueen shirts. "Okay then," Allie said. "I'll set up a time with your dad so I can take you bra shopping."

Jack shot her a grateful look, then grabbed the green dress from her arms. "Please, let me get this. It's the least I can do, since you're taking my kid bra shopping and going with me to the reunion."

She started to protest, then stopped herself. "Thank you," she said. "I accept."

The smile he gave her was enough to have Allie questioning exactly what she'd just agreed to.

# CHAPTER EIGHT

"This room makes such a lovely little hair salon," Skye said as she curled a lock of Allie's hair around a contraption that looked like she'd taken it from a space station.

Allie shifted a little on the high-backed barstool Skye had parked in front of the mirror in a small, sunlit room on the first floor. Her grandmother had always called it the Maple Room for a tree that used to be right outside the window.

But the tree was flat on the ground now, the victim of a bad windstorm several weeks ago, according to Skye. Allie still hadn't rounded up an arborist to haul it away.

"I always loved the light in here," Allie said. "My grandma used to read in that corner over there when we didn't have guests staying in the room."

"You must miss her a lot."

Allie started to nod, but stopped as Skye wrapped another section of her hair around the curling iron. "I do. I keep picking up the phone to call her, and then realizing I can't."

"I never knew any of my grandparents, but I always thought of Vicky as the grandma I wish I had."

"It still smells like her in this room," Allie said. "She used to keep these big vases of roses everywhere in the house."

"It's potpourri. I bought some with rose petals in it, and your grandma loved it so much that I started buying huge bags of it so the place would still smell like home whenever the nurses brought her to visit." She met Allie's eyes in the mirror and gave her a small smile. "Sorry, I don't want to make you cry when we just got your makeup perfect."

"It's okay. I'm not much of a crier."

"Still, I'll come up with something better to talk about." Skye seemed to think for a moment. "What's the latest on the woodpecker situation?"

"I took pictures of the damage and showed them to a guy at Home Depot after Jack left yesterday," Allie said. "He told me I should put up a bunch of pinwheels and metallic streamers to scare them away."

"Is that why the front of the house looks like a Mardi Gras party?" Skye laughed and released Allie's hair. "I thought you were just getting into the spirit of your reunion."

"Nope, it's for the woodpeckers. And Jack's reunion, not mine. I'm just going to keep him company."

"Mmm," Skye murmured, sounding dubious. Or maybe it was just the bobby pin she'd stuck between her teeth. She used it to anchor a curl into a little upsweep she'd created at the crown of Allie's head, then picked up another lock to twirl around the barrel of the curling device. "So you graduated from college at different times, but you went to high school together?"

"Yes. He was my date to the senior prom."

"No kidding? So you were high school sweethearts."

"Sort of," Allie admitted, not sure how much of the story she wanted to tell. "We were friends all through middle school and high school, but just friends. Prom was kind of our first official date, but we dated in secret for about nine months before that."

"Why in secret?"

Allie shrugged, a little embarrassed at the memory. "I didn't want my parents to know. My family was sort of—"

"Protective?"

"Yes," Allie agreed, though that wasn't what she'd been about to say. *Prominent. Judgmental. Pretentious.* Take your pick, and none of them were that flattering. She still remembered the first time she'd broached the subject of Jack with her mother.

*"I've been seeing this boy,"* she'd said. *"Actually, we've been friends at school for a long time. He's really cute and smart and funny and—"*

*"What do his parents do?"* Priscilla's scowl had sent a burst of ice water through Allie's arms.

*"I—um, I'm not sure. His mom is a secretary at an elementary school, I think. His dad isn't around."*

*"And this boy—"*

*"Jack."*

*"Jack,"* her mother had repeated, pronouncing the word like a disease. *"Where's he going to college?"*

*"Um, he's not sure yet. Maybe community college for a couple years to save money, and then—"*

*"So it's not serious, then."*

The words had been a statement, not a question. Allie remembered the flare of anger in her belly, but she'd tamped it down. *"I want you to meet him."*

And so he'd met her parents. Her father had been guarded, but charming. Her mother had been chilly, and had remained chilly for the next two years, through family dinners and Jack's surprise scholarship and the two of them moving in together and the engagement and—

"Turn a little to your right," Skye said, jarring Allie back to the present. "Perfect. I just want to make sure I've got the other side even."

"I really appreciate you doing this."

Skye beamed at her in the mirror. "No problem. Every woman should look gorgeous for a reunion, even if it's not her own. Will you know people there?"

"Maybe a few. I'm really just going for Jack."

"Jack." Skye grinned and wrapped another lock of hair around the curling iron. "Was he that hot in high school?"

"No. I mean—he was hot, yes. Really hot. But it was more of a youthful hot. Less edgy, you know what I mean?"

Skye nodded. "I know exactly what you mean. His eyes—they look old, but not in a bad way. Sorta soulful. Like he's *seen* things."

"Yes. That's it exactly."

Allie fingered the edge of the sheet Skye had draped around her to keep any wayward hair products off her dress. She thought about what Jack's eyes might've seen, things she hadn't been a part of. A life that had unfolded completely without her.

"Tell me about the guy you were dating," Allie said. "The one who was living here with you when my grandma hired you. Brody?"

She watched Skye's expression turn solemn in the mirror, but she didn't look heartbroken. Just a little wistful.

"There's not much to tell," Skye said. "He just woke up one day and said he didn't love me anymore."

"I'm sorry," Allie said. "Sometimes it happens that way."

"Yeah. I didn't take it very well at first. I emptied his underwear drawer on the front lawn, sent him pleading text messages at all hours of the night. That sort of thing."

Allie smiled at her in the mirror. "Pretty sure we've all done things we're not proud of at the tail end of a relationship."

"True." Skye bit her lip. "Actually, can I confess something?"

"Go right ahead."

She curled another lock of Allie's hair around the barrel of the curling iron, then twisted it slowly toward the crown of her head. "Brody came from this really wealthy family. Tons of money, tons of nice things.

After he took off, he just left a bunch of stuff here. And, uh—I might have hidden some of it in the attic."

Allie's arms prickled. She took a deep breath, unsure exactly what Skye was telling her. "Here? In this house?"

Skye nodded, but didn't meet Allie's eyes. "I was a little worried when I saw you up there the other day. I thought you might have found it and since we didn't know each other well yet, I guess—" she shrugged. "I didn't want you to jump to the wrong conclusion about me."

Allie's heart was pounding hard in her ears, but she kept her voice even. "What conclusion would that be?"

"I don't know. That I'm the sort of person who'd steal."

"Steal," Allie repeated, too stunned to form a complete sentence. "So that's where it came from?"

"It's not exactly stealing," Skye said. "It's been six months and he's never asked about it, so it's pretty obvious he's forgotten he even left it here."

Allie tried not to let her eyes boggle. A million dollars in cash? Surely even the richest bastard wouldn't forget something like that. She licked her lips, trying to come up with an appropriate response.

"So . . . do you have any plans to return it to him?"

Skye shrugged. "If he asks about it, I guess." She met Allie's eyes in the mirror. "Are you mad?"

"Mad? I'm not mad. Just . . . confused, I guess."

"So was I, the first time I saw them."

"Them?" It occurred to Allie that they might not be talking about the same thing. She started to ask about the sex toys, then remembered her blunder with her father. For crying out loud, what the hell was everyone doing hiding things in her grandma's attic?

Fortunately, Skye seemed oblivious. "Right. I mean, it's not every day you stumble upon a collection of antique bongs. Some he brought back from travels around the world—Thailand, Guatemala, I think there's even one from Russia in there. The one that has the elephant with a giant penis wrapped around his shoulders and—"

"Um, yeah." Allie couldn't decide whether to feel relieved or . . . well, more confused. But she knew she couldn't let Skye know there was anything else to be concerned about in the attic, so she flashed her a friendly smile. "Don't worry. Your secret's safe with me."

"Thanks." Skye beamed, then took a step back and surveyed her work. "All done! What do you think?"

"Oh, wow." Allie turned her head from one side to the other, admiring the cascade of soft waves Skye had created for her. Her hair was loose and wavy, with a few curls pinned up in a beautifully haphazard twist. Skye had used some sort of magical product that made her hair silky instead of crunchy, and it smelled amazing. The whole effect was rather delicate and romantic.

"I love it," Allie said. "You're very talented."

"Thank you!" Skye beamed as a black-and-white tuxedo cat twined itself around her bare ankles and made a soft little mewling sound. Its tail spiked straight up like a fluffy pipe cleaner as it sniffed a piece of paper lying next to the chair. The tail swished once, twice, before the cat grabbed hold of the paper and took off running.

"Dammit, Marilyn!" Skye started to run after her, then stopped. "Oh, whatever. It was just a piece of junk mail this time."

"This time?"

"She steals. Paperwork, gloves, rolls of toilet paper—anything she can carry in her mouth and run away with."

"Where does she put it?"

Skye shrugged. "My bedroom sometimes. Other times she'll take it to the other cats like gifts."

"I've never heard of something like that."

"I always figured it's a polydactyl thing—sort of like a six-fingered discount?"

Allie laughed as Skye leaned forward and wrapped one of Allie's curls around her finger, twisting it so it laid just so. "I still can't believe you're going to your reunion with the first guy you ever kissed. That's so romantic."

"It's really not like that."

"Not like what?"

"Not like we're together or anything. Not like that, anyway."

Skye gave her a serene smile and nodded. "Still, I think it's very sweet."

"I guess. So are you dating now? Or is it still too soon after Brody?"

"Oh, I'm dating a little. A couple months ago I even tested out the waters dating women. Just a few Tinder hookups here and there, nothing serious."

"Really?" Allie couldn't decide whether to feel scandalized or intrigued.

"It was fun for a few weeks, but honestly, it didn't do much for me. Dating girls, I mean. I think I just like penises a little too much to ever—"

"Hello!"

They both turned to see Wade standing in the doorway. He wore a blue Armani suit and the same smile he'd wear if he came home from work to find a porn flick being filmed in his living room.

"Thank you, ladies," he said, folding his arms over his chest and smiling at Skye. "I'm going to dream about that conversation for the next week."

Allie rolled her eyes. "Don't you know how to knock?"

"I did, but no one answered. And there was a sign out front inviting me to come in."

"It's left over from the bed-and-breakfast days," Skye said. "I left the door unlocked for when Jack gets here. Sorry. I'm Skye, by the way."

"Wade," he said as he reached for her hand.

Allie caught the dazzled look in his eye, along with the contrast of Skye's flowery sari skirt and bare feet beside Wade's Armani suit and silver cuff links. Their hands were still joined, and Skye's smile had turned goofy.

Wade lifted her hand to his lips, brushing a soft kiss over her knuckles before nestling her hand back into the folds of her skirt. "It's a pleasure to make your acquaintance, Skye. Allie told me she'd met the caretaker of the place and that you were doing her hair, but she didn't mention you were so—enchanting."

Skye blushed prettily, and Allie glanced at Wade, ready to tell him to knock it off. But the look on his face was just as smitten as the one on Skye's. What the hell? Wade dated polished socialites, not free spirits.

But the way he was looking at Skye suggested he might be reconsidering.

"You're sweet," Skye said. "How do you and Allie know each other?"

Wade leaned back against the wall and crossed his ankles. "We go way back. Tell me about yourself, Skye. Are you from Portland?"

"Born and raised. I'm finishing up at cosmetology school and hoping to get a job at one of the salons downtown. How about you?"

"I'm from Seattle, originally, but I moved out here ten years ago to take a job at Solomon Ashe and Associates."

"You're a lawyer?"

"Don't hold it against me. That reminds me—"

He turned to Allie, who had started to think they'd forgotten she was here at all. Wade reached into the side pocket of his briefcase and pulled out a large manila folder with the law firm's name on it. "Here's that stuff you were asking about on asset forfeiture laws and estate taxes."

"Oh—right, thank you."

He lifted one eyebrow in a silent question, and Allie shook her head. *Not now,* she telegraphed, willing him not to ask any questions that would lead Skye to suspect there was a giant trunk of cash in the attic. Not that she'd told Wade about it, either, but she had asked a few vague questions and enough hypotheticals to pique his interest.

Luckily, his interest seemed more piqued by Skye at the moment. "So, Skye," he was saying. "Since Allie's running off to have fun with her old fiancé tonight, I don't suppose you'd be interested in having dinner with me?"

Skye smiled and began winding the cord around the fancy hair curler. Her own long curls fell over her face, and Wade stared like she was the most exotic creature he'd ever seen. Allie tried to remember some of the women he'd dated over the years. There'd been plenty, but she couldn't think of any who looked like Skye.

"I think I'm free," Skye was saying. "What did you have in mind?"

"Something different. I like the blue in your hair, by the way."

"Thanks. I've been thinking of switching to pink, but I'm still loving the blue."

"It's great. Very unique. Goes with your name."

"You're right, it sort of does." Skye looked pleased that he'd noticed, and Allie couldn't help feeling charmed by their flirtation.

"So how about it," Wade said. "Dinner? With me? Tonight?"

Skye smiled. "Okay. Have you been to Marrakesh?"

"In Morocco?"

"No, I mean the restaurant. It's this slightly cheesy little place over on Northwest 21st where you sit on the floor and eat with your hands. There's a belly dancer on weekends, and the staff dresses in traditional Moroccan attire. Like I said, kinda cheesy, but I love the place."

"Sold!" Wade grinned. "That sounds perfect."

Allie stood up and set Wade's envelope on top of the maple dresser. She pulled the bedsheet off and folded it neatly before setting it on the empty barstool. Then she straightened the peacock-green dress. She'd worn it here, not wanting to mess up her hair by pulling it on afterward. Jack was picking her up from the B&B in about ten minutes.

"Whoa, Albatross!" Wade had finally glanced away from Skye and was looking at her. "Nice dress!"

"Thank you."

"That color's great on you."

"Totally," Skye agreed. "I told her she looks like Jennifer Garner." She shifted closer to Wade, seemingly drawn to him. "Did you just call her Albatross?"

"Allie Ross the Albatross," Wade repeated, smiling fondly at her. "The bird who'd rather fly alone."

Skye gave Allie a sympathetic smile and shrugged. "Nothing wrong with that. It's good to be a strong, independent woman."

"Amen, sister."

"Are you two going to hug now?" Wade asked. "Because I'd really like to see that. Especially if there's a boob grab involved."

"You're ridiculous." Allie slugged him in the shoulder, then picked up the envelope again and moved through the door. "Thanks again, Skye. Really, you did an amazing job. You're sure I can't pay you?"

"No way. You're doing me a favor here. I needed the practice."

"Thanks again."

"You look gorgeous. Kinda glowy or something."

"Glowy," Wade repeated, looking her up and down with a critical eye. "You haven't been snogging the guy already, have you?"

Allie rolled her eyes, which was mostly a move to avoid eye contact with Wade. She knew he could see right through her. She held up the envelope as she made her way out the door. "I have a few minutes before Jack gets here, so I'm going to go look through this."

"Call if you have questions about it," Wade said.

"I will. Thanks again. Both of you!"

"You're welcome," Skye called.

Allie headed down the hall and into the kitchen, a familiar space that reminded her of dainty teacups and her grandmother's shortbread cookies. She felt a pang of sadness and took a few deep breaths to get it under control.

She set Wade's envelope on the counter, hesitating a little. She'd been deliberately vague when she'd asked him to dig up some info on inheritance laws and Oregon statutes on found property. He was her best friend, but it seemed unwise to just blurt out the fact that she'd stumbled upon a million dollars in cash. Given his connection to her parents' case, would he be required to report it? Allie wasn't sure, so she figured better safe than sorry.

She pried open the clasp securing the envelope, careful not to wreck her new manicure. A thick stack of papers was inside, and Allie pulled it out and stared at the first page.

*Lost, Unclaimed, or Abandoned Property Laws, ORS §98.005 . . .*

"Hello? Allie, are you here?"

The papers fell from her hands as Jack's voice rang out from the foyer. *Crap.*

He called out again, his voice getting closer now.

"I'm in here!" Allie shouted as she dropped to her knees and began grabbing pages. They were hopelessly out of order, a blur of words like *forfeiture* and *encumbered property* and *theft by deception*. She stuffed them into a pile, not sure why she felt so guilty, but knowing Jack was going to walk into the room at any moment.

"Allie?"

She turned to see him standing behind her. His eyes were locked on her ass, and he had a funny look on his face.

"Well," he said, his voice a little strained. "Can't say I expected to see you on your hands and knees this early in the evening."

◆　◆　◆

Jack wanted to kick himself for saying something so suggestive to Allie when their connection was still in the realm of tepid friendship. It was the sort of thing he could have gotten away with sixteen years ago, but not now. Not with all this history between them.

Lucky for him, she didn't seem offended.

"Very funny," she muttered as she continued scooping papers into a haphazard pile.

"Here, let me help you up." He reached a hand down to her, half expecting her to swat it away.

But she let him hoist her to her feet by one hand as she clutched a disheveled stack of papers in the other.

"Thanks," she said. "You startled me."

"Sorry about that. I knocked on the front door, but when no one answered, I saw that sign telling me to come in."

"Right, I need to get that taken down."

"Remind me the next time I'm here with my tools and I'll get rid of it."

He watched a hint of color seep into her cheeks, and he wondered if she was thinking about the last time he'd been here with his tool belt. He was considering making another suggestive comment when a flash of black and white tore through the room.

"Marilyn, no!"

The animal—was it a skunk or a cat?—snatched something off the floor and streaked around the corner, its fluffy tail trailing behind like a taunting battle flag.

Allie took off running, which was quite the feat in ridiculously high heels. Jack had no idea what was going on, but he followed anyway.

"What are we chasing?"

"A cat!" Allie yelled back as they tore around a corner and down a hall. "A thieving polydactyl."

"That sounds like a lesser-known Shakespeare title."

"The brat stole one of my pages."

"An irreplaceable page from a bestselling novel you're writing?"

"What? No, it's just something I need."

The fluffy black tail disappeared around another corner and through a doorway, and Allie scrambled after the kleptomaniac creature. Jack followed suit, skidding to a halt as he saw Allie down on her hands and knees beside a bed. She was peering under the dust ruffle, and Jack knew he should probably stop staring at her ass and help. Any minute now. Just one more second and—

"Come here, you little sneak."

Jack stepped forward, shaking off the ass-trance. "Want me to grab her from the other side?"

"Sure, or maybe you could just chase her toward me."

Jack walked around to the other edge of the bed and dropped to his knees, wondering if she felt as awkward as he did about kneeling next to a bed with a person he'd slept with for two years. Probably not. She had other things on her mind, obviously.

He lifted the dust ruffle and peered underneath. A pair of glowing yellow eyes peered back at him, daring him to make a move. The cat clutched a sheet of paper in its teeth, whiskers fanning over the pages like black streaks of ink. The cat stared at him for a few beats, then gave a muffled meow.

"Here, kitty-kitty-kitty," he coaxed.

"Her name's Marilyn."

"Do you really know all their names now?"

"Not all of them, but she has that little Marilyn Monroe beauty mark on her cheek."

"Ah, I see that now." Jack reached under the bed and tried to grab the cat. She scooted back and gave another meow, this time dropping the paper.

"Got it!" He snatched the page, sending the cat skittering backward toward the headboard. She gave a halfhearted hiss, then sat back and began to clean her ears with one of her catcher's-mitt paws.

Jack stood up, ready to walk around the bed and help Allie to her feet again, but he saw she was already standing. They were separated by the width of a queen-sized mattress, and there was something strangely intimate about it. Like they were a pair of lovers on the brink of crawling into bed together instead of two exes on their way to a college reunion.

They stared at each other across the mattress, both of them still a little breathless from the chase around the house. Allie looked at him, her palm trailing absently over the blue coverlet.

She was the first to speak. "Sorry about that. Thank you for the help."

"No problem. Your hair—"

"Oh, God—did I mess it up? Skye's going to kill me." She put her hand up to touch it, and Jack shook his head.

"No, that's not it. I just meant it's beautiful. I didn't notice before, but I've never seen you wear it like that before."

"Oh. Thanks." A flush crept into her cheeks, and her palm drifted over one of the pillows. Was she thinking the same thing he was? Remembering a different bed, a different reason for the heavy breathing and mussed hair? The way they used to—

"Can I have it?"

"What?"

Allie stretched her hand out and gave him an expectant look. "My page. The paper the cat stole."

"Oh. Yes, of course." He started to hand it to her, then glanced down at the words.

*ORS 98.005 Notice/Report Requirements*

Allie stretched out to snatch it out of his hand, but Jack drew it back. He was probably being a nosy asshole, but he was curious.

"'A person is always required to report found money or property (ORS 98.352 and ORS 98.376) or to pay or deliver unclaimed property to the Department of State Lands, unless the property interest vested prior to August 20, 1957 . . .'"

"I was just finding out more about the laws pertaining to found property," Allie said, interrupting his reading. "It's no big deal."

Jack looked up from the words to meet those dark-green eyes. "So you're thinking of reporting the cash to the authorities?"

"Yes. No. I don't know."

"But you're supposed to?"

"I'm not sure yet. The laws are kind of complicated, and I haven't had time to read all that yet."

He frowned. "So where's the money now?"

"Shhh!" She glanced toward the doorway, and Jack glanced over, too. "Skye's here?"

"And Wade, too."

An unwelcome flicker of jealousy burned in his chest, which was stupid. Wade was just a friend. Besides, it's not like Allie entered a convent when they split up.

He was still staring at the door like an idiot when he felt Allie tug the paper from his grip. He turned to see her kneeling on the bed in front of him, sliding the paper out of his sweaty fingers.

"Thank you," she said.

She didn't move back right away. They were almost nose to nose, and Jack felt something stir inside him at the sight of a beautiful woman in a cocktail dress kneeling in front of him on the blue silk duvet. She was a little flushed, and he wished like hell he knew what she was thinking. Her gaze held his, and he could feel her breath coming fast. From chasing the cat or from something else?

He started to reach for her, and her eyes flashed. She licked her lips.

"Ready to go?" She drew the page up between them, the world's most ineffective shield.

He nodded, not quite ready to break the spell. "I'm ready."

For what, he had no idea.

# CHAPTER NINE

Jack turned the key in the ignition of his Audi Q5, then glanced over at Allie to make sure she'd buckled her seatbelt. He wasn't used to having anyone in the passenger seat beside him. Paige still rode in back, much to her annoyance, but he was holding firm on that one. Everything he'd read from the American Academy of Pediatrics said it was safer for a child to remain in the backseat until she was at least thirteen. Maybe thirty-six.

"All set?" he asked.

Allie nodded. "Nice car."

"Thank you. It just arrived yesterday."

"It's new?"

"No, I had it brought up here by a moving company. Time was a little tight, so Paige and I flew to Portland and had most of our household stuff sent by a moving company."

"That must have been expensive."

He glanced at her, trying to figure out if there was any sort of judgment or admiration in the words. They seemed harmless enough, so Jack decided to let it pass. He concentrated on easing the car away from the curb and pointing them toward the restaurant where the event was being held.

They were both quiet a moment, the silence in the car broken only by the sound of rainwater shushing beneath the tires and the wiper blades squeaking against the windshield. He breathed in Allie's perfume and wondered what she was thinking. He didn't have to wonder long.

"So do you really want me to take your kid bra shopping?"

Jack nodded, then realized she was looking out the window instead of at him. "If you're up for it. I mean, I'm sure you're busy—"

"No, it's okay. I just meant—well, I've only met her a couple times. Isn't there someone closer to her?"

"Just my mom, and like I said, she still kind of treats her like she's a baby. If this bra thing has to happen, I'd rather it happen with someone who's going to treat her like a maturing little girl."

Allie turned from the window and gave him an appraising look. "Wow, that's very adult of you."

He laughed. "Having a kid makes you grow up pretty fast." He thought about that for a moment, then glanced over at her. "Having a daughter especially."

"How so?"

"Maybe it's different in two-parent households. When you're a single dad raising a little girl, you spend half your time feeling like some sort of Viking protector, and the other half pretty sure you're screwing up six ways to Sunday."

"I hardly think you're screwing her up," Allie said. "She seems like a well-adjusted kid."

"Thanks."

"Not that I've been around a lot of kids."

He grinned. "So your observation is meaningless?"

"I wouldn't say that, exactly. But I was always a bit of a daddy's girl, so I think I'm qualified to assess father-daughter relationships. Yours seems pretty solid."

"Thanks. It is." He didn't say anything right away as his thoughts mixed with the splash of rainwater outside and he tried to figure out the words that went along with what he was feeling. "That's the thing about being a dad. When she's young, she's your little girl. You play games and make each other laugh and spend most of your time feeling like the center of each other's universe. But then the universe gets bigger— friends, school, social stuff—and you worry you're not enough for her. That no matter how amazing your bond is, it's still stupidly inadequate for everything she needs to make it through that awkward transition from little girl to young woman."

"Wow." Allie bit her lip. "I guess I never thought about that."

He shrugged. "Maybe it's not the same with all dads and daughters. It might just be me."

She looked at him, her green eyes clear and bright. "Like I said, I'm not the best judge on the planet. But from where I stand, you seem like you're doing great."

"Thank you. That means a lot."

She went quiet again, and Jack thought about how nice it felt to talk to someone about this. He talked with his mom about Paige, of course—who would be picking her up from a birthday party, or whether it was time to switch her from Flintstones Vitamins to something more grown-up, but not conversations like this. He usually avoided discussing his daughter with Lacey, and since Lacey had made it clear she wasn't interested in a relationship, he'd kept contact to a minimum between the two. No sense getting Paige's hopes up for something permanent, or having her imprint on a new mother figure like an orphaned baby duck. It was a moot point now anyway, since Lacey had zero interest in relocating to Portland.

Allie seemed to read his thoughts. "So your girlfriend—"

"Definitely not my girlfriend."

"Whatever. Your *lady friend*, then—did you guys cut things off when you moved?"

"Pretty much."

She nodded, and Jack wondered what she was thinking. If she'd ask him anything else about his love life these past sixteen years, and what he was willing to volunteer.

"My mom wasn't a huge fan of Lacey," he said.

Now where the hell had that come from?

Allie looked at him and smiled. "How does she feel about you spending time with the woman who broke your heart sixteen years ago?"

He shrugged. "Guarded," he admitted. "But she always thought highly of you. Even after we split."

"She sent me a card during my parents' trial," Allie said. "Said she was thinking of me, hoped I was doing okay. That she knew how close I was to my mom and dad, and that she knew I loved them no matter what."

Jack nodded. "I always envied what you had with your family. Both parents present and accounted for. Loving grandparents. The whole mess."

"My grandmother adored you." The fondness in Allie's voice was unmistakable. "Said every woman needs a man who lights her up inside and leaves her glowing after he's left the room." She grinned. "Grandma could be a little passionate."

"You don't say." Probably best not to bring up the sex toys. "Your mom couldn't stand me."

"She didn't hate you." Allie pressed her lips together. "Just didn't think you were the right choice. My dad liked you, though. Still does."

Hearing that made Jack feel warm from the inside out, like he'd swallowed a shot of whiskey. "I always wished I had a dad like yours."

The sad look Allie shot him had Jack questioning whether it was smart to share this much. They were still easing back into their friendship, after all. But when she spoke, her voice was tinged with compassion, not pity.

"I remember that story you told me," Allie said softly. "About the time your dad decided the two of you should hitchhike from Portland to Vegas. You were what, five?"

Jack gave a tight nod. "Almost six. By the time we finally got there, he was tired of hanging out with me, so he told me to sleep in the car while he and the driver—some guy we'd just met named Buddy—went into the casino and got wasted."

Allie grimaced. "God, I can't even imagine how your mom must've felt getting that phone call."

Jack shook his head and gripped the steering wheel tighter. "*I think I lost the kid, but I'm sure he's around here someplace,*" Jack muttered in his closest approximation of his father's voice. Then again, he hadn't heard that voice for years. His memories were fuzzy.

"You think he remembers any of that?" Allie asked. "That trip or the things he did?"

"I have no idea. I hardly ever think about him."

It sounded lousy saying it out loud, but it was true. He'd written his father off years ago, and with good reason.

"The trip wasn't all bad," she said in a voice as soft as the rain outside. "Your hitchhiking adventure, I mean. I remember you telling me about how he stopped at a truck stop along the way and gave you a whole handful of quarters to run the jukebox all night. Chased away anyone who tried to have a turn. You told me he picked you up and danced with you when you made it play 'Boot Scootin' Boogie.'"

A pang of sadness hit him square in the gut. Jack glanced at her, surprised she'd remembered that detail. He'd forgotten it himself. Leave it to Allie to focus on the good parts of the story. To push aside the ugly ones and hold tightly to the prettier pieces of memory.

He couldn't think of anything to say, which was just as well since they'd arrived at Bumble. He started for a parking spot in back, but remembered Allie's high heels and drove around for a few minutes until he found one closer. He pulled into it and shut the car off, but didn't pull his keys from the ignition right away. He sat there for a few seconds longer, mentally steeling himself.

"So . . . what's the plan here?" Allie asked.

He turned to look at her. "How do you mean?"

"Do you need me to pretend to be your girlfriend, or am I just an old pal?" She shrugged. "I'm good either way."

"No, I don't want to lie. But I guess—maybe we don't need to volunteer details?"

She laughed and tossed her hair. "I see. So you're saying there might be a situation in which it would behoove you to have a girlfriend on your arm, but then again, maybe you'd rather be free to pick up chicks?"

"No, it's not that at all."

"It's okay, Jack." She smiled, and he knew she meant it. "I'll play it however you want. Maybe we need a cue."

"A cue?"

"Yeah. Like if we get in there and you want me to play your old buddy, you scratch your chin. And if you want me to play your girl-friend, you—"

"Grab my crotch?"

"Very funny." Allie grabbed the door handle. "Come on. We're already thirty minutes late. Better get in there."

She pushed her door open, and Jack unbuckled his seatbelt, not sure he was ready for this. Not sure he was ready for any of it.

◆　◆　◆

Allie smoothed down the front of her dress, feeling oddly self-conscious. It wasn't her reunion. That didn't mean she wouldn't be judged, though.

She glanced over at Jack, who was looking a little gray. She started to reach for his hand, but remembered they weren't pulling out the boyfriend-girlfriend card unless he gave the signal. What was the signal again? She started to ask, but Jack grabbed the door handle and yanked it open with surprising force.

"Whoa, there," she said, jumping back so the door didn't hit her in the face. "You okay?"

"Yeah, why wouldn't I be?"

He let the door fall shut, and Allie pulled her jacket tighter around her shoulders. The rain had stopped, but it was still chilly outside. Still, she got the sense Jack wasn't thrilled to be going inside. "I guess you just seem a little nervous about going in there."

"Maybe a little," he admitted.

"How come? You're wildly successful, you still look hot, you have a great kid."

He smiled, but it didn't quite meet his eyes. "Thanks. That was a good pep talk. I needed it."

She couldn't tell if he was joking or not, but he seemed sincere. "What's it like, anyway?" he asked. "I've missed all my other reunions. This will be my first."

"That makes two of us."

"Really?"

She shrugged, determined not to get defensive about it. "I got mono right before our ten-year high school reunion, so I couldn't make it to that."

Okay, so it wasn't entirely true, but Jack didn't need to know the rest of the story. That she'd been embarrassed about dropping out of law school, about breaking her engagement. She'd expected to have kids and a brag-worthy career and a big house in the West Hills, but she hadn't achieved any of that by the time her reunion came around. It had just seemed easier to skip it.

"Anyway," she said, "I never bothered with the college reunions, either."

"How come?"

She shrugged. "Life just turned out differently than I expected."

"Allie, people's dreams change all the time."

"Not mine," she said, and the words came out with a little more vehemence than she'd intended. "Anyway, there was also that whole business with my parents. I didn't want to have to answer questions about it."

"I guess I can understand that." He glanced at the door, but made no move to reach for it.

"Jack." She laid a hand on his arm. "We don't have to go in there if you don't want."

"No, I want to," he said. "Of course, I might prefer shoving bamboo under my fingernails and soaking my hands in grapefruit juice."

Allie giggled. "Or removing your eyelids with pliers?"

"Definitely preferable. Same with sticking a hot fork in my eye and twisting."

"Oooh, ouch." She studied his face, noticing some of the stiffness had started to leave his expression. "How about eating six jars of mayonnaise in one sitting?"

Jack laughed. "Using my toothbrush to clean litter boxes at your B&B."

"Disgusting." She grinned at him. "So just out of curiosity, why are you doing this?"

He sighed, seemed to be deciding something. "Does it make me a shallow jerk if I admit it's because I want everyone to see I turned out well?"

"Nope." She offered an encouraging smile. "You're not a shallow jerk. I promise. That's probably why most people are here."

"What if I flat out say I kinda want to rub their noses in it?"

"Maybe a little bit of a shallow jerk. It's okay, though. Your secret's safe with me."

He nodded, and the look he gave her was so full of gratitude she thought her heart might burst. "I guess that's not the whole truth. Honestly, I just want to make sure I can do this."

"How do you mean?"

He shrugged. "Being around groups of people who knew Caroline—it used to be hard, especially right after she died. I haven't done it much in the last decade."

"Oh, Jack—" Allie felt her eyes prick with tears, but she was at a loss for what to say.

"It's okay," he said. "It's been almost ten years. It's not like I'm still in the depths of grief or anything. It's just—this is sort of a test, I guess. To make sure I can handle it."

"I believe in you," she said. "Let me know if there's anything I can do to make it easier."

He grinned. "You already are. You're here with me." Jack took a deep breath and reached for the door again. "Okay. Let's do this."

He gestured for her to go ahead of him, so Allie walked through first. The foyer was empty, but Allie could hear the thud of bass so loud she felt it in her head. They followed the sound down a dim corridor, moving together toward the pulsing music. As they reached a doorway, Jack seemed to hesitate.

"You've got this," Allie said.

"Okay." He didn't sound convinced, but he moved forward anyway.

They stepped into a dimly lit room packed tight with bodies and the smell of red wine and nervous energy. She felt Jack stiffen beside her, but he was surveying the room, getting the lay of the land.

The space was dotted with tall bistro tables draped with black table-cloths and a single purple iris in a silver vase at the center of each. A bar on the left side of the room already contained a cluster of people laughing a little too loudly. On the other side of the room stood a buffet table adorned with silver trays offering mushroom caps, crudités, charcuterie, and fancy little pastries filled with something that looked like salmon mousse.

Jack started toward the food, but Allie reached out and touched his elbow. "Three o'clock," she murmured, nodding in that direction. "Someone's heading this way."

"Shit," Jack murmured as the guy drew closer. "I can't remember his name. Brock or Brent or Brett or—"

"Jack, my man! Good to see you again." The guy did one of those fancy handshakes only men seemed to know. Some sort of handclasp melded with a shoulder clap and a chest bump. Allie stood back and hoped the guy didn't notice how forced Jack's smile looked.

"Good to see you . . . uh, man," Jack offered. He looked like he needed a lifeline, so Allie threw him one.

"Hi there," she said, reaching out a hand. "I don't think we've met before. I'm Allison."

The guy grinned and pumped Allie's hand. "Bryce. Great to meet you."

"You, too, Bryce."

He turned back to Jack, and his expression changed. So did his tone, switching to a timbre that reminded Allie of a late-night DJ counseling a caller on his marital woes. "Listen, I heard about what happened. I just want to say—"

"Wow, are those Swedish meatballs?"

Allie blinked, then followed Jack's gaze to the buffet table. She looked back at him, perplexed, but willing to play along.

"Yes," she said, barely missing a beat. "I think they are. Would you like me to get you some?"

"Actually, I'll go with you." His voice was tight and a little too fast. "I want a lot of them. Bryce—it was great seeing you again. I hope you don't mind if I—"

"No, of course," he said, clapping Jack on the back again. "We'll talk later. I don't want to stand between a man and his meat."

He wandered away, blending back into the crowd. Allie turned to Jack. "Come on," she said. "Let's get those meatballs."

They'd taken three steps toward the buffet table when a trio of women approached. The instant they spotted Jack, the one dressed in a silver-sequined gown let out a soft gasp and put her hand over her heart. The other two tilted their heads to the side and gave identical sympathetic headshakes, looking like well-coiffed parrots. One wore a bright-red gown and the other a strappy little number in purple chiffon.

One of the two—whose face seemed frozen by astonishment or Botox—marched forward with such purpose that Allie had to step out of the way to avoid being trampled under the strappy, bloodred Jimmy Choos that matched her dress.

"Jack Carpenter," she said in a voice that reminded Allie of an audition for the dramatic lead in a high school play. "We were wondering if you'd be here. How *are* you, honey?"

The woman in purple chiffon was still doing the sympathetic headshake, but Silver Sequins dropped her hand from her heart and put it on Jack's arm. "We were so sorry to hear about Caroline. How awful that must have been for you."

"And you have a little girl, too," Purple Chiffon added, making a sympathetic *tsk* noise that showed a flash of crimson lipstick on her teeth. "If there's anything you need—anything at all—"

"Uh, thanks," Jack said, shooting Allie an imploring look. She tried to read his mind, not sure if he wanted her to introduce herself or fade into the crowd. She watched as Jack reached up to scratch his chin, and she tried to remember which cue that was. Friend or girlfriend? God, why hadn't they spent more time nailing down the body language?

He seemed to be wrestling with the same question, then reached a conclusion. She watched as his hand dropped to his waist, then slid down for a subtle crotch grab.

She stifled the urge to laugh as she stepped closer to Jack. A look of intense relief crossed his face, and he put his arm around her shoulders like it belonged there.

"Hi, I'm Allie," she said. "Jack's girlfriend?"

The three women stared at her. Silver Sequins blinked hard, making her lashes stick together like a pair of mating spiders.

"Oh," murmured the one with lipstick on her teeth. "Well, my. That's—that's wonderful."

"Absolutely lovely," Botox added. "I've been so worried imagining you all alone, a grieving widower."

"Nope, I'm doing great!" Jack said, perhaps a little too enthusiastically. "Business is booming, I've launched my own app development firm—"

"And your little girl?"

"Paige is great," Jack said, shooting Allie a look she couldn't quite read. For lack of anything better to do, she put her hand on Jack's ass. Might as well get something out of playing the role. He looked down at her and gave a smile that looked shaky, but genuine.

"Yeah, Paige is ten now," he continued, sounding more steady. "Doing well in school, and she grew two inches in the last six months."

Botox went for the heart clutch again, and Allie admired the deliberateness with which she splayed her fingers over her cleavage. "It must be so hard for her without her mother," she said, and the other two women did the sympathetic *tsk* again. "I can't imagine—"

"Actually," Allie said, snuggling closer to Jack. "We've been doing a lot of counseling as a family, and the therapist says Paige is coping wonderfully."

All three of them eyed Allie, not sure what to make of this outsider interfering with their right to comfort a grieving widower. She'd clearly screwed up their narrative.

"How about you," Jack tried. "How are things going with all of you?"

"Just great," Botox said. "But really, Jack—it must be so heartbreaking to lose someone that way. And so young!"

"Right," he said, and Allie looked up to see him tug on his tie. A faint sheen of sweat dotted his forehead, and she wondered if she should just pull a fire alarm to get them out of here.

Instead, she turned back to the women. Before she could take her own stab at redirecting the conversation, Silver Sequins chimed in.

"Well," she said, shooting a morose look at Jack. "I know it can take years to get over something like that. The love of your life, the mother of your child—that's just not something you ever bounce back from."

"Ever," echoed Botox, with a pointed look at Allie.

She willed herself not to let the barb sting, and looked to Jack for a cue. He responded by planting a kiss on her forehead.

"Right," he said. "Actually, Allie and I went to high school together. We were even engaged back when we were—what, eighteen, nineteen?"

"Nineteen," Allie supplied, wondering if he really didn't remember or just wanted the moral support of having someone complete his thought.

"Much too young back then," Jack added. "But we're older and wiser now."

"Much wiser," Allie agreed, wondering if she should take her hand off Jack's ass at some point.

"I see." Silver Sequins glanced at the other women for direction on how to proceed. "Well, then. I think I see someone else we need to greet. Ladies?"

Botox touched Jack's arm again, lingering a little too long before glancing at Allie. "It was very nice to meet you, Hallie."

"The pleasure was all mine," Allie managed, thanking her parents for the gift of easy lies. Jack held her tight against him until the women strutted away in search of meatier gossip.

The second they were out of earshot, she slipped out from under Jack's arm and looked up at him. "Are you okay?"

"Yeah. I'm sorry." The sheepish look on his face was a surprise. "I thought having you as my human shield might eliminate that."

Allie smiled. "I think you underestimated the female need to wrap a grieving widower in the billowy comfort of her bosom."

He snorted. "Is that supposed to turn me on? Because it kind of does."

She laughed, glad to hear the old Jack cracking through the surface. This had to be hard, dealing with the sympathetic looks and whispered conversations every time he encountered someone from his past. Losing her grandmother was one thing, and Allie could relate to having lost someone close. But a spouse—the parent of your child—she couldn't imagine.

"You sure you're okay?" she asked. "If you want to duck out, I wouldn't blame you a bit. We could be sitting in a booth at Rigatelli's splitting a pizza in fifteen minutes if you say the word."

"Tempting," he said. "But I made it this far. I want to stick it out."

"Okay then. Let's get you those damn meatballs."

She grabbed his arm and began towing him toward the buffet table. "You know, I was kidding about the meatballs," he said. "But they do look pretty good."

Allie skimmed the sign, her fingers still wrapped around Jack's arm. "They're in a cabernet sage sauce. Yum! Oh, look." She pointed at the sign, still trying to distract Jack from the forced somber conversation. "Looks like it's catered by Meg Delaney. She's a bit of a local celebrity. Wrote a famous aphrodisiac cookbook."

"Really?" Jack's interest seemed to pique, and Allie tried not to read too much into it. He was a guy, after all.

"Ooh!" Allie pointed to another platter. "Make sure you grab some of those bacon-wrapped apricots."

"Good call." Jack picked up a plate and began loading it with meats and cheeses, a few pieces of prosciutto-wrapped melon, a slice of bruschetta, something that looked like Brie in phyllo with raspberries.

Allie grabbed a plate of her own and added a little of everything, conscious of her Spanx digging into her ribs like a hot fork. Jack reached the end of the line and nodded toward an empty bistro table. "If you want to call dibs on that, I'll go get us some wine."

"Perfect. I'd love Pinot Gris if they have it."

"Coming right up."

He slid his plate into her hand, then headed off toward the bar. Allie walked over to the table and set the plates on it, careful not to tip Jack's meatballs onto the pristine black tablecloth. She picked up a baby carrot and surveyed the room, scanning for faces she recognized. In a way, she was glad not to see anyone she knew. It was easier this way, letting Jack's college memories stay separate from her own.

A few feet away, a group of women all seemed to be smiling a little too broadly, laughing with forced enthusiasm. Then again, who was she to judge? She'd enlisted a fake fiancé to show Jack and his nonexistent wife just how happy and well adjusted she was over a clam dinner she really couldn't afford. She was hardly in a position to cast stones.

She looked back at Jack, who was making conversation with another guy in line at the bar. He laughed at something the other guy said, and she admired the way his eyes crinkled at the corners. They hadn't done that in college, and it added a dimension to his face that hadn't been there at eighteen.

Allie picked up a crab puff and took a small bite, careful not to dribble crumbs down the front of her dress. Nothing itched like phyllo stuck in a lace bra cup.

"Excuse me, are you Allison?"

She turned to see a slender, dark-haired woman in a black dress. Her well-manicured nails clutched the stem of a glass of white wine, and Allie wondered if Jack had sent her over to deliver it. She finished chewing her crab puff, embarrassed to be caught with her mouth full. She nodded in response, wishing she had something to wash down the flaky pastry.

"I'm Allie," she said, swallowing the last of the crab puff. "Sorry about that. Are you one of Jack's classmates?"

The woman gave a primal snarl Allie mistook for laughter. That was probably why she didn't jump back fast enough.

"You bitch!" the woman growled, lunging at her. Allie moved back, but she wasn't quick enough. Not to avoid the fierce slap, or the icy splash of white wine hitting her square in the face.

# CHAPTER TEN

Jack turned at the sound of the shout, half expecting to see one of his old fraternity brothers sticking a frog down someone's shirt.

What he didn't expect to see was Allie looking like she'd just run through a lawn sprinkler in her dress. Standing beside her was his late wife's sister. From the look on her face, Missy was extremely mad or extremely drunk. Maybe both.

Abandoning his spot in line, he sprinted across the room.

"—and a whore and a tramp and a skank-wad and a hussy and a—"

"Try harlot," Allie offered, swiping a wet curl off her forehead and shooting Jack a warning look before turning back to face Missy. "And maybe charlatan. That has a nice ring to it."

"What's going on here?" Jack asked. "Allie, are you okay?"

"Oh, right!" Missy snarled. "It's all about how your *slut* is doing. Not about my sister!" She sputtered and grabbed the edge of the table, swaying like a whiskey-soaked daisy in a windstorm.

Allie looked remarkably calm for a woman fending off an attack from an intoxicated stranger. She wrung something that smelled like Chardonnay from her hair and turned to look at Jack. "Your sister-in-law came over to introduce herself. It seems Missy is upset by my presence here this evening."

"Bitch!" Missy snapped, then kicked off her shoes. She started to topple, and Jack reached out to steady her. She shook off his hand and glared at him, then jabbed a finger into his chest. "And you're a traitor!"

"Missy," he said, trying to keep his voice calm. "What are you doing here? Your mom said you guys were stuck in Cleveland."

"You wish!" she slurred. Jack drew his hand back, and Missy turned the wagging finger on Allie, swaying there for a moment with the digit wiggling back and forth like a hooked worm. Allie just stood there, her expression as calm and unruffled as if Missy had just asked for her goulash recipe.

"I really like that color of nail polish," Allie said. "OPI, right?"

"Scallop!" Missy shouted.

Allie seemed to consider that. "Is that a cross between a skank and a trollop?"

"Slut!"

"You already used that one, but try again," Allie offered.

The room around them had fallen silent, and everyone had turned to stare. Jack stepped closer to Allie and lowered his voice. "I'm so sorry. Missy's um—had a little trouble since her sister passed. And I didn't expect—"

"It's okay," Allie said, wiping another wet curl off her forehead as she kept a wary eye on Missy. "These things happen."

Jack found that hard to believe, but maybe Allie had wine dumped over her head more often than he did. He grabbed a black cloth napkin off the table beside them and handed it to her. He knew he owed about a thousand apologies to everyone here, but he had no idea where to start.

Allie took the napkin without comment, and Jack tried not to stare as she mopped at her cleavage.

Missy rocked unsteadily on her feet. "How dare you!"

It wasn't clear who she was speaking to, but since the conflict clearly stemmed from Jack, he figured he owed it to them to step in. "Missy, how about we talk about this like—"

"Liar!" she snapped. "You said you'd love her forever and ever and ever and ever and no one else. No one!"

"Right, and I had every intention of doing that, but—"

"Missy?"

They both turned to Allie, who had finished mopping off. She set the napkin down and looked straight at Jack's former sister-in-law. "I'd really like to hear about your sister," she said. "She sounds like an amazing woman. What can you tell me about her?"

"She wasn't you!"

"That's true," Allie agreed, shooting a warning glance at two of Jack's fraternity brothers who looked like they might be plotting to wrestle the inebriated woman to the ground. Allie shook her head, and the two men fell back, looking as confused as Jack felt. "What are some of the things you loved most about your sister?"

"She was smart," Missy slurred. "And pretty. Prettier than you! And so funny and nice and—" Her eyes went a little glazed, and she seemed to trail off in mid-thought.

Allie gave an encouraging nod, and took a step toward her. "What do you say we find you someplace to sit down and—"

"No!" She smacked Allie's hand away, and the two fraternity brothers moved forward again. Allie gave them a warning look, but stayed where she was.

"We need to fight!" Missy announced.

"Okay, Missy," Jack warned. "That's enough. Why don't we—"

"Are you envisioning a fistfight?" Allie asked calmly. "Or were you thinking of something like fencing or maybe a duel? You have very nice muscle tone, so maybe arm wrestling would be a bit unfair, but I'm open to negotiation."

"Fight!" Missy insisted, wobbling again as she took a step toward Allie. "Gotta defend my sister's honor."

Allie put her hands out, but the gesture seemed less like self-defense and more like an effort to show she was unarmed. "Of course," Allie agreed, taking a small step back. "But neither of us is dressed for a really good fight at the moment."

Missy stopped moving and looked down at her dress. It was blue and shimmery and a little rumpled. "Huh," she said.

"Tell you what," Allie said. "Let me take a look at my schedule, and we'll find a time that works for both of us to brawl. Sound okay to you?"

Jack stared at her, too dumbfounded to say anything. Missy was frowning in concentration, and Jack had a strange hunch Allie's strategy was actually working.

Allie reached behind her for the beaded handbag she'd brought with her, keeping one eye on Missy the whole time. Jack stepped closer, ready to intervene if Missy pounced.

But Missy had gone quiet. As Allie pulled out her phone, Jack's former sister-in-law watched with intense concentration. "Let's see, I'm pulling up my calendar," Allie said.

Jack squinted at the screen Allie had pulled up. He half expected to see her dialing 9-1-1, but honest to God, she'd pulled up her calendar. "It looks like I'm open next Tuesday or Wednesday after five," she said. "Would either of those times work for you?"

Missy frowned, then looked down at her hands. "I forgot my phone."

"No problem. You can let me know later."

"Oh my God, Missy!"

Jack turned to see Missy's husband, Gary, rushing into the room. He wore a gray suit and a look of utter horror. "Honey, we talked about this," he said as he rushed to her side. "I just called a cab and it'll be waiting out front in five minutes. Why don't we go out and get some fresh air?"

Missy stared up at her husband, then gave a feeble nod. "Okay."

Jack's former brother-in-law turned to him and gave an apologetic grimace. "I'm so sorry. I only left her here for a couple minutes so I could call a cab—"

"It's fine," Jack said. "I know she's had a tough time."

Gary turned to Allie and raked his fingers through his hair. "I want to apologize on my wife's behalf. She's not normally like this. She had a little too much to drink and—"

"Not a problem," Allie said, slipping her phone back into her bag. "I've had to handle similar situations before."

Jack frowned. "You've fended off other attacks by drunk sisters of your ex-fiancé's late wife?"

Allie gave him a look. "I said *similar,* not identical."

"Really, I'm so very sorry." Gary looked around, seeming to realize for the first time that they'd become the center of attention. "I'm going to get her back to the hotel now."

Jack stepped aside to let them pass. "Good to see you, man," he murmured. "Maybe we can grab pizza or something if you're in town for a few days. Paige would love to see you guys."

Gary grimaced. "Maybe when she sobers up."

"Good plan."

The whole room stared as Gary and Missy made their way to the door. As soon as they disappeared through it, everyone began murmuring again. Jack stepped closer to Allie, not sure where to begin.

"That was unbelievable," he said.

"Well, she's grieving. People do strange things when they—"

"No, I meant you. Defusing the situation like that? I've never seen anything like it."

"Thanks." Allie smiled and peeled the sticky top of her dress away from her chest. "I've done a lot of coursework in handling workplace conflict."

"The way you negotiated with her—you would have been an incredible lawyer."

Her smile vanished and she gave him a cool look. "Well now I'm an incredible Certified Association Executive," she said. "And I happen to be pretty good at it."

"I'm sure you are," he said quickly, pissed at himself for managing to offend her. "I didn't mean to suggest that being an attorney is the only good use for conflict management skills. I just meant that was pretty impressive."

"Thanks." Allie peeled the dress off her chest again, then seemed to give up. She sighed and glanced around the room. "I hope that didn't embarrass you too much."

"Me? You're the one who had wine dumped over your head. I'm so sorry that happened."

"It's okay. Any idea where the restroom is? I might want to mop up a little."

Jack slid an arm around her shoulder, not caring that the wine soaked through his sleeve. "I think fate is trying to tell me something."

Allie stared up at him, her expression wary. "What's that?"

"That I'm not meant to be at my reunion."

She shook her head and grabbed the napkin off the table behind her. "I don't want you to leave on account of me." She made another attempt to mop at her bare arm, which only seemed to spread the sticky liquid around. "We've been here less than thirty minutes. Surely you want to spend time reconnecting with everyone. Really, Jack, I can just catch a cab—"

"Allie," he said, leaning close enough for her hair to tickle his nose. "The only person I give a shit about reconnecting with is standing right here, dripping wine on my shoes. Now let's get out of here."

◆　◆　◆

Allie had planned to have Jack run her back to the B&B so she could pick up her car and head home alone for a shower.

But things unfolded a little differently.

"Where did she say those cat pills were?" Jack asked as he rummaged around in her grandmother's kitchen cupboard.

*My kitchen cupboard now*, Allie amended silently as she picked up her phone to scroll through messages. She found the text she'd gotten from Skye a few minutes ago and read through it again.

"The cupboard right next to the refrigerator," she said. "Top shelf."

"Got 'em."

Jack pulled the bottle out of the cupboard, along with the object Skye had described in her text as a *pill rocket*.

"You don't have to do this, Jack," she said. "I'm the one who told her to go ahead and stay out all night. I'm the one who agreed to pill the cats."

"And you're also the one who dealt with my crazy sister-in-law." He set the pill supplies on the counter and folded his arms over his chest. "I could pill a hundred rabid cats and still not make up for tonight."

"You had to deal with her, too," she pointed out.

"Yes, but I'm dry. You, on the other hand—" He gestured to her still-sticky dress. "Go shower, Allie. I'll take care of this."

"But you shouldn't have to—"

"I mean it," he said. "You have a change of clothes here?"

She nodded. "Yeah. I've been keeping some stuff in the Laurelwood room. I thought it would make it easier to get work done around the place if I can stay the night sometimes."

"Then go get cleaned up. Seriously. I have this handled."

Allie hesitated, then nodded. "Thank you."

She turned and walked down the hall, stifling a giggle as she heard Jack's deep baritone crooning, "Here, kitty-kitty-kitty . . ."

The coaxing was followed by a howl of feline protest and Allie paused in the hallway, straining to hear if it was Maestro's shrill screech or Maggie's.

"You're officially a crazy cat lady if you can distinguish one cat from another by its voice," she muttered to herself as she stepped into the bathroom and pulled the door closed behind her.

Stripping off her wine-soaked dress, she wondered what Skye and Wade were up to. She'd practically had to order Skye to go ahead and stay out as late as she wanted, even after the cat caretaker had admitted her reluctance to cut the night short for a round of cat pilling. Was she having fun? Was Wade on his best behavior? Allie had to admit, she'd never seen her best friend looking so smitten over a woman. True, Wade and Skye had only just met, but there was a certain spark between them that went beyond the romance of an "opposites attract" chemistry.

Allie plucked her phone out of her handbag on the bathroom counter and sent a quick text to Wade.

*Got Skye's message about staying out a little late. You're treating her well?*

There was no immediate reply, which made sense if they were getting along as well as Allie suspected. Well, maybe that was good for both of them. Lord knows Wade could use a kindhearted woman in his life, and Skye—well, Skye was a sweetheart who could probably benefit from dating a stable guy like Wade. The rest was none of Allie's business.

She climbed into the shower and let the water sluice over her, rinsing away the sticky Pinot Gris residue and all the goop Skye had used to style her hair. By the time Allie had stepped out of the shower, there was a new text from Wade.

*Skye's perfect. Treating her like the goddess she is. Holy shit, Albatross. Where have you been hiding this woman?*

Allie smiled, then noticed she had another text from Skye.

*Thanks again for taking care of the kitties. And for introducing me to Wade. Kinda diggin' this guy . . .*

The message trailed off there with a bunch of hearts and a couple emoticons that looked like praise hands or sausages or . . . well, maybe it was best not to look too closely.

Allie finished toweling off her hair, then pulled on a pair of yoga pants. She started to don one of her tank tops with a built-in shelf bra, which would give her the luxury of not wrangling herself into underwire, but she wasn't ready to be braless in front of Jack, so she hooked her lacy La Perla and wriggled her arms through the straps.

She pulled on a mint-green fleece zip-up she'd left here earlier in the week. It wasn't fancy, but it was comfy. Hadn't she earned some of that this evening?

Her phone buzzed again, and Allie picked it up expecting to see more news from Wade or Skye. Instead, it was a number she didn't recognize. She opened it up to a sea of emoticons that put Skye's earlier collection to shame. There were smiley faces, clapping dogs, flowers, and a string of colorful donuts. The colorful emojis were followed by a few simple words:

*My dad gave me your number so we could plan our shopping. So excited!!!!!!!!!!*

Ah, it must be Paige. Allie smiled to herself, then glanced at the clock on the wall. It was after eight, and she wondered if the girl was already snuggled in bed or if she got to stay up late watching movies or playing games with her grandma. She typed out a quick reply:

*I'm excited, too! Can I look at my schedule and talk to your dad and text you some possible times tomorrow?*

The little bubbles popped up on screen to tell her the girl was typing a reply.

*YES!!!!!!*

The word was in all caps and followed by another string of colorful emojis. Allie smiled and tucked the phone in the pocket of her fleece. She hesitated at the door, listening for the sound of howling cats. It was silent, and she wondered if Jack had finished and slipped out to go home. She hadn't actually invited him to stick around, and he'd probably be eager to get back to his place and tuck his daughter in for the night.

As she made her way down the hall barefoot, she realized she was psyching herself up to find him gone. She turned the corner into the kitchen, simultaneously relieved and annoyed by her relief at seeing those broad shoulders hunched over the counter. His tie was rolled up on the counter with his cuff links at the head of the coil like a pair of snake eyes. He'd tossed his suit jacket on a chair in the corner, and rolled up his shirtsleeves to reveal impressively muscled forearms.

"Hi, Jack," she said, smiling a little as she remembered the shared joke they had in high school.

He turned and grinned at her. "Hijacking is illegal," he said, and held out one of her grandmother's good Riedel wineglasses. "So is allowing a woman to have white wine dumped over her head but never letting her have a glass for herself. Here."

He tipped up a wine bottle and filled her glass nearly to the brim with pale straw-colored liquid. Allie leaned back against the counter, a dark-chocolate granite her grandmother had picked out when she'd remodeled eight or nine years ago. The cupboards were original, and Allie had helped her grandma paint them a honey-hued off-white just a few years ago. God, it felt weird to be here so much without her.

"You thinking about your grandma?"

Allie blinked, then nodded. "How did you know?"

"This kitchen reminds me of her. All the antique copper over there and the vase of dried roses."

"I always thought it was the prettiest room in the house," she said.

"It is. I think that's why it reminds me of her."

A soft warmth spread through her, and Allie lifted the wineglass to her lips. "Wow. This is terrific." She took another small sip, feeling her shoulders relax for the first time all night. "Where'd you find it?"

"The backseat of my car."

"The backseat of your car must be a different place now than what I remember."

He laughed, and Allie felt a faint flush creeping up her neck and into her cheeks. It was probably the wine, or maybe the realization that she'd fallen back into the habit of flirting with Jack Carpenter without even realizing it.

But he was smiling at her and didn't look uncomfortable with it, so Allie relaxed and took another small sip.

"True enough," Jack said at last. He lifted his own wineglass in a mock toast to her. "Actually, I picked up my wine club shipment earlier today. Just hadn't gotten the chance to take it home yet."

Allie caught the bottle by the neck and turned the label toward her. She recognized it as one of the nicer vineyards in the Dundee Hills area about thirty minutes from Portland. Sunridge Vineyards made excellent wine, and most of it didn't sell for less than seventy-five dollars a bottle. Even a Pinot Gris like this probably went for upwards of sixty dollars. It wasn't the sort of thing she could afford these days. She thought about remarking on that, but decided against it, not wanting him to think she was hung up on money.

"It's very good," she said. "Thank you for sharing."

"Thank you for attending my disastrous reunion with me. Sorry it didn't quite go like I'd hoped."

"No, *I'm* the one who's sorry. I'm thinking it might have gone better if I hadn't joined you."

"Definitely not true. The building could have caught on fire and it still would have been better with you than without you."

She felt a smile tugging at the corners of her lips and lifted her glass to hide it. She took another sip of wine and glanced around the kitchen.

"Did all the cats run and hide after you got out that pill rocket?"

"Yes, but they came right back after I busted out a can of tuna."

"Smart man," she said. "So everyone's been dosed with the necessary heart medicine or kitty Prozac or whatever the hell that was?"

"Yep. Clever of Skye to have a whole binder complete with cat photos and recommended dosages. There was even something that looked like a feline family tree."

"You're kidding."

"Nope. I found it in the cupboard right next to the pills. Some of the handwriting looked different, so maybe your grandma was the one who put it together."

"I'll have to check it out sometime. So it really went okay?"

"More or less." Jack held out his right arm and Allie studied the ripple of muscle and the whorls of dark hair she knew would feel deliciously soft under her fingertips. It took her a few seconds to realize she was supposed to be checking out the web of scratches on his forearm.

"Yikes." She grimaced and looked up at him, relieved to see he didn't look too upset about it. "Sorry about that."

"It's okay. I think I started to get the hang of it after the third cat. The trick is apparently to do it fast before they can start plotting an exit strategy."

Allie laughed and went over to the pantry. Back when Rosewood operated as a B&B, her grandma kept the place well stocked with all kinds of gourmet eats. Most of what was in there now belonged to Skye, though Allie had brought some things over in the last few days.

"Sorry, I don't have much to nibble on," she said.

"We should have grabbed a to-go box at the reunion."

"How do you feel about Ritz Crackers?"

"I feel good about them. I'd feel better if we took this little wine and cracker party into the parlor."

"Deal. You take the wine, and I'll throw some of these on a plate with some Laughing Cow cheese wedges I brought over yesterday."

"Perfect."

He turned and walked toward the parlor while Allie got the snacks together. She was glad he'd picked the parlor, since it offered the most privacy. Skye's room was up on the third floor, but the parlor on the main floor had always been Allie's favorite space in the house. It backed up to the Laurelwood room, which was the one she'd claimed for herself during the last round of cleanup. It was cozy with a big rosebush right outside a window that streamed rivers of natural sunlight. Sleeping there in the big, antique four-poster bed reminded her of her grandmother.

Scooping up the plate of crackers, Allie headed into the next room. Jack had already seated himself on the sofa and was holding a photo in an ornate silver frame. She couldn't see the photo itself, but knew from the frame which one it was. An image snapped more than twenty years ago in the outdoor courtyard of the B&B. She was sitting at a table draped with a white-linen tablecloth, her parents beaming from either side of her as her grandma set a plate of tea sandwiches on the table.

Jack looked up and smiled. "I forgot you were such a cute kid."

"Thanks. I was pretty close to Paige's age in that one."

"No kidding?" He looked at the photo again, his expression a little faraway this time.

"I heard from her, by the way," Allie said. "Paige, I mean. You must've given her my number?"

"Yeah, sorry—I meant to tell you. I hope that's okay?"

"No problem. She's a sweet kid."

"She's pretty excited about the bra shopping."

"I could tell." Allie tucked one bare foot up under her on the sofa. "So," she said, taking a small sip of wine. "Is your sister-in-law always like that?"

Jack sighed and picked up his own wineglass. He spun it around by the stem, but didn't take a sip. "She's struggled a lot since Caroline died, but nothing like that."

"Are she and Paige pretty close?"

"Not really. They live in Chicago, and Caroline's parents are in Florida, so Paige isn't super tight with anyone on her mom's side of the family."

"Seems kind of funny that Missy would have such a problem with you dating another woman."

He shook his head. "That's not it exactly. She doesn't want to see me with *you*."

"Me?" Allie frowned. "But I've never even met her."

"Caroline may have mentioned you once or twice." Jack cleared his throat and used his thumbnail to rub a spot on his dress slacks. "Sisters talk, I guess."

"How do you mean?"

"It always bothered Caroline a little that I was engaged before. I guess when Missy heard you were there, she sort of flipped her lid."

"How do you know all this?"

He picked up a cracker and began smearing it with cheese. "I heard from Gary—her husband—when you were in the shower. Apparently Missy started sobering up on the way back to the hotel. She wanted your address so she could send flowers and an apology note."

Allie fought the urge to grimace. "Please tell me you didn't give that woman my address."

Jack laughed, though it was a sad little laugh. "No. I told her it was the thought that counted, and I'd pass her apology along."

Allie picked up a cracker and nibbled on the edge. Part of her wanted to know more about Jack's marriage and family and everything that had happened the last sixteen years. Part of her wanted to bury her head in the sand.

But she'd done plenty of that lately, so she took a deep breath. "How did you meet your wife, anyway?"

He looked at her a moment, assessing. Allie ordered herself not to blink, not to flinch, not to do anything that would prompt him to gloss over the story or give her a half-baked version of it. Jack set his wineglass down.

"You really want to know?"

"Yeah." Allie held his gaze. "I think I do. You and I were so close for so many years. It seems weird not to know such a big thing about you."

He nodded, then picked up his glass again. "I wasn't in a great place after you and I split up," he said slowly. "Screwed around for a couple years, generally being an asshole."

"Screwed around, like . . . with your life, or you mean sexually?"

"Yes."

"Got it." She gave a tight nod, pleased with herself for not reacting. This was his history, after all. She had no claim to him beyond their engagement sixteen years ago.

"Anyway, I met Caroline in a sandwich shop in Tigard when I tried to pick her up. She totally shot me down."

Allie grinned and took a sip of wine. "I think I like her already."

Jack gave a small smile and shoved the whole cracker into his mouth, cheese and all. "Yeah, you probably would have liked her. She didn't put up with shit from anyone, especially me."

"So you convinced her to go out with you?"

"Not right away. Actually, I didn't see her again for three months after that. I went back to the sandwich place every week hoping to bump into her again, and eventually I did."

Allie nodded and took another tiny drink. At this rate it would take her five hours to finish a single glass of wine, but she didn't want to be tipsy for this conversation. Didn't want to blurt something stupid or ask questions she wasn't ready to have him answer. "So did Caroline ask why you were stalking her?"

"Nah," he said. "But I did tell her it was fate that we'd run into each other again, so she should probably go out with me or risk angering the gods."

"Not a bad pickup line."

"Yeah, it worked. She gave me her number and we went out later that week."

"And she fell instantly, madly in love with you and the rest is history?" She was careful to keep any trace of snark from her tone, but he looked up anyway. She gave him a small smile, an unspoken reassurance he seemed to understand. He nodded and kept going.

"No, she called me a loser and told me to call her when I had my life together." He gave her a shamefaced grin. "I may have had too much to drink at dinner."

"Nice." She laughed. "So then what?"

"I took her advice. Went back to school. Got serious about the video game I'd been trying to develop. Moved out of my mom's basement. A year later, I called her again."

Allie felt something twist deep in her gut, but she forced herself to keep breathing. So what if he wasn't willing to get his shit together for her, but he did it for another woman after pursuing her with such dogged determination? It wasn't a reflection on her. It was a sweet, romantic story about the mother of his child. Nothing more.

"Was she happy to hear from you?" she asked.

"Not at first. But I convinced her to go out with me, and I think she could see right away that I was different. We started dating for real after that. I was still going to school, and she was in her first year of grad studies for architecture. We ended up moving in together during my last term of college."

"And then you got married?"

"And then she got pregnant," Jack said. "The marriage came pretty quickly after that."

"Oh." She wasn't sure what to say to that. There were a million way-too-intrusive questions she could pose, but she couldn't imagine herself asking any of them out loud. This was Jack's history, and Caroline's, too. Allie had no right to expect him to fill in all the gaps for her, or to volunteer anything he didn't share readily.

Jack leaned back on the couch, spreading his arms wide across the back of it. When he looked at her, there was something thoughtful in his expression. "I always wondered if we would have gotten married otherwise, you know?"

The *we* threw Allie for a second, and she thought he was talking about the two of them. When she realized what he meant, she hoped he didn't see any of that on her face. "You mean if Caroline would have married you if she hadn't gotten pregnant?"

"Yeah," he said. "But when Paige came along, it was amazing."

"Really?" Allie bit her lip. "People always say a baby can drive a big wedge in a relationship. Especially when you're young like that."

"I know. We heard all the statistics and I was braced for it to be pretty tough. But it wasn't like that with us. We loved being parents."

"That's wonderful." Allie tried to swallow the lump in her throat, but it wouldn't go down. She tried forcing it with wine, keeping her gaze on the rim of the glass so she wouldn't have to look Jack in the eye. She breathed in the tangy, citrus scent of Pinot Gris until the sharp stabs of unspoken memory began to dull. "So Paige was just a baby when her mom died?"

"Eighteen months."

"It was a car accident?"

He nodded. "She was in the car alone. I'd stayed home with Paige so Caroline could go to some craft fair with her girlfriends. A guy blew through a stop sign when she was on her way home. She was dead before the ambulance even got there."

"Jack." She rested a hand on his knee. "I'm so sorry."

"Thank you." He picked up his wine and took a small sip. "I've asked Paige if she remembers her mom at all. She says she does, but I'm not sure that's true. Not that she's lying or anything. I just wonder sometimes if she remembers the *idea* of her. The stories I've told her or that her grandparents and Aunt Missy have shared."

Allie nodded, then noticed her hand was still on his knee. She drew it back, feeling foolish. Jack looked up and held her gaze for a moment. Then he shifted on the sofa, bringing him a few inches closer.

Their knees were touching now, and it felt more intimate than any kiss they'd shared.

"Is it weird to hear this stuff?" he asked.

Allie started to shake her head, then changed directions, nodding just once. "Maybe a little. I don't know. I guess I sometimes wondered what you've been up to all these years, but I mostly thought in terms of your job or where you might be living."

"Not about my love life?"

She shook her head. "Not really. Not because I wasn't interested or I didn't care. I guess I just didn't want to go there. It was easier to picture you frozen in time, sitting there on that futon with a bewildered look on your face."

He laughed, even though he probably had every right to take offense at her response. He reached out to grab a cracker, and his arm brushed her knee, sending goose bumps all the way up her thigh.

"That's funny. I've gotta admit, I was always pretty curious where you ended up. I could never find much on Google or Facebook, but a friend of a friend told me you'd gotten engaged in law school. I guess I figured that was it."

She nodded, and glanced down at the knee of her yoga pants. There was a frayed thread sticking out of the seam, and she thought about tugging on it, but changed her mind. No sense in unraveling everything.

"Yeah," she said at last. "That didn't really work out."

"Have you ever been married?"

"No. Just engaged." She hesitated, not sure how much to volunteer. Only days ago, she'd been preparing to introduce a fake fiancé and crossing her fingers Jack didn't know anything about her parents' crimes. Was she really ready to let her guard down?

Then again, the guy had been baring his soul to her all evening. It hardly seemed fair to offer platitudes in return. She looked up to see him studying her with interest.

Allie took a deep breath. "I got engaged three times."

His brows shot up. "No kidding?" He must have sensed her bristling, because he softened his expression to one with a lot less judgment. "So, three times counting me?"

Allie shook her head as heat crept into her cheeks. "Four times, counting you."

"Wow."

A flicker of defensiveness flared in her chest with that single, disapproving syllable. Or maybe she was reading too much into it. She was readying a retort, but he beat her to the punch.

"I didn't mean it like that," he said. "I mean, that's not the same as being married four times."

"Right." Her voice was tight, but she hoped she'd kept the shame out of it.

"I guess I'm just surprised."

"That I had so many engagements, or that I never followed through on them?"

"Both, I guess. I mean, I guess I always assumed you'd be married by now." He seemed to hesitate. "Do you mind if I ask why you're not?"

Allie shrugged, oddly nervous now that he was the one asking the questions. "The guy after you I met in law school, and he forgot to mention he had another girlfriend on the side. The next guy was sweet and smart and had everything going for him, but we got into this big fight when we went shopping for our first piece of furniture together—"

"A loveseat?" He offered a small smile, and she couldn't tell if he was teasing or just trying to lighten the mood.

"An ottoman," she said.

"Damn ottomans. They'll get you every time."

Allie forced a smile and took a small sip of wine. "Anyway, it became clear we had different ideas on conflict resolution."

"So you split up over an ottoman?"

161

"It wasn't just the ottoman. It was a major disconnect in the way we each approached disagreement. It was about respecting each other's differences and how our lifestyles fit together."

"That's a lot to assign to an ottoman."

Allie sighed. "It just wasn't the right fit."

"Okay." Jack nodded, seeming to digest that. "What about the next guy? What went wrong there?"

She looked down at her wineglass, wondering why she hadn't mentioned this before. Wondering if she should have mentioned it before now.

"I already told you," she said slowly. "Wade and I had zero chemistry."

# CHAPTER ELEVEN

There was a faint buzzing in the back of Jack's brain, and he didn't know why.

Okay, he kind of knew why. He took a slug of wine, buying some time before he responded. "You were engaged to Wade?"

"Yes."

"But I thought—I thought you said that was fake."

"It was fake the other night. But not six years ago."

Allie began carefully spreading cheese on a Ritz Cracker, and he wondered if she was avoiding his eyes on purpose. "We dated for less than six months and we were only engaged for about three weeks," she said. "We really didn't even get started planning a wedding. It felt more like a business arrangement than anything."

"How romantic."

The bite in his voice was unmistakable, and he kind of hated himself for it. Allie looked up, and he couldn't tell if it was anger or hurt in her eyes. He braced himself to do battle. To have her fire back something about his judgmental bullshit so he could retort with an asshole comment of his own. It was a pattern he knew well, and he was ready to do his part.

But she didn't take the bait. "Wade and I were great friends from the start. We thought maybe we should be more than that, and we did a pretty good job convincing ourselves for a couple months. But the chemistry just wasn't there, and I think we both knew it. It ended fast, and on good terms."

Something flared in Jack's chest—pride? Jealousy? Neither of which he was entitled to in this particular case. "No chemistry," he said. Repeating it didn't make it sound any less intimate, so he decided to just ask what he was thinking. "So you're saying he's lousy in bed?"

Her cheeks went faintly pink and she raised an eyebrow at him. "I'm not saying that at all. Just that we weren't good together." She took a sip of wine, not meeting his eyes. "He dates a lot of women. He's got a bit of a reputation for it, actually. I'm sure he makes plenty of women swoon."

"But not you."

He deliberately omitted the question mark in his tone, not sure he wanted her to answer and disagree. Some small, dickhead part of him wanted to just believe the guy never made her cry out and arch her back the way she used to do with him. That Jack had been the only one to hear that soft little whimper she made right before she toppled over the edge.

Allie looked at him. She set her wineglass down, and he thought she was going to kick him out. He deserved it. He drained his own glass and set it on the table a little harder than he meant to, bracing himself for the words.

But instead of pointing him to the door, Allie grabbed his hands. She held them both in hers, thumbs gliding over his knuckles for a moment as she looked in his eyes.

"I'm sorry."

Jack blinked, pretty sure he'd heard her wrong. "What?"

"I said I'm sorry."

"What on earth for?"

"For the way I broke our engagement. I know this is the path guys go down in their minds—'Was it because I sucked in bed?' or 'Did I not make enough money for her?' Now that I've had a few broken engagements and a lot more life experience, I know those are the things men think. I'm sorry if you felt that way."

Jack swallowed, even more pissed at himself now. Annoyed by the stupid lump in his throat. Annoyed by the fact that he was being such a bastard right now. Mostly though, for still caring so much.

"It's fine."

"No, it's not," she said. "I treated marriage and engagement too cavalierly for a long time. That wasn't right, and I'm sorry you had to bear the brunt of me growing up and figuring everything out the hard way."

He nodded and felt a dull ache in his chest. "I'm sorry, too." He cleared his throat. "For a lot of things sixteen years ago. But especially for right now. For being a jealous prick. You listened to me go on and on about my marriage without batting an eyelash. I should have been as gracious about it as you were."

Allie gave him a small smile, the one he used to call her Cheshire cat look. "I'm just a better actor than you are."

He laughed. "I guess that's always been true." He hesitated, not sure he had the right to ask what he wanted to. "So did it make you feel jealous? The stuff I told you, I mean."

"Not jealous, exactly. I guess it's more wistful. Like I missed out on something I always thought I'd get to be part of." She shrugged and looked down at their interlaced fingers. "That's true for a lot of things, I guess."

"It is." He cleared his throat. "But I guess we probably have to accept the fact that we've both had a few serious relationships with other people these last sixteen years. We've fallen in love with other people, made life plans with other people, maybe even had sex with other people."

Allie quirked an eyebrow at him. "Let's not jump to any conclusions."

He grinned. "I'm just saying it's possible."

She shifted positions again, her knee bumping his. Like a pig, he wondered if she had a bra on under that little tank top she wore. She'd zipped her fleece jacket up tight over it, but he could see glimpses of creamy, pale flesh at her neckline. The view was making him dizzy, so Jack looked away.

That's probably why he didn't see the kiss coming.

But he did feel it. He felt her breath warm against his throat, smelled shampoo and white wine. He turned and found his lips against hers, almost as though the whole thing happened by magic.

And there was something magical about it for sure. He sure as hell hadn't seen it coming, but it had always been like Allie to pull a rabbit out of a hat before he even realized she was holding a damn hat.

He kissed her back, tentatively at first, then with more hunger. She slid her fingers into his hair, pulling him closer to deepen the kiss. She was leaning into him, practically on his lap now. He pulled her the rest of the way onto him and guided her thighs to either side of his so their bodies pressed together at the core. She moaned and hugged her legs around him.

Jack broke the kiss, though he was still too stunned to form a complete sentence. "What on earth—"

"I've been wanting to do that all night," Allie said. "All week, really."

"Well, do it again, then."

She did, and Jack kissed her back with less hesitation this time. Her hair was still damp, and he twined his fingers in it, amazed at how silky soft it felt. She smelled like honey and sunshine and her lips were softer than he remembered. Her breath came fast now and she was making soft little sounds in the back of her throat. He wondered if she'd meant to make this a quick peck, but it snowballed into something else.

But there was no stopping it now. Not for him, anyway. He thought about being in the attic with her, the way she'd moved her hands to the hem of her shirt to lift it up. Without even realizing it, he found his own hands there, tunneling beneath the soft fabric of her tank top. He walked his fingers up her spine, taking his time, feeling each vertebra one by one until he reached her bra clasp.

He broke the kiss to look into her eyes. "I was wondering if you'd bothered with a bra."

Allie grinned back. "I was wondering if you could still unhook it one-handed."

"Wonder no more."

He flicked it open with a quick pinch, rewarded by the tiny gasp of pleasure he'd nearly forgotten. Claiming her mouth again, he slid both palms around her rib cage, moving them so he cupped one breast in each hand. They seemed fuller now, or maybe he was remembering wrong. They felt perfect and lush, the curve of them filling his palms exactly.

Allie groaned and pressed tighter against him, against the fly of his dress slacks the way she'd done that long-ago prom night in the backseat of his rusty Toyota. He felt dizzy all over again, the blood pounding in his brain as she ground herself against him. This time, it was Allie who broke the kiss.

"I know dry humping was kinda sexy when we were seventeen," she breathed. "But maybe we could move things to the bedroom this time?"

Jack stroked his thumbs over her nipples, eliciting another gasp from Allie. "You sure there's time before your curfew?"

"Mmmhmm." She planted a kiss on his earlobe, the spot that still made him crazy even now. "Just this once."

He wondered if she was being flirty or setting the terms of this encounter. Either way, it didn't matter. He wanted her, *needed* her. And one way or another, he was about to have her.

Sliding his hands out from under her shirt, he cupped her bottom. As he stood, she wrapped her legs around him even as she began to protest.

"Jack, you can't—"

"Yes, I can."

Allie flushed and tossed her hair out of her face. "I might weigh a little more than I did in college."

"And I might be a little stronger than I was in college. Now which way are we going?"

"That way," she said, nodding to the doorway just off the parlor.

Jack pivoted and carried her there, careful not to trip over the shoes she'd left lying near the nightstand. A cat looked up from the gold-silk-upholstered chair in the corner, then yawned and rested its head on its paws again. Jack used his heel to kick the door shut, then laid Allie on the bed as gently as possible.

He followed close behind, easing himself down on top of her. She began unbuttoning his shirt with surprising haste, and he wondered where he'd left his tie and cuff links. She pushed the fabric off his shoulders, pausing to trace the fiery lines of the tattoo on his ribs. Her eyes met his and she smiled.

"It's beautiful," she said. "Paige was right. It's a lot like mine."

He nodded and slid a hand into the small of her back, skimming the spot where her own flame tattoo was branded.

He'd never wanted her more.

Jack got to work ridding her of the extra layers. Fleece, tank top, yoga pants—all of it ended up in a heap at the foot of the bed.

When he reached for her again, there was nothing between them but heated skin. He skimmed a hand down her body, starting at her breasts and trailing over her belly, over her hip, between her thighs. She moved one arm down to cover her stomach, and he watched her start to arrange herself into some sort of flattering pose.

"No," he said, gently drawing the arm back. He placed a trail of kisses where it had been, worshiping every inch of her. "You're so beautiful, Allie. I love your body."

She laughed, and he wasn't sure if she believed him or thought he was feeding her a line. It was true, though, dammit, and he wanted her to know. "So perfect." He planted another row of kisses down her center, skimming over her right hip and then back to her belly button. He only meant to tease, knowing she needed more foreplay than he'd offered her so far.

But Allie grabbed his wrist and pressed his fingers into the warmth between her legs.

"Touch me," she whispered, her voice cracking with intensity.

"Jesus, you're wet."

"I want you," she panted. "Right now. *So much*, Jack."

Had she been this assertive in college? Jack didn't think so. He knew he'd been her first, and she'd always seemed a little shy. Even after they'd been together for years, she was rarely the one to initiate things in the bedroom.

But she was initiating now, and it made Jack dizzy with desire. He slid a finger inside her, marveling as she arched up off the bed. He stroked deep inside her, pressing the heel of his hand against her pubic bone and trying not to let the word *pubic* throw him off his stride with thoughts of his inquisitive kid asking about pubes.

"Jack, please."

He smiled down at her, knowing damn well what she wanted, but needing to hear those words. "Please what?"

"Please," she gasped again, closing her eyes as he angled his finger to hit something that sent her arching off the bed.

Allie wasn't the only one who'd gained experience the last sixteen years.

"I want you inside me," she pleaded.

That was enough for him. He started to move on top of her, nudging her thighs apart with his own. He hesitated.

"Uh, Allie?"

"What?"

"I don't have a condom. I wasn't exactly planning for this."

She grinned and pushed a stray lock of hair off her forehead. "Nightstand," she said. "Hurry."

God bless the girl. He hurried to tear open the packaging and sheathe himself, pretty sure he'd never been this eager to be inside a woman, not even her. "Please tell me you stashed this in there and I didn't just grab a rubber that belonged to your grandma."

She laughed and pulled him on top of her. "It's mine."

There was an echo of something in that word. *Mine.* He remembered whispering it to her in the darkness, driving himself inside her. *You're mine. Always. Mine.* She'd murmured it back, binding them together with youthful oblivion and naïve lust.

There was none of that now. They both knew what they were getting into, and they wanted it anyway. As Jack slid inside her, he felt something shatter in the back of his brain. He stilled for an instant, wanting to savor the moment, to get himself under control.

Allie drew her legs up, heels pressing into the mattress, as she arched up to meet him. "Please, Jack. Fuck me."

*Oh my God.* Was this really Allison Ross?

He opened his eyes, just to be sure, and saw her smiling up at him. "I've never wanted anyone so badly," she murmured.

"God, you're killing me."

He began to move then, slow strokes at first. He'd been cocky at the start, eager to prove he had better stamina than his eighteen-year-old self. But he may have overestimated his own skill, or maybe he'd underestimated Allie.

"You feel so good," he groaned into her hair, driving into her harder.

"So do you."

He slid deeper inside her, losing his grip on reality as he lost himself in the sensation. There was a loud hum vibrating his eardrums, and he was pretty sure he'd have to stop soon or change positions or think about operating systems or UX testing or the World Series or—

"Jack, I'm close."

He knew that plea. Had it ever happened this quickly before? He didn't think so, but he sure as hell wasn't complaining. He drove into her again, teetering on his own brink.

"That's it, Allie," he whispered, kissing her ear. "Come with me."

He'd never said something like that before, not to her anyway. But the words seemed to spark something inside her. She cried out, arching tight against him.

It was Jack's cue to let go, and he did, letting the first wave of pleasure grab hold and pull him under. He drove into her again and again, not sure whose shudders he was feeling and wondering if they'd melded together into one sensation.

When the last wave subsided, he felt her go still. He rolled to his side, pulling her with him. She smiled and came willingly, her cheeks flushed with pleasure.

"Well," she said softly. "You've developed some serious skill in sixteen years."

He laughed and drew her closer. "You, too."

"Gotta admit, I thought we had a pretty decent sex life back then. But that was—holy shit."

He laughed and planted a kiss on the edge of her temple. "I think I've heard you swear more in the last fifteen minutes than I have in my whole life."

"What do you expect when you fuck me like that?"

"Good Lord. Why is that such a turn-on?"

"If I knew it would be, I would have cursed at you years ago."

He smiled and stroked his fingers through her hair. His heartbeat was slowing back down, and a few brain cells were beginning to buzz back to life. He lay quietly for a moment, not sure what to say next. What did this mean? Was she expecting something now, or had this just been for fun?

At that moment, she angled up to look at him, and her smile sent tiny daggers of warmth right into his core. He leaned down and kissed her, thinking maybe he didn't have to figure it out now.

◆ ◆ ◆

Allie was alone when the woodpeckers woke her around eight the next morning, their beaks rattling the cedar outside her window like miniature jackhammers.

"For the love of all things holy," she muttered, pulling a pillow over her ears.

She lay that way for a long time, savoring the fuzzy memory of Jack kissing her sometime after midnight before crawling out of bed and dressing silently in the darkness.

"*Sorry to be that guy,*" he'd murmured against her hair when he'd kissed her again. "*I need to be there when Paige wakes up.*"

"*Mmhm,*" Allie had mumbled without opening her eyes, drowsy with post-sex glow in her bliss nest of feather duvets and Egyptian cotton sheets.

Warmed by the memory, Allie pulled the pillow off her head and turned to snuggle the one Jack had used. It smelled like him, all woodsy and earthy, and the memory of last night made her smile.

That had been . . . different.

And the same, in some ways. In sixteen years, she'd never once allowed herself to conjure memories of what Jack was like in bed or how his sexual prowess might've changed over the years. Sure, there were occasional flickers of memory the first time she'd gone to bed with someone else. The feel of different thumbprints on her flesh, or a hitch in breathing that tickled her eardrums with familiarity. But it's not like she'd had many lovers over the years, and she'd gotten engaged to most of them.

Remembering the flash of jealousy in Jack's eyes, she hugged the pillow tighter. Okay, so he hadn't been thrilled to hear about her serial engagements. It's not something she felt proud of. Not something most people knew. The idea of getting married had always been appealing to her, ever since she was a little girl sitting in the parlor of the B&B holding a silver-framed photo of her parents' wedding.

*"That was such a perfect day,"* her grandma used to tell her, beaming down at the photo. *"Your mother looked like an absolute princess, and your dad was so handsome."*

Something about that fairy tale had always tugged Allie's heart-strings. She'd wanted that for herself, even after visions of Snow White and Cinderella had been replaced by thoughts of Vera Wang and Dom Pérignon. The look on her parents' faces in that photo had driven her to want what they had, at any cost.

Then again, her parents' union had turned out to be a criminal partnership as much as a blissful romance. Maybe that wasn't the best example.

Allie rolled over again, heaving herself out of bed this time. She thought about showering, but a tiny, silly part of her wanted to savor the scent of Jack on her skin for a little while longer. She tugged on her yoga pants and tank top again, shivering a little at the memory of him stripping them off her body. She skipped the bra this time, feeling deliciously vulnerable and powerful all at once.

Padding barefoot into the parlor, she spotted the empty wineglasses and a few scattered crackers that looked like they may have been gnawed on by feline teeth. She scooped everything up and carried the whole mess toward the kitchen, pausing as she caught sight of her reflection in the hall mirror. She looked like a woman who'd been thoroughly ravished. Her cheeks were flushed and her hair was a snarled mess, but instead of looking slovenly, it looked like a style she might've seen in a lingerie catalogue. Allie smiled and continued on, rounding the corner into the kitchen.

"Hey there!"

Allie jumped, her grip on one of the wineglasses loosening. Skye reached out and caught it easily, setting in on the counter with a grin before diving back into her cereal bowl.

"Nice reflexes," Allie said as she set down the cheese plate and the other wineglass.

"Thanks." Skye's smile went a little wider as she chewed a mouthful of cereal. "Looks like you had a good night."

Allie felt her cheeks start to redden before she realized Skye was nodding at the wine bottle. "Oh, yes. Right." Allie tucked the empty bottle in the recycle bin. "Yes, it was terrific wine."

"Tell me about it. I dated the winemaker there like ten years ago. He made some killer Rieslings, too."

"I'll have to check those out." Her face felt hot, so Allie opened the fridge and pulled out the carton of eggs she'd brought over earlier in the week. She found a nub of butter in an orange dish, then turned to rummage for her grandmother's favorite copper skillet.

"I bought some really great bread at the farmer's market yesterday," Skye offered. "If you want some toast with that."

"That sounds great. Can I make you a scrambled egg or two?"

"I'd love one. Thanks!"

They were behaving like awkward new roommates, which was sort of what they were. Still, it felt weird to be in that position after so many years of living on her own. Allie got to work cracking the eggshells, beating the eggs with a heavy-duty whisk and the gourmet white pepper her grandma always used. She poured the whole mess into the skillet and turned down the heat.

"Thanks again for pilling all the cats last night," Skye said.

"No problem. I take it you had a good dinner with Wade?"

"Oh Lord! That man is amazing."

Allie turned to see Skye beaming with the same look Allie had seen on her own face in the hallway mirror just a few minutes ago. She felt a pang of nostalgia for her college years, for the sequence of female roommates she'd lived with after she and Jack had split. Something inside her shifted, a quiet little thawing.

"Yeah." Allie grinned and gave a little wave of her spatula. "Wade's amazing. Jack's amazing. Sounds like this is a pretty amazing morning for both of us."

Skye laughed. "Very true." She seemed to hesitate, twirling the spoon in her now-empty cereal bowl. "I was thinking of this thing with Wade as a fling, you know? I had kind of a dry spell after Brody left, and I've been easing back in with some casual hookups. It works if everyone's on the same page."

Allie nodded, even though she wasn't all that familiar with casual hookups. It had never been her style, which was probably why she'd ended up engaged to so many men she barely knew.

The other woman was looking at her intently, so Allie just nodded. "Of course. So did something change your mind about that with Wade?"

Skye shrugged. "I don't know. This morning—" she stopped there, and her cheeks went faintly pink. "I probably shouldn't talk about this, huh? You're his best friend and all."

"It's okay. I mean, if you want to talk about it, I promise not to tell him anything you don't want me to."

Skye seemed to hesitate, twirling the spoon again. Then her face broke into a grin. "I'm just thinking it could be more than just a hookup. Like an actual relationship."

Allie swallowed hard, then turned to stir the eggs so she wouldn't have to meet Skye's eyes. Shit. This could be bad. "Wade *is* a great guy," she said. "But uh—I'm not sure he's really. Um, I mean he kinda—"

"He fucks a lot of girls?" Skye laughed and Allie turned with a start to see the other woman grinning like a cat that ate a canary. "Yeah, I know. Even if he hadn't told me, I know the type. I can spot a man-whore from a hundred miles away. I've even sought them out."

"Right," Allie said, relieved not to have to break this to her gently. "He's a good guy, and he's not insensitive or anything. He's just not really one for commitment. He tried it a couple times, and said it wasn't for him."

She stopped there, remembering the blaze in Jack's eyes last night when she'd mentioned the engagement. It didn't seem like her place to share that detail with Skye, so she left it at that.

"I totally get it," Skye said. "I'm kind of into the casual thing myself. But this morning, I don't know—things feel a little different. For him, too, I think."

Allie wanted to believe it. Wanted the glow in Skye's cheeks to be reciprocated on the other end. Before she could say anything, Skye held out her phone.

"Here. I don't normally share private text messages from guys I've just hooked up with, and maybe this is weird since you're his best friend and all, but I kinda want your take on this."

Allie found herself reaching for the phone, spurred by a touch of voyeurism and the thrill of having a girlfriend to share secrets with. After her parents' arrest, she'd started avoiding old friends. She'd hated watching their faces for pity or judgment or both, and it had become easier to keep to herself.

This past week with Skye, she'd realized something vital had been missing in her life. She had a female friend, and part of her felt fiercely protective. She looked down at Skye's phone, wanting to be proven wrong about Wade. Wanting him to be truly smitten for once. She didn't have much hope, but his words to Skye stopped her flat.

*You are fucking amazing. I woke up feeling like I've been hit on the side of the head with a 2x4 made of happy. God, I'm talking like a fucking Hallmark card. Look what you've done to me, woman. When can I see you again?*

Allie stared at the words, taking them in. She felt a slow smile spread over her face.

"Well?" Skye's tone was hopeful, and Allie looked up to see a little crack in the bravado she'd worn just a few moments ago. "It's cheesy, I know. But is it just a line? Does he say that sort of thing to all the girls? Lay it on me, I can take it."

Allie shook her head and handed the phone back. "I've known Wade for six years. Cross my heart and hope to die, I've never seen him write anything remotely like that."

The grin that flashed on Skye's face was like the sun coming out. "I was hoping for that."

"Seriously. He dates a lot of women, and he can be a passionate guy. But he's never that effusive. *Never.*"

Skye tucked a blue curl behind one ear. "You're not just saying that?"

"No way. The man's got it bad."

"Good. Because so do I."

Allie laughed. "Congratulations."

"Thanks!" Skye cocked her head to the side. "So how about you? Is this thing with Jack serious, or is it just a fling?"

Allie gripped the spatula tighter, not sure how to answer. "I guess it's too early in the morning to say. I mean, it's kinda new. Well, not new. I mean, I've known him forever, but not this version of him, you know?"

"Right. But what do you *want* to have happen?"

The hopefulness in Skye's voice was contagious. Allie hesitated, not sure what to say. She felt deliciously happy, happier than she'd felt in ages. She couldn't wait to see Jack again, and the thought of kissing him made her spleen do somersaults in her abdomen.

She wondered what he was feeling. Was it just a fling for him, or something more? Which did she want it to be?

"Hey, Allie? I think your eggs are burning."

"What? Oh." Allie whirled around to see smoke billowing from the copper skillet. Dammit. She snatched it off the burner and dropped it into the sink, scraping halfheartedly at the mess glued to the bottom. "Crap. They're goners."

"Sorry. My fault. I distracted you with all that boy talk."

She laughed. "Don't worry, I was plenty distracted on my own." She reached for the faucet handle, but Skye stood up.

"Actually, let me see if I can salvage any of that for the cats."

"Really? I wouldn't have thought of feeding eggs to cats."

"The vet says they're a good protein source. Especially for some of the older guys."

As if on cue, two cats appeared in the kitchen and began twining themselves around Skye's ankles. A tiger-striped one named Kenny and a chubby, Creamsicle-colored cat named Luna. Their oversized paws made velvety thumps on the hardwood floor as they circled Skye's bare feet in perfect synchronicity.

"I'm gonna miss these guys," Skye murmured. "Big sweeties."

"You could always stay," Allie offered. "Once I get the B&B back up and running, I'll still need the help."

"Thanks. I'll think about it. But I kinda want to venture out on my own, you know? Be open to new experiences, new jobs, new people?"

Allie nodded and turned to the cupboard filled with pots and pans, grateful she had more eggs and an abundance of good skillets in her grandma's kitchen.

But mostly grateful she'd avoided Skye's question. The one about what she wanted. She wanted Jack, plain and simple. Wanted him so much she practically ached with it.

And that was a scary place to be.

◆ ◆ ◆

"Okay, you little bastards," Allie muttered an hour later. "Time to get serious."

She shoved one last battery into the eighties-era boom box and jammed the flap closed. Tucking the oversized stereo under one arm, she turned and crawled down through the attic door. This was the first time she'd been up here since Friday, and she knew she'd been avoiding it on purpose. Part of her didn't want to look at the money, didn't want to think about what she should do with it. Part of her was afraid to open any more boxes, not sure what the hell else she might find.

Most of her just wasn't sure what to do, at least not about the money.

But she had an idea what to do to make her grandma's house better, so she was focusing on that.

As she made her way down the ladder, she felt her ankle wobble. She was almost to the bottom and tried to jump the rest of the way, but two hands grabbed her shoulders and steadied her.

"Careful there, Albatross!"

Wade's voice was as familiar as his hands on her arms, though neither gave her chills the way Jack did. But it was good to have him here now, especially since it meant she hadn't fallen the last twelve inches to the ground. As her feet touched the floor, she pulled the boom box to her chest and turned to face her friend.

"Thanks," she said. "I probably need a spotter if I'm going to keep using that ladder."

"You probably need a neon-pink Members Only jacket and some Aqua Net hairspray."

"What? Oh, you mean the boom box?"

Wade slid a finger over the cassette buttons and gave a low whistle. "That thing is vintage. Were you planning to stand outside someone's window blasting a Peter Gabriel song?"

Allie laughed and brushed a dust bunny off her shirt. "You're not too far off the mark, actually."

"Oh yeah? Wait, don't tell me—you're heading to Jack's house so you can serenade him with the song you danced to at your high school prom."

"No. I'm taking it out on the back deck to try a new strategy for getting rid of the damn woodpeckers."

Wade quirked an eyebrow at her. "My idea was more romantic."

"I don't need romance right now. I need the woodpeckers to stop making holes in the house."

"Maybe when you're done, I can borrow that sometime."

"What for?" Allie started down the hall, then waited for him to fall into step beside her. He did, and they stomped down the stairs together.

"Skye told me this story last night about the guy who broke her heart in high school," Wade said. "Dumped her right in the middle of a slow dance to some Coldplay song. I thought it might be cool to surprise her sometime, maybe show up with a corsage and ask her to finish the dance with me."

Allie glanced over to see him grinning like a love-drunk teenager. She couldn't help but feel happy for him, even though her own romance was a little less mushy at the moment.

It was almost noon, and she still hadn't heard a peep from Jack.

"I think the slow dance sounds cute," she said. "Cheesy, but cute."

"Good cheesy or just cheesy cheesy?"

The thought of Jack and cheese made her think of last night's wine and cracker party, along with everything that happened afterward. She found herself smiling for real, so she flashed it at Wade as they reached the bottom of the stairs and turned right. "Good cheesy. I take it you're here to see her?"

"Yeah, she's just getting ready," he said. "We're going to brunch someplace in the Pearl District. Then we're checking out an exhibit at the Portland Art Museum."

"The last time I heard you sound this excited was when you bought that silly gold Corvette."

"It's not a Corvette, it's a Jaguar. And it's not gold, it's Spacedust—a custom color—so it was worth the excitement."

"And is Skye?"

"If you must know, my excitement about Skye makes the Jag excitement seem like one of those party favors that you blow and the little paper thing comes out flat and just flops around." He frowned. "I think I might have lost something in that metaphor."

Allie stopped at the door to the back deck and studied her friend. "Wow. You're not kidding, are you? You've got it bad."

He shook his head and held up his hand. "As God is my witness, I think I'm in love."

"Holy shit."

He grinned. "I know, right?"

She shook her head, trying to get a handle on this. "You've known her less than twenty-four hours."

"When you know, you just know."

The sincerity in his voice made her heart swell. For him, for Skye, for love in general. Crazy or not, Wade was sincere. She couldn't help but be happy for him.

When Allie and Wade had dated, they'd never *just known*, not even when they'd gotten engaged. It had seemed like a reasonable next step—two attractive, well-educated young adults with lawyer parents and the same ideas about how life should unfold. It had seemed like a good idea at the time.

"I'm happy for you," Allie said. "Really, I am."

Wade grinned. "Thank you."

"Now let's go scare some damn woodpeckers."

"Right."

She pushed the door open, half expecting him to retreat back into the house, but he followed her outside instead. The air was crisp and a little muggy, and the smell of damp leaves was thick in the air. Birds were chattering all around them, but the cheerful twittering had ceased to sound cheerful to Allie. Several birds were scattered through a nearby oak tree, and Allie glared at them, wondering which of the little assholes was responsible for the latest round of destruction to her grandma's house.

She set the boom box on the picnic table and switched it on.

"So explain to me what you're doing," Wade said. "How is a vintage ghetto-blaster going to get rid of woodpeckers?"

"I'm hoping to scare them away with loud music."

"This is really your best idea?"

"No," she muttered as she began to turn the dial. "My best idea was the fake owls, but the little assholes just pecked holes in their faces."

"Ouch."

"Then I tried pinwheels. And streamers."

"I thought it was looking rather festively tacky around here."

Allie glared. "It's time to step things up a little."

She cranked up the volume on the boom box. There was a clatter of static, followed by the high-decibel blare of a DJ's voice.

*"You're listening to Portland Sex Radio, and today we're going to be talking about polyamory, the Portland orgy scene, and the six kinds of orgasms you should be having right now."*

Allie smacked her hand on the volume lever and glanced at the neighboring houses. No sign of anyone stirring at the sound of high-decibel porn, but it wasn't worth taking chances. She spun the dial to change the station.

"Hey," Wade protested. "I wanted to hear that."

"Get the podcast," she muttered, still flipping for a new station.

"So, speaking of orgasms," Wade said, "I hear you and Jack brought the party home last night."

Allie ignored him and glanced back up into the oak tree. The birds that had dotted the branches were beginning to collect on the deck railing, their chirping more ferocious now. A few new feathery bastards swooped in and landed on the fence. Sparrows, maybe, or some sort of jay. Maybe not woodpeckers, but what the hell did Allie know? She should probably get a bird identification book.

She settled on a station broadcasting something pop-y with a tinny beat. Was that a Justin Bieber song? She wasn't sure, but she cranked it up anyway, then turned to Wade. He was apparently still waiting for her response to his question about Jack and orgasms, which she had no intention of answering directly.

"I take it Skye told you about our conversation this morning?" she said.

"What? No, she didn't utter a peep. She told me last night that you and Jack had the cats handled, which I took to mean he was here with you. I filled in the blanks as soon as I saw your just-got-laid grin."

"Great," Allie muttered, glancing at the porch rail. A dozen more birds had gathered, little speckled brown and tan ones. They cheeped and chattered in time with the music, one of them pausing long enough to raise its tail and poop on her grandma's prized rosebush.

Allie sighed and spun the radio dial again. She found some classical music—Beethoven? That should do it—and turned up the volume a little.

"So what did Skye say about me?" he asked.

Pleased he'd moved on from wanting to discuss Jack, Allie dropped her hand from the boom box and regarded him with a stern look. "I'm not sharing private girl talk with you, Wade. If she didn't spill the dirt on my date, I'm certainly not telling you anything she might've told me in confidence."

"Fair enough," he answered. "At least tell me if she's even a tiny fraction as into me as I'm into her. Which is actually saying a lot, because I'm really fucking into this girl."

Wade's normal cocky cool was gone, replaced by something much more vulnerable. The chatter of birds around him gave the whole scene a hopeful, Disney tone. Allie sighed, always a sucker for fairy tales.

"Yeah," she said. "She's into you. *Really* into you. And that's all I'm going to tell you, so stop pestering me."

"Yes!" Wade gave an awkward fist pump and an out-of-character foot shuffle. A handful of birds startled behind him, fluttering up in a burst of feathers and squawking.

"Do that again," Allie said. "You're scaring the birds."

"I'll pass. But maybe you should try some different music. I think they're kind of enjoying this stuff."

Allie glanced around. True enough, the feathered rats seemed to have multiplied. Fat little blue ones and a couple redheaded ones she thought might be cardinals. She spun the dial again, settling on something that sounded like Frank Sinatra.

"So," Wade said. "Did you have a chance to look through any of the materials I brought you yesterday? The legal stuff about found goods?"

Allie nodded and shot a quick glance at the house. No sign of Skye. Still, she wasn't sure she wanted to have this conversation. She would have almost preferred talking about Jack.

"Yeah, I skimmed through it this morning," she said. "Thanks for digging that up."

"You're welcome. You sure you're not willing to tell me what you found?"

Allie hesitated. She thought about some of the passages she'd read this morning in the packet of information he'd given her. Her single year of law school had done nothing to prepare her for the sea of legal jargon she'd read in the text of ORS 98.352 and ORS 98.376 and a gazillion other Oregon Revised Statutes pertaining to lost, unclaimed, and abandoned property.

*A person commits theft by receiving if the person receives, retains, conceals or disposes of property of another knowing or having good reason to know that the property was the subject of theft . . .*

Which wasn't to say Allie really thought the money was connected to her parents' crimes, but still. She had no way of knowing for sure.

"Earth to Allie?"

"What?" she glanced back at Wade in time to see him watching her with an odd expression. Behind him, another cluster of birds had gathered in the cherry tree, their chirping nearly drowning out the sound of "Old Blue Eyes." Frankly, Allie was relieved. She'd always hated Sinatra. She turned the dial again, this time settling on a country western station.

Wade stepped closer, possibly to speak in confidence, or maybe to avoid the crow hovering on the roofline just over his shoulder. "Look," he said. "I know you said you don't want to tell me too much about what you found, and I can respect that."

"Thank you."

"But can you at least give me a hint?"

The blare of twangy music and the lyrics about exes in Texas made an awkward backdrop to this conversation. He was still looking at her, expecting a response, so Allie sighed.

"I'm not sure I should say much," she said. "I read all that stuff you gave me about ORS 98. There's that stuff about witnesses or other people being legally bound by the notice or report requirements, and I was worried about—"

"Right, right . . . theft by deception, probable cause, yada yada yada. I know the law. Still—" Wade cleared his throat. "Can you at least tell me by any chance if whatever you found needs to be . . . laundered?"

Allie felt the hair prickle on the back of her neck. She licked her lips. "Laundered?"

Wade glanced toward the house, then quickly back to Allie. She thought she heard Skye's hair dryer going upstairs, but Wade took a step closer and lowered his voice anyway.

"Yes, *laundered*," he said. "You know."

"I—um. I guess it's possible. I guess I'm not sure how I'd know."

He frowned. "You didn't look closely at it?"

"You can tell by looking?" Allie felt her brow furrow. "How?"

He gave an awkward little laugh. "For starters, I guess I was thinking maybe you saw the stains."

Allie's mind was reeling. She tried to remember something she'd seen on *Dateline* about the dye packs used by banks in robberies. The teller would stick something in the bag of money that would stain the cash when the robber tried to remove it. Or was it about staining the robber's hands? Maybe that's where the phrase, *caught red-handed* came from? God, why hadn't she paid more attention to that TV special?

Wade was looking at her intently, and she tried to imagine him robbing a bank. She couldn't picture it. Then again, she couldn't picture her parents stealing money from a bunch of innocent investors.

She answered carefully. "I—uh—I guess I didn't think to look for stains."

"Right, of course not," he said. "And I suppose you didn't smell it?"

"Smell it? What on earth would that tell me?"

Wade frowned. "Well, mostly that my client spent entirely too much time in a cigar bar."

"What?"

"Though the cum stains were really the bigger issue. That, and the threat of a DNA test."

Allie stared at him. "What the hell are you talking about, Wade?"

"The dress. A custom Versace, one of a kind. Extremely expensive. I assumed you of all people would recognize it."

Allie stared at him. "Versace," she repeated, trying to buy herself time to figure out what the hell he was talking about.

"My client said it was worth six or seven grand. I hid it in your grandma's attic a few years ago when I came over for dinner in the middle of that divorce case from hell. Your grandma asked me to help her move some boxes up there, so it was a convenient spot." Something in her face must have registered utter disbelief, because Wade stopped talking and frowned at her. "Wait, what were *you* talking about?"

"The dress, of course." Allie took a deep breath and turned the radio dial again. She kept spinning it until she found something that sounded like acid rock, with a lead singer that screeched like someone had his testicles in a vise. Allie kept her gaze down until she was sure she could safely look Wade in the eye. He was still frowning when she glanced up.

"Look, I just couldn't believe you'd think I'd go around sniffing other people's smelly clothes," she said. "Your secret's safe with me. Want to tell me about it?"

He eyed her for a few beats, probably trying to assess if she was full of crap. Allie kept her expression flat.

"It's no big deal," Wade said at last. "Not anymore. I meant to come back and grab it, but then the client and her husband worked things out and decided to terminate divorce proceedings. She asked me to burn it, but by then you and I weren't dating anymore, and it seemed unnecessary to go digging it up again. To be honest, I'd kind of forgotten about it."

"Right." Allie nodded and glanced toward the fence. More birds had gathered there, and this time she was pretty sure she saw a woodpecker. At least she assumed it was a woodpecker. It had a long, pointy beak and little beady eyes. It was looking at her like it knew she was up to no good, or maybe she was just projecting.

She turned to Wade again. "Anyway, the dress is safe. I left it right where I found it. You can go get it if you want."

"I suppose I should. It's apparently worth a lot of money." He was still watching her, and Allie resisted the urge to squirm. He'd never been that perceptive, but maybe he'd figured out—

"I found some money, okay?"

She'd blurted the words before she'd had a chance to think them through. The second they were out of her mouth, she felt relieved. Wade was a lawyer. He could fix this, couldn't he?

He frowned at her. "What do you mean you found some money?"

"Here. At the house. In the attic. That's why I was asking you all those questions."

"How much money?"

Allie swallowed, feeling guarded now. "A lot."

"Like—more than two hundred and fifty dollars?"

Allie nodded and watched Wade's frown deepen. "How much are we talking, Albatross?"

She opened her mouth to answer, not entirely sure what she was about to say. Lucky for her, Skye chose that moment to step out onto the deck looking radiant and lovely in a red-and-gold sari skirt with a white T-shirt knotted at the hip. She wore big hoop earrings and gold sandals with laces up the ankles, and she was beaming at Wade like he'd just offered her the keys to his Jag.

Wade snapped his attention to Skye, and Allie had never felt more relieved to have another woman steal the limelight.

"Good God in heaven." Wade pantomimed stabbing himself through the heart, his distress at Allie's confession all but forgotten. "You're stunning."

It would have sounded like a line if Allie hadn't been watching his face to see the absolute adoration there. It almost took her breath away.

Skye laughed and took his arm. "Thanks." She glanced at the radio and frowned. "I didn't realize you guys were fans of the Bloody Buttholes."

"We're not," Allie muttered, glancing up at the eaves where a woodpecker had begun hammering at the cedar siding. "But apparently the woodpeckers are."

"You ready to go?" Wade planted a kiss on Skye's forehead, his conversation with Allie seemingly forgotten.

"Anytime you are." Skye looked back at Allie. "Sorry about the woodpeckers. If it helps, I could maybe talk to a friend of mine who works with birds at the zoo."

"Really?" Allie felt her hopes rising. "You think she might know something about woodpeckers?"

"I don't know. She works with penguins, so I guess that's not the same thing."

"I'm getting desperate," Allie said. "At this point, I'll try anything."

"Even the Bloody Buttholes," Wade said. "Come on, let's get going."

The two of them walked off together arm in arm, and Allie watched them go. Skye's hand was tucked in Wade's back pocket, and she leaned toward him as though drawn by magnets. As they rounded the corner, Wade reached out to brush a curl from her face, his hand lingering longer than necessary on her cheek. The whole tableau made Allie's heart feel like a warm, gooey puddle in the center of her chest.

Okay, so Wade and Skye had known each other less than twenty-four hours, and yeah, it seemed like an odd match. But maybe this would be it for Wade. When he and Allie had split, he'd never seemed sad about it. She hadn't been, either, so she didn't take it personally. Though it hadn't worked between them, Allie had always held out hope he'd find someone. Maybe Skye was it.

Maybe they'd ask her to be a bridesmaid or to read a poem at the wedding. Maybe she could bring Jack, and he'd turn to her after the ceremony and whisper—

Her phone buzzed in the pocket of her hoodie. She fumbled it out, snagging her wristwatch on the fleece. Freeing it at last, she held it up and glanced at the screen. She felt her heart skip a beat when she saw *Jack Carpenter* on the readout.

Then it stopped altogether when she read the words.

*Made a mistake.*

*Plz don't text me, K?*

# CHAPTER TWELVE

Jack walked into the living room to find two of the three most cherished females in his life sprawled on opposite ends of the sofa, each with an iPhone in her hand.

His mother looked up at him and smiled. "I really like this new Kegel reminder app your team developed," she said. "It's good for ladies my age who need to strengthen their pelvic floors, so we don't tinkle."

"What's a pelvic floor?" Paige asked as she glanced up from her own phone.

Er, make that *Jack's* phone.

"Paige," he said in his most stern voice. "What are you doing with my phone?"

"Well mine's not working right now, so—"

"I know yours isn't working right now," he said through gritted teeth. "And do you think that might have something to do with the fact that you deliberately ignored me the two thousand times I told you not to take your phone into the bathroom?"

His daughter's bottom lip quivered a little, and Jack resisted the urge to back down. Some lessons she had to learn the hard way.

"Well, yeah, but—"

"No buts," he said. "Your phone is a privilege, and you lost that privilege when you splashed water on it."

"But I didn't think a few drops of water would ruin it like that."

"We'll know in a few hours if it's ruined. You did the right thing putting it in rice like I showed you. But you did the wrong thing by taking it in there in the first place, and you're also doing the wrong thing by using my phone right now without asking."

Her eyes had gone a little watery, but she stuck out her jaw anyway. "But I had to text Allie," she said. "We were making plans to go bra shopping and I had to tell her that I messed up and I couldn't text her like I said I would."

An uneasy feeling tickled the center of Jack's gut. He held out his hand. "Give me the phone, please."

Paige got up and walked over, setting it in his palm. "I'm sorry, Daddy."

"We all make mistakes," he said, scrolling back through his daughter's texts to see that very word jumping out at him.

*Made a mistake.*

*Plz don't text me, K?*

Oh, shit. He scrolled down, his gut hitting rock bottom as he read Allie's reply:

*Total mistake, for sure! Was thinking the same. Won't text you again.*

Jack felt nauseated. He stared at the words, trying to make sense of them.

"What's wrong, Daddy?"

He looked down at his daughter to see her staring up at him with a concerned look on her face.

"Honey," he said slowly. "When you use someone else's phone to send a text message, you need to tell them it's you and not the person whose phone you're borrowing."

"But Allie knew it was me," Paige protested. "She even seemed like she knew about how I messed up and got water on the phone."

"It does seem like that, doesn't it?"

*Total mistake, for sure!*

Jesus Christ. Did she really feel that way, or was she just responding to what she thought he'd said? He was too old for this sort of guessing game.

He glanced again at his daughter's worried face. He ordered himself not to panic, to stay focused on this teaching moment with his kid. The rest could wait for later.

"Paige," he said slowly. "What are some of the lessons you've learned here this morning?"

His daughter scuffed her turquoise Converse sneaker on the carpet and scrunched up her forehead. "Not to take my phone in the bathroom," she mumbled. "And not to use your phone without asking."

"And?"

"And not to text people without telling who I am."

"Right. Now come here."

He stooped down and opened his arms, and Paige stepped into them. He hugged her tight, and heard a small sniffle close to his ear. She clung to him like a baby koala, her bony angles and the scent of strawberry shampoo overpowering the poised young woman who insisted she needed a training bra. Paige squeezed him back, and Jack wondered how he ever thought he knew what love was before he had a daughter.

"All right," he said as he released her. "I want you to go to your room and think about what you've done. When I come get you, we're going to talk about consequences and what other privileges you'll be giving up besides the phone."

She nodded. "Okay, Daddy." She turned and walked away.

He straightened up and turned to see his mom watching him from the couch. She set down her phone and patted the space beside her.

"Very nice, son."

"Thanks." Jack sighed and walked over, dropping into the space beside her. "It's going to get harder, isn't it?"

"Yes," she told him. "But you can handle it."

"I wish I had your confidence."

She put her hand on his back and rubbed a slow, circular pattern the way she used to when he was a little boy who couldn't sleep. "You're already ten times the father your dad ever was," she said. "You grew up without any sort of male role model at all. It's nothing short of miraculous that you turned out to be such an amazing dad."

He smiled and put his hand on hers. "That's because I had a mom who was badass enough to be both parents."

She laughed and put an arm around him, rocking a little. "I did my best."

Jack raked his fingers through his hair and glanced at his phone. The message wasn't lighting up the screen anymore, but he could still picture it in his mind.

*Total mistake, for sure!*

Dammit to hell.

"Trouble in paradise?" his mom asked, reading his mind.

Or reading his text messages. He could never really hide anything from her.

"Yeah," Jack muttered and flipped the phone face down. "I guess I need to make a phone call."

"I take it you and Allie are seeing each other again?"

"I don't know. Maybe. It's complicated."

"I can imagine. I've seen that look in your eye all week."

"What look?"

"The one you used to get when you were seventeen years old and you sat by the phone waiting to hear if her parents would let her go out with you that night."

He snorted at the memory, thinking life might've been easier before the advent of cell phones. "Yeah, it might be a little like that. I'm not so sure she wants to hear from me right now."

"She always had her pride," his mom said, and he wondered how much she knew. "It was one of the things you always loved about her. Also one of the things that got in the way, if I remember right."

"That's probably true for both of us."

His mom patted his knee and looked up at him, her expression serious. "You want a little unsolicited advice from the person who not only incubated you for nine months, but watched you navigate every great romance of your life?"

Jack smiled. "Depends. Will this person feel obligated to describe her episiotomy as a way to emphasize the challenges of raising me?"

"Not this time." She pressed her lips together the way she often did while trying to think of the kindest way possible to suggest he remove his own head from his butt. "Go see her in person."

"Who, Allie?"

"Yes, Allie. I don't know if Paige messed something up or if you messed it up yourself or if Allie did. It doesn't matter. What matters is that you probably can't un-mess it using the same tool that caused the mess in the first place."

She likely had a point. Still, what was he supposed to do? "I can't just show up on her doorstep."

"Sure you can. It's better that way. No phone calls. No text messages. No Spacebook messages. Just real, old-fashioned, face-to-face dialogue."

He laughed, both at the earnestness of her reply and her blending of Facebook and Myspace. Still, he felt pretty sure his mom was oversimplifying things a bit. She obviously didn't realize Allie had just told him they were better off not starting down that road again. If that's how she really felt, was it really his place to convince her otherwise?

*Maybe.*

He cleared his throat and lifted his eyes back to his mom's face. "You're okay watching Paige for an hour?"

She smiled. "I insist."

♦ ♦ ♦

As soon as Jack had worked out his daughter's punishment and doled out at least a million hugs and snuggles, he told her he needed to run an errand.

"Are you going to see Allie?" she asked.

He smoothed her hair back from her face. "Why would you think that?"

"Because you have *that look*."

"Jeez," he muttered, not bothering to ask what look she was talking about. "You're as bad as your grandma."

Paige grinned, obviously taking it as a compliment. "Can you find out if Allie wants to take me shopping this week? Like maybe she could pick me up after school and we could have ice cream or something and then go to the mall."

"We'll see." He kept it vague, not wanting to get her hopes up. If Allie meant it about last night being a mistake, what did that mean for their friendship?

"I love you, Daddy."

"I love you, too, Noodle Clump."

She giggled and squeezed him tight, fortifying him with a hefty dose of bravery as he set out to talk with Allie about last night.

But standing on her doorstep now, he felt his bravery trickling from his forehead and springing up under his arms. God, did he always have to sweat when he got nervous?

He took a few deep breaths, getting his bearings. The air smelled spicy, like wet leaves and fresh bark dust. There was a clay pot of geraniums next to the front door, their carrot-scented red blossoms a cheerful contrast to the pale-yellow siding on the house. The white plantation shutters looked like they'd gotten a fresh coat of paint, and Jack wondered when Allie had found time to do all this. Must have been sometime today, since he hadn't noticed it the night before.

He took one more deep breath and turned his attention back to the door. He knocked once, then waited. The sign telling him to come right in was gone, so all he could do was stand there. He felt itchy in his own skin, uncomfortable and awkward.

No one answered, so Jack knocked again. He was on the brink of ringing the bell when he heard a thud on the other side of the fence. Frowning, he walked to the edge of the yard and approached the gate. It was slightly ajar, so Jack pushed it open and stepped into the backyard.

The second he saw Allie, he realized this was about to be more awkward.

"Allie, hi." He looked her up and down, trying to keep his own reaction in check as she stared down at him from the edge of the deck. "Um, wow."

"What?" Her tone was flat.

"I've never seen you wear combat fatigues before."

She flipped up the visor on the helmet she wore, revealing a guarded expression and one very bruised eye. "Can I help you?"

Jack's stomach lurched. "Oh my God. Are you okay?" He moved closer, stepping up onto the deck for a closer look. "Who the hell gave you a black eye?"

"The stupid woodpeckers!"

He blinked, then looked her up and down again. The camouflage getup wasn't something she'd picked up at a local hunting store. It looked old, maybe vintage military. Jack returned his gaze to her face, wincing as he took in the shiner again.

"A woodpecker hit you in the face," he said slowly, trying to understand.

"No," she said with exaggerated patience. "The woodpeckers made holes in my house, so I went up to the attic and found all this camo gear and an old BB gun, so I thought maybe I could take care of the woodpecker problem the old-fashioned way."

"With a BB gun."

"Right." She reached behind her and lifted the weapon, and Jack took a step back. "But not only did I miss, the gun backfired the first time I tried to shoot it and it hit me in the face."

"Jesus," he said, wishing he could reach out and soothe her bruised skin. But he sensed his touch wouldn't be welcome at the moment. "That's awful."

"And then the cops showed up, because apparently it's illegal to fire a pellet gun in the city limits," she continued. "So now, on top of a black eye, I have a police record."

"They arrested you?"

"Of course not." She waved a hand, looking wild and a little desperate. "But now there's a record out there of the police coming to my house and talking to me, which is pretty much the same thing."

"Pretty much." Part of him wanted to hold her. Part of him wanted to laugh at the absurdity of it all. Most of him managed to hold it together as he stood there on her back deck trying to keep a straight face. "Were you really going to shoot a woodpecker?"

She gave a heavy sigh. "Probably not. But I did think I could hit the fence *near* one and maybe scare it away."

"What did you hit instead?"

"I shot the nipple off my neighbor's Venus pond statue."

"Ouch."

"They weren't amused."

"Probably best you only got one shot off," he said. "I think your aim might leave something to be desired."

"Right. Well, I should probably get back to—"

"Allie, can we talk for a minute?"

"What for?"

"I wanted to talk about that text message."

"What text message?"

He sighed. "Nice try. Can we maybe sit down or something?"

"Actually, I'm kind of busy."

"Could you at least put the gun down then? I want to talk to you."

She seemed to hesitate, then lowered her weapon, such as it was. "What?" He heard her try to infuse the syllable with anger and bravado, but it came out sounding defeated. It was enough to buoy him just a little.

"Allie, I didn't send that text message this morning. The one that said I made a mistake?"

She glared at him. "What are you talking about? Is your phone in the habit of sending regretful morning-after messages all by itself?"

"No," he said slowly. "But my ten-year-old daughter *is* in the habit of using it to send regretful morning-after messages after she drops her own phone in the sink."

"What?"

"You text-dumped my kid, not me."

All the color seemed to drain from Allie's face. "Are you serious?"

"Yep. Want to reread the message in that context?"

He didn't give her a chance to respond, whipping his phone out of his pocket before she could say anything. He flicked it on and scrolled quickly to the text messages. "Here, take a look. 'Made a mistake.'" He held it out to her, forcing her to take it. "The mistake was taking her phone into the bathroom when I've repeatedly told her not to."

"Oh."

"And 'Plz don't text me, K?' First of all, did you honestly think I'd give you the brush-off with improper English?"

Allie was still staring at the screen, eyes fixed on the words there as she took them in with this new context. "That did seem weird," she admitted.

"Come on, Allie." He held out his hand, and she handed his phone back. Jack shoved it back in his pocket, relieved to see the softening in her expression. "You know me. Would I really text you something like that the morning after we slept together?"

The color seemed to come rushing back to her face, or maybe that was just the bruise setting up. "That's just it, Jack. I don't know you. Not anymore. Hell, text messaging wasn't even a thing when we dated. I have no context for how you operate in a modern relationship. For all I know, this is how you blow off all your one-night stands."

"It wasn't a one-night stand," he said. "Not to me, it wasn't."

He waited for her to respond. To tell him she felt the same, and that maybe there was hope of them spending more time together in the future. She seemed to hesitate, and he remembered what his mother had said about Allie's pride sometimes getting in the way. Maybe he could make this easier.

"Look, Allie. Last night was unexpected. It was amazing. It wasn't something I was thinking about when I looked you up a couple weeks ago, I'll be honest. But I really want to see where things might go."

She still hadn't said anything, and Jack wondered if he'd overstepped. If she really had meant it when she'd said it was a mistake. He was sweating again, and he wished he knew better how to read this modern version of Allie. When she spoke at last, her voice was quiet.

"I didn't mean it," she said.

He swallowed hard, hoping she meant this morning's text message and not everything the night before. "You mean about last night being a mistake?"

She nodded. "Yeah. I was pretty hurt when I thought that's what you were telling me."

"I'm sorry you thought that. I can see why you would."

They stood there in awkward silence for a few beats, and Jack wondered where this round of apologies left them. Were they back where they'd ended last night, or someplace new?

When Allie reached for his hand, something surged inside him. "I'm glad you came here," she said. "Not just right now, though that's good, too. I mean I'm glad you're back in Portland. I'm glad you looked me up."

"Me, too."

"And I'd like to keep seeing you." She bit her lip. "I mean—if that's what you want."

"I want." He smiled at her. "I really like you, Allie. A whole lot. More than I did when I loved you."

She laughed out loud and brushed her hair from her face. "Same here. I like you a lot more than when I loved you."

He leaned in to kiss her, then bonked his head on the damn visor. "Ow."

"Hang on," she said, and wrestled the helmet off her head. "There, that's better. Pucker up, buttercup."

"Such a romantic," he muttered, but bent to kiss her anyway.

The kiss was slow and soft and sweet and left him wishing she'd invited him inside so they could see where this went. But he couldn't stay. He had to get home to—

"Paige," he said, breaking the kiss.

"Um, what?"

"My daughter."

She blinked at him. "I'm aware that your daughter is Paige. I'm just not sure what that has to do with kissing me."

Jack raked his fingers through his hair. "No, I just remembered. Paige wanted me to set a time with you to go bra shopping. Are there any afternoons this week that might work for you?"

Allie reached into her pocket and pulled out her phone. She tapped the screen a few times, then began scrolling. "Well, my boss insisted I take a few days of bereavement leave this week, but I was planning to use it to repaint the downstairs bathrooms and maybe go see my parents. In between prison visits, I need to find time to get my hair trimmed and do some grocery shopping." She glanced up and gave him a small smile. "Of course, I still have to pencil in a time to fight your sister-in-law."

Jack stifled a groan. "She sent me another apology this morning."

"Don't mention it." She waved a dismissive hand, then looked back at her phone. "I have an early meeting on Thursday, which means I could leave work by three-thirty or four. What if I picked Paige up right after that?"

"I can drop her off here to make it easier. And thanks, Allie. Really. This means a lot to her. And me."

"No problem." She shoved her phone in her pocket and looked at him again, her expression somewhere between amused and contemplative. "You know, when I imagined our fairy tale happily-ever-after together, I didn't picture myself wearing combat fatigues and talking with you about buying a training bra for the daughter you had with another woman."

"Sorry," he said. "Sorry you didn't get your fairy tale."

"It's okay," she said, though her expression was still wistful. "Fairy tales are probably overrated."

"True enough." He lifted her hand to his lips and kissed the knuckles, the courtliest gesture he could muster. "But maybe if you keep kissing me, I'll turn into a prince."

# CHAPTER THIRTEEN

Allie's week went by in a blur. The days she went to her office were a flurry of meetings and spreadsheets, memos and presentations. She had a big convention coming up in two months, but there was still plenty of time to plan. Her co-workers were understanding, and her boss told her to take more bereavement days if she needed them.

She'd taken to spending nights at the B&B so she could make better progress on the fix-up projects she'd identified with a little help from Jack. She was determined to do most of the work herself, and spent evenings watching YouTube videos on everything from resealing travertine floors to reconditioning leather sofas. Then she put her new skills to the test, scrubbing and polishing and working her way through the dilapidated house with a trail of mutant-toed cats behind her.

Jack helped when he could, stopping by after work to lend tools or muscle or some combination of the two. Sometimes he'd bring Paige, and sometimes they'd both stay for dinner. There was an undercurrent of something new and different between them. They weren't "back together," exactly. It was more like they were together for the first time.

By the time Thursday rolled around, Allie felt a delirious mix of accomplishment, exhaustion, and excited energy. She'd been home for twenty minutes, waiting for Jack to drop off Paige for the bra shopping, when the doorbell rang. She smoothed down her dress and hustled to the front door, giddiness coursing through her at the thought of seeing Jack again.

But it wasn't Jack at the door.

"Hey, Albatross."

"Wade." She stepped aside, allowing him to pass. "I don't think Skye's home from class yet. You can wait in the parlor, though."

"Actually, I wanted to talk to you for a sec."

"Oh?"

"It's about the money."

There was something serious in his voice, and Allie felt a shiver run up her spine. "Okay. Come on in."

She turned away so he wouldn't notice and headed toward the parlor, feeling him close behind her. Once she reached the doorway, she gestured toward the sofa. Wade sat awkwardly, resting his hands on his knees. He must have come straight from work, but he'd left his suit jacket behind somewhere. He yanked on his tie to loosen the knot, but didn't take it off.

"Can I get you some water?" Allie asked. "Or a beer or something?"

"I'm good." Wade patted the space beside him. "Have a seat, Albatross. You're making me nervous hovering like that."

"You're making me nervous looking all serious." Even so, she sat down beside him, bristling with tension.

Wade sighed and raked his fingers through his hair. "Look, we haven't had a chance to talk alone since that day on the back deck. When you mentioned finding money somewhere in this house?"

"Right. It's been kinda crazy around here."

Which was partly Allie's doing. She'd done her best to avoid him, pretending to be on the phone when he stopped by to see Skye, or hunkering down in her bedroom with Jack when the happy couple was in the family room binge-watching *Outlander*. Allie knew she was burying her head in the sand, afraid to hear what he might have to say.

But it was clear she'd run out of opportunities to put off hearing Wade's lawyerly lecture. "Lay it on me," she said heavily. "What did you want to say about the money?"

Wade cleared his throat. "Look, you know property law isn't my specialty. But I did a little more research this week and found out some things you should probably know about ORS Chapter 98."

Allie nodded and fought the urge to glance at her watch. "Okay. Jack's bringing Paige by to go bra shopping in about ten minutes, so maybe you could give me the short version?"

His eyebrow lifted a little at the mention of bra shopping, but he didn't say anything. "You didn't tell me the amount you found, but you said it's more than two hundred and fifty dollars, right?"

"Right." Allie swallowed, not sure what she'd say if he pressed for more.

"Under Section 98.005, any person who finds money or goods valued at two hundred and fifty dollars or more and the owner of those goods is unknown, the finder is required by law to give notice in writing to the county clerk within ten days."

Allie felt herself go cold. "Notice?"

"Written notice. Within ten days of the finding. And within twenty days, you're required to publish an ad in the local newspaper once a week for two consecutive weeks stating the general description of the money or goods found, the name and address of the finder, and the date by which they must be claimed."

"But—but—that's insane," Allie sputtered. "And totally old-fashioned. Besides, I'm not just going to put an ad in the paper saying, 'hey, I've got a million dollars cash in my attic—is it yours?'"

Wade blinked. "A million dollars?"

"Hell."

"Jesus, Allie—I assumed ten-K, max. Are you shitting me?"

"I didn't mean to say that." She kind of had, though. She'd been carrying the secret for days, and she desperately needed to tell someone. Someone besides Jack.

"Who else knows?" he asked quietly.

"Jack. He was there when I found it."

Wade nodded. "That makes it more complicated."

"You're not kidding," she muttered, though she wasn't thinking about the law.

"No, I mean legally," Wade said. "I'll need to look it up, but I'm pretty sure Jack's bound by the same reporting requirement. If you prevent him from getting in touch with the county clerk or putting the ad in the paper or whatever, there's a chance you could be charged with theft by deception under ORS Section 98.005."

"What do you mean *prevent*? Like I tie him up and tell him he can't do it?"

"The law isn't explicit there, but no. I think simple coercion would be enough to make the case."

"Or omission? Like not telling him that's what I'm supposed to do?"

Wade nodded, his expression grim. "Yeah. Something like that."

Allie swallowed hard and tried to think. She glanced at the window over her shoulder. She'd cracked it open to let the blossom-scented breeze ripple through, and a trickle of sunlight pooled on the back of the sofa.

She turned back to Wade. "What if it's my grandma's money? What if she left it to me on purpose?"

"Allie." His tone said plenty, and so did the fact that he'd called her by name instead of *Albatross*. "We both know this isn't about you wanting to keep a million dollars to yourself."

"Maybe it is," she said. "I could buy a lot of shoes with that."

Wade shook his head. "You're thinking the same thing I am."

"What's that?" she asked, forcing him to say it so she wouldn't have to.

"We both know a lot of money magically vanished before your parents went to trial. If they get out on appeal, that's a nice little nest egg just waiting in the family coffers."

Allie shook her head. "But maybe that's not it. Maybe my grandma left it to me free and clear. The will says I get the house and its contents, right?"

"Right. But not if those contents aren't hers to give."

Allie nodded and didn't say anything. If the money was dirty, if her parents had squirreled it away somehow, she knew damn well they could say farewell to any hope of early release. Of returning to their normal lives and rebuilding like they might have hoped.

And even if it wasn't dirty—if her grandma really, truly had tucked it away for her—there was no way to prove that. Then she'd just be getting her parents in trouble for nothing.

"I need more time," she said. "To figure out if maybe someone in my family knows where it came from. Maybe it's a legit thing."

"How long has it been?"

"Six days."

He frowned. "You don't have much time left. Not according to the law, anyway."

"I know." She curled her fingers into the brocade fabric of the sofa, finding comfort in the familiar lines of the pattern. "But I want to be sure. Before I go blabbing to the county clerk or putting up a billboard telling everyone to come get the money, I want to find out if there's a legitimate reason it's there."

Wade lifted an eyebrow at her. "Legitimate, or illegitimate?"

"Wade."

He held up his hands in mock defense. "I'm on your side, Albatross. But we can't let this drag out for very long, okay? There's more at stake here than I realized when you first told me about it."

Allie nodded and looked down at her hands. "I know that."

The doorbell chimed, and Allie bolted off the sofa like it was on fire. She hurried for the door, not sure if she was more eager to see Jack or to escape the conversation with Wade. She threw open the front door to see father and daughter standing on the front porch.

"Hey, there," she said, beaming at both of them with a smile she hoped didn't look too guilty. "Good to see you guys."

"Hey, Allie!" Paige beamed up at her, and stretched out her arms for a hug. Allie obliged, delighted by how unabashedly friendly this kid was.

Allie straightened up, not as sure how to greet him. This whole thing still felt a little awkward, and she wasn't sure whether to treat him like a boyfriend or an old pal, especially with Paige standing there. Did she shake his hand or hug him?

She was still pondering it when Jack solved the dilemma by brushing a quick kiss on her cheek and grinning at her. "Thanks again for doing this."

"No problem. You know I love any excuse to shop."

"I definitely remember."

Allie turned to Paige. "You ready to go, Miss Thing?"

The girl had stooped down to pet BeeGee, who had flopped on his back like a fluffy disco ball with all four paws in the air. Paige looked up with her palm still resting on the furry belly. "Actually," she said, enunciating the word with an extra syllable. "I was hoping maybe I could use your bathroom."

"Oh. Yes, of course. Right this way."

Allie started down the hall, then rounded the corner and pointed Paige toward the powder room. The girl scurried in, closing the door behind her. Allie started to move back toward the foyer, part of her hoping Wade would take the hint and stay put. Something about having him here felt awkward, and she'd just as soon pretend they hadn't been in the middle of a secret conversation about stolen cash just thirty seconds ago.

But as they passed the threshold of the parlor, Allie's hopes sunk. Wade stepped out and greeted them with a wave. "Hey, there," he said, pumping Jack's hand a few times. "Good to see you again."

"Yeah," Jack said, frowning. "You, too."

There was a flicker of something in Jack's expression, something so faint Allie might have imagined it. She glanced into the parlor and remembered the window behind the sofa was open a few inches. Had he heard her conversation with Wade? Did he know about the reporting requirements or what that meant for him?

Or was he just annoyed at seeing her alone with Wade?

Wade's expression was blank, which was no help at all. She studied Jack's face instead, fighting to keep any traces of guilt from her expression.

But Jack was still looking at Wade. "Haven't seen you for a while," he said. "How's it going?"

"Good, good. How about you?"

"Not bad." Two thin frown lines appeared between Jack's brows, but he was still smiling. "I thought Skye said last night that she had a late class today."

"She did," Allie said, trying to keep her tone breezy. "Wade just stopped by for a minute to visit with me."

Jack's gaze swung back to her, and Allie fought to keep her spine straight. She was determined not to look guilty. Wade was her best friend. She had nothing to feel guilty about. Not the conversation about money or Jack's hang-ups about her engagement history or—

"Hey, Wade!"

Paige came bounding out of the powder room, and Allie breathed a sigh of relief.

"Hey!" Wade offered her a high five, which Paige returned with a hearty smack. "How's my favorite oenophile?"

Paige giggled and twisted her braid between her fingers. "Is an oenophile someone who knows a lot about birds?"

"No, but you're close," Wade said. "A bird expert is an ornithologist. An oenophile knows about wine."

"Oh." Paige looked thoughtful. "I've been learning about birds in my new school and Grandma bought me this really cool bird book."

"Excellent!" Wade replied. "Hey, Albatross—here's who you need to consult about your woodpecker problem."

Paige crinkled her nose and looked at Allie. "Albatross?"

She rolled her eyes. "That's Wade's nickname for me. Allie Ross the Albatross."

"The bird who'd rather fly alone," Wade said, and Allie watched his gaze slide knowingly between her and Jack.

"I haven't learned about that kind of bird yet," Paige said. "I'll look them up in my book. But I'm pretty sure woodpeckers are in there. Do you know what kind?"

Allie shook her head. "I'm not sure, but I know they're destroying this house."

"Really?" Paige was wide-eyed, and it occurred to Allie that she was being a touch dramatic in her description of the situation.

"Well, not destroying, exactly," she amended. "They're making a lot of holes. And big messes. And loud noises."

Paige frowned. "You should find out what kind they are. I can bring my book if you want."

"That would be great," Allie said. "I guess I didn't even think about there being a lot of different kinds of woodpeckers."

Jack put a hand on his daughter's back, and the pride in his expression was almost enough to mask the darkness that had flitted across his face moments before. "You girls ready to get going?"

Paige grinned. "Yep. Want me to drive?"

"Ha!" Allie said, grabbing her keys off the little hook in the hallway. "Maybe in about six years."

"Deal!" Paige said, and Allie wondered what the odds were they'd still be in each other's lives then. Not wanting to dwell on that, she turned to Jack. "How about I bring her back to your house around six?"

"That sounds good. I've got some errands to run anyway. Why don't you just text me when you're leaving the mall?"

"I can do that."

"By the way, my mom asked if you could stay for dinner."

"Oh," Allie said. "Well, I don't want to impose—"

"Please stay!" Paige grabbed her hand. "She's making paper salmon, and that's the best."

"That's salmon *en papillote* to fancy people," Jack said, and for a moment Allie wondered if he was setting her apart on purpose. Fancy snobs like Allie and her ilk, versus regular folk like them. But it was silly to read that much into such a simple comment.

"That sounds nice," Allie said, not committing one way or the other.

"You can have wine, too," Paige added, grinning at her father. "What kind, Daddy?"

Jack smiled and took his cue. "How about a rosé? Something cacophonous with hints of expired bathtub caulk and slightly wilted bib lettuce."

Paige dissolved in peals of laughter as her father reached into his back pocket for his wallet. He pulled out a few bills, folded them over, and handed them out to Allie. "Here. This is for the you-know-whats," he said.

"Dad." Paige rolled her eyes. "It's a bra shopping trip, not a spy mission."

"I was trying not to embarrass you in mixed company," Jack said, glancing at Wade.

Wade pantomimed covering his ears. "I hear nothing, I know nothing."

Allie laughed and stole a glance at Wade. He still had his ears covered, but he gave her a quick wink. She realized he was sending her a message.

*I have your back about the money. I'll keep my mouth shut for now, but you need to deal with it.*

Message received. Allie nodded, then looked at Jack.

A dark cloud passed over his face, and Allie felt a shiver run down her spine.

◆　◆　◆

Allie felt like a poorly attired chauffeur driving to the mall in an eighteen-year-old car with a ten-year-old girl in the backseat. She kept shouting conversational tidbits over her shoulder so Paige wouldn't feel ignored, but all Allie had managed to do was discover the kid wasn't terribly interested in the Portland mayoral race or the new windows on the KOIN Center.

By the time they reached the mall, Allie had a hoarse voice, a mild case of anxiety, and a growing sense of unease about how to fill thirty minutes before Paige's appointment with the professional bra fitter.

"Sorry about getting us here so early," Allie said as she guided her young charge through the front doors of the mall. "I was expecting the traffic to be worse."

"It's okay," Paige said. "It seemed bad to me. Like when that guy pulled his car out in front of you."

Allie grimaced. "Right. Can you please not repeat those words I yelled? Especially not to your grandma or your dad or your teacher or—"

Paige looked up at her blankly, and Allie had the sinking sensation that she was the worst person on earth Jack could have trusted with his child for the afternoon. Honestly, she'd just never been around kids. The few times she had, there'd always been a parent or some other adult who seemed to know the ropes. Allie had always assumed her instincts would kick in as soon as she had children of her own. Since that hadn't happened, she was left feeling wholly unprepared to be in charge of any creature that didn't walk on four legs and scratch the furniture.

Spotting a familiar tea shop up ahead, Allie felt a flutter of hope. "Would you like to get some tea with me?"

"Tea?" Paige's tone suggested a mild suspicion she was being offered crack.

Crap. Was tea not allowed? Caffeine or something?

"You could have herbal tea," Allie decided. "Chamomile or peppermint or maybe lemon verbena."

"Okay. Thank you."

The girl gave her a polite smile, and Allie guided her into the little café. The smell of coffee and sugar cookies was heavy in the air, and Allie felt her frayed nerves start to quiet down. She stepped up to the counter and tried to look confident and adult instead of like someone pretending to be those things.

"What can I get you?" chirped a girl with three rings in her nose and a name tag that declared her name to be Danica.

"Earl Grey, please," Allie said. "Venti."

"And you?"

Allie glanced down to see Paige biting her lip. "What's a venti?" she asked. "I might want one of those."

"Here." Allie picked up the laminated menu and scanned the list of teas. "They have a few different herbal teas. Do any of these sound good to you?"

She pointed to the column on the right, and Paige studied the words for a moment. "I'd like the mango one, please."

"Got it," Danica agreed, then looked at Allie. "Maybe a short?"

It took Allie a moment to realize she was supposed to make the decision. That a woman walking around with a kid was expected to be adult and authoritative instead of utterly fucking clueless about what size tea was appropriate for a ten-year-old girl. "Oh. Yes, I think that's good. Thank you."

"You want room at the top?" the server asked.

"Actually, I prefer a bit of steamed milk blended right into the Earl Grey."

"I meant on her drink," Danica said. "For ice. To cool it down so she doesn't burn her mouth."

"Right. Of course, yes."

God, she was supposed to know stuff like this, wasn't she?

She looked down at Paige, expecting to see judgment or disbelief that her father had let someone this ill-prepared be in charge of her well-being.

But the kid just smiled at her. "Want me to find a table?"

"That would be great."

Allie paid for the drinks and took a few calming breaths. This would be okay. She could handle this. She'd grown up with competent, loving women guiding her through her own childhood. Her mother and grandmother used to take her out like this all the time. It's not like she was an idiot. Just a little new at this, that's all.

By the time she had the drinks, she'd managed to talk herself down. She had another quick flash of panic when she didn't see Paige right away, but her heart rate slowed as she spotted the girl at a corner table.

Paige waved her over, then accepted the cardboard cup Allie handed her. "Thank you."

"You're welcome. I wasn't sure if you take cream or sugar or anything." She pushed a few packets across the table, just in case.

"I'm not sure, either," Paige said. "I've never had tea."

Allie picked up her own cup and pried off the lid so she could blow on it. "My mom used to take me for tea all the time when I was your age. Well, maybe a little older. I always liked cream and sugar."

Paige nodded as she used a little wooden stir stick to swirl about eighty pounds of sugar into her drink. "My mom's dead."

Allie winced. "I know. I'm sorry. *Really* sorry."

"It's okay." Paige gave her a small smile that nearly broke her heart. "May I try the cream, too?"

Allie handed her some and tried to think of a safer topic of conversation. Something that wouldn't remind the kid she was motherless or in the care of a woman with dubious child-care credentials. Luckily, Paige picked up the slack.

"So you must like cats a lot, huh?"

Allie took a small sip of tea. "Actually, I'd never even had a cat until a couple weeks ago."

"How come?"

"My parents wouldn't let me when I was growing up. They said they were dirty and messy and ill-tempered. My grandma always loved them, though."

"So she let you play with hers?"

"Yes." Allie felt a twinge of wistfulness as she remembered running around the house dragging the silk tie from her grandmother's robe with Stumpy scampering after it. "My grandma was the best. Funny and smart and sophisticated. A little nuts, but in a good way."

"My grandma's pretty great, too."

Allie fished the tea bag out of her cup and set it on her napkin. "Your dad's mom?"

"Uh-huh."

"Do you see your other grandma much? Your mom's mom?"

"No. Grandma Sarah's in Florida."

"And your Aunt Missy is in Chicago?"

"Yeah."

The girl sounded distracted, and Allie looked up to see Paige staring at the mannequins across the mall aisle at Victoria's Secret. Their shiny bosoms jutted out toward the window like pink satin torpedoes, and Paige gaped at them with an expression somewhere between mystified and fearful. Allie touched the girl's arm.

"We're not going there," she reassured her. "The place we're going is a little more discreet."

"Discreet," Paige repeated, her gaze fixed on a bra covered in gold sequins.

"I'm of the opinion that a woman's bra shouldn't set off metal detectors."

"Good idea." She looked up at Allie and smiled. "So you know my Grandma Louise?"

"I do. I used to go over to your dad's house for dinner sometimes many, many years ago."

"Back when you and my dad were boyfriend and girlfriend."

"That's right."

Paige blew into her own mug of tea, though Allie could see flecks of mostly melted ice cubes drifting on top. "Did my grandma make corned beef for you?"

"She did. With carrots and cabbage and baby potatoes. It was amazing."

"She still makes that. It's my favorite." Paige took a big slurp of tea. "Did your mom make corned beef, too? When my dad came over for dinner, I mean."

"My mom's not much of a cook," Allie said, crossing her fingers Paige wouldn't keep going with this line of questioning. In all honesty, Priscilla Ross had never once invited Jack to dinner. "My grandma used to make really nice dinners, though," she added. "At the bed-and-breakfast where all the cats are now. She'd make stuffed quail and coq au vin and all kinds of other pretentious-sounding foods."

"What's pretentious?"

Allie laughed. "My family. It's kind of a fancy way of saying *stuck up*."

"Pretentious," Paige repeated. "A pretentious way of saying stuck up."

"Exactly."

Paige seemed to consider that for a while. "You don't seem pretentious."

"Thanks. I've had a long time to work on it."

The girl went quiet again, and they both sipped at their tea in silence for a bit. Allie glanced at her watch. They still had ten minutes to kill.

"Did you know my mom?" Paige asked.

Allie choked on her tea. She caught herself quickly, hoping Paige wouldn't notice. "No," Allie said, coughing a little. "I never knew your mother."

She sat there stupidly, trying to think of something to say. What did someone even say to a child who'd lost her mother? Surely a smarter, more experienced woman could come up with something. Allie was drawing a blank.

But she gave it her best shot. "Do you remember your mom at all?" she asked softly.

"I think so. Maybe a little. She was pretty, like you, but her hair was kinda curly and shorter. Also, she could do this funny thing with her elbows where they bent the wrong way."

"You mean she was double-jointed?"

"Yeah," Paige said. "Me, too. Look."

The girl proceeded to demonstrate, flipping her arm back so it seemed to hinge the wrong way. Allie grimaced. "Ouch."

"Nah, it doesn't hurt." Paige flipped her arm back the right way and grinned. "My dad says my mom could do it with her shoulders, too. I don't remember that. I don't really even remember her voice."

Allie swallowed hard, utterly charmed and heartbroken for the girl all at once. "I'm sure she loved you very much."

Paige nodded. Her expression was a little wistful, but not terribly sad. "Me, too."

"I wish I'd met her." Allie realized with a start that it was true. She would have liked to know the sort of woman Jack would marry, the kind he'd choose to raise a child with, even if that plan hadn't turned out the way they expected.

She wanted to offer more, but she wasn't sure what else to say. Maybe it was best to have conversations like this in small pieces, eking out little bits of history at a time.

Paige tipped her cup up, draining the last of her tea. Allie realized she hadn't finished even half of her own drink, but they only had five minutes left until the appointment. She put the lid back on her tea and stood up. As she pushed in her chair, Paige stood up and did the same.

"You ready to do this?" Allie asked.

Paige nodded. "Yep." She smiled again, wider this time, and Allie felt a faint tug in her belly. Some thread of connection that hadn't been there thirty minutes ago.

"Let's go."

She led the way down the mall corridor and through the doors of Nordstrom. They rode the escalator up, talking more comfortably now than they had an hour ago. As Allie stepped up to the lingerie counter, Paige did likewise, standing on tiptoe so she could lean forward on her elbows.

Behind the counter, a woman in a starched white shirt and navy pencil skirt stood with her back to them, sorting through a pile of lacy push-up bras. Allie slid her keys from her purse and put them back again, hoping the small jingle would catch the woman's attention.

Nothing.

She cleared her throat. Still nothing. She glanced at the little gold bell next to the cash register, but felt rude ringing it like she was summoning a butler.

"Hi, there," she tried at last.

The woman spun around, flipping her glasses off her face and onto the counter in front of them. Paige stared at them.

"Sorry to startle you," Allie said. "We have an appointment with Eleanor for a bra fitting."

"Éléonore," the woman corrected, snatching the spectacles off the counter and situating them on her nose once more. "Not Eleanor, *Éléonore*. It's French."

"Right," Allie said, glancing down as Paige took a step closer and gave Allie a skeptical look. "We have a four-thirty appointment with *Éléonore*."

"I am Éléonore," she announced the way someone might declare herself to be the Queen of England. "And you are?"

"Allie. Allison Ross. And this is Paige Carpenter. We have an appointment to be measured for a—"

"Brassiere?"

She pronounced it with a heavy French accent, even though the rest of her speech—save her name—was perfectly American. It took Allie a moment to figure out what she was saying.

"A brassiere," Allie repeated. "Right. We need proper measurements for a brassiere."

She felt ridiculous pronouncing it in her own fake French accent, but Éléonore seemed satisfied with the request. She eyed Allie up and down and made a little *tsk-tsk* noise. "Yes, I can see you need a little help."

Allie frowned and resisted the urge to cross her arms over her chest. "The fitting isn't for me. It's for my—for—for Paige here."

Paige gave a small giggle and stepped on Allie's toe. Allie fought to keep a straight face as Éléonore shifted her attention to Paige. She peered at the girl over the top of her glasses, frowning.

"I see," said Éléonore. "How old are you, Paige?"

"Ten," Paige replied, glancing at Allie. "I'm ten, but I'll be eleven in June."

"Hmmm," Éléonore replied, now eyeing Paige. "And I suppose this is your first brassiere?"

Paige glanced at Allie, then back at Éléonore. "Um, I think so?"

"I'm going to be taking a lot of measurements today," Éléonore continued. "I trust you are comfortable with this?"

"Well, sure," Paige replied. "Are your hands cold?"

"I beg your pardon?"

"My friend, Emma, said when she went to get her bra, the lady had really cold hands. So I was just wondering if your hands were warm or cold."

"Here," Allie offered, thrusting her paper mug of tea into Éléonore's hands before the woman could object. "This might help."

Éléonore scowled, but didn't set the mug down, so Allie considered it a win. The woman looked back at Paige, still assessing.

"A good brassiere is like a fine Bordeaux," Éléonore said. "It's well-structured, elegant, and supremely smooth."

Allie gritted her teeth, wondering if she should have just taken Paige to Victoria's Secret. At least there they had some cute things, and they wouldn't be subjected to the palpable disdain of Éléonore. The woman seemed to be going out of her way to use words Paige couldn't possibly know, and that pissed Allie off.

But Paige just smiled and tossed her braid over her shoulder. "A good Bordeaux has notes of chocolate cupcake and Colgate toothpaste," she announced. "Do you have any bras with those things?"

Allie snort-laughed in a most unladylike fashion, causing Éléonore to swing her gaze back to her.

"Will you be joining us in the dressing room for the fitting?" Éléonore asked.

"Oh, um—I guess that's up to Paige."

"Yes," Paige said, reaching out for Allie's hand. "She'll be joining us."

"I see," Éléonore said. "You do understand that bra fitting is an art and not a science?"

"I like art and science both," Paige replied. "But writing is my best subject."

"Just like your dad," Allie said, squeezing the girl's hand at the memory of Jack, bleary eyed and rumpled, as he slaved over essays for college scholarships. "He used to love writing essays in high school. Everyone else hated them, but your dad—"

"And how does your mother feel about things like padding, push-up, and underwire?"

Allie blinked and glanced at Paige. Paige looked back at her, seemingly at a loss for words for the first time since Allie met her. The girl gave a tiny shrug, so Allie looked back at Éléonore. "*My* mother is in prison, but she strongly favors all of those things," she replied.

"And my mother is dead," Paige supplied. "So I don't think she cares."

Allie squeezed the girl's hand and leveled a look at Éléonore. "Why don't we just go with whatever Paige would like to have on her body?"

Éléonore looked alarmed for a moment. Then she sniffed and spun on her heel. As she marched toward the dressing room, Allie leaned down to whisper to Paige. "Are you okay? We don't have to do this if you don't want."

"I'm fine," Paige answered. "I want a bra."

"I know, but that woman—"

"Éléonore?" The girl pronounced the name with a dramatic flair, rolling her eyes as she said it.

"Éléonore," Allie repeated as the woman turned the corner into the dressing rooms. "She's a little intense."

"I can handle intense."

"I can see that," Allie said, more impressed with this kid than she'd been with anyone she'd ever met.

Paige glanced toward the dressing rooms, then back at Allie. "What's a brassiere?" she whispered.

"It's a bra for snobby people."

"Can we tell her I just want a plain old bra?"

"Definitely," Allie said, putting her arm around the girl as they started toward the dressing room. "And for the record, I don't think you need padding or push-up or any of that stuff."

"Okay. But maybe not just plain? Maybe one with stripes or lace or something."

"I'm sure that can be arranged. Only instead of stripes, we'll have to call them *rayures*. And instead of lace, we have to say *dentelle*."

"*Dentelle*," Paige repeated, trying it out. She reached up and plugged her nose, then tried again. "*Dentelle*," she tried again, sounding a lot more authentic than Allie had after four years of college French.

"Perfect," Allie said, and guided her young charge toward the dressing room.

# CHAPTER FOURTEEN

Jack felt his pulse kick up at the sound of familiar female voices outside the front door. Even though he'd seen Allie two hours ago, even though she'd texted to say they'd finished shopping, something inside him stirred with excitement at the thought of seeing her again.

Was it really less than two weeks ago that he'd sent that first email and spent the whole week filled with a different sort of anxiousness? The urge to show her up, to rub her nose in how well he'd turned out.

Now he just wanted to wrap his arms around her and kiss her and—

". . . And that lining on the inside helps conceal your nipples if it's cold out," Allie was saying as she pushed open the door. "So that's helpful for modesty."

Jack grimaced. Hearing Allie discuss nipples might have been a turn-on if she weren't talking to his preteen daughter.

"Hey, Daddy!"

"Hey, kiddo!" He held out his arms and she rushed forward so he could swoop her into a bear hug. Would she ever stop being this affectionate with the people she loved? He hoped not, but he'd gone through a definite "don't touch me" phase in middle school. Of course, that had more to do with his dickhead father walking out than with any real aversion to affection. He'd sure as hell gotten used to affection when he started dating Allie.

In the doorway, Allie stood smiling at him with her arms weighted down by shopping bags. She held something that looked like a bakery box in one hand. Seeing his gaze on it, she stepped closer and held it out. "Snickerdoodles," she said. "Paige said they're still your favorite."

There was something almost unbearably sweet about Allie remembering his favorite dessert and his daughter knowing it now, and Jack felt a wobbly lump in his throat. It almost made up for the sour feeling he'd had in his gut when he'd seen Wade back at Allie's place a few hours ago. He knew it was shitty, but something bugged him about coming face-to-face with a guy Allie had slept with, loved, planned a future with at one point in the not-so-distant past.

Jack knew he needed to get over himself, so he reached out to take the box from her. "Thank you. I suppose I have to save these until after dinner, huh?"

"Life's short," Allie said. "Eat dessert first."

"Good idea!" Paige reached for the box, but Jack swooped it up and out of her grasp.

"No way," he said. "That rule doesn't apply to growing girls."

"No fair." She pretended to pout, but Jack could see she really didn't care. "Where's Grandma?" she asked.

"She's upstairs playing with my new app that lets her race her friends to see who runs out of toilet paper first."

"Excellent," Paige said, scooping up the shopping bags Allie had set at the bottom of the stairs. "I'm going to show her my new bras."

She scampered up the stairs, leaving Jack simultaneously relieved and wistful that his little girl no longer had an interest in showing him her purchases. He got it, and truth be told, he would have been uncomfortable seeing a bunch of bras his kid planned to wear. Still, it felt strange being on the edge of this precipice into Paige's adulthood.

As soon as Paige was gone, he turned to Allie. "How'd she do?"

"Really well. I took her to a professional bra fitter at Nordy's."

"That's a real job title?"

"Yep. At first I thought the whole thing might be kind of awkward, but Paige handled it like a champ."

"I'm not surprised. She's not exactly shy."

Allie laughed. "That's putting it mildly."

"I'm sure this was the highlight of her week. Thanks for doing that."

"No problem. That's an inquisitive little girl you have there."

Jack laughed and set the bakery box on the table behind him. "Sorry. We're still working on recognizing what's appropriate to ask a stranger."

Something flickered in Allie's eyes, but her smile didn't waver. "I wouldn't say I'm a total stranger. We've been bra shopping. We've shared a snickerdoodle. We've bonded."

"Very true," Jack agreed, wishing he could tell her he hadn't meant to make her feel like an outsider. But the moment was gone, so instead he said, "Thanks again for doing that."

"It was my pleasure." Allie glanced at her watch. "I should probably get going. I was going to work on touching up the grout in all the second-floor bathrooms tonight."

"You're not staying for dinner?"

"You really want me to?"

"Of course. Why would you think otherwise?"

She seemed to hesitate, glancing toward the stairs before meeting his eyes again. "I don't know. You seemed a little . . . *bristly* earlier."

He thought about denying it. The old Jack would have. He'd have gotten defensive, maybe thrown it back on her with some stupid accusation of his own.

"Sorry," he said. "I've just got a lot on my mind."

"Want to talk about it?"

He shrugged, wondering if he should just swallow his stupid insecurity about Wade. But she'd asked, and he owed her an answer. "I don't know. Isn't it weird sometimes hanging out with a guy you used to sleep with? Someone you'd planned to marry at one point?"

Allie frowned, but seemed to consider it. "A little, I guess. But since I'm sleeping with him again now, I guess that makes it—"

"Wait, what?"

Her brow furrowed. "We're talking about you, right? About the fact that we have a history together?"

He laughed in spite of himself, shaking his head. "I wasn't, actually. But thanks for the heart attack."

"Wade?" Allie raised an eyebrow at him. "You were talking about Wade?"

"Yeah, I guess so. I know I'm being a jealous prick, but it rattled me a little. Knowing you used to be engaged to him, and that you're still so close."

"But in a different way," Allie said, reaching out to hook a finger in his belt loop. He knew she didn't mean it to be suggestive, and it wasn't. It was more possessive, and something about it made Jack relax a little.

"Besides," Allie said. "Wade is with Skye now."

"I know. Like I said, I know it's not reasonable. I'm being a jealous prick, and I'm sorry."

Allie nodded. "How's Lacey?"

The question caught him off guard, and he almost laughed. "Lacey?"

"The woman you were sleeping with up until a few weeks ago. The one who texted you just a few days ago to say, and I quote, 'Miss you and that big, thick c—'"

"How did you know about that?"

Allie smirked and tugged the belt loop. "About the text message, or about your big, thick—"

"About the text," he interrupted, though truth be told, he did sort of want to hear her take on the other thing. "How did you know about that?"

"Relax, Jack. I'm not snooping on your phone. The message popped up on your screen Sunday when you handed me your phone so I could reread that message from Paige."

"Ah," he said, wondering if Allie's casual indifference was real or a front. She'd never had the jealous streak he had, but she still used to seem bothered when he brought up his first girlfriend or when girls in his college classes touched his arm and told him he was too young to be engaged. "Lacey's fine. I think."

"Hey, it's none of my business," Allie said with a shrug. "You and I have only been hanging out for a little while. It's not like we agreed to be exclusive or anything."

Something flared in his chest. Something primal and possessive. Something that had him pulling his phone out of his pocket and flicking it on. He scrolled to *Lacey* in his text message history, then held the phone out to her.

"Read," he said.

Allie rolled her eyes. "What are you, a caveman?"

"Read," he insisted, still holding the phone out. "Please."

"Jack, I don't need some sort of reassurance that—"

"Please," he said again, softer this time. And this time, it worked.

Allie took the phone from him, and he watched her eyes move back and forth as she skimmed the words on the screen. Her forehead creased, and he couldn't tell if it was worry or confusion or something else. When she looked up, it wasn't either of those things he saw in her eyes. It was amazement. Exactly the emotion he'd hoped to see there when he'd come back to town two weeks ago, but for a different reason.

"You told her you're back together with your old girlfriend and asked her not to contact you anymore?"

He nodded and took the phone back, sliding it into his pocket as he reached for her. "That's right. I'm all in, Allie."

She seemed to hesitate, then nestled into his arms. Jack held her against his chest, thinking about how right she felt there. She tilted her head back and looked up at him, and he lost himself in those green eyes for what felt like the millionth time.

"Are you?" he asked. "All in? I mean I know we didn't talk about exclusivity or anything, and it's kinda soon, but—"

"Yes," she said, smiling up at him. "I am."

He kissed her then, so damn grateful that he almost didn't see the flicker of worry in her eyes, almost didn't feel the pang of hesitation in his own gut.

*Almost.*

♦  ♦  ♦

Allie looked up as her mother swept majestically into the room, making her grand entrance with an attractive young man by her side.

Granted, the young man was a prison guard, and Priscilla wore handcuffs instead of the thick gold bracelets she used to favor. Even so, there was a regal air to her mother's presence. Allie stood, resisting the urge to curtsy.

"Mother," she said as the guard unlocked the cuffs and gestured toward the adjacent table. Allie leaned in for the customary, brief hug they were permitted at the start of a meeting. Then they seated themselves on opposite sides of the table.

"Allison, dear, did you have someone new do your hair?"

She nodded and touched a hand to it, trying not to take it personally that the question hadn't included a compliment. "Yes, Skye. The woman Grandma hired to take care of the house."

"You let a housekeeper do your hair?"

Priscilla's tone suggested Allie might as well have allowed a busboy to perform her tonsillectomy, but Allie held her tongue on that account. "She's a student at one of the beauty schools, and she does really great work."

"Hmph. I suppose the layers do frame your face nicely."

It was the closest thing to approval that Allie was likely to get, and she sat wondering how soon she could steer the conversation to the real reason she'd come.

"I didn't expect to see you again so soon," her mother said. "It's only been ten days this time."

"Yes, but the last time was a special visit so we could talk about Grandma. This is our regularly scheduled visit."

"I see." Priscilla folded her hands on the table, her fingernails looking perfectly manicured and polished. "It's nice to see you again."

"You too, Mom." Allie glanced at the guard. He was standing a little farther away than normal, probably trying to keep a closer eye on the amorous-looking couple in the far corner. Something about the closeness between the two made her think about Jack, and she found herself blurting out the one thing she hadn't intended to tell her mother at all.

"I'm seeing Jack Carpenter again."

She looked back at her mom in time to see her eyes narrow the tiniest bit.

"Really." The word came out dry and crackly, not a question as much as a disdainful statement.

"Yes. He has a ten-year-old daughter."

Priscilla gave a familiar put-upon sigh. "And let me guess—he sees her every other weekend and complains about how much he has to pay in child support."

"No, Mother," Allie said, ordering herself to keep her tone even. "The girl's mom is dead. Jack's been raising her alone from the time she was just a baby."

That wiped the judgmental sneer off Priscilla's face. Her hands went flat on the tabletop, and the frown lines deepened around her mouth. "I'm sorry to hear that."

"And Jack's actually quite wealthy now." Allie felt annoyed with herself for saying so, for giving a damn about the fact that Priscilla would obviously care about Jack's financial status. For *caring* that Priscilla would care. Still, she couldn't seem to make herself shut up. "He's the owner of a successful app development company. I looked up the sale prices on some of the games and apps he's sold. Some have gone for well over a million dollars."

"Well," Priscilla said, looking suitably chagrined. "I guess sometimes things don't turn out exactly like you expect."

Allie nodded, clenching her own hands tight in her lap. "You're right. They don't."

Neither of them said anything for a moment. Allie studied her mom's face, noticing for the first time that they had identical lines at the corner of their eyes. She'd never seen them before on her mother, and Allie guessed it was something Priscilla had previously kept hidden with Botox. Not much of an option in prison.

Allie shot another glance at the guard, who was moving in to separate the couple now that the woman was practically sitting on the man's lap. "Break it up, you two," he said.

Allie looked back at her mother. This was her chance.

"Mom." She leaned closer, lowering her voice. "You looked more closely than Daddy did at Grandma's financials, right?"

Priscilla frowned. "Did my attorney tell you to ask about this?"

"What?" Allie blinked. "No. I mean—that's not why I'm asking."

"Why are you asking?"

"Grandma's will—your attorney was the one who prepared that, right?"

"What are you driving at, Allison?"

Allie swallowed hard. "I found something in Grandma's attic. And I'm wondering if she ever mentioned it to you."

The flicker in Priscilla's eyes was unmistakable. She knew something, Allie was sure of it.

When Allie's mother spoke again, her voice was almost a whisper. "So you found it."

"Yes." Allie hesitated. "I'm not talking about sex toys, either. Or love notes. Or collectible bongs or semen-stained Versace gowns or—"

"What on earth are you babbling on about?" Priscilla stage-whispered.

"I just wanted to make sure we're on the same page here," Allie said. "That we're talking about the same thing."

She stared into her mother's eyes, so deep and green and so much like the ones that stared back at her every time she looked in the mirror. Her mother stared back, seeming not to blink at all.

"So you found the money," Priscilla said flatly.

Allie wasn't sure she heard her right at first. Her voice was so low, and the declaration was so unexpected after this many false alarms with everyone stashing things in the attic. Allie just stared, at a loss for words.

"I'm not surprised you guessed the combination," Priscilla said slowly. "You always were a smart one. Or did you pry it open with a crowbar?"

Was that a backhanded compliment or a test of some sort? Allie gave a tight nod. "I figured out the combination."

"Good. So now you know."

"Know what?" Allie leaned forward, her hands shaking a little. "I have no idea where it came from or who it belongs to or—"

"It belongs to you, Allison," she said. "The fact that your grandmother used your birthdate as the combination should have made that obvious."

Ice sluiced through Allie's veins. She couldn't breathe for a moment. Couldn't even think of what to say next.

Which was fine, since Priscilla was still talking. "As for where it came from, that's inconsequential. The fact of the matter is that it's your inheritance. The will was very clear about that. The contents of the home, the home itself—it's all yours."

"But—but—" Allie shook her head, not sure where to start. "That kind of cash doesn't just magically appear. Where did it come from?"

"Are you questioning your grandmother's honesty, Allison?"

"Of course not," Allie said, then bit her lip. She left the rest of the words unspoken.

*I'm questioning your honesty, Mother.*

"Your grandmother was always very smart with money," Priscilla continued. "Remember when she bought up all of those properties in West Linn during the recession? She made a fortune on those deals."

"I remember," Allie said, though it had never occurred to her until now to consider who had to lose out for her family to profit. Allie cleared her throat. "So what am I supposed to do with it?"

Priscilla laughed. "Spend it, of course. I don't recommend putting it in the bank. Obviously from the way your grandmother chose to store it, she intended to have you keep it that way. A safe deposit box might be smarter, but you could always just leave it in the attic. But bottom line, it's yours to spend."

"Spend," Allie repeated, baffled by the idea of having that kind of money to her name. "I—I guess I'm just not used to the idea of having that sort of cash lying around."

Her mother made a *hrmph* sound and rolled her eyes. "No, but you might have. If life had gone differently."

Allie curled her fingers inward, digging her nails into her palms. It was possible her mom was lamenting her own incarceration, but Allie didn't think so. It sounded like a jab about her daughter's earning potential or her lack of a husband. It could have been any number of insults, but Allie didn't feel like having that argument right now. She had so many more questions to ask. She opened her mouth to voice one, but her mom cut her off.

"Have you spoken to your father lately?"

Allie hesitated. "Yes. I went to visit him a few days ago. He sends his love."

A faint smile crossed her mother's face, and Allie watched closely, wondering if it was an act or the real deal. "That's nice. And his appeal—I trust that's all going according to plan?"

"As far as I know. We don't really spend a lot of time talking about it."

Her mother raised an eyebrow. "What do you talk about?"

"Work. Family. How he's feeling."

"And how is he feeling?" The hardness in her voice was a contrast to the softness around her eyes, and Allie wondered what the hell went on behind her mom's brittle exterior.

"He's sad," Allie said. "He misses Grandma. He misses you. He misses his freedom."

Priscilla's eyes began to glitter, and she looked up at the ceiling as though contemplating the gaucheness of florescent light fixtures. "I see," she said. "You know, Allison—"

"Time's almost up, ladies!"

Allie jumped. She hadn't even noticed the guard approaching, hadn't realized they'd been talking this long. She leaned closer to her mom, wanting to say so much more. Wanting to hear more. Not words, exactly, but something else. Something that had been elusive throughout the entirety of their mother-daughter union.

But when Priscilla looked back at her, the mask was in place again.

"Take care, Allison." Her mother stood, then leaned in to air-kiss her on one cheek, then the other, her lips barely grazing Allie's skin.

◆  ◆  ◆

The money was still weighing heavily on Allie's mind the following Friday. She wanted to believe her mom. She *did* believe her mom, dammit.

Which changed whatever she had to do from a legal standpoint. She was under no obligation to report the cash. She could sit tight for a while and take her time deciding whether to invest it or tuck it in savings or pay off debts. She had plenty of options. Plenty of time.

So why did the little voice in her head keep telling her it wasn't that simple?

Well, she had other things to dwell on. Jack was coming to dinner, the first time in ages she'd see him without Skye or Paige or Wade or Jack's mom or someone else close by, making them censor their conversations and cut short the lingering touches.

This time, they had the whole evening and the whole B&B to themselves. This time, Skye was on a romantic overnight getaway in Seaside with Wade, and Paige was staying the night with a classmate. Allie had nearly twenty-four hours of alone time with Jack, and she planned to make the most of it.

She threw open the door at eight o'clock and grinned up at him. He wore a blue-gray shirt that brought out the color in his eyes, and he held a bottle of wine and a bouquet of daisies in the same hand.

"Hey, sexy," she said, stretching up on tiptoe to kiss him hard and deep.

Jack responded with enough enthusiasm to leave her breathless. By the time he'd kicked the door shut, she was halfway to shimmying out of her panties and letting the appetizer burn.

"Wait," she said, breaking the kiss and pushing against his chest. "I want you."

Jack grinned, his familiar, dimpled grin, and Allie felt herself melting. "I think you just established that," he said, setting the daisies and wine on an end table and reaching for her again.

"But I also want razor clams," she said.

"Razor clams?" Jack's hand tightened on her waist. "Fresh?"

Allie nodded. "A co-worker drove to Cannon Beach this morning. Dug up her limit in the first twenty minutes, but her dinner plans fell through at the last second. She said they'd go to waste if I didn't take them, so I couldn't say no."

"You know the way to my heart." Jack kissed her once more, then scooped up the daisies and wine and headed toward the kitchen. He had the flowers in water and the top off the wine before Allie could get the glasses out. While he filled them up, Allie pulled crisp, fragrant bread slices out from under the broiler and began rubbing each one with a clove of garlic.

"That smells amazing," Jack said as his lips brushed her neck, making Allie shiver.

"It's that bruschetta my grandma used to make," she said. "I remember you liked it."

"Loved it. I can't believe you remembered." He reached out to grab half a cherry tomato from the bowl in front of her, and Allie gave his hand a playful smack.

It felt good to be here with him in this kitchen where so many of her happiest memories lived. If they'd gotten married sixteen years ago, would Jack have ended up laced through all of those stories in Allie's mind? Would he have carved the Thanksgiving turkey with her father or helped Paige make pumpkin pie at the massive granite island?

*No, dummy. Paige wouldn't have existed if you guys had gotten married.*

The thought gave her pause, but Allie pushed it out of her mind as she ladled the tomato-basil mixture onto each piece of toast. "Want to enjoy these in the living room with a glass of wine before I put the razor clams in?"

"Perfect. I let Paige choose the wine, by the way. We decided it's bumpy with notes of kumquat and parakeet droppings."

Allie laughed. "I can't believe a ten-year-old has heard of kumquat."

"Are you kidding? She loves them."

"I'm impressed you've raised such an adventurous eater."

"We have this tradition we call Fear Factor Friday," he said, scooping up both wineglasses as Allie picked up the tray of bruschetta and led the way to the couch. "Every Friday, we try some experimental new food that maybe sounds a little weird or scary."

"Like what?"

"Oh, like stuffed grape leaves or carpaccio or whole Dungeness crab that we clean ourselves."

"What a cool idea." Allie set the plate down on the coffee table and Jack handed her a glass of wine before seating himself on the sofa.

"I think it's a big part of the reason she's never been a picky eater," he said. "From the time she was really little, I had her tasting things like artichoke and escargot and gazpacho—stuff that would make most kids turn up their noses."

"But you made it a game." Allie took a bite out of a piece of bruschetta. "Very smart."

"Thanks. Not everything's been a hit. She still hasn't forgiven me for the frog legs or the fried chicken liver."

"You win some, you lose some."

Jack laughed and popped a bite of bruschetta in his mouth. "True enough."

"You've turned out to be a pretty awesome dad."

"Thank you."

Allie finished off the bruschetta and took a sip of wine. She felt nervous all of a sudden, and it had nothing to do with Jack's hand on her bare knee.

"So," she said, dusting crumbs off her shirt as she struggled to keep her tone casual. "Speaking of parents, did I tell you I visited my mom last weekend?"

"You did, but we never got a chance to talk about it. How's she doing?"

"Good. She's good." Allie cleared her throat. "I finally got a chance to ask her about the money."

Jack picked up another piece of bruschetta and didn't say anything. Allie watched him chew slowly, and she wondered if this was his way of buying himself some time, of not blurting out the first thing he thought. He was still touching her knee, so that seemed like a good sign.

"And did she know about the money?" Jack asked.

235

"Yes," Allie said. "She did."

"Let me guess." Jack picked up his wineglass and swirled it around, his expression more guarded than it had been five minutes ago. "Your mom told you the money's yours free and clear. That you should just spend it and not worry about things. Is that about right?"

Allie gritted her teeth and fought the urge to argue. So what if he'd used almost the exact words her mother had? She took a small sip of wine, willing herself not to react. "That is what she told me."

"Did she say where it came from?" Jack asked. "Or did a million dollars cash miraculously drop from the sky?"

Allie frowned. "Why are you being so snarky about this? The money was in my grandmother's home—a home she willed to me, along with its contents. The combination on the chest was my birthdate. Don't you think that adds up?"

"You're kinda dodging the real issue here."

"Which is?"

"Which is the fact that no one's saying where the money came from." He took a bite of bruschetta, and Allie wondered if they were both continuing to sip and eat as a way to make this whole conversation feel less acrimonious than it really was. Jack was still touching her leg, and they sat close together on the sofa.

Allie took a deep breath. Sixteen years ago, this would have been a fight by now. She was determined not to let it escalate. "My family has a history of making a lot of money," she said. "My grandfather made a killing on Portland real estate in the eighties."

"And your parents made a killing on unsuspecting investors thirty years later. Just because they made a lot of money doesn't make it legit."

Allie frowned. "Maybe we should talk about something else."

His palm curved over her leg, and the look he gave her was almost sympathetic. "Allie. I know you always love to believe the rosiest, happiest version of a story, but don't you think you're taking it a little far here?"

"No, I don't." She narrowed her eyes. "Don't you think you're being a little suspicious?"

Jack sighed and took a sip of wine. He didn't say anything for a long time, and Allie began to fidget. She picked up a piece of bruschetta, then set it down again.

When Jack spoke again, his voice was softer. "I have a legal team on retainer for my company. They usually work on stuff related to app development, but I asked them to help me with a little legal research a couple days ago."

"Oh?" she tried to sound casual, but her hands were shaking.

"I had them pull up information on Oregon's found-property laws."

"You mean the same information Wade dug up for me?"

"Right," Jack said, his voice even. "I wanted to read it for myself. Have you read the whole text of ORS Chapter 98?"

Allie nodded. "Yes."

"So you know what it says about your obligation to provide notice to the county clerk within ten days and in the newspaper within twenty days."

"I read the laws," Allie said, doing her best to summon the lawyer voice she'd worked on up until she'd dropped out of law school. "But the notification rules only apply if you don't know who the money belongs to. And I know now that it belonged to my grandmother. And now to me."

Jack raised an eyebrow. "On your mother's say-so."

"And the fact that my own birthdate was the combination on the lock. Doesn't that seem significant?"

"Maybe not as significant as the fact that the amount in that trunk isn't too far off the mark of what was unaccounted for during your parents' trial."

She shouldn't have been surprised he'd know the details. It had been in the paper, of course. Still, she hadn't expected him to go reading up on old court cases and statutes Allie would just as soon forget.

"Look, Allie—I'd love for that money to be yours. I really would."

"It's not about that, Jack." Allie heard her voice start to quiver, but she was determined not to get choked up. "I'm not counting out fistfuls of hundreds and thinking about buying Prada handbags and a condo in Lake Oswego."

"So what is it about?"

Allie sighed. "It's about wanting to believe that's not dirty money. That my family did something good by leaving it to me. That my grandma really cared that much."

He didn't say anything for a long time. When he finally spoke, his voice was softer. "I understand what you're saying. But I'm just trying to keep you safe. To make sure you're acting within the parameters of the law. That we both are. You know this affects me, too. I was there when you found that money."

"I know that. And I also know it's been fourteen days when the law says I'm supposed to do something within ten."

"Right." Jack sighed. "You and I are the only two people who know the exact dates, though. I'm fine keeping quiet a little longer to buy you some more time, but you should really—"

"Wade knows about the money." The second the words left her mouth, Allie watched Jack's expression darken. "He's a lawyer. I had to talk to someone."

"Isn't he a divorce attorney?"

"He still knows the law. And he's done some work in estate planning and even criminal cases."

Jack pressed his lips together for a second. "I think I'd feel better if you consulted someone else. I can have someone from my legal team talk with you at no charge."

"I appreciate that," Allie said. "And I'll certainly consider it."

"I'm glad."

"Can you tell me something, though?" Allie cleared her throat. "Is this because Wade doesn't specialize in this type of law, or is this because I was engaged to Wade?"

Jack looked down into his wineglass, but didn't take a sip. When he looked up again, the silver-blue of his eyes seemed darker. "A little of both," he admitted. "But also that you didn't tell me about the engagement until right before we slept together. Not even when we were baring our souls over whipped cream and mud masks that night or when I was spilling all my intimate stories on the way to my reunion."

"You're right," Allie said softly. "I suppose I should have mentioned it sooner."

Jack sighed again. "I guess it doesn't help that you're still so close with a guy you used to sleep with. A guy you loved and made plans with and thought you'd spend your whole life with at one point. I'm working on the jealousy thing, Al, but it'll probably always bug me just a little."

Allie felt something soften inside her. She put her hand on his, and Jack's gaze swung back to hers. "You're forgetting something, though," she said.

"What's that?"

"I might have loved Wade once. Not the right way, exactly, but it was a kind of love. I might have even loved those other two guys I was engaged to."

He raised one eyebrow. "Is this supposed to be helping?"

Allie leaned close and brushed her lips over the edge of his jaw. "I've never loved any of them *twice*. But I'm falling for you all over again, Jack. Maybe even harder this time."

She drew back in time to see his eyes widen ever so slightly. Allie felt her heart slamming against her ribs. Maybe it was too soon to start trotting out the L-word. She hadn't flat-out said she loved him, but close. Maybe she'd said it too soon or—

"I'm right there with you." Jack smiled. "I've been feeling it since the moment you opened your apartment door."

Allie grinned as a rush of warmth flooded through her. "I'm so glad."

He squeezed her hand. "And I want us to be smart this time around. Honesty and trust and open communication."

Relief washed through her, warmed by the simple bliss of hearing those words. Of knowing he felt the same way she did. That maybe they really could have a second chance to get things right this time.

Jack leaned in to kiss her again, and Allie met him halfway. She slid her fingers into his hair, loving the feel of his chest pressed against hers, his breath coming faster as she ran a hand up his thigh.

Jack kissed her hard and deep with an urgency that left her breathless. Allie closed her eyes and tipped her head back, savoring the gentle brush of kisses down the middle of her throat. As pleasure coursed through her, his words were still echoing in the back of her mind.

*Honesty and trust and open communication.*

But for now, she pushed them aside, and reached up to unbutton Jack's shirt.

# CHAPTER FIFTEEN

Jack woke up sometime around three in the morning. At first, he couldn't remember where he was. The sheets felt softer than his own, and the room smelled like lavender and furniture polish. He kept his eyes closed while his brain fumbled groggily for a location or the reason he'd woken up in the first place. Was Paige okay? Did she have a stomachache or need a glass of water or—

A soft hand skimmed over his chest and Jack opened his eyes, then relaxed under Allie's touch. He felt his heartbeat slowing, then speeding up again as he remembered what they'd spent the last couple hours doing, and why he wouldn't mind doing it again. Rolling toward her, he kissed her bare shoulder, then her collarbone, then the soft little hollow under her ear.

Allie smiled in her sleep, but kept her face buried in her pillow. "Mwahter mpho?" she mumbled.

"What?"

She rolled her face toward him, but didn't open her eyes. "Was that your phone buzzing?"

It dawned on Jack that maybe that's what had woken him up. He spotted the device on the nightstand and stretched over Allie to grab it.

His thoughts reeled with worst-case scenarios. Maybe Paige had gotten hurt at the sleepover, or maybe his mom had fallen or—

His brain skidded to a halt as he read the words on the screen. He stared at them for a few moments, opening and closing his eyes a few times to clear his vision. Without a word, he set the phone facedown on the nightstand and laid back down beside Allie. He pulled her against him so they were face-to-face in the darkness, then stroked a hand over her hip.

"I just missed a call from my father."

He spoke the words quietly, almost as though he hadn't committed to saying them aloud. They dropped like bricks onto the bed between them, cold and unfamiliar in the dim glow of the clock radio.

He watched Allie's eyes flutter open, and she stared at him for a few beats, studying his face. Jack kept stroking the side of her body, soothing himself with the feel of her skin.

"Your father?" Allie murmured. "I didn't realize you were in contact with him."

"I'm not," Jack said. "I spoke to him once sixteen years ago. Then again ten years ago."

Her brow furrowed as the timeline seemed to register. She reached up and brushed the hair off his forehead, but she didn't ask anything. Didn't push for details about the call just now or the ones in the past. Something about that made him feel safe. Trusted. Loved.

So Jack found himself spilling the details. "You know he left when I was six and I didn't talk to him after that."

"Right," Allie murmured, still touching the side of his face. "I don't remember him calling a single time when we were together. Not on your birthdays or when you graduated from high school or when we got engaged."

Jack took a deep breath. "I called him about two weeks after you and I split up. I was floundering and not sure what to do. I thought maybe he'd have some sort of fatherly advice to offer."

"Did he?"

Jack snorted. "Not especially. Told me to pull my head out of my ass, which was probably sound advice in retrospect."

"But probably not what you needed to hear right then."

"Exactly." Jack breathed in and out in the silence, taking himself back to the next time he'd called. It was six years later, and he'd been in a much different place.

"I called again to invite him to my wedding," he said. "Caroline was pregnant, and I was excited about that. Excited about graduating from college. I just felt like life was coming together for me. I was the first college grad in the family and I was going to be a father. I guess I wanted my own father to know that."

"That makes sense." She drew her hand down over his shoulder, her movements slow like she was soothing a cat. Jack's hand was still on her hip, and there was something so intimate about talking this way in the darkness, about touching each other with such familiarity. "So how did that conversation go?" she asked.

Jack breathed in and out again, savoring Allie's palm gliding over his shoulder. "It took him a second to even recognize my voice," he said. "Then before I could even tell him anything, he said, 'Let me guess— you either knocked someone up, you need money, or both.'"

"Jesus," Allie said. "What did you say?"

Jack shook his head, feeling the sting of those words all over again. "I hung up. I never told him anything. Not about the wedding or the graduation or about Paige."

"You mean he doesn't know he's a grandfather?"

He shrugged as Allie skimmed the back of her hand over the side of his face. "I don't think so," he said. "I never told him, anyway." He swallowed hard and stopped stroking her hip. He let his hand rest there, palm cupping the smooth roundness. "The thing is, he wasn't totally wrong. I *had* knocked someone up. And deep down, I was kind of hoping he'd offer to loan me money. Maybe for a down payment or to help with the wedding or something."

"That's not so far-fetched," Allie said. "After a decade of not paying child support, it's the least he could have done for you."

He sighed. "Even so, I guess he was right about me after all."

"Jack, no." Her hand drifted up to his jaw again, and he leaned into her touch the same way he found himself leaning into her words. "Look at everything you've done for yourself, without the tiniest bit of help from him. You have a good education, an amazing career, an awesome kid. And that last one is all you. You managed to become a great dad without any dad of your own as a role model."

He closed his eyes, letting her words and her touch calm him. He was suddenly more tired than he'd been in weeks, or maybe months. He felt himself starting to drift off to sleep.

Allie's voice pulled him back. "Did he leave a voicemail?"

Jack opened his eyes, disoriented again. He reached over and picked up the phone again, then squinted at the screen. "Yep," he said. "One new voicemail."

He could see her face in the glow from his phone screen, and he watched her throat move as she swallowed. "Do you want to know what it says?"

Jack stared at the screen. His thumb hovered over the options. *Play. Call back. Delete.*

He stared at them, watching as his vision blurred and the choices jumbled together. *Play. Call back. Delete.*

"No," he said.

Then he pressed his thumb to the screen, making his choice with a single touch.

*Delete.*

The words vanished from the screen, and Jack set the phone back down on the nightstand, then pulled Allie against him.

♦  ♦  ♦

The next time Jack woke up, light was seeping through his eyelids despite the faded brocade drapes Allie had drawn the night before. With his eyes still closed, he reached out for her, craving the feel of her skin and the warmth of her body on a lazy Saturday morning.

But his palm found only the empty sheet.

He opened his eyes and glanced at the clock on the wall. It was just after seven, which seemed odd. Allie had never been a morning person, preferring to snooze until ten or eleven in their cozy little college apartment.

He looked over at the door to the bathroom and saw it wide open. While Allie might have changed a lot over the years, there was no way she'd ever be a woman who'd pee with the door open. He glanced around the room, taking inventory. Her phone was on the nightstand, right next to his. He thought about the deleted voicemail from his father and felt a cold tingle in the center of his chest.

He rolled over, putting his back to the phone and looking around for more traces of warmth. He couldn't remember what Allie had been wearing the night before, but the clothes he'd been wearing were folded neatly on a chair beside the bed. He remembered Allie pulling the shirt off his shoulders, yanking at the buttons like his sleeves were on fire. The thought made him smile.

Feeling warmer now, he rolled over again and grabbed his phone, intending to send an "I love you" text to Paige or maybe scroll through Facebook while he waited for Allie to return.

Instead, he found himself staring at a text message from his father. *Please call. I've been a shitty dad, but I have something to tell you.*

Jack stared at the words, breathing in and out while he waited to see how they'd register with him. He felt—*nothing*. Absolutely nothing. Not anger, not sadness, not nostalgia. Just a total absence of any feeling whatsoever.

He started to delete the message, then stopped. Maybe he'd want to reply later. Something terse and unsentimental, or maybe a dismissive note saying he was much too busy for phone calls.

Pushing thoughts of his father from his mind, Jack sat up and ran his fingers through his hair. Maybe Allie got hungry and decided to make breakfast, or maybe she was watching YouTube videos about caulking bathtubs or polishing doorknobs. It wasn't outside the realm of possibility that she was refinishing the dining room table right now.

He got up and pulled his jeans on, not bothering with shoes or a shirt. It was warm in the house, and as far as he knew, the two of them had the place to themselves until evening.

"Allie?"

His voice bounced off the parlor walls as he moved into the kitchen. No sign of her there, though he noticed she'd cleaned up after their midnight razor clam binge.

He moved from room to room, scoping out the whole first floor before heading upstairs to poke around the second floor.

"Allie?"

Still no response, but he felt a gust of cool air as he emerged onto the third floor. He glanced up to see the attic door open and the ladder propped beneath it.

He made his way to it, keeping his steps quiet as he climbed. It was chillier up here, and he was already regretting not pulling on his shirt or socks. He suppressed a shiver as he boosted himself through the opening and looked around.

Allie was leaning against the trunk, and Jack felt a flicker of annoyance. Two weeks, and the trunk full of cash was still just sitting there.

She had her back to it, and it seemed symbolic somehow. Like she hoped it might vanish altogether if she pretended it wasn't there.

She looked up then, and her green eyes went wide. Then she smiled. "Jack. You startled me. Everything okay?"

Something about her smile seemed off, but maybe it was just early. He clambered the rest of the way into the attic and padded across the beams to sit beside her. She wore a beige cashmere cardigan that looked like something her mother might've owned, and Jack brushed the fabric aside to plant a kiss on her bare shoulder.

"You're up early," he murmured as he slid the cashmere back in place.

"A woodpecker woke me up right at dawn," she said. "Figured I'd come up here and get some work done."

He looked down to see an old cigar box in her lap. "Are those the love letters?" he asked. "The ones your dad told you about?"

"Actually, no. They belonged to my grandmother. I was kind of hoping I'd find something referencing the money."

"Any luck?"

She shook her head. "No, but I did stumble over some interesting stuff. Apparently she worked as a burlesque performer before she met my grandpa."

Jack laughed. "No kidding?"

"Nope. I'm not even sure my parents knew about it. Also, she may or may not have had an affair with Ernest Hemingway sometime in the late forties. I'm still reading to figure it out."

Jack let his gaze stray to the trunk, and he felt his smile starting to fade. "I guess you've got a lot of secrets buried up here in this attic."

He stared at the trunk for a few more seconds, hoping she'd get the message. Hoping she'd acknowledge the need to do the right thing, the *legal* thing. She had to know that was her only option, didn't she?

But Allie wasn't looking at him. She was looking down at the box in her lap, a pair of lines creasing the fair skin between her brows.

"Allie?"

"Yeah?" She looked up, and Jack watched the mask fall into place. Her expression was completely bland, so devoid of emotion she was almost serene. She was so convincing, he almost believed she was just fine. But Jack knew better.

"What's on your mind?" he asked.

He reached up to tuck a few strands of hair behind her ear. She was beautiful like this with no makeup and her cheeks flushed with the cold air. He expected her to blow off his question, or to tell him she was just tired.

Instead, she took a deep breath and glanced at him again. "You remember what you were saying last night? About honesty and trust and open communication?"

Jack nodded as a slither of ice crept down his arms. "Yes."

"I want that, too." Her gaze dropped to her lap again. "Moving forward. I don't want there to be any secrets between us. Anything else kept hidden in the attic."

Jack glanced at the trunk again, but something told him that's not what she meant. Seeming to read his mind, Allie shot a glance over her shoulder.

"It's not about the money, Jack. I'll deal with that later—" She paused, probably waiting for him to chide her for the undefined *later*. Jack held his tongue, waiting for the other shoe to drop.

"So what is it?" he finally asked.

She looked up, and something in those dark-green eyes made his heart stop cold. She held his gaze for a moment, and it seemed as though neither of them was breathing.

"There's something else I need to tell you." Her voice was barely audible, less audible than the sound of her swallowing. "Something that happened sixteen years ago."

The ice floes in Jack's veins turned sluggish, and he felt like he'd stopped breathing altogether. He knew whatever came out of her mouth next was going to be bad. A game changer. He had the same feeling he'd had that day she'd walked into the living room and stared down at him sitting on their old futon. She'd leveled him with a look that chilled him to the bone, even now, all these years later.

As he looked into those dark-green eyes now, he had the distinct sensation of sinking.

"Okay," he said. "Let's hear it."

# CHAPTER SIXTEEN

Allie's pulse was pounding so hard she thought her brain might explode. Her hands had started to shake, so she pressed her palms together and slid them between her knees. She couldn't look at Jack. Couldn't meet his eyes at all if she wanted to get these words out.

"Allie?" he said. "What is it? What did you need to tell me?"

Something about his tone told her he already knew it would be bad. She just had to say the words. Just had to put them out there so he could know everything and they could put it behind them and move on.

She wasn't sure where to start, so she took a deep breath and dove in.

"Back in college, I was thinking about ending things between us for three or four months before I actually did it." She spoke the words slowly, her gaze still fixed on her knees. "I just kept thinking we were in different places in our lives and it didn't feel right. I'd start to get up the nerve to do it, but then you'd go and do something sweet like putting together one of your treasure hunts, and I'd start thinking things would work out okay."

Jack didn't say anything, but reached over and rested a hand on her thigh. It was a comforting gesture, one she probably didn't deserve. She dared a glance at him, and saw his expression was guarded.

"You cheated on me." His voice was flat.

Allie sat up straighter and shook her head. "No. No, that's not it."

"I can handle it if that's what happened, Allie. I mean, it was a long time ago, and I always wondered about you and that guy from your chem lab—"

"No!" Her voice sounded sharp, and she took a few deep breaths to soften it before she spoke again. "I swear, Jack. There was never anyone else."

"Then what?"

Allie took a shaky breath. She had to just say it. It was time to put it out there, to stop keeping secrets. *Honesty and trust and open communication.* Isn't that what he'd said?

"So six or seven weeks before we broke up, I realized I was a few days late. My cycle was always like clockwork, so I knew something was up. I thought it was stress at first. We had midterms and I was having doubts about us, so I guess I just tried to convince myself it was nothing."

"Oh." A stunned silence followed, and she knew he was putting the pieces together. "It wasn't nothing."

The words weren't a question, and Allie knew he'd already figured it out. Part of it anyway. She pressed on, needing to tell him the whole story. "It wasn't nothing," she confirmed. "Still, I waited a few more weeks. I guess I thought—well, I suppose I was in denial. I just kept thinking things would turn out fine, that it was just stress or a side effect of being new to birth control pills. I spent almost a month trying to pretend nothing was wrong. That it was all going to be okay."

She waited for him to point out that was what she'd always done. Just buried her head in the sand and hoped for the happily-ever-after that never came. He didn't say it. He didn't say anything at all.

Allie took a shaky breath and continued. "Anyway, I bought a test at that drugstore by our apartment. The one with the—"

"It came up positive."

251

She nodded, squeezing her fingers together. "Yes."

He was silent again, and Allie finally got up the courage to look at him. Her heart squeezed tight in her chest like someone had wrapped a rubber band around it. Jack's expression was blank, but a tiny muscle twitched along his jaw. She wanted to reach up and smooth it with the tips of her fingers, but she kept her hands pressed tight together between her knees. She could feel his hand tensing on her thigh, but she couldn't read his expression at all.

"You never told me," he said.

"I didn't." Her voice was practically a whisper. "I knew if I told you, you'd convince me to stay. You were so hell-bent on getting married and starting a family while we were young. I knew you'd talk me into going through with it."

"Going through with it," he repeated.

His face had gone a little paler. Maybe it was the cold, but Allie didn't think so. She'd been holding back the tears up to that point, but she felt them pooling in her eyes now. She blinked hard and looked up at an overhead shelf until her vision cleared. She took another breath.

"I made the appointment that weekend you went to that music festival at the Gorge. I went by myself. I didn't tell anyone. There was this counselor who stayed with me the whole time, but I didn't feel like talking about things, so I mostly just talked about law school applications and the high price of olive oil and whether or not the Blazers would go to the playoffs." The words tumbling out of her mouth sounded absurd and jumbled, so she forced herself to take a few deep breaths. "After it was over, I caught a taxi back to our apartment. I felt nauseated for the first couple days, but after that I was mostly back to normal. By the time you came back from Washington—"

"You had an abortion."

Allie gave a slow nod. She was struck by the abruptness of his words. By his need to say them aloud. To put them out there in the hollow, chilly air between them. She'd never done that, not once in sixteen years.

"You had an abortion without talking to me about it," he said. "Even though we lived together. Even though we slept in the same bed every night. Even though we were talking about spending our *lives* together at that point."

"Jack, I know," she said, and her voice sounded too high to her.

She'd always wondered if the story might affect him like this. She'd guarded the secret so tightly that she'd almost put it out of her mind. But he was hearing about it for the first time. She reminded herself of that. That he'd been a part of things, too, even though he hadn't known.

She forced herself to meet his eyes, to not look away this time. The silver-blue irises glittered in a sharp streak of sunlight that slashed through the chilled air. His eyes weren't cold. They weren't even angry. They were the eyes of someone who'd just watched a close friend run over his dog, then back up and do it again.

"I'm sorry," she said, and her words were barely a whisper.

She glanced down at his hand on her thigh, studying the ridges and bumps and the little scar he'd gotten on that long-ago camping trip. With no matches or lighter, he'd tried to start the fire by rubbing two sticks together. He'd rubbed and rubbed and rubbed for what seemed like hours, but hadn't even made smoke that way. Just a gash in his hand when he slammed the sticks down in frustration. The futility of it made her want to cry, though she knew that's not where the tears were coming from at all.

When Jack finally spoke, his voice came out crackly. "I'm sorry you went through that," he said. "I—I guess I don't know what to say. It must have been hard."

Allie nodded again, not trusting herself to form words.

"I imagine it was scary and sad to go through that alone," he said, and she nodded again like a dumb puppet.

He drew his hand back, breaking contact with her for the first time since this conversation began. Allie felt herself shiver. He didn't say anything else. Not for a long time.

"We went looking at wedding venues that week," he said.

Allie looked up, surprised he'd remembered that detail. "Yes. I—I guess we did."

"It was that same week," he said. "Because I'd loved that damn concert at the Gorge so much I suggested we find a place near that. But you wanted to keep the wedding closer to home. I remember you saying that. That you wanted it to be a place that held meaning for both of us."

"That's right," Allie said, wondering why she'd forgotten until now.

"We must have visited six or seven places that week. And you went through it all knowing you wanted to split up," he said. "So much so that you hid a pregnancy from me. An abortion."

Allie's eyes were stinging and her throat felt thick and tender. "I'm sorry."

He dragged his fingers through his hair, and the helplessness of the gesture pulled the breath out of her lungs.

"Allie," he said, and the crack in his voice made her chest ache. "I can't believe you didn't tell me. I would have wanted to know. To be involved. To at least talk with you or comfort you or—"

"I understand," she said. "But Jack—I made the best decision I could at the time. I knew we couldn't get married, and I didn't trust myself not to cave if you begged me. Don't you see? I couldn't have done things any differently."

She watched his throat move as he swallowed. Then he gave a sad little headshake. "That's not what bothers me most, Allie. Not the abortion. Not what happened sixteen years ago. I'm bothered about *now*."

"What do you mean?"

"This—this—pattern. This habit of hiding things. Of cheerfully going through the motions and covering up anything that doesn't fit the story you've written in your mind."

"I don't—"

"You do," he said, hurt still flashing in his eyes. "You pretended Wade was your fiancé, and then you said you were just friends. Only it turns out he actually *was* your fiancé at one point, and you neglected to mention it. And then there's this money—" He gestured toward the chest, a wild look in his eye. "Were you even going to tell me about the reporting requirements? About the fact that I'm as legally bound as you are to report it to authorities?"

"I thought if I just waited—"

"How long?" he demanded. "How long are you planning to sit on this, Allie? To pretend it's not here? To convince yourself of some ridiculous fairy tale about your grandmother squirreling it away instead of accepting that your parents are thieves and this money is part of that."

The words felt like a kick to the chest. Allie blinked back the tears, struck by the fact that he was right.

"Jack," she whispered. "I'm sorry. I should have said something."

Her apology sounded hollow, and she wasn't even sure what she was apologizing for. Wade? The money? For not telling him about the pregnancy? All of it?

He was staring at the trunk again, though she sensed he wasn't really seeing it. She could tell his mind was someplace else, someplace outside this attic, outside this moment entirely.

When he met her eyes again, it was like he'd already left the room.

"It's always going to be like that, isn't it?" he asked softly.

"Like what?"

"You covering up anything that doesn't mesh with the perfect version of events that you've mapped out in your mind. You with all your secrets and me sitting here wondering when you plan to clue me in or drop the next bombshell."

"Jack, no." She shook her head, though she couldn't think of any argument to counter what he'd just said. "I can earn your trust, Jack. Please. I can work on it."

"I don't think so," he said. "You've had a long time to figure out how to be forthcoming, Allie. If it doesn't come naturally for you, it's never going to."

"But we all have secrets, Jack."

"I know that. And I don't need to know every last deep, dark secret in the bottom of your soul. Everyone has things they keep private. But I can't spend my life worrying that you're leading this parallel existence and keeping me out of it."

Allie was still struggling to think of what to say when he stood up. The sight of him towering over her, shirtless and distraught, was enough to undo her. She felt a tear slide down her cheek, and she swiped at it with the back of her hand.

"I'm sorry, Allie. I'm sorry for what happened sixteen years ago. I'm sorry you felt like you had to go through that alone." She watched his throat move as he swallowed, seeming to force himself to form more words. "And I'm sorry this was painful for you to tell me just now. I appreciate you finally letting me know."

"Jack—" She reached her hand up, imploring him to take it. Willing him to sit back down and talk through this.

His gaze dropped to her hand and stayed there for a few heartbeats. He didn't take it. Then he met her eyes again.

"I can't be pulled back into this," he said. "Into the secrets and the half-truths and the need to ignore anything that disrupts the storyline." He swallowed again, and she saw his eyes glittering in the sunlight streaming through the dormer window. "I'm sorry, Allie. I can't."

With that, he turned and walked away.

◆　◆　◆

For more than a week, Jack ignored his phone.

He used it to swap "I love you" texts with Paige, and to find out when she needed to be picked up from a playdate. He even used it to test apps for his company, now that most of his crew was up and running in the new Portland office.

But the calls from Allie went straight to voicemail.

So did the ones from his father, who had continued to send messages imploring him to get in touch.

The irony wasn't lost on Jack. The thing that made him angriest with Allie was the same damn thing he was doing now. Avoiding conflict. Pretending things were peachy-fucking-keen when they weren't at all. When there was a giant, gaping hole in the middle of his chest that he knew damn well hadn't been there the last time he and Allie split up. He didn't know why it seemed to ache more this time around, but it did.

But she'd *lied* to him, dammit. Not just sixteen years ago, when he distinctly remembered her telling him she needed to skip the concert to study for exams. She'd lied about Wade. She'd lied about the money. Lying by omission—by *avoidance*. That was still lying in Jack's book. It was something he couldn't live with day in, day out, for the rest of his life.

"Daddy, you're doing it again."

Jack snapped his attention back to his daughter. She was sitting across the dining room table twirling a rainbow-striped game spinner and giving him a look of mild annoyance. They were playing Life, a board game she loved almost as much as he had at her age.

"I'm doing what?" he asked.

"You're wrinkling the money." She reached over to pry two paper bills from his hand. "You've already put wrinkles in three fifty-thousand-dollar bills."

Jack frowned. "Have I pointed out that's not an actual form of currency in the real world? Like you probably shouldn't expect to put a down payment on a home with a single bill."

Paige rolled her eyes, giving him a glimpse of the teenager she'd be very soon. "You've mentioned that several thousand times. Now stop being a grump and hand me an action card."

"Say please," Jack said as he flipped the top card off the stack. "And I'm not being a grump. I'm stewing."

"*Please*," Paige repeated, and at first Jack thought she was being sarcastic about his grumpiness, which he should probably own. But she was just taking his cue about the manners, which Jack would have noticed if he weren't so busy stewing. "And thank you," she added as she studied the card he'd handed her. "It says, 'Ballet rehearsal: Pick an opponent. Both twirl like a ballerina and spin.'"

"It does not say that."

"Does so."

She held the card out to him, and Jack heaved a sigh. "I swear they never made us do stuff like this in the old version of the game."

"Things change," Paige said as she hopped out of her chair looking positively giddy. "Get used to it."

Jack stood, too, and he had to admit it was tough to stay grumpy with a ten-year-old twirling in circles in front of him. He lifted his hands over his head and spun in his best approximation of a pirouette. His elbow smacked the bookcase, and he felt mildly dizzy, but he found himself smiling.

Paige finished her dance, then plunked down and twirled the spinner. "Eight!" she announced.

Jack spun and got a five.

"That's another fifty Gs for me," Paige announced. "Plus a hundred K at the end."

"When did you start talking like a ten-year-old gangsta?"

She grinned. "Your turn, Daddy."

Jack spun, then moved his game piece six spaces to the *get married* spot. He caught himself wincing before he had a chance to stifle the reaction. If his daughter noticed, she didn't say anything. Just handed him a pink peg to stick in his blue plastic car.

"You have to spin for wedding cash now," Paige ordered.

"Yes, ma'am." Jack fumbled his new wife into the slot, feeling awkward and distracted and totally fucking useless.

The pointer landed on a black space, so Paige forked over a hundred thousand dollars and took her turn spinning. "Another action card," she announced. She stretched across the table to grab it this time instead of waiting for him, which was probably smart. "'Fired for sneaking your cat into work,'" she read. "'Return your career card to its deck, shuffle the deck, and take the top two cards.' Awesome, I get a new job!"

"Good," Jack said. "I think that police officer thing was going to your head."

"Says the guy who picked 'Fashion Designer' over 'Pilot.'"

"What? I need a creative profession."

That earned him another eye roll. "Remember what Grandma said about not taking the game so literally?"

She pronounced it *lit*-rall-ee—three syllables instead of four, another one of Caroline's quirks. How had his wife done that? Managed to infuse her infant daughter with linguistic idiosyncrasies through eighteen months of murmured lullabies and bedtime stories? It was a trick Jack would never understand, but there was a soft comfort in hearing his late wife's voice tripping from their daughter's tongue. It assured him he'd managed to do something good in choosing a mate and a life and a—

"I think I'll be a rocket scientist," Paige announced. "And before you say it, I know that's going to be hard with four kids."

"Not if you've got a partner pulling his share of the weight."

She stared at him, then shook her head. "It's a game, Daddy."

"Right." Jack spun for his turn, landing on a stop sign that ordered him to choose between *Family Plan* and *Life Path*. For chrissakes, what was this? A fucking Ouija board? He hesitated.

He was still hesitating when his phone buzzed on the table beside him. It was facedown on the table, and he resisted the urge to look at it. Paige's eyes darted to the phone and Jack watched her brow furrow. "You're not going to answer?"

"Nope. I'm with you. Remember how we discussed staying focused on the people you're with in real life and not blowing them off for the people on your phone?"

"Yeah. I just thought—" She stopped there, biting her lip. "I thought it might be Allie."

"It might be," he admitted as the phone fell silent. "But we talked about this, remember? Allie and I decided it would be best if we stopped seeing each other."

Paige glanced at the phone again and frowned. "You both decided, or just *you* decided?"

He tried not to flinch. She'd asked the question without any trace of judgment, but he felt guilty anyway. He leaned back in his chair and sighed.

"Look," he said at last. "Sometimes it just works out that one person just can't stay with another person no matter how much they might both wish it were different. That's just the way life works."

His daughter stared at him, fiddling with her plastic car. She seemed not to notice she'd just dumped out her boy-and-girl twins, landing one in the path of an oncoming vehicle and the other in the middle of the ocean.

"When you were boyfriend and girlfriend with Allie before, who did the breaking up?"

Jack swallowed. "You mean sixteen years ago? You're asking if Allie broke up with me or if I broke up with Allie?"

Paige nodded and grabbed one of the twins by the head before jamming it back into the car. "Yeah. Did you break up with her, or did she break up with you?"

"She broke up with me," he admitted. "Sixteen years ago, I still had a lot of things to figure out."

His daughter seemed to consider that for a moment as she stabbed the other twin into the backseat. "So did you break up with Allie this time?"

Jack hesitated. *Honesty*, he thought. *You promised her honesty.*

"Yes," he said. "This time, I broke up with Allie."

He braced himself for the question. For the "why" he knew was coming. But that wasn't the next word out of his daughter's mouth.

"So you're even," she said. "And now you can make up."

The simplicity of it was so sweet it made his chest ache. "It doesn't work that way, honey. I wish it did, but—"

"But what? I know you love Allie and Allie loves you. It *should* work that way. It just should."

Her voice quivered a little, and Jack put his hand on hers. "It should," he said. "You're right. But one thing I've learned in life is that it's pretty frustrating to spend your time hung up on how things *should* work. To get so invested in how you thought things would go that you forget to deal with the way things really are."

Paige stuck the end of her braid in her mouth and looked at him. He wondered how much of it she understood. How much any of it really meant to her.

Hell, Jack wasn't sure *he* understood.

At last, Paige got out of her chair, came around the table, and put her arms around him. "I love you, Daddy."

Jack's chest felt tight as he wrapped his arms around her and hugged hard. "I love you, too, sweetie. So much."

He breathed her in, feeling simultaneously hollow and filled to the point of bursting. He gave her a quick squeeze, making her squeak a little.

"Daddy!" She giggled and sprung back, whacking his phone with her elbow. They both watched as the gadget flipped end over end, coming to rest with a smack on the hardwood floor.

Jack looked at the screen, then at his kid. "You are *so* lucky right now that I spent the extra eighty bucks for the LifeProof case."

"Sorry."

"It's okay," he said, planting a kiss on her forehead. "Things happen."

The phone began to buzz again, and Jack lunged for it. But he wasn't fast enough. Paige grabbed it first, glancing at the screen as she held the phone out to him.

"Who's Deadbeat Dickhead?" she asked.

Jack gave an inward groan as he picked up the phone. He'd programmed his father's number into his contacts eons ago on a whim, certain he'd have no occasion to use it. Several times he'd reminded himself to delete it, but he'd never gotten around to it.

Probably for the same reason he hadn't deleted Allie yet.

He tapped *ignore* on the screen, or at least that's what he tried for.

"Hello? Son, is that you?"

*Oh, shit.*

Jack stared in horror at the screen as his father's voice blared at him and the speaker function lit up like a beacon.

"I uh—"

Paige stared in wonder, and Jack fumbled at the screen, doing his damnedest to take the stupid thing off speakerphone.

"Look," his dad said quickly, rushing to get the words out. "Before you hang up, I just need to say something to you."

"Who is that?" Paige whispered as Jack jumped up and started for the other room. He tripped over the gym bag he'd tossed next to the coat closet and cursed his own clumsiness, his stupidity for not blocking the number, his inability to turn off the goddamn speakerphone—

"Jack, I know I've been a shitty dad," he said. "But I want you to know I'm dying. I'm dying, son."

# CHAPTER SEVENTEEN

Allie clasped her hands together on the battered gray table and looked at her father. "So that's pretty much it," she said. "We broke up. Again. I guess I don't have things figured out after all."

Her father curled his hands around hers and squeezed tight. The sympathy in his eyes made Allie's chest feel like someone was standing on it. "Oh, sweetie," he said. "I'm so sorry. I wish there was something I could do."

Allie felt the tears welling up in her throat again, but she swallowed them back. "Thanks, Daddy. It feels nice to talk about it. To be able to tell someone."

She tried not to think about the irony of it all. Telling her secrets, opening her mouth and spilling her guts—that's what prompted the breakup in the first place. Maybe Jack hadn't explicitly meant for her to bare her soul to a parent in a green jumpsuit, but still. She was capable of opening up, dammit. Able to be honest and forthright.

All right, fine. That wasn't the whole truth. The fact that she hadn't been honest *before* was what obviously bothered Jack. She could understand that. But couldn't he understand she'd had her reasons for keeping secrets? About the pregnancy, the broken engagements, the money—

"Speaking of money," she said, even though they hadn't been.

Her father blinked in surprise. "What's that, honey?"

"There's something else I wanted to ask you about."

"What's that, Alliecakes?"

She licked her lips and glanced at the guard, who was standing a good ten feet away eyeing an inmate pressed close to a very pregnant visitor. The guard wasn't looking at Allie and her father, but that didn't mean he wasn't listening.

It didn't matter, though. Allie had to get this over with. Had to put it out there once and for all and let the chips fall where they may.

Turning back at her dad, she took a deep breath. "Remember last time I was here when we talked about me poking around the attic?"

Her father frowned. "You didn't get hurt up there, did you?"

"No, that's not it. I—um—well, I found something up there."

"Besides those old love letters?" He chuckled. "Boy, I wouldn't mind getting a look at those again. Your mom and I used to dream about buying a boat together and sailing off to—"

"No, Daddy—this isn't about the letters. I found a trunk in the attic. The old steamer trunk that used to be in the blue room."

"Right, you mentioned that before. You said it was locked?"

Was it her imagination, or did something shift in her father's expression? A flash of unease, but it was gone in an instant. It might have been nothing.

"The trunk was locked," she said, "but I figured out the combination. There was money in it, Daddy. A lot of money. I didn't know where it came from, so I thought about it for a really long time—longer than I should have, I guess. And then when I went to visit Mom, I—"

"You talked to your mother about this?"

Her father's face had gone ashen. Allie stared at him, and it dawned on her he didn't look surprised at all. Not about the money, anyway. And why was the first question out of his mouth about her mother?

"I, um—yes. Yes, I did." Allie cleared her throat. "And Mom said the money was legitimately Grandma's. But something didn't feel right about that. I don't mean to disparage Mom, but she was the one who orchestrated the whole Ponzi thing, so it just didn't add up, you know? Anyway, I started looking into what I needed to do from a legal standpoint."

"Oh, Christ." Her father dragged his hands down his face like he was trying to erase his features. "You got lawyers involved?"

Allie stared at him. "Daddy?" Her voice cracked a little on the second syllable, so she lowered it to a whisper. "You know something about this?"

Her father glanced at the guard. The guy had his hand on his radio as he leaned down to say something to the heavily tattooed inmate with the pregnant visitor. None of them were looking at Allie and her dad. None of them could see the stricken look on either of their faces.

When her dad turned back to her, his expression was resigned. "Yeah," he said at last. "I know about the money."

Part of her didn't want to ask. Didn't want to know the truth. A little voice in the back of her mind told her to keep believing the story her mother had told. That her grandma had owned the cash free and clear, and now, so did Allie.

But Allie was done listening to that voice.

"Mom hid it up there, didn't she?" The question seemed to surprise them both, and Allie wondered where her sudden bluntness had come from. Jack, or maybe Paige.

The thought of never seeing either of them again made Allie's gut twist, and she pressed on, needing to hear the whole truth. "It's okay, Daddy," she said, reaching for his hand again. "Look, the courts already know Mom was the one pulling all the financial strings. Maybe this will help with your appeal. Maybe when you tell them you had nothing to do with the money or with—"

"Allie, honey." Her father shook his head, a little sadly, it seemed. "You've got the story all wrong, Alliecakes."

She blinked. "What do you mean?"

265

Her father gave a heavy sigh and leaned forward with his elbows on the table. "I guess I'm not surprised. This is the way Priscilla wanted it. I told her it was a bad idea, but then everything got complicated and—"

"What are you talking about?"

He clasped his hands together and brought them down like a slow hammer. "Your mother didn't hide that money up there, Allie. And she wasn't the mastermind behind the investment scam."

"Who was?"

"Me."

She stared at him, pretty sure she'd heard wrong. "What?"

He unclasped his hands and put them over hers again. "The funds, the investments, the plan to skim a little off the top—that was all my doing. When I got in over my head, your mother caught on. She tried to help me fix things, but by then it was too late."

"I don't understand." Allie swallowed hard, her throat making a funny click. "So *you* hid the money up there?"

"No. That was your grandmother."

"She was *in on it*?"

Her voice came out louder than she meant it to, but the guard didn't turn. There was a frantic feeling building in her chest, like something with sharp claws scrambling to get out.

"No, baby. Your mom was telling the truth. Your grandma tucked that money away for you."

Tears filled her eyes, though Allie had no idea why. For her grandmother's sacrifice? For not believing her mom? For the evaporation of the image of her father as the kindly, unlucky victim in her mother's crime?

She stared at the ficus tree in the corner, at the trio of dead leaves on the floor beside it. A heating vent switched on, sending the brittle carcasses tumbling into the wall.

Allie looked back at her father. "You mean the money's legitimate?"

He looked down at his hands. "It started out that way. Grandma tucked it away for years and years. She never really trusted banks or

266

investors or lawyers." He gave a hollow little laugh. "Considering the way things turned out with me, it seems her fears were justified."

"So what happened?"

"I knew she'd been socking money away for you, so when things went south with the investments, I tried to get my hands on it. I thought if I just had a fresh infusion of cash, I could course correct. Launder it through the system, pay off the people who needed to be paid off, and eventually restock the coffer."

"But Grandma found out?"

"No. Your mother did." He sighed. "She was mad as hell, but by then I was in too deep. She didn't want me to go to prison, of course. She tried to get the money back out, but it was too late. We got caught."

"You mean *you* got caught." She was looking at her father differently now, seeing someone she hardly recognized.

"Yeah, I guess you're right there." He scrubbed his hands down his face again, looking incredibly tired. "The whole thing was my deal from the start. Your mom was just trying to help me get out of it."

"So—so—Mom took the fall? To help take pressure off you?"

Allie's brain felt like it was spinning inside her skull, and it occurred to her she had more in common with her mother than she'd realized. Misjudging a man, making self-destructive decisions when it came to love—Allie hadn't sucked that out of her thumb.

"It was something like that," her father was saying. "Anyway, I've been trying to make it right. That's what all these meetings with the lawyer have been about. Not an appeal. An attempt to turn it around, maybe negotiate a lighter sentence for your mom."

Allie frowned, still trying to make sense of it all. "But I told you about finding the chest the last time I was here," she said. "You didn't seem to know anything about it."

He shrugged and gave a guilty look. "I was hoping you'd take my advice and stay out of there. Figured if the money was still there when I got out, I could help you invest it or something."

There was a sick feeling in the pit of her stomach. She stared at her father, then shook her head. "This can't be real."

"We all make mistakes, Alliecakes. Some of us just do a better job than others at covering it up."

Allie swallowed hard. "I guess that's true."

"I'm sorry." He started to reach for her hand, then stopped himself. He placed his palms on the table and sighed. "I'm sorry you believed in me and I let you down."

Allie nodded. Her arms prickled with gooseflesh. She stared at her father and felt a rush of anger and confusion and guilt and fury and sadness all mixed together in one big, salty, powerful wave.

"I love you," she told him. "But I'm not sure I like you very much right now."

"That's understandable."

Her throat felt raw and there was a good chance she was going to lose her lunch. She scrubbed her damp palms down her thighs and stood up. Her knees were wobbly, but her legs still held her.

"I have to go," she said.

Her dad stood, too, frowning as he glanced at the still-unmoving guard. "You won't do anything rash, will you?"

She shook her head, feeling sorry for him while at the same time wanting to grab the cactus in the corner and thread it up his nostril.

"I'm going to do the right thing," she said. "After this long, that's not rash at all."

◆　◆　◆

"Don't put that in your mouth."

"Sorry." Allie handed the pen back to Wade, but he waved it off with a shudder.

"Keep it," he said. "Now that it's covered in your cooties."

Allie sighed and set the pen down. "So now what happens?"

"Now we wait for the county clerk to call us back and we go from there."

"And I'm still within my twenty-day window to post it in the newspaper."

"Correct," he said. "Do you want help with that?"

Allie hesitated. "I want to do it myself. I think—I think that's important."

Wade nodded. "Okay. Let me know if you need me to proofread."

"Thanks."

He reached across the desk and gave her hand a friendly squeeze. "You're doing the right thing, Albatross."

"Then why does it feel like I just hit myself in the forehead with a cricket bat?"

"Have you ever held a cricket bat?"

"No." She frowned. "I might be confusing it with that thing hockey players use."

"A stick?"

"Right."

"You've played hockey?"

Allie picked up the pen and tossed it at him. "It was a metaphor, Wade."

"You used *like*, so technically I think it's a simile."

"I don't care what it is. It feels lousy."

"Right." He grabbed the pen from where it had landed in the Zen garden on the corner of his desk, which probably screwed up Allie's Zen six ways to Sunday. He set the pen back in his chrome desk organizer and looked at her. "Sometimes doing the right thing feels really fucking shitty."

"That's deep."

"I'm a lawyer, not a guidance counselor."

Allie chewed the inside of her lip and glanced up at the wall where Wade had all his law degrees in expensive-looking frames. She

269

remembered sitting here in this office six years ago, looking at those frames and imagining a future with the sort of man who'd earned those degrees. A man who'd worked his way up the career food chain and had the fancy ties and the sleek leather office furniture to prove it.

"I did care about you," she said, dragging her gaze to Wade. He looked surprised, and Allie wondered if she'd said the words for his benefit or for her own. "When we were together, I mean. I might not have loved you the way you're supposed to love someone you marry, but I always thought you were an amazing guy."

"I am, of course." He grinned at her, then leaned back in his chair. "Don't sweat it, Albatross. No offense, but I never lost much sleep over us."

"Ouch."

"That didn't hurt."

"You're right," she admitted. "I wanted it to be right. With us, I mean. And the other guys."

"The ones who weren't Jack."

She ignored him. "I guess I just got too caught up in looking for the puzzle pieces that seemed like the right color or pattern instead of looking for the one that actually fit."

"Now that's a metaphor."

Allie shook her head. "I'm sorry about you and Skye."

"It's fine." He waved a dismissive hand. "Water under the bridge."

The breakup had been swift and amicable, only days after the pair had returned from their romantic beach getaway. Allie got the sense she was more upset about it than Wade or Skye were.

She sighed and propped her elbow on his desk, letting her chin sink to the back of her hand. "I still can't believe you two are over."

"Believe it, babe. It was good while it lasted, but the whole thing ran its course."

"But that's not how it was supposed to go!" The vehemence in her voice and the fact that she'd just smacked her palm on the desk made her sound a little crazed. Wade raised an eyebrow. Allie sighed and folded her hands on the desk. "I just mean you two seemed so good together," she said. "I thought this was really it."

"Sometimes the story doesn't end the way you think it will," he said. "Doesn't mean it was a bad story to start with."

"Will you please stop talking like a motivational card?"

He laughed and steepled his hands in front of him. "Heard from Jack lately?"

"No." Heat crept into her cheeks, but she shook it off. "He won't take my calls."

"Need me to beat him up?"

"No. Thank you, but that won't be necessary."

"Good. I kind of liked the guy."

"I don't."

"Yes, you do." Wade put a hand over hers. "That's why you're taking this so hard."

Allie shrugged and looked away. "He was right, you know. I should have been straightforward with him from the start."

"Probably," he agreed. "But at least now you know that. You can admit it and say you're sorry, while he's still over there sulking like a little bitch."

"Be nice," Allie warned, though she felt more sad than angry.

"Sulking like a kid who dropped his Popsicle on the pavement," Wade amended.

"That's not any better."

"That's as good as I'm going to get." He let go of her hands and placed his on either side, palms down on the polished wood. "You did your best, Albatross. You spilled your guts, you learned some lessons, and you did the right thing in the end. Now the ball's in his court."

"We're back to the hockey analogies."

"That's a puck."

"Whatever." Allie frowned. "So you're saying it's over with Jack. That there's nothing I can do."

"I'm saying if you love someone, set them free—"

"—if he comes back, it's meant to be." Allie rolled her eyes. "And if he doesn't—"

"I call in a client with mob ties and we fit the bastard with concrete galoshes."

Allie folded her arms over her chest. "I don't think that's how the saying goes."

Wade grinned and leaned back in his chair. Picking up the little rake from his Zen garden, he began making fine little lines in the sand.

"Have a little faith in the guy, Albatross. After this many years, I think he's earned it."

# CHAPTER EIGHTEEN

The smell of antiseptic hung over the room like a sticky net as Jack stood looking at his father from the end of a hospital bed. This was his first time visiting his father's home, and he rested his hands on Paige's shoulders, not sure if he was trying to lend his daughter strength or trying to bolster his own.

"You sure you want to be here?" he whispered to her.

His little girl nodded and looked up at him. "He's your dad and you're my dad," she whispered. "So we should all be here."

That all made sense in a weird way. The hospice nurse had told them it was fine to wake his father, but Jack wasn't ready yet. Ten feet away between a brown refrigerator and an overgrown asparagus fern hovered his dad's wife, Barbara. She was a mousy woman only a few years older than Jack who looked at them with wary eyes that made him think of a cat that had its tail stepped on too many times.

The thought of cats made Jack wonder what Allie was up to and how she was getting along. He missed her a helluva lot more than he'd expected to, which pissed him off. She'd lied to him, dammit. Shouldn't he be over her by now? He'd had a tight feeling in his chest all week, and he knew it had little to do with his decision to visit his father.

Jack cleared his throat too loudly. Just like he expected, his dad's eyes fluttered open. He stared at Jack for a good five or six seconds while Jack stood rigid with his hands on Paige's shoulders.

"Son."

There was no tenderness in the word, but something about it made Jack's spine feel like it was made of rubber. He kept his posture erect and nodded. "Yes."

He wasn't willing to call the guy *Dad*. Not now. Not after this many years and this many missed opportunities for connection. The old man had had plenty of chances to reach out, to prove himself as a father.

He'd never taken one of them.

But standing here now, staring at the withered man under a tatty cotton blanket, Jack felt some of the anger seep from his pores. He didn't have to like the guy, but he could at least acknowledge the DNA that linked them.

"This is my daughter, Paige," Jack said slowly. "Your granddaughter. She's ten."

For once, Paige didn't rush forward with handshakes or hugs. Jack wondered if she sensed her father's trepidation, or if it was the presence of tubes and wires that held her back.

"Hello," Paige said softly. "I'm sorry you're sick."

The man laughed, a good two or three seconds of joviality before a racking cough seized him. Barbara jumped from behind the fern, but the old man waved her off.

"I'm fine, I'm fine," Jack's father grumbled. "Sick, yeah. Dying, if you want to get right down to it. That's okay, though. Probably deserve it."

Jack tightened his hold on Paige's shoulders, but said nothing. His daughter glanced up at him with wide, silvery eyes, and Jack felt his heart crack down the middle. His father had the same damn eyes. He didn't have to look at his dad now to know that.

"So," the old man said. "Looks like you went and had a kid of your own despite having a total fuckup for a father."

He felt Paige flinch under his palms, and Jack held her tighter. Barbara frowned in the corner, but didn't say anything. Jack gritted his teeth. Then he cleared his throat again and squeezed his daughter's shoulders.

"Paige is a straight-A student," he said. "She's also the goalie for her soccer team. She plays the violin and won an award for—"

"So what?"

Anger flared hot and sour in Jack's chest. He'd never wanted to punch his father as much as he did right then, and he'd wanted to punch the guy plenty. He opened his mouth to tell the old man to go fuck himself, but he didn't get the words out.

"I didn't mean that like it sounded," the old man muttered. "Good for you, kid. You're smart. Just like your old man."

"Thank you," Paige said, and the simple, sweet sincerity of her response cooled Jack's temper from inferno to red hot.

The old man coughed again. "All I meant," he continued, "is why do you give a shit what I think? You've obviously showed the whole world you're educated and successful and a better dad than I ever was. Why do you feel like you've gotta prove anything to me?"

Jack stared at him. He didn't know what to say. "I don't—"

"Look, kid—I was a shitty father. 'Scuse me, young lady. What was your name again?"

"Paige."

"Paige," he repeated, nodding. "Nice name. Sorry about the cursing. I do that too much. I also smoke too much. And drink too much. Probably how I ended up like this."

"That's okay," she said. "It's all right to do shitty things as long as you say you're sorry."

The old man dissolved into another laughing-coughing fit, and Jack thought about chiding his daughter for cursing. Either that or hugging her for doing a damn better job than he was at knowing how to respond to his father.

"That's right," Jack's father said, nodding with what looked like newfound respect. His gaze drifted from Paige to Jack and held there. "I am sorry, by the way. For everything."

Jack swallowed hard. He wanted to hang on tight to the anger that had been his security blanket for so many years, but what was the point?

"Thank you," he said tightly. "I *am* a good father." Why the hell did he say that? He wanted to grab the words out of the air and stuff them back down his throat, but Paige was grinning at him.

"You're okay and all," she said. "But I still think Brad Pitt might be a cooler dad."

Over in the corner, Barbara smiled. Jack's father gave a bitter-sounding chuckle that may have been another cough. Then his gaze swung back to his son, and those silver-blue eyes locked with Jack's for the space of several breaths.

"I would have screwed you up, you know."

Jack blinked. "What do you mean?"

"I was a shitty person back then," the old man said. "Well, I'm still a shitty person, but I was shittier. If I'd stuck around, if you'd been raised with me in your life? You would have turned into a prick just like me."

"I doubt that very much." The words came out soft, not icy, and Jack wondered how he'd meant them to sound.

He also wondered if there was a sliver of truth to what his father said. "It still would have been good to know you," Jack said. "To have some contact with you, at least."

"It wouldn't have. Trust me on that." Another cough racked the old man's body, and Barbara hustled forward to adjust the pillows. He stopped coughing and looked at Jack again. "Look, me walking out? It was the best thing I could have done for you."

Jack didn't know what to say. Part of him wanted to stay angry. He had more than thirty years of fury built up inside him, and he wanted to let it out somehow. For so many years, he'd dreamed of telling his father off. He'd scripted an impassioned speech where he told his dad exactly what he thought about his failures as a father and a human.

But right now, he couldn't remember a damn word of it.

He was still deciding what to say when Paige stepped forward. Jack stood frozen, hands cupping the space where her shoulders had been as his little girl walked to the edge of the bed with halting steps.

The old man turned to look at her. Jack held his breath, ready to step forward if his father said anything shitty.

But the old man said nothing. Just watched as Paige pulled a chair from the dining room table and dragged it next to the bed. Three pairs of adult eyes watched as the girl seated herself, folded her hands in her lap, and looked at her grandfather.

"How old was my dad when you saw him the last time?" she asked.

"Six and a half," the old man answered with no hesitation. "It was August twelfth. Summer break."

Paige nodded, seeming to digest this information. Jack's hands felt useless and floppy, so he put them behind his back and stood like a marine at military rest.

At the head of the bed, Paige spoke again. "Tell me about him."

"Who?" The old man frowned, but Jack saw something soften in his eyes.

"Tell me about my dad," Paige said with no trace of impatience. "I want to know what my dad was like when he was a kid."

The old man seemed to hesitate. Jack held his breath again. Over in the corner, Barbara looked like she was doing the same.

Paige unfolded her hands and lifted one, resting it on top of the old man's gnarled one. All of them stared—Jack, Barbara, Jack's father. Then the old man looked up and met his granddaughter's eyes.

"I remember this one time when your dad was five," he said. "I wasn't around much by then, but I wanted to spend time with him. Do some bonding, you know?"

Paige nodded. "Yeah."

"Anyway, we decided to hitchhike to Vegas. Just me and your dad, a couple guys seeing the west together. Man stuff."

"That sounds fun." Paige was watching with rapt attention, her hand still on her grandfather's.

"We had us a time!" the old man said, and there was a spark in his eyes that stirred Jack's memory. Something warm and comforting in the archives of his childhood. "Sleeping under the stars, eating beef jerky for dinner and telling ghost stories. We caught rides with truckers who let your dad blow the horn at pretty girls."

Jack stood frozen. He'd forgotten the jerky. Forgotten the horn. Forgotten everything but being left. Not just in the car, but after that.

"So then what happened?" Paige asked.

The old man looked up and met Jack's eyes. Neither blinked. Neither said a word.

Jack's dad looked away first. He took a heavy breath and lifted his gaze to his granddaughter's. "I screwed everything up when I—"

"A lot of adventures," Jack interrupted, stepping forward to put his hand on Paige's shoulder. He looked at his father and gave a small nod. "Tell her about the jukebox, Pop."

◆　◆　◆

On the car ride home, Jack couldn't stop stealing glimpses at his daughter in the rearview mirror. He didn't know whether to be more impressed by her bravery, her empathy, or her conversational skills.

Seeming to sense his gaze on her, Paige met his eyes in the mirror. "What?"

"You." Jack smiled and directed his gaze back on the road. "You did good in there, kid."

"Grandma says I'm charming."

Jack laughed. "That you are." He signaled right and got into the slow lane to let traffic by. "Thank you, by the way."

"For what?"

"For teaching me something important in there."

"You mean how to do the armpit fart noise? I learned that from this girl in my class who went to summer camp."

He laughed again and shook his head. "Yeah, I think your grandpa was pretty impressed."

"I could tell."

"I actually meant the other thing," he said. "The fact that you talked to him in the first place. That you didn't just stand there with your thumb up your butt like I did."

"Ew," she said with a giggle. "Well, you guys were being really boring. I thought someone needed to talk."

"You're right. And I appreciate that it was you. That you're able to find the good in people instead of getting hung up on the worst in them."

"Yeah." Paige fell silent again, and Jack glanced in the mirror to see she'd gone back to gazing out the window.

"I've been reading my bird book," she said.

"Oh?" The subject change threw him a little, but it was a welcome diversion. Birds seemed like an easier topic than cancer or death or forgiveness.

"Want to hear about the albatross?" Paige asked.

She was still staring out the window, and Jack couldn't read her expression at all. Was she thinking of Allie, or just choosing a bird at random?

"Sure," he said carefully. "Tell me about the albatross."

"Well," she began as Jack merged off the freeway toward downtown. "There's lots of different kinds. The snowy albatross and the black-footed albatross and the waved albatross. The royal albatross is the biggest one. When a baby royal albatross starts flying, it takes off and goes around the world a bunch of times all by itself without ever touching the ground."

"Really?" Jack found himself fascinated, and he wondered if Wade had known any of this when he'd given Allie her nickname. *Allie Ross the albatross, the bird who'd rather fly alone.*

"Yeah," she said. "They do that for, like, five years, all by themselves. Just catching stuff in the ocean and making these big circles all the way around the world. But you know what's cool?"

"What's that?" He glanced in the mirror again, trying to get a read on her.

She met his eyes and smiled. "When the royal albatross goes back to where it was born, it spends a long time finding the one albatross it likes best of all."

"They mate for life?"

Paige frowned. "What's that?"

"Like only one other albatross for the rest of its life."

"Oh. Yeah, they do that. Anyway, when they're trying to find their husband or wife, they meet a bunch of different albatrosses. They flap their wings and make weird noises. Then they go off with one other albatross and they make a nest to see if they really like each other."

"And then they lay eggs?"

"Nope," Paige said. "Then they leave each other."

Jack glanced at her in the rearview mirror. "What do you mean?"

"I mean they take off. In opposite directions. The girl bird goes one way and the boy bird goes the other, and they spend a whole year flying by themselves around the world."

"Seriously?"

"Yeah, but you know what's cool? They come back to the same place. Always. And they land within a few hours of the other albatross, even though they've been away for a year and they went to all different places. But they come back and they make a nest and they have babies and then they do it all over again. But they always come back."

There was a tightness in his chest that hadn't been there before. He kept his eyes off the mirror, not wanting her to see how undone he felt in that moment. Not wanting to believe this was anything other than a simple story about birds.

"That's amazing," Jack said at last.

"It is." Paige was quiet a moment, and Jack glanced at her again. She was fiddling with the end of her braid, twisting and untwisting the rubber band, not looking at him. "I also learned some stuff about woodpeckers."

"Really?"

"Yeah." She looked up then, meeting his gaze in the mirror. Then she grinned. "I think I know what kind Allie's got."

"What kind?"

"I think it's called a northern flicker. It's got red right here by its eye and speckles on its body and these black feathers here like a necklace."

Jack gripped the steering wheel tighter, feeling his heart starting to thrum in his ears. "That's good. That you can identify the kind of bird. Nice work."

"Uh-huh," she said, giving him a smile he could have sworn looked just like Allie's Cheshire cat smile. "And I think I know what to do about it."

# CHAPTER NINETEEN

Allie handed a cup of chamomile tea to Skye and sat down beside her at her grandmother's dining room table.

Across from them, Wade peered into his own teacup and swirled it around. "There's no bourbon in this?"

"Just milk and sugar." Allie stirred her own brew with one of her grandmother's tiny teaspoons, then set the utensil on the saucer.

"This looks great," Skye said as she blew into her own cup. "Not the tea. That looks great, too, but I meant the table."

"Thanks," Allie said. "It took a few tries, but I finally got all those scratches out and got the stain pretty close to what it used to be."

"It's better, I think," Skye said. "Warmer. It looks more friendly. More like you."

Allie smiled as a fluffy orange cat named Matt hopped into her lap and arranged himself across her thighs. He began to knead her with his oversized paws, making biscuits on the knees of her jeans. Allie took a sip of tea and reached for the box at the center of the table.

"You're still snooping?" Wade asked, making Skye roll her eyes.

"It's not snooping," Skye told him. "It's her own history. Love letters between her mom and dad and her grandma and grandpa."

"Or between grandma and one of her many lovers," Wade pointed out. "Granny got around."

Skye swatted at him, but Allie wasn't offended. "I thought it might be creepy, reading all this mushy stuff between family members, but it's not at all. It's actually giving me some great insights."

"What, like the importance of burning all your dirty secrets before your grandkids find them?" Wade suggested.

"No," Allie said. "That love stories are complicated. No matter how perfect they look from the outside, there are ups and downs and ins and outs and—"

"Whips and chains," Wade added helpfully.

Skye gave him another swat, but Wade dodged back this time, so her blow landed on his chest instead of his shoulder. "Nice pecs," Skye said, patting his chest before she drew her hand back. "Don't be a jerk."

"Don't be a nag," he replied, snatching her teacup. He took a small sip, then shuddered as he handed it back to her. "You didn't get bourbon, either."

"Are you guys sure you don't want to get back together?" Allie said, trying to keep the hopeful note from her voice. "You're pretty much the perfect couple."

"Thanks, but no thanks." Skye picked up one of the sugar cookies Allie had baked earlier that day. "But we'll be friends forever."

"The story of my life," Wade said, not sounding terribly bummed about it.

Still, Allie couldn't help but wish for the happily-ever-after, even if it wasn't going to happen. Not for Skye and Wade, and certainly not for her and Jack. After almost two weeks, she'd given up hope.

No, that wasn't true. She hadn't given up hope, exactly. She might not ever. Even now, knowing this stupid Pollyanna complex was probably her downfall, she couldn't help it.

But she had given up calling him.

"The place is looking great, Albatross," Wade said. "You're pretty close to having it back up and running as a B&B?"

"Getting there," she said. "It won't be the same as when grandma ran it, but I think it'll still be pretty nice."

"It'll be better, I think." Skye leaned down to scoop up a lanky tabby with a swoop of orange fur under his nose that looked like a Hitler moustache. "Especially since these guys all get to stay."

"You might want to keep Kitler there from creeping into guests' rooms," Wade mused. "He'll have them shouting 'Sieg heil' over breakfast and making swastikas out of bacon."

Allie smiled and sipped her tea again, grateful for the comfort of good friends, good tea, and a whole lot of cats to keep her mind off Jack. She'd stayed busy in the weeks since he'd walked out of her life. She'd followed through on her legal obligation to post the money, leaving it to Wade to handle the crazies trying to lay claim to the cash that was tucked away in a safe deposit box now. She still wasn't sure who to believe about the origins of the cash, but she had to trust the law to run its course.

She'd also visited her parents, helping as much as she could with her dad's effort to set the record straight in hopes of earning a shortened sentence for Allie's mom. She'd had a few long talks with her mother, their hands clenched tight together with a box of tissues on the table between them.

*"I love him so much, Allison,"* her mother had murmured as she dabbed at the corner of her eyes. *"Your father. Even when he did things I didn't agree with, he's still the best man I've ever known."*

*"I get it."* Allie had swallowed hard, still struggling to come to terms with her own feelings about her father. *"I love him, too."*

*"When you love someone as much as I love your father, you don't always make the smartest decisions."*

Allie had nodded and handed her mother another tissue. *"I know. But you can always try to make better ones once you figure that out."*

But no matter how many talks she had with her parents, no matter how many miles she put on her car or coats of paint she put on walls at the B&B, she still missed Jack. And Paige, for that matter, much more than she'd expected to. She thought about them every day, wondering if the girl was settled in at school and if Jack's company was off and running in the new city.

"Don't you think that's kind of weird?"

Allie shook herself back to the conversation, aware that Skye had just asked a question. "What's weird?" she asked.

"I haven't heard the woodpeckers all morning," she said. "Or last night, for that matter. What did you try this time?"

"I haven't tried anything," Allie said. "Well, not since the pepper spray incident."

Wade snorted into his teacup. "Who knew you had to pay attention to which way the nozzle was pointed?"

"Or that woodpeckers don't actually have taste buds," Skye added.

Allie rolled her eyes. "Real supportive, guys."

Still, Skye had a point. When was the last time she'd heard the woodpeckers? She'd been busy for several days refinishing the table, working late into the night with earplugs to protect her from the angry buzz of the electric sander. She hadn't exactly been listening for the birds. She started to stand up, earning a grumpy meow from the cat on her lap.

"Sorry, buddy," she said as she set him on the ground. "I have to check something."

The cat growled and trotted off as Allie headed for the front door. She pulled it open and stepped out onto the porch, breathing in the scent of mossy earth and the honeysuckle that twined around the porch railing. Still clutching her teacup, she walked to the end of the deck and looked up at the side of the house.

It took her a moment to realize something was different.

The cedar boards above the front window still looked like they'd been riddled with bullets. But right above that, centered perfectly between the eaves, was a birdhouse.

A hand-painted birdhouse. A hand-painted, pale-yellow birdhouse with white, arch-top plantation shutters.

She was still staring up at it when Wade and Skye walked out onto the porch.

"Allie?" Skye touched her elbow. "What is it? What's wrong?"

"Look."

She pointed to the birdhouse and both of them stared up at it.

"Hey, check it out!" Wade laughed as a speckle-chested bird with red markings near its eyes popped out through the front door. "That's seriously the longest pecker I've ever seen."

Skye snorted. "It's called a beak, dummy."

"It's a woodpecker," Allie breathed. "He built me a woodpecker house."

Skye grabbed her hand and squeezed. No one asked who *he* was.

The little bird with the black bib of feathers on its chest squawked once and ducked back inside.

"That's brilliant," Skye said. "Give them a house so they'll leave yours alone."

"I actually saw that on a nature show once," Wade said. "Woodpeckers beat the shit out of people's houses because they're looking for a place to roost. Give them a safe spot and they'll leave your house alone."

Allie looked at him and rolled her eyes. "You're remembering this just now?"

"Oops." Wade shrugged and spun his teacup around in his palm.

Allie returned her gaze to the birdhouse as a soft warmth spread from her chest through her limbs. She took in the craftsmanship, the detail, the thought that had gone into something so utterly simple yet so completely beautiful.

"I have to go." She turned and ran into the house.

♦ ♦ ♦

"What kind of wine would go best with this dinner?"

Jack looked at Paige, then down at his bowl of mac and cheese. "Pepto-Bismol?"

"No," Paige said, with a dramatic eye roll. "Come on, Daddy. You're not doing it right."

*The story of my life*, Jack thought.

But at least his kid was trying to connect with him, so he did his best to rally. "Let's see . . . how about a Chardonnay? Cuddly with overtones of deer scat, Elmer's glue, and shavings from the floor mat in a 1968 Oldsmobile Cutlass."

Paige erupted into laughter, and Jack felt better. Not great, but better. He might not have won back the woman of his dreams, but he did have the best kid on the planet.

He shoveled up a bite of pasta. Admittedly this meal was not one of his shining moments of parenting, but he'd had a busy week. Researching the best possible domicile for a northern flicker woodpecker had been time-consuming enough, but building it to the precise specifications he needed had taken a good chunk out of his week. Paige had helped, of course, and they'd worked together between schoolwork and visits with Grandma at her new apartment. Paige had been the one to paint it, her small brush skimming over the arched top of the tiny shutters as she'd smiled up at him with a smear of yellow on her cheek.

No matter what, he had that memory. Plenty of others, too.

"Chardonnay's good," Paige said. "Or maybe a Merlot. It would be crusty with hints of bubblegum and the fuzz off a tennis ball."

"Very nice," Jack said, and held up his plastic cup of orange juice to toast her.

"Thank you." Paige grinned and spooned up the last bite of her dinner. "May I please clear my plate?"

"After you eat two more slices of apple."

She shoved both in her mouth at the same time, then stood up and headed toward the kitchen.

"Don't forget to rinse the bowl before you put it in the dishwasher," he called.

"Roger that," she said, saluting him from the doorway. It was a phrase Jack had heard Wade utter countless times, and hearing it from his daughter should have annoyed him. Instead, he just felt empty. Jesus, was it possible he missed Wade, too?

Paige had just set her bowl on the counter when the doorbell rang.

"I'll get it!" she yelled, halfway to the door before Jack had a chance to finish chewing his too-large bite of mac and cheese. He wasn't expecting company, and his stomach did a stupid flip at the thought that it could be Allie.

But that seemed impossible. He'd put up the birdhouse four days ago, sneaking over when he knew she'd be at work and Skye had class. For the first couple days, he'd waited. Allie wasn't the most observant person in the world, so maybe she needed time to notice.

After four days, though, it seemed clear she was still angry. Angry or hurt, probably both. She had every right to be. She'd spilled her guts and he'd shot her down. She'd shown him how to see the best in things, and he'd insisted on pointing out the worst. She'd tried to reach out to him and he'd ignored her like a big, grudge-holding ass. Was a birdhouse really going to fix all that?

"Daddy?"

"Yeah, baby?"

"There's no one at the door, but there's an envelope with your name on it."

"Can you bring it here?"

She trotted across the living room and deposited it on the table in front of him. Goose bumps rippled up his arms the second he saw his name scrawled on the pink paper in Allie's swoopy, cursive script.

"What is it?" Paige asked.

"I'm not sure." He grabbed his butter knife and slit it open, heart thudding in his ears. A single piece of paper fell into his lap. Jack picked it up with fingers that felt numb and useless.

"What does it say?" Paige leaned close, and Jack angled the card away from her to shield the words. He didn't know what to expect, what he might have to explain to Paige after all this. He needed to see the message for himself first.

But as he took in the words, a slow smile spread over his face. He read them twice, just to enjoy the lovely lilt of her cursive across the pale-pink paper.

"I'm super thankful," he read aloud. "Go look in the tank(ful)."

Paige frowned. "What does that mean? Like a fish tank? We don't have a fish tank."

Jack stood up. His heart was racing now, and his brain was only a few steps behind. Tank? Like a piece of military equipment? Tank top? Toilet tank? She wouldn't have risked sneaking into the house for a treasure hunt, so it had to be something outside—

"Gas tank," he said, and hurried out the front door.

Sure enough, there was another small envelope taped to the inside of the fuel door covering his car's gas tank. This one was white with little roses along the top and his name was scrawled in the same loopy script across the front. He yanked it off and ripped it open faster this time, tearing the corner of a rose-flecked card.

"'You're pretty adorable,'" he read. "'Go look by the doorbell.'"

Paige cocked her head to the side and leaned over his elbow to read the words for herself. "I'm not sure that really rhymes," she said, but Jack was already running back toward the front porch.

A pale-yellow envelope was tucked up under a shingle, which is probably why he hadn't seen it before. He snatched it with shaking hands and tore it open to read the words aloud.

"'I love you still. So damn much, Jack. Go look in the rosebush.'"

"That *really* doesn't rhyme," Paige said. "She could have tried *windowsill*."

A familiar laugh rang out from the edge of the house, and Jack looked up to see Allie stepping out from behind the rosebush. She wore a green sundress and a killer smile. Her hair was loose around her shoulders, and the setting sun made a halo behind her.

"I could have used you an hour ago, Paige." She smiled at his daughter, then slid her gaze to Jack's. He felt the full force of it deep in his gut. "I'm not much of a poet, as you may recall."

"It's perfect," he said, hardly daring to move. He couldn't believe she was standing here in front of his house looking pale and nervous and so damn beautiful he couldn't breathe. "*You're* perfect."

Her laugh was sharper this time. "Definitely not. But at least I can admit that. I can admit it and work on it and try to do better each time."

"I can do that, too," he said, taking a step toward her. "I'm sorry, Allie."

"So am I."

"I'm sorry I didn't recognize that people need to handle things in their own way," he said. "That there's a time for the coldest, hardest, truest version of a story, and a time for the one that just lets you get up in the morning and put your clothes on and brush your teeth and go about your day until you can deal with the other version."

Allie shook her head, and he watched her throat move as she swallowed. "I'm sorry, too," she murmured, tears glittering in her eyes. "For a lot of things. But mostly for not trusting you with the truth. For not trusting myself with it. I've been working on that."

"I know," he said. "I saw the newspaper." He'd almost reached her now, and he held out his hand palm up. She laced her fingers through his, and Jack pulled her closer. "We've got plenty of time to talk about who's the sorriest and how we plan to do better."

Allie squeezed his fingers with hers, then looked at Paige. "Is this okay with you? If your dad and I date each other again?"

"Uh-huh," she said. "He's been very grumpy."

"Thank you for the birdhouse," she said, then turned her gaze back to Jack. "Both of you."

"Does it work?" he asked. "Are they leaving your house alone?"

Allie nodded. "They've moved in already. No one's heard a bird pecking for days. Who knew that's all it took?"

"Paige did," Jack said, reaching over to ruffle his kid's hair.

"I read it in my bird book," the girl said. "We found the plans online for a flicker house. We got the right bedding in there and everything."

"Smart kid," Allie said.

"About a lot of things." Jack watched as his daughter's cheeks turned pink, and pride swelled so big in his chest that it nearly cracked his ribs.

He lifted Allie's hand to his lips and planted a kiss across her knuckles. "I'm so glad you're here."

"Me, too." Her eyes flashed with sunlight and the green sundress fluttered in the breeze.

"Are you guys going to kiss now?" Paige asked. "Like for real. None of that hand-kissing stuff."

"We'll get to that eventually." Jack's fingers were still linked with Allie's, but he reached up and brushed a windswept bit of hair off her forehead. "I've been reading about your mom's appeal. The headlines make it sound pretty dramatic. Your dad's laying it all out there."

"It's been a busy couple weeks," Allie said. "It's going to get messy, but he's trying to do the right thing. That counts for something."

"It does," he agreed. He let go of her hand and slid his arms around her, pulling her against his chest. Breathing in the Chardonnay scent of her hair, he had to remind himself she was really here. That he was really holding her again. Her arms cinched around his waist, and they stood there holding each other so tight he felt his ribs creak. But Jack didn't need to breathe deeply. He just needed this, right here, right now.

"You guys want to be alone?" Paige asked.

"Nope." Allie drew back and stretched out an arm. "You should be part of this, too. Group hug!"

Paige giggled and wrapped her arms around both of them, and they stood there on the edge of the driveway like some mutant three-headed creature made of tangled limbs and twisted hearts.

When Jack finally pulled back, he looked down at the two amazing females who made his heart feel whole. "So we're all in this together?"

"Uh-huh," Paige replied, then craned her neck to look at Allie. "You good with that?"

"I'm good with that," Allie said, then stood on tiptoe to kiss him.

# EPILOGUE

"Cut it out, Jack!" Allie tried swatting him away, which did no good at all. He kept his body pressed against her back, his mouth on her neck, and his hands wrapped around her very pregnant belly.

"No way," he said. "I keep missing it when he kicks. I'm determined to feel it this time."

Allie laughed and wiggled against him, which probably did more to encourage than dissuade. Truth be told, it felt damn good, so she was in no real hurry to escape.

"You're going to feel my foot to your butt if you don't go pick up Paige," she said as she dropped into the chair in front of the computer. "Come on, I need to finish processing all these reservations before she gets home."

"Au contraire." Jack bent down to kiss her neck again. "Your mom offered to pick Paige up. Apparently they had a date at some fancy English tearoom. They've been planning it for weeks."

Allie felt a warm bubble in the center of her chest. Much more pleasant than the heartburn that had been plaguing her for most of this pregnancy. Jack leaned down to smooth his palms over her belly some more, and Allie gave up trying to organize all the online reservations that had come in that morning for the B&B.

"Hey, guys!" Skye swooped into the room in a flutter of purple tie-dye, then swooped back out just as quickly. "Sorry," she called from behind the door. "I didn't mean to interrupt sexy time."

"It's fine, we're not getting busy in the parlor," Jack called, lowering his voice as his lips brushed Allie's ear again. "Not this time, anyway."

Allie took another swat at him, but he moved away in time and flopped back onto the couch. Two big orange polydactyls—Maestro and Matt—hopped up on either side of him, flanking him like fuzzy bookends. Jack looked so perfect there—so much a part of this home and this life they'd reconstructed together—that Allie wanted to fold herself onto his lap and kiss him six ways to Sunday.

But Skye swept back into the room again and deposited a stack of mail beside Allie. "It's another batch of fan mail for the cats," she said. "Looks like we need to make some more of those paw-print postcards."

"Really? We went through all six boxes already?"

"Crazy, right?" Skye tucked a blue curl behind one ear. "Maybe we can make the paw-print stamp with one of the other cats this time. Luna or Marilyn might be good."

Allie nodded and glanced down as one of the cats in question scampered across the carpet. "I still can't believe people get so nuts about getting paw-tographed letters from famous cats."

"So should I order a few thousand more?" Skye asked.

"Already on it." Jack stood up again and returned to his spot beside Allie. "And I'll also process all those reservations after dinner."

"Someone's on the ball today." Skye grinned at Allie. "Need anything at the store? I have to run out anyway, since I'm out of cuticle cream in the salon, and the guests in the Laurelwood room ate all the cream cheese this morning."

"Please don't mix up the two," Jack called as she headed toward the door.

"I'll do my best!"

As Skye vanished from the room, Jack turned back to Allie. "Come on. There's something I want to show you."

She looked up at him. "Are we going somewhere?"

"Not leaving the house, if that's what you mean."

He pulled her up and out of the chair, and Allie felt a tingly swoop in her belly. "Don't you dare try to pick me up, Jack Carpenter," she said. "You'll break your back."

"Relax, woman. Come with me willingly and I won't have to carry you anywhere."

Allie would have followed him off the end of a dock with her pockets filled with rocks, though she couldn't do it all that quickly in her current state. Why had no one told her that being eight months pregnant felt a lot like swallowing an angry watermelon?

Jack towed her out of the parlor and into the foyer, rounding the corner toward the stairs. "Wait," Allie said as her gaze landed on the framed collection on the wall. "Hang on a sec."

He let go of her hand, and Allie paused to straighten the framed letter from Ernest Hemingway. The words—and the legally documented authenticity of it—were a big part of what had put the Rosewood B&B on the map. She owed it to Ernie to at least make sure things looked tidy.

"I still can't believe we own Ernest freakin' Hemingway's cats," Jack said as Allie touched the edge of the framed feline family tree next to the letter. Her grandmother's handwriting was tidy and flourished, and Allie felt a pang of nostalgia.

"Not all of them," she reminded him. "Just some. Enough to make them a historic attraction, anyway."

"Good enough for me." He caught her hand again. "Come on."

Allie let him pull her away from the documents, which was fine by her. She'd had plenty of time to study them in the eighteen months since she'd found everything in the attic and pieced it all together. About the cash her grandmother really had squirreled away for her, a mixture of smart investments and a few sizeable contributions from one famous literary figure. It was payment for the care and feeding of his favorite felines, though apparently Ernest had vastly overestimated the cost of cat kibble. Either that, or he'd been exceptionally grateful for some of the other things Allie had read about in the letters.

She preferred not to dwell on that part of the story.

As Jack pulled her up the stairs, Allie thought about how damn lucky she was. She had a husband who loved her and the best step-kid any woman could ask for. Her father might still be in prison, but things were better now that her mom could visit him. Each time Allie saw their eyes light up or watched them hold hands across the familiar gray table, she learned a little more about love and forgiveness and all the things that made marriages survive the worst stuff life throws at them.

She rested a hand on her belly now as Jack towed her down the second-floor hallway. Looking at him, she felt a swell of gratitude so fierce it took her breath away. Or maybe that was the exertion of climbing stairs while incubating a baby the size of a small rhinoceros.

"Where are you taking me?" she asked. "I thought you said I wasn't allowed in this wing because the paint fumes might be bad for the baby."

"I lied," Jack said, turning to face her with his back to a closed bedroom door. "Sorry about that."

His grin told her he wasn't the least bit sorry.

"So there's no paint?"

"No paint. Not right now, anyway." He brushed a strand of hair off her forehead. "But I wasn't lying about renovating. I promise the new master suite will be ready before the baby's here."

"I don't mind, Jack. As long as we all have beds to sleep in, I'm not picky."

"Never thought I'd hear Allie Ross say those words."

"That's Allie Ross Carpenter, thank you very much." She stood on tiptoe and kissed him, and Jack pulled her close to deepen the kiss.

Well, *close* was a relative term.

"Ooof," he said as the baby belly bumped him squarely in the crotch. "Cock blocked by my own spawn."

Allie laughed. "Not the last time, I'm sure."

"Come on." Jack let go of her and reached for the door. He turned the knob to the room Allie hadn't set foot in for months. When they'd first reopened the B&B for guests, they'd set aside this wing of the house for their own quarters. The plan had been to renovate eventually, but between the wedding and the pregnancy and the unexpected flood of guests, they hadn't had time.

Or Allie hadn't had time, anyway. It was clear Jack had been up to something. As they stepped into the room, she took in the magnitude of the *something*.

Brocade drapes—exact replicas of the ones her grandma had purchased so long ago—lined the windows. They were open now, letting slabs of yellow sunlight spill across a blue duvet the color of a robin's egg. The carpet had been ripped out to reveal freshly refinished hardwood floors that gleamed like honey in a sunbeam.

Her gaze drifted to the far wall and Allie felt her heart stop. "Oh my God!" She stared at the fireplace. It was magnificent. Rustic brick lined the edges and the interior, and a rough-hewn wood beam gleamed above it. She stepped forward for a closer look and found herself skimming a palm over the mantle where their wedding photo rested.

"The brick is vintage," he said. "I bought it from a guy who claims it came out of an old house on the same block as the Hemingway House in Key West. And the mantle—I made that myself. It's from that old maple out back that came down in the windstorm a while back."

"Jack, it's beautiful." Allie's eyes filled with tears as she turned back to face him. "I can't believe you did this."

"You always said you wanted a fireplace in your bedroom." He smiled and closed the distance between them, taking her hand again.

"And this one burns gas or wood. So we can do it the old-fashioned way, or just flip the switch."

Somewhere downstairs, Allie heard the muted thud of footsteps, the slam of the front door, and Paige's voice chatting excitedly with Allie's mother. She heard her mother laugh, and knew she'd hear over dinner how utterly charming her granddaughter was.

Up here, the room smelled like cinnamon and fresh linens. The fireplace glowed warm and inviting beside them, and Allie stretched up to loop her hands behind Jack's neck. "I love you so much."

He grinned. "Because I light your fire?"

"Because you light my fire and battle my woodpeckers and feed my mutant cats."

"And knock you up," he said. "Don't forget that part."

"I couldn't possibly."

"I love you, too, Allie."

His lips touched hers, and Allie felt the same spark she'd felt at seventeen years old. Jack slid his hands into the small of her back, angling her sideways so they fit together just right. Like two puzzle pieces that had always belonged together.

Like two birds come home to roost at last.

# ACKNOWLEDGMENTS

I couldn't do this author thing without a seriously kick-ass team of experts behind me, and I owe a huge debt of gratitude to all of you. Thank you to Michelle Wolfson of Wolfson Literary Agency for steering my career, making sure we don't hit any really big icebergs, and keeping me supplied with barf bags and a life preserver. I'm also thankful for my agency sistah, Lauren Blakely, for all the hand-holding, butt-patting, and general career advice.

Huge thanks to my amazing Montlake editors, Chris Werner and Krista Stroever. You deserve big props for making me a better writer and helping polish this story from "Meh" to "Oh yeah!" I'm also grateful to Anh Schleup, Jessica Poore, Kimberly Cowser, Marlene Kelly, Rachel Adam, Hannah Buehler, and the rest of the Montlake team for doing such a bang-up job getting this book into the hands of readers, and for making me feel like an author rock star (minus the leather pants and drug habit).

My critique partners and beta readers played a crucial role in shaping this story and its characters, and I'm so thankful for Linda Grimes, Cynthia Reese, Kait Nolan, Bridget McGinn, Minta Powelson, and Maegan MacKelvie. It's a thankless, unpaid job you do for me, and I hope you know how much I appreciate it. You ladies are amazing.

I'm enormously indebted to Sophia R. Grotkin for lending your legal expertise and answering all my idiotic questions about found-property laws and nitty-gritty lawyer stuff. Any errors or embellishments are mine alone.

Thank you to my cats, both polydactyl and normal-pawed. Luna, Kenny, Marilyn, Maestro, Maggie, and Matt the Cat—please don't sue me for using your names and likenesses, and please don't hack hairballs onto my keyboard.

Big hugs to the folks at the Royal Albatross Centre in Dunedin, New Zealand, for teaching me about these amazing birds, and to Doug La Placa for teaching me what *not* to do in the event of a woodpecker infestation.

Big thanks to Shelby King for all the brainstorming, bullshitting, and Portland research. I'm also grateful to Sandra Giarde, CAE, for joking that no one ever writes a heroine who's a Certified Association Executive, and then telling me everything I needed to know about Allie's job. Thank you to Allison Murphy of Utilitu Sewing & Design for mending my crotch, lending your name, and not finding it weird that I paired you with your dead cat. Huge thanks to Judah McAuley for lending depth to my deadbeat dad storyline with your own personal anecdote, and to Danny Thomas for inspiring the father-daughter chat in the barbershop.

Thanks to Valerie Warren, Kevney Dugan, Nate Wyeth, Hank Therien, Jason Lusk, Lisa Sidor, Linda Orcelletto, and everyone else at Visit Bend for your incredible flexibility and understanding. Balancing a day job and an author career would be impossible without you guys there to steady me when things start to topple.

Thank you to my parents, David and Dixie Fenske, and to Aaron "Russ" Fenske and his lovely wife, Carlie Fenske. Family connections are the bedrock of this book, and I'm so happy to be linked up with you.

Thank you to Violet Zagurski for inspiring many little pieces of Paige, and for being the best stepdaughter on the planet. Early readers claimed Paige steals the show in this book, which seems fair since you stole my heart six years ago. I'm also grateful to Cedar Zagurski for being an amazing stepson and all-around awesome dude. I look forward to the day you drive me out into the desert and leave me, because I'm pretty sure you'll make me laugh the whole way there.

And thank you to Craig Zagurski most of all. Like Allie, I never in a million years imagined myself marrying a single dad. I'm so glad you showed up and proved to me over and over that the best things in life are the surprises no one saw coming. Love you, babe.

# DISCUSSION QUESTIONS

1.  What do you think of Allie's reasons for breaking things off with Jack sixteen years ago? Did she do the right thing? How would their lives have unfolded differently if she'd gone through with the marriage back then?

2.  How have Jack and Allie changed since they first dated in high school? How are they the same?

3.  Jack grew up with a devoted single mother and a deadbeat, absentee father, while Allie was raised by wealthy parents whose seemingly happy marriage harbored several big secrets. In what ways are Jack and Allie affected by their upbringings?

4.  Allie has several secrets she's kept hidden from Jack, but the one she reveals in the attic comes as the biggest shock to him. Do you think she should have told him sixteen years ago? How might that have changed the direction of their lives?

5. Jack clings fiercely to his anger at his father throughout the story. Do you think he forgives him by the end of the story? What role does Paige play in the arc of Jack's feelings about his dad?

6. Paige has moments of being precocious and insightful, and moments of being a typical ten-year-old girl. Have you known girls like Paige? In what ways is her personality shaped by having a single father and a mother who died when she was a baby? In what ways do you think Allie might influence her in the future?

7. Birds are a significant symbol throughout the book, both in Allie's battle with the woodpeckers and in the albatross nickname she's been given by Wade. How did your perception of those birds and their habits change throughout the story?

8. Jack tends to focus on the darkest pieces of memory and the negative aspects of a story, while Allie desperately wants to see things through rose-colored glasses. Are you more like Jack or Allie? Is one or the other a more challenging way to navigate the world?

# ABOUT THE AUTHOR

Tawna Fenske is a *USA Today* bestselling author who writes humorous fiction, risqué romance, and heartwarming love stories with a quirky twist. Her offbeat brand of romance has received multiple starred reviews from *Publishers Weekly*, one of which noted, "There's something wonderfully relaxing about being immersed in a story filled with over-the-top characters in undeniably relatable situations. Heartache and humor go hand in hand."

Tawna lives in Bend, Oregon, with her husband, step-kids, and a menagerie of ill-behaved pets. She loves hiking, snowshoeing, stand-up paddleboarding, and inventing excuses to sip wine on her back porch. She can peel a banana with her toes and loses an average of twenty pairs of eyeglasses per year.

To learn more about all of Tawna's books, visit www.tawnafenske.com